HEADING OVER THE HILL

JUDY LEIGH

Boldwood

First published in Great Britain in 2020 by Boldwood Books Ltd.

This paperback edition first published in 2021.

1

A CIP catalogue record for this book is available from the British Library.

Paperback ISBN: 978-1-80280-367-9

Ebook ISBN: 978-1-83889-573-0

Kindle ISBN: 978-1-83889-574-7

Audio CD ISBN: 978-1-83889-566-2

Digital audio download ISBN: 978-1-83889-568-6

Large Print ISBN: 978-1-83889-571-6

Boldwood Books Ltd.

23 Bowerdean Street, London, SW6 3TN

www.boldwoodbooks.com

For Cait

1

'Maggot Street? You have to be kidding me, Billy.'

Billy clutched the steering wheel of the old Transit, swinging the van around a corner, and then whirled his eyes towards his wife, who was huddled next to him, her purple lace-up boots on the dashboard. 'Margot Street, darlin'. Mar-go. As in Margot Fonteyne, the famous classical ballet dancer of the 1960s.'

'As in "Am Mar-go-ing to like this place?" I don't think so at all.' They turned the bend too sharply and, as Dawnie indicated the maze of houses on the estate, she leaned across to Billy, almost obstructing his vision, her voice incredulous. 'Look at it, Billy. It's just a pile of boring terraced houses.'

Billy grinned, extending a hand to pat Dawnie's knee. 'It's just a six-month let, my darlin'. The first of May to the last day of October, with an option to stay on if we need to. I just went online, like we agreed, and picked something convenient and cheap for us, just for now. We'll take our time to buy the house we really want – a big rambling one, on the coast looking over the rolling waves, in time for Christmas. Log fire, beams on the ceilings. It'll all be just dandy.'

Dawnie wrinkled her nose in answer. 'I thought it'd be great to live here in Barnstaple, by the sea, away from the frozen north. I thought it'd be a great place for two seventy-year-old misfit hippies to do our own thing in the wilds of north Devon. But this group of identical terraces, Billy: look at it. It's all net curtains and plastic faux-wood front doors. The residents are going to hate us here.'

'Don't fret, my pet,' Billy chuckled. 'It'll be deadly. Think about the advantages. Lindy and Stewie and the kids have our house in Bolton. It's big and ramshackle and ideal for them – so close to the shops and schools. And now my da's money is in the bank from his place in County Mayo, God rest his soul, so that makes us cash buyers. We can pick wherever we want. And I want something peaceful, where we can hear the sea when we open the window and look up at the moon.' Billy stared at her meaningfully, raising his bushy eyebrows. 'We're in charge of our lives for once. The kids are settled; it's a new start for us, and the pictures of the seaside properties on the internet look grand. We came here years ago and loved it: remember that summer in Staunton Sands when the kiddies were little? And if the worst comes to the worst and we don't like it here or we can't find the place we want by the end of six months—' He gave a big shrug, his shoulders moving like two giant hills. 'Then we can move on again. We could always go to Ireland. I've still a cousin over there.'

'I've got nothing against this area: it's just this horrible street. Look at it,' Dawnie exploded, scratching her head. She was wearing the long blonde wig today and her scarlet sunglasses; she thought she'd dressed perfectly for the early summer sunshine that glinted and dazzled her through the windscreen of the red Transit. But now she wasn't sure, staring out of the window at this tidy row of terraces, net curtains at the windows, neat hanging baskets by the doors. People could be quick to judge. Then she folded her arms, came to a decision and let out a long breath. 'Oh, sod them all, Billy. I mean, if the neighbours are going to dislike us just because of your long hair and leather jacket and my wild wardrobe, then they aren't worth worrying about.'

Billy rolled the Transit around another bend into a narrow row of neat terraces. 'I bet they're all lovely people, darlin'. You just have to trust in the beauty of human nature. I'm sure they'll all be wonderful, our new neighbours.'

Dawnie slid the red glasses up onto her forehead and beamed at him. 'Ah, you're right, Billy, as usual. We're going to love it here. And here we are – look: this one is ours, the cute little brick one right in the middle with the white plastic door. Number thirteen, Maggot Street.'

* * *

The floral curtains on the upstairs landing window of number eleven Margot Street twitched briefly. A hand held the material back, leaving a gap just wide enough to peek through. A man in his seventies, his hair grey-brown and thinning on top, peered through his spectacles with eager eyes as he leaned forward. A woman appeared behind him, resting her chin on her palm and frowning. She was considerably shorter than him, her ample figure encased in a flowery dress not dissimilar to the curtain material. At the end of her legs, which were sheathed in tan-coloured nylon tights, was a pair of comfortable brown slippers. She leaned closer. 'Is that them, Malcolm? Our new neighbours?'

'I certainly hope not. It's a red Transit van. Must be builders come to make good any damage left by the students, or whatever those three young men were who lived there before.'

'Darren and Jason and the other one? Oh, I'm so glad they are gone. The smells that used to come through the walls sometimes – awful smells. Goodness knows what those young men used to cook: all sorts of strange ingredients, no doubt.'

'They were probably smoking cannabis – especially if they were students.' Malcolm didn't move. 'Or cooking foreign food. I don't like foreign food.' He sniffed. 'Apparently the new tenants are an older couple. Perhaps they're our age, Gillian. In their seventies. Sensible people who – oh, my goodness.'

'What is it, Malcolm?' Gillian patted her short white hair to check the hairspray had kept it in stiffly in place. 'Can you see them?'

'There's a man, the driver, in a leather jacket. He has long grey hair in a big ponytail. He looks like a thug; he's huge. He's going to the back of the van and he's getting something out – something large, I think – goodness me, is that a motorcycle in there?'

'Let me see, Malcolm, You're in the way. I can't see.'

'Don't push me, Gillian. Wait your turn. It can't be the new neighbours. Oh, he's getting luggage out of the van first. There's someone coming to help him...'

'Is it them?' Gillian craned her neck. 'Is it the new people, moving in next door?'

'Oh, will you look at that woman?' Malcolm caught his breath.

Gillian assumed he'd seen an attractive woman and was ogling her. She pushed her husband to one side. 'Let me see.'

A woman in a red mini dress and a denim jacket appeared around the side of the van. At the end of long skinny legs, she wore huge purple lace-up boots and her flowing blonde hair came almost to her waist. She was tugging a large case.

Malcolm coughed. 'Well, would you believe it? She's no spring chicken...'

'And dressed like that – just look at her,' Gillian muttered.

They stared together, their hands gripping the curtains. Then, at the same time, they caught their breath and jerked backwards, almost slipping down the stairs. The blonde woman had seen them; she was staring up through red sunglasses and was smiling, waving her hand maniacally and yelling, 'Yoo-hoo. Hello, we've arrived.'

Malcolm tutted softly to himself. 'No, Gillian – that's not them. There must be a mistake. They surely can't be the new neighbours.'

* * *

Across the road at number fourteen, a dark-haired man in his early fifties was putting out the recycling boxes, which were stacked with folded cardboard. It was a job he liked to make sure was completed early, in case he forgot to do it. Work at the garden centre was hectic during the summer months and it was important to have a routine for everyday jobs like dustbins. He couldn't ask his mother to do strenuous chores. Besides, he was strong: he worked out regularly, so it made sense for him to take out the bins. He placed two green plastic crates carefully, one on top of the other, adjusted his tie and pushed his hands into his pockets.

He frowned. Two people had just emerged from the red Transit across the road. A large man with long grey hair tied in a ponytail, wearing a leather jacket and jeans, was rolling a motorbike down two planks of wood, grunting. The dark-haired man paused, shoved his hands deeply into the pockets of his loose trousers and squinted, staring across the road. His mother would be calling him for her second cup of tea but he wanted to find out who the neighbours were. He'd make her a drink as soon as he went inside: at eighty-six, she had every right to be demanding. He leaned forward, watching the big man grunt and struggle. The man caught his eye and smiled across, shouting something that sounded a little like, 'Will you give me a hand here?'

He had an accent, Irish or Scottish; the dark-haired man thought he must be from somewhere in the far north. It might be safer for the time being to pretend he hadn't understood. He shrugged and fiddled with the cardboard in the recycling box, neatening the edges. A voice called to him from inside the house, his mother's voice, the tone firm despite her advanced years. He could hear her distinctly.

'Vinnie, can you come back in here, love? It's getting draughty with that door open. What are you doing out there for so long? Come on in, I need another cuppa.'

Vinnie straightened his tie and glanced in the direction of the struggling stranger and the motorbike. It was a classic, the machine; glossy black paint, with beautifully chromed forks and spokes. Vinnie nodded: it was a lovely bike, and he imagined how nice it would feel to own one. For a moment, he was astride the machine, aviator sunglasses on his face, the engine rumbling between his knees, cruising along the road to the soundtrack of 'Born to be Wild'. He imagined his dark curls lifted on the breeze, his frame encased in leather. It would be good to own a bike, to feel the wind in his hair, to be independent.

Suddenly, he heard a shriek and he lurched backwards. A woman in a red mini dress, her blonde hair almost to her waist, had joined the man and was laughing, shrieking something towards the upstairs window of number eleven, helping the man to steady the motorbike. She jerked her head to look at Vinnie and his mouth dropped open. Behind the sunglasses, the woman was no youngster: she was older than him, probably, and he was fifty-two. He gasped, as she caught his eye and waved a hand wildly.

'Ey-up, handsome,' she shrilled. Vinnie felt his heart lurch. She had a northern accent and clearly wasn't lacking in confidence. 'You could pop over and give us a hand rather than just stand there gawping. If you keep staring at me like that, the wind will catch you with your gob open and you'll stop like that forever.'

The man with the ponytail mumbled something to her, his voice a soft rumble. Vinnie didn't wait to find out what he was saying. The man was big and burly and might be dangerous. Vinnie knew it was safer to walk away from confrontation. He twisted round, called, 'Just coming, Mam,' and ambled into the house. As he closed the door, he could hear the woman's voice chuckling, peals of loud laughter in his ears. He could never tell what women meant when they laughed like that. Sometimes it meant that they were attracted to you. After all, she had invited him over and called him handsome. For a fleeting moment, Vinnie wondered if the blonde woman had been the big biker's wife. But she was more likely to be his sister or his friend. She had paid Vinnie a compliment in front of the big man: if she was his wife, she'd never have done that.

Vinnie paused in the hallway and felt his heart lurch. He had been loved more than once. More than one woman had stroked his soft curls and commented on the beauty of his huge brown eyes and long lashes. But there was no one now, no one to whisper words of affection in his ear. The women at the garden centre were mostly married or too young for him. Vinnie shivered. He wondered if the blonde woman had found him attractive and wanted to get to know him. But it was hard to read what women meant when they gave you their full attention like that. Sometimes it meant they liked you; sometimes it meant that they liked you a lot. Vinnie scratched his scalp through the soft curls and wandered into the lounge to see what his mother wanted.

* * *

Dawnie watched the man rush back into his house across the street, slamming the door behind him. Laughter spluttered from her mouth. 'I've upset one of them already.'

Billy wrapped a bear-sized arm around her. 'Ah, but you couldn't upset anyone, darlin'. We'll get the Harley inside, will we?

Then perhaps we can have a good look round the house, get our bearings. I'm hungry.'

'And I'm dying for a brew, gasping. Come on then, Billy. Steady as she goes.'

They pushed the motorbike, Billy guiding the handlebars and Dawnie shoving the seat from behind. It fitted well enough into the hallway, with enough space for a human, even Billy's size, to squeeze through the gap. Billy closed the front door with a dull clunk and took Dawnie's hand.

'The bike's safe now. It won't be stolen, locked in here with me. But we'll get a big garage in the next place.' Billy gave Dawnie a sheepish grin. 'This is our home, my darlin' – for the next few months. Tell me, how well has your husband chosen?'

'Maybe I shouldn't have left it all to you.' Dawnie screwed up her face. The lounge smelled musty. There was a blue sofabed, faux-leather and squishy enough. The TV was nothing special, not like the huge one with surround sound they'd left at home for Lindy and her family. The mantelpiece was old-fashioned white tiles, and below it was a gas fire. Dawnie sniffed meaningfully, wrinkling her nose in disgust, and tugged Billy into the kitchen. It was old-fashioned and poky; the white cooker had clearly not been cared for. The gas rings were rusty and there was still a circle of dried-on gravy encrusting the enamel. The floor was covered in thin linoleum in a black and white square pattern, like a tattered chess board. There was a small fridge, a microwave, an old washing machine and a scratched stainless steel sink with a dripping tap.

Billy grabbed her in a little waltz. 'We can cook up a storm in here.'

'It reminds me of my mother's old place in Daubhill years ago. The style is the same 1950s chic.' Dawnie planted a little kiss on Billy's nose. 'But home is where you are, my lover. I'll get my own stuff in here and maybe we can chuck some paint on a wall or two, change the curtains and...'

'And it'll be grand, while we look for the place of our dreams... It's what we need, darlin'. Our own place – me and you and some peace and quiet.'

Dawnie forced a smile. 'Peace at last, just the two of us, Billy, you and me...' She cuddled up to him as he wrapped her in a bear hug. She was thinking about her daughter Lindy Lou and Lindy's husband Stewie and their daughter Fallon and her three children at the rambling Victorian semi in Little Lever. She imagined baby Milo, his face contorted, screeching as he often did, and seven-year-old Willow throwing a tantrum as she smeared her mouth with her mother's crimson lipstick. This house felt too small, too quiet in comparison. It was going to be difficult living so far away from her huge brood. Dawnie forced a quick grin, wriggling closer into Billy's warm embrace.

'Home is where you are, Billy. And it's the beginning of a new adventure. We've talked about it for ages: the sea and how it'll bring you some calm and you'll sleep better. I'll miss the old place I expect, from time to time, but this is only temporary, and it'll give us time to get to know the area. Yes.' She smiled up at him. 'This is perfect for now. Let's phone for a takeaway. There must be somewhere local, and we can crack open a bottle. What do you think?'

Billy lifted her up with ease and, as the mini dress hitched itself further up her thighs, she wrapped bare legs around him. 'I think I'm the luckiest man in the world.' He kissed her lips. 'My lovely wife.'

She nibbled his ear, her voice deliberately provocative, teasing him. 'We haven't checked the bedroom yet.'

Billy chuckled, a deep grumble from beneath his ribs. 'I hope there's a good bed upstairs. The one online on the landlord's photo looked strong enough to take an eighteen stone man... and his seven and a half stone woman...'

'I'm eight stone two.' She wriggled down from his grasp, adjusted the blonde wig so it sat straight on her head and then grinned. 'We'd better give it the once over, though.' She cocked her head to one side. 'Come on then, Billy, I'll chase you up the stairs.'

He turned to go just as the bell chimed two long notes in a deafening *ding-dong*. Billy turned to his wife, his forehead creased in confusion. 'Well, and who can that be now? We've just moved in... and we don't know anybody.'

2

Billy opened the door to see two women, huddled closely together, smiling. One was tall and blonde, the other short and dark, probably in their fifties. They both wore jeans and identical pale blue sweatshirts. The shorter one with curly dark hair to her shoulders wore gold-framed glasses. The taller one had smooth hair, a blonde bob, and colourful earrings made of red and blue beads. They opened their eyes wide as soon as Billy filled the door frame.

'I'm Audrey from next door, number fifteen. But please call me Aude,' the blonde one explained. 'And this is Sylv.'

Sylv grinned as the wind lifted her dark curls over her face. She leaned forward, holding out a Pyrex cooking dish with a tea towel over it. 'You're new here, just moved in, aren't you? I thought you probably wouldn't have had time to make anything to eat or do some shopping, so we brought you this.' She thrust the dish into Billy's hands. 'It's vegetable lasagne with lentils.'

'It's lovely. Sylv's special recipe,' Aude insisted, thrusting her hand out and offering a bottle of wine. 'And I brought this. It's red. Italian.'

Dawnie had joined Billy at the door, and she clutched at the wine eagerly. 'That's proper nice of you. Do you want to come in and have a glass with us?'

'Oh, we won't, not today.' Sylv's gold-rimmed spectacles had slipped forward and she pushed them back on her nose. 'You must be so busy, right in the middle of moving in.'

Aude held out a hand. 'But it's great to meet you, er...'

Billy grasped her fingers in his huge paw, then turned to Sylv and shook her hand. 'Billy. Billy Murphy. And this is my wife, Dawnie Smith.'

'Oh, you're Irish, Billy,' Sylv beamed. 'How lovely.'

'From County Mayo, originally. My dad and my brother lived there all their lives.' Billy shrugged huge shoulders. 'But I moved away years ago. I came to Manchester when I was a young man, and I've moved around a lot. Ah, but the accent's not so strong now.'

'Oh, it's a lovely lilt,' Aude insisted, turning to Dawnie. 'You're not Irish, are you, though?'

'Bolton born and bred, love.' Dawnie held up the wine. 'We have a house up there. My daughter and her husband are living in it at the moment, their daughter and my great-grandchildren too. We're looking to buy ourselves a home somewhere here, on the coast.'

'Oh, the coastline is superb,' Sylv nodded. 'There are some beautiful properties in this area. Or you could buy this house. Tell the landlord you like it and stop here and live next door to us. It'd be great to have some permanent neighbours. People don't normally stop here for very long.'

Billy frowned. 'And why would that be?'

Aude rolled her eyes, her gaze encompassing the direction of the house next door, number eleven. She lowered her voice, as if afraid to be heard. 'Ah, not everyone gets on with the neighbours next door to you.'

Sylv shrugged. 'Oh, they're all right. Don't pay any attention to him next door to you. He likes a little grumble, that's all. We tend to ignore him.'

Aude poked Sylv gently with her elbow. 'Moaning Malcolm won't bother Billy here – Billy's twice as big as he is.'

Sylv nodded. 'And you look like you can stand up for yourself, Dawnie. Don't take any grief from *her*.'

Dawnie folded her arms. 'I'm not likely to.'

Billy lifted the lasagne in the dish. 'Ah well, thanks for the pot of food.'

'My pleasure,' Sylv cooed.

'And the wine: that's very decent of you,' Dawnie enthused.

'Well, it's good to meet you both. We'll pop by again, when you're moved in and settled.' Aude gave Sylv a little push. 'Come on, Sylv, there's another lasagne waiting in the oven for us.'

'Nice to meet you, Dawnie, Billy.' Sylv gave them a little wave as the women walked away.

'What lovely people.' Billy closed the front door behind him. 'Well, that's our dinner sorted now.'

Dawnie nodded. 'Good to have such nice neighbours. Shall we have a look at that old oven in the kitchen and see if we can get the gas lit?'

Billy hugged the Pyrex dish to his chest. 'I'll do that, Dawnie, love. You see if you can find a bottle opener and some glasses. I have a big thirst on me all of a sudden.'

The bottle was half empty by the time Dawnie and Billy had managed to make the ancient oven work. Another bottle from their own supplies had been opened when Dawnie dipped a large serving spoon in the lentil lasagne, ladling the thick mixture on two plates. By the time Billy spooned the last scrapings from the Pyrex dish onto his plate, the second bottle was empty too. Dawnie leaned back in her seat and rubbed her tummy. 'I think we will like it here, Billy.'

Billy ran a thick finger around the Pyrex dish, licking rich tomato sauce. 'Wherever you are, darlin', then I'm happy. But yes, I think it's a good place.'

'I wasn't so sure when you suggested it, by the sea, miles away from Lindy and Fallon and her little ones. But I think it's the right thing to do now we're older, to live somewhere beautiful, by the coast.'

'It's our time now, darlin', to be sure. The kids should have their own lives. They can have our house and we'll buy one here from Da's money. It makes sense. Let the young ones have their independence.'

Dawnie nodded. 'I mother them too much. Smother them.'

Billy licked the last smear of tomato sauce and lentils from his fingers. 'You've been a good mammy to our two, for sure.'

'We don't hear much from Buddy, especially since he split up with that Mandy. I wasn't so keen on her.'

'He has the travelling bug. He's forty-four, darlin'. He's his own man now.'

Dawnie pulled a sad face. 'Where is he now? Kansas City?'

Billy's chuckle rumbled. 'Following the yellow brick road, making a living wherever he lands, meeting up with other musicians, playing his guitar and singing, I guess. But he's doing his own thing, making his own way. And he texts us sometimes, once in a while.'

'Not often enough,' Dawnie frowned. 'But he could come back to live in the basement in the Little Lever house if he was tired of travelling. Buddy's a single man with no responsibilities.' She sighed, a shuddering ache from the bottom of her lungs. 'Lindy Lou's brood will be all right living in the house, and she'll take over the organisation. She's like me, good in a crisis, and her Stewie's not the best provider. He has to look after Fallon and her three kids now, too. He and Lindy are in their forties but he still can't hold down a job for more than six months.'

'Ah, but Stewie's a good man, really. I've always liked him. He's an eco-warrior, a man of principle. Besides, he has a savage collection of guitars and he's a good fella for a jam session.'

'But why couldn't she hook up with an accountant or a doctor: someone with a bit of money? She's taken so much on, looking after Fallon and her little ones.'

Billy breathed out. 'Fallon's always been a handful, hasn't she, ever since she was born. She's unpredictable; they've always had a time of it with that one.'

'It was because she was their only child, Billy. The sweetest baby – she was so cute. They spoiled her rotten. I did, too.'

He pulled his steel grey curls free from the long ponytail and shook his head. 'She reminds me of myself at a young age, Fallon. She's a wild one. But she has those babies already and there's only her to look after them.'

'And Lindy Lou's a grandma at forty-six. It's ridiculous. I'm sure she'll miss my support.'

'We keep talking about this, darlin', but nothing will change. Fallon has the three kiddies and, thanks to us, they all have a roof over their heads now. Lindy and Stewie will be just dandy by themselves. Let's leave them to it, will we?'

'But it's my fault, Billy.' Her eyes filled. 'I brought Lindy Lou and Buddy up to be independent. I was too much of a hippy, letting the kids paint their walls any way they wanted, growing their hair and dressing them up and then they were dragged from school to school. And you were never there with us, Billy; you were always away.'

'I know that, darlin'. It couldn't be helped. But you did a grand job with them both, you know that. Ah, don't fret yourself.' He wrapped an arm around her, pulling her against his chest. 'You've just had a few glasses of wine tonight and you feel a bit tearful. You know how it is sometimes after a jar or two.'

Tears were trickling down Dawnie's face. She wiped them away with the back of her hand. 'Fallon's twenty-three. That's no age to have one kiddie, let alone three. And all of them have different dads.'

Billy sniffed and offered a mischievous grin. 'Maybe she just likes the variety?'

'She was still at school when she fell pregnant with Willow. Caleb was the result of her holiday trek to Thailand, and who knows what bush little Milo crept out from under?'

Billy stood up, sliding back his chair and picking up the lasagne dish. 'I'll give this a wash and we can return it to the women next door tomorrow. They were grand, the neighbours at number fifteen. Will I dig out some of the home brew and let them have a few bottles?'

'That'd be a nice gesture: and maybe a couple of bottles for the people on the other side next door. What did Aude and Sylv say they were called?'

'I can't remember.' Billy watched the cold tap water splash into the Pyrex dish. 'We'll call on them in the morning and introduce ourselves.' He began to scrub the dish clean with thick fingers. Dawnie put her head in her hands.

'This house needs a makeover. I think I'll ask the landlord if I can spruce it up a bit, paint the walls. What about a mural in that little living room? Something swirly and psychedelic?'

'Let's not do too much to it, just a coat of paint and put one of my photos up. It's best not to change it much if we're only here for six months. The landlord doesn't know I've the Harley stowed in the hallway. Perhaps it's a good idea to keep a low profile.'

'I'll just paint the bedroom, then, and maybe the lounge.' Dawnie brought her hands together, as if praying. 'A nice calm blue colour, like cornflowers, perhaps a feature wall in deep blood red, vermillion, the colour of passion?' She grinned at Billy. 'Six months is a long time to be staring at magnolia.'

He made a low noise, a sound between a groan and a yawn. 'It's gone ten o'clock, darlin'. I'm bushed. We'll turn in – it's been a hard day and the driving was tough – all motorways and then the long road with the twists and turns.' He began to dry the Pyrex dish. 'I'd rather be on the bike than in the Transit any day.'

'Yes, it's bedtime for us, Billy. Tomorrow is our first day in north Devon.' Dawnie stretched her arms above her head. 'It's exciting. When will we start looking at houses? Soon, I hope.'

'I thought we might get up with the lark tomorrow. I've a spot of cleaning and tinkering to do on the bike. I just need to adjust the carburettor. In the afternoon, we could take it out for a spin and drive round the coastline. Maybe we can see what little villages we like the look of and then next week we'll start our house search properly. What do you think, darlin'?'

'Perfect.' Dawnie's eyes fell on a red suitcase. 'I'll go up, shall I, Billy?'

He nodded. 'I'll be up after you in five minutes.'

Dawnie dragged the suitcase into the hallway and bumped it up the narrow staircase with the floral green carpet into the main bedroom. The walls were grubby magnolia; the double bed was just a divan and a mattress beneath a window with thin red curtains. Dawnie gazed around her, talking softly to herself.

'I hope we're not paying much for this. I should've discussed it all properly before we moved.' She sighed. 'In fact, I should've got more involved in the whole thing really, looked at the website, made decisions like a proper wife. But oh no, I just concentrated on Lindy Lou and Fallon and the kiddies and said, "You sort it out, Billy, love, I'm sure it'll be fine." This house is a right dive. I should have organised somewhere for us instead of leaving it to Billy, bless him.'

Hands on hips, she stared at the wardrobe, the dressing table, heavy square-shaped wooden furniture from the early twentieth century. Both had seen better days. There were ring marks on the dressing table, the size of beer glasses. A handle on one of the drawers was broken. Above her head, a thin cord held a bare light bulb. Dawnie grinned as she gazed around: she'd have the place looking like home in no time. She'd already decided to give the bedroom furniture a rub-down with sandpaper and paint it a smart cream and powder blue.

She glanced at the bed and called out to Billy. 'The bedding's still in the van. Or it might be in that little living room with the rest of our boxes. I'll go and get it in a minute. I'll do myself first.'

Dawnie wasn't sure if Billy had heard her or not: it was likely that he was absorbed in something else. She smiled: Billy could only ever do one thing at a time. She opened the large red case and lifted out several items encased in tissue paper, placing them gently on top of the dressing table. Silky hair of various colours, black, brown, red, electric blue, stuck out from the wrapping. Dawnie pulled off her long blond wig and placed it carefully on top of the other wigs. She ran her fingers through her thick hair, a platinum pixie cut, making it spike attractively round her small face. Without the wig, she seemed even tinier, sparrow-like. She tugged a round box from inside the case, placing it at her feet and searching inside. 'Ah, here we are. I can't live without my products.'

She held up a bottle of liquid and a huge wad of cotton wool and proceeded to cleanse her face, placing the items back in the box. She delved back into the case and lifted out a pair of tiny pink pyjamas, shorts and a vest top decorated with lace.

'Oh, and we'll need toothbrushes. They are in here somewhere.' Dawnie stuck her head under the lid of the red case and rummaged in its depths before bringing out two electric toothbrushes and some toothpaste.

Heavy footfall on the landing announced Billy's arrival. He stood in the room, his arms full of bedding. 'I thought we'd be needing these, darlin'. I'll just make the bed up, will I? Have you seen the bathroom yet?'

'No, is it all right?'

'Bath with a shower over it, basin, toilet. It's just dandy.'

'Is there enough space for my products?'

Billy shrugged his big shoulders and dumped the bedding onto the mattress, proceeding to stuff pillows into cases, shaking out a sheet and finally flapping a huge duvet with a guitar print in black and white onto the bed. He turned to Dawnie, who was in the short pink pyjamas.

'Should I get the drums in now, do you think?'

'They'll be safe in the Transit until tomorrow.'

'What if someone steals them? My kit's worth a bit. There's the cymbal John Coghlan used to play in the seventies.'

Dawnie grinned. 'We'll get them in tomorrow, first thing. Don't worry, love, there's a big lock on that Transit. There's no need to lose sleep...'

Billy's face was anxious. 'I should've brought them in once the Harley was indoors. If the neighbours hadn't called round with the food, I'd have brought them in then.'

Dawnie went over to Billy, reaching up and kissing his lips. 'They'll be fine. The beard needs a trim, Billy.'

'Okay. I'll set up the drums tomorrow in the spare bedroom.' He was thoughtful for a moment. 'Have you got the toothbrushes?'

Dawnie handed him a brush and the toothpaste. Suddenly, they both froze, listening. There was a noise, a sharp clicking sound downstairs. Billy frowned. 'Was that someone at the front door?'

'Did you lock it?

'I was sure I did.' He turned to go.

'I'll go, love. I'll get us a glass of water each, shall I? I'm thirsty after the wine.'

'Will I come down with you, darlin'?'

'Don't be soft. You clean your teeth. I'll check the door and bring us a nice glass of cool water.'

Dawnie padded down the stairs in bare feet, glad of the carpet's shabby softness. She stood at the bottom of the stairs and flicked on the light. Billy had locked the front door; a big bolt was securely fastened across the top. Dawnie turned to go, then she noticed a slip of paper on the floor. She squeezed past the Harley with an easy twist of her hips, bent down and picked up a folded note. She called up the stairs. 'It was the letter box, Billy. It's probably just a welcome note from one of the neighbours – maybe they wanted to tell us what day to put the bins out.'

Dawnie unfolded the paper and stared at the writing. It was in an old-fashioned style, a cursive hand, in navy fountain pen ink. She frowned and read the note again.

> *To whom it may concern. Please move your van. It is parked too close to my property and it leaves me insufficient space to move my own vehicle. If you do not comply herewith, it may be necessary for me to telephone your landlord.*
>
> *Regards,*
>
> *M. H. Frost (Number 11, Margot Street)*

Dawnie studied the note for a second, then squashed it into her fist, squeezing it until it was a small ball. She clenched her teeth. 'M. H. Frost of Maggot Street, eh? I'll give you insufficient space all right.' She threw the litter on the floor, the glasses of water forgotten now. She turned on her heel, snapping the light switch as her feet stomped up the stairs.

3

'Your boiled egg is ready, Malcolm.'

His thin fingers twitched at the curtains. 'Just a minute.'

Gillian picked up a cloth and wiped it across the marbled work top, scrubbing at imaginary crumbs. Then she reached for the teapot. Her short white curls were tidily brushed and fastened with a neat hair grip at one side, to prevent them falling across her fore-head. 'Malcolm.' She poured weak tea into china cups and added milk. 'Your three-minute egg...'

'All right, Gillian.' The tense note in his voice told her to refrain from further cajoling or nagging: he would often say, 'You're nagging me again, Gillian.' She sighed and sat down, cutting the top of her egg with a small knife and watching the golden yolk drip over the side of the small egg cup. She wondered whether to reach for a napkin and wipe it clean.

Malcolm leaned forward and pressed his nose against the living room window. He adjusted his glasses, and blinked. 'He's out there again. He's getting something out of the van.'

Gillian opened a packet of butter carefully. With precision, she scraped a tiny amount and pressed it on a slice of pale toast, staring at the table in front of her.

'What's he got? It looks like a box, a big square box. He's getting it out. He's carrying it into the house. It looks heavy and precious. He's carrying it very carefully.'

'I'm not sure about that note you sent last night, Malcolm. It wasn't very neighbourly.'

'If he doesn't move that van today, I'll be true to my word, I'll ring... oh, good God.'

'What is it, dear?'

'There's a woman out there with him.'

'The blonde one in the mini dress?'

'No, another one. She must have a twin: this one is just as small and skinny but she has long black hair, and she's wearing a pair of tight leather trousers. Not very seemly.'

'Malcolm...'

'Come and look, Gillian. I think he might have two wives. A bigamist: perhaps that's what he is.'

Gillian took a bite of toast. 'Your egg...'

'Good Lord, she's carrying a cymbal.'

'What sort of symbol, Malcolm? Do you think they are druids? Warlocks?'

'It's some sort of drum-shaped thing, Gillian. I wouldn't be surprised if he's not one of those dodgy antique dealers who do the shabby chic stuff – you know, coffee tables made out of old tyres and recycled trash. That sort of thing.'

'Come and have your breakfast, dear.'

Malcolm turned. His brow was furrowed beneath the thin grey hair. His dark suit, grey shirt and tie were impeccable, but his clothes hung from his frame, sparse and ill-fitting. He groaned. 'I have a bad feeling about these neighbours, Gillian. A bigamist who deals in dubious antiques, that's what we have living next door to us now. And he must be at least six feet four, with all that hair and a big beard. It's a worry. I mean – this is our *home*.'

Gillian offered him a smile as weak as the tea. He moved slowly towards the table. 'They aren't young people. He must be sixty-something at least. Almost as old as we are, Gillian.'

She nibbled a piece of pallid toast. 'I'm seventy-four.'

He sat down sadly. 'They're old enough to know better, not to behave like teenagers, like students.' He bashed his egg with a spoon, cracking the shell open. Inside, the yolk was deep yellow and hard. 'I'm not going to put up with any nonsense, Gillian. I'm going to write it all down in a list. Day one, large newcomer parks too close to our parking space and it would be difficult to get the Honda Jazz out. He then takes a motorcycle into the house. Day two, bigamist neighbour brings junk and antiques into the house, probably bought from a dubious source. I'll log it all down, every day.' Malcolm lifted his cup and took a sip of tea. It was tasteless and tepid.

They chewed in silence, Gillian thinking about the white carpet that covered the whole floor in the lounge and kitchen diner, and how it needed hoovering. She was proud of the fact that she cleaned each day. The roast needed to be put in the oven soon: Malcolm liked his meat well-cooked and his roast potatoes crisp on the outside. She wondered whether to make a fruit crumble for pudding or whether to offer ice cream from the freezer. She glanced across at the mantelpiece, at a photograph of a young man in uniform, and sighed. It was best to put James out of her mind this morning and concentrate on getting things done.

Malcolm was planning a file on the neighbours. He would begin it today, filling in yesterday retrospectively. He would write it all by hand, logging activities and the times they occurred. It was a shame, he thought, that he didn't own a mobile telephone, as he could take photos on one, although he wasn't quite sure how it worked. He could use a computer – he had one in the third bedroom, now his office – but it was only for emailing and researching. Technology didn't interest him much, although now he could see a use for it. He had a video camera somewhere, probably in the loft: that might be useful for filming the neighbours. He could film them from the landing window and achieve a reasonable angle without being noticed. Malcolm frowned at the thought of the footage of Billy he might get, the sort of antisocial or illegal behaviour he could capture on film.

Gillian interrupted his thoughts. 'Have you eaten enough, dear? You haven't finished your egg.'

He grunted. 'The yolk was hard. It was overcooked, Gillian.'

Suddenly, the door knocker echoed loudly: there was someone outside, bashing at the door. Malcolm sat bolt upright. Gillian glanced at him, her eyes wide. 'Who's that?'

Malcolm moved swiftly to the window, edging behind the curtains and peering out like a secret agent. He took a deep breath. On the other side of the net curtains, he could see two figures. One was the woman in leather trousers and a matching jacket, her hair a mass of black curls to her shoulders. She was wearing a pair of heart-shaped sunglasses in lurid blue. The other was the big man, his hair, now free of the ponytail, reaching his shoulders in grey unruly curls. He was carrying a plastic bag. Malcolm kept his voice low. 'It's them.'

'Who? Who?'

'Shhh, Gillian, you sound like an owl.' Malcolm adjusted his position. 'It's the big man next door and his second wife. And they've got something in a bag.'

Her voice rose. 'A gun? A dead animal?'

Malcolm frowned. Gillian had been watching too many detective programmes on television. The door knocker resounded again, louder. Malcolm could see the huge giant of a man in his leather jacket and dark jeans lift a ham-sized fist to make himself heard. The woman said something and laughed. Malcolm held his breath.

'Don't answer it, dear.' Gillian's voice was a low hiss.

'I don't intend to. He might be dangerous,' Malcolm whispered back, his eyes wild.

There was no sound for a while except the persistent ticking of the clock on the mantelpiece. Then Malcolm breathed out. 'They're moving away.'

'Back to their house?'

'Yes. No. Good Lord.'

'What's happening, Malcolm?'

'It's the woman. She's taken the bag off him. She's going across the road. Oh, Vinnie Stocker is outside his house at number fourteen. He's putting out more rubbish into the recycling bins although I've no idea why he does that at the weekends since the bin men don't come until Monday. Oh, she's talking to him. He's talking back. The big man has gone over to join them. The big chap is shaking his hand and giving him the plastic bag.'

Malcolm felt a light touch on his shoulder. Gillian had come to stand behind him. 'What's in the bag, do you think, dear? Drugs?'

'I dread to think. He was going to offer it to us. Whatever he has in that bag, it doesn't bode well. I'll update my file: neighbour and second wife offering unknown substance to other neighbour in broad daylight.'

* * *

Across the road, Vinnie peered inside the plastic bag. 'Thank you. Is it, you know, Irish?'

Dawnie giggled. 'It's stout, if that's what you mean. Packs a proper punch, though.'

'It does, for sure,' Billy nodded. 'I have gallons of the stuff under the stairs. I make it myself. It's nice to have a bottle or two of a night, while I'm watching TV.'

'I'm partial to a bit of beer. My mam likes milk stout.' Vinnie's face was anxious as he clutched the bag of bottles to his chest. He scratched his dark hair, pushing back a long fringe that almost covered his eyes. 'She likes port, too.'

'Well, try her on the home brew,' Billy suggested. 'If she likes it, I'll bring her a few bottles round.'

Vinnie smiled at his new neighbours, glad of their company. 'Thank you,' he muttered. 'Oh, and I'm Vinnie Stocker by the way. Vinnie, most people call me, although I was christened Vincent. Vincent David Thomas Stocker. My mum's Dilys Stocker, Dilly, she's eighty-six.'

'She won't thank you for telling us that.' Dawnie held out her hand. 'Maybe we can meet her next time. I'm Dawnie Smith and my husband is Billy Murphy.'

Vinnie shook her hand and glanced at Billy. 'Irish. I see.' He brought his lips together and nodded. 'Billy. Dawnie.'

'You're lucky our neighbours weren't in,' Billy chuckled. 'I already gave a few bottles to the ladies in number fifteen. But the man at number eleven was out and then you came outside...'

'Didn't we see you yesterday?' Dawnie pushed her black curls back from her face and adjusted the sunglasses.

Vinnie frowned. The woman who had shouted to him yesterday, who had paid him her full attention, had been a blonde. Dawnie was very similar to her: Vinnie assumed there must have been two women, sisters perhaps, with different coloured hair. Dawnie, the dark one, was the wife and the blonde one was Billy's sister-in-law. He wondered where the blonde sister was at the moment, and how he might ask the questions about where she lived and if she was single.

Billy wrapped an arm around Dawnie. 'Right, darlin'. We're off on the bike after I've sorted the carburettor. It's a lovely day for it.'

Vinnie breathed. 'You have a Harley Davidson. I'd love to see it properly, close-up...'

'Right you are, Vinnie, I'll give you a shout and you can come and help me do a couple of little jobs. I clean and polish it every Sunday.' Billy patted his shoulder and Vinnie winced.

Dawnie brayed loudly. 'Maintaining the bike is more important than cleaning the house. Come on then, Billy. Let's get organised and then we can head off to the coast.'

Vinnie watched them turn and walk back to number thirteen, their arms around each other. He wondered if he had made friends. He smiled and, as he turned back to the house, he began singing to himself. It was the chorus of 'Born to be Wild'. As he disappeared into the darkness, he made some low motorbike sound effects, imagining Dawn's lovely sister clinging to him as he roared along the road on his own bike, and his grin broadened.

Vinnie placed the bottles in the kitchen. 'I'm here, Mam. Do you need anything?'

His mother's voice had a soft Welsh lilt. 'Come in and close the door, Vinnie. I'm freezing in here.'

Vinnie was thoughtful for a moment. The woman with black curly hair, Dawnie, was Billy's wife; the blonde woman in the mini dress, the sister who called to him yesterday, must definitely be single and interested in him. She had called him handsome. He wondered if she lived with them, the blonde. She was attractive, full of energy. Vinnie wondered what her name was. He hoped she might be looking for love. A soaring feeling lifted his lungs, a little bit like bubbles or a happy tune, and he imagined himself friends with Billy, helping him with the Harley Davidson, going for a ride as a pillion passenger, having dinner with Billy and Dawnie and meeting the blonde sister and falling in love with her.

It would be good to have someone to care for. It had been a while since Sally. He had loved Sally best, and she had hurt him the most. She had turned out to be everything his mother had warned him about. But there had been others he had loved too, loved and lost, because, as his mother often told him, he picked girls who were fickle. But maybe Dawnie's sister was looking for true love.

Vinnie worried about his mother for a moment. She depended on him. But if he married the blonde sister, perhaps they could both live with his mother. Vinnie hoped they'd all get on. He wandered into the lounge. His mother was listening to a news programme on the radio, huddled in the armchair. She was a small woman but she was not frail. She wore comfortable trousers, a loose sweater and a pair of heavy-framed glasses and her hair was long and pale, wound around her head and fastened with a clip.

'Where have you been, Vinnie? I do wish you wouldn't leave the door open, mind. It gets so draughty in here with it all open.' Dilly tugged at the rug over her knees to prove the point.

'Sorry, Mam.'

'I thought I'd make us a lovely shepherd's pie for lunch. There's some meat in the fridge, I think.'

'I can do it, Mam.'

'Don't be silly. I may be in my eighties, but I'm not senile. I can move about this house as fast as you can when I put my mind to it.'

'Just trying to help, Mam.'

'Well, don't make me feel like I'm decrepit. I'm not. Just make sure I don't bump into the furniture, mind, or forget anything, that's your job. What were you doing outside all this time?'

'I was talking to the new people over at number thirteen. They seem nice.' Vinnie watched his mother's reaction. She leaned forward, squinting at him with her good eye.

'Who are they? Are they local people?'

'No, he's called Billy and he's Irish, Mam. She's from somewhere up north.'

'She's the cat's mother, is she?'

'Sorry, Mam, she's called Dawnie.'

'Young, are they?'

'They might be my age, fifty-something, probably even older, in their sixties. I don't know.'

'What did they want then?'

'He gave me some home brew. Stout. He makes it himself.'

'What did he give you beer for? Is it no good?'

Vinnie beamed. 'He says it's lovely, Mam. He said we could have more if we like it. They are really nice. They're going out for a ride on his motorbike, down to the sea. I think the woman called Dawnie has a sister.'

His mother stared at him. 'Well, my boy, we'd better sample some of this lovely stout before I make lunch, I think.' She wriggled in her seat. 'Go and fetch two glasses, will you, and a bottle of your new friend Billy's best beer. And while you're at it, bring my eye drops.'

'All right, Mam.'

Dilly watched him go, leaning forward. Her stronger eye was not too bad, but the other one was weak now, mostly just misty. She smiled. Vinnie was a good boy and she was lucky to have him home with her, helping her. But he needed friends: she could sense he was lonely and that she wasn't enough for him, not really.

'What would I do without you, Vinnie?' she called out. She always told him the same thing and she meant every word. He was her treasure. She pulled the blanket over her knees. It was cold in the house, even though it was summer now. She wished she could go out and about more, like her neighbours across the road on the motorbike. It would be great to see the coast again and take in the scenery. Life was for living, she always said, but she wasn't having the best of life, not nowadays. She was mostly indoors, in the armchair, squinting at the television.

She liked the action movies best: Arnold Schwarzenegger, Clint Eastwood, Sylvester Stallone and Bruce Willis. Without the television, life could be a bit dull, although Vinnie did his best for her. But there wasn't much fun, not now. She was often tired at the end of the day, her limbs aching and stiff, and her movements were slower now than they used to be. She wasn't sure how much longer she had left but she wished she could enjoy it all a bit more. She used to enjoy company, friends, going out, having fun. But those days were gone, in the distant past. She'd forgotten what it was like to have fun.

4

'Watch where you're going, Billy. Here's the turn for Saunton.'

Dawnie thought he was going too fast so she shouted into his ear through the crash helmet. The loose silk strands of the black wig blew against her face and tickled her cheek as she heard his voice drift back to her on the wind.

'Don't worry, darlin'. I know the way.'

The engine slowed to a dull throb and Billy leaned the Harley to the right at the crossroads. They accelerated again, passing houses, a single shop and a group of farm buildings. Then tall trees leaned across the road and grass verges tapered on both sides.

Dawnie leaned her helmet against the hard leather of Billy's jacket and closed her eyes. Things were changing fast, she knew that; she was entering another chapter of her life and, like Billy's Harley increasing its speed along a narrow road, Dawnie felt that she had no control over where she was going. She gripped her arms around the tree-trunk thickness of his waist. She missed the children, much more than she could explain.

She closed her eyes and thought of Buddy, her youngest, now forty-four, but still her baby. He was tall like his father but artistic, moody, thoughtful, easily hurt. He'd had a string of unsuccessful relationships. The last woman he'd been seeing for over a year, Mandy from Farnworth, had broken his heart by going back to her husband and two children. Dawnie had never liked Mandy: her gaze was too bold, her hand on Buddy's arm too possessive, too confident. And she had hurt him so badly that he'd left his home two months ago and now he was wandering across the United States, playing his guitar and apparently trying to find himself. He was lost, her sweet, sensitive son. He'd probably marry a flaxen-haired banjo-playing vocalist from Wichita, settle down in Topeka and she'd never see him again. Dawnie sighed. It was different for Billy: he didn't feel the same about the children. He'd never been there when she'd wiped their tears, bathed scraped knees or been erratic about bedtimes. She'd done most of the parenting of Buddy and Lindy Lou by herself, so it was no surprise that she felt so alone without them.

Bereft, that was the word. Living in Little Lever with Lindy Lou and her brood had driven her crazy at times. The noise had been a constant buzzing in her head: laughter, screaming, shouting. But it had been thriving family banter, Lindy nagging Stewie to wash the dishes, or Lindy yelling at Fallon because Milo needed his feed and her daughter was still in the bathroom doing her hair. Dawnie had been at the centre of it all, playing Superman with little Caleb, and dancing to pop music with Willow while Billy cooked a huge family hotpot. It was impossible to be lonely in such a busy house.

And yes, there had been times when she'd craved a moment with Billy all by herself, when she watched him sharing a pint with Stewie, discussing global warming, his brow set in a frown, or when he made up the rocking cradle for Milo in Fallon's room, or while he was teasing Lindy Lou about her short skirts, which were exactly like her own. Then, she'd wanted Billy all to herself, and now there was just the two of them she was not disappointed. They had plenty of time to share. But, she thought, wasn't that just the way life came around and bit you on the bum? Now that she had quality time with her husband, she was missing the children.

Dawnie heaved a sigh and blinked tears, squeezed her eyes closed, then opened them wide and peered over Billy's shoulder. Ahead, the road was curving downhill and to the left there was an expanse of intense blue. The sea stretched out, blending into sky. Dawnie bit her lip. This was her future now, open, new and fresh for the taking. She had to grasp it with both hands. It was what Billy needed. It would bring him the peace he craved. It was what they'd said they both wanted. Dawnie had been sure that was what she wanted most. She was almost sure.

Billy's voice drifted back to her. 'Saunton Sands. There isn't a soul around. We'll stop and have a walk, will we, darlin'?'

The Harley chugged slowly down a winding path, turning left into a car park and stopping next to a van where a young man was half wearing a wetsuit, rubbing a towel over his bare torso and damp locks. Billy nodded to the surfer and brought the bike to a standstill, pulling off his helmet. Dawnie did the same, rubbing her hand over the dark curly strands of her wig to make sure the style wasn't flattened. The surfer glanced at them and then glanced away, throwing the towel in the back of the van before lifting up his surf-board. Billy offered a hand to Dawnie. 'Let's walk down to the sea.'

She slipped her small hand into his huge paw, feeling his fingers encase hers, keeping them warm. They walked past an ice cream shop, over cobbles towards the beach. The sands were an infinite expanse, stretching towards rising waves, a glittering line of sea and a vast cloudless sky, a merging of deep dreamy blues. Dawnie sighed. If they moved near to here, they could walk on the beach every morning, their faces pressed by the bracing breeze. Dawnie felt healthier already, gulping the cold air that reached the back of her throat.

She was lost in thought for a while; it looked exactly the same as when she and Billy had brought their youngsters, more than forty years ago. This would be an ideal place for Lindy Lou to visit with Fallon and the little ones: they'd have a great time playing on the beach. To the left, sand dunes rose in little hillocks and, behind them, more towering hummocks of sand. Dawnie imagined Willow and Caleb rushing up the mounds screaming, their voices thrown into the air by the wind that billowed in their t-shirts as they slid down the sandy helter-skelters on the seats of their jeans. Dawnie could picture their faces laughing against the breeze, their eyes screwed up small, just as her own children had done. A sigh made a hard ball in her chest, and she let it out slowly.

'Penny for them, darlin'?'

She shook her head, making her anxious thoughts rattle. 'I was just wondering about Lindy Lou. I hope she'll be all right. I wondered if we shouldn't send her some more money...'

He wrapped an arm around her shoulders. She shivered, small and fragile. He took a breath. 'I gave them some money before we left. Lindy and Stewie both have jobs now. She enjoys working on the school dinners with the others – it's good company for her, and Stewie's just started in the plastics factory...'

'That can't be easy...' Dawnie bit her lip. 'What with him being an eco-warrior.'

Billy chuckled. 'It's only until he finds something better.'

'It's always been the same with Stewie, Billy. He likes to move from one job to another. But at least he always comes home every evening for Lindy and Fallon.'

'I know, Dawnie.' Billy squeezed his arm around her, as if making up for his past absence. He frowned. 'I know it was tough on you in those days.' His face remained thoughtful for a moment, then he grinned. 'But it's our time now. You and me, here by the sea, fresh air, a new start, the open road to our future... I need the peace and quiet, darlin' – you know that.'

Dawnie felt the tears blur her vision again and the constriction in her throat made the next words difficult. 'Should we go up and visit them in a week or two? Just to help Fallon out with the kiddies?'

'Let's leave them be for a while, will we? Let them stand on their own feet while we try to find ours again?' His grip tightened on her shoulder. 'You and I fall in step just grand together, don't we?'

Dawnie looked down at her feet on the sand. She and Billy were moving forward, their feet beating the same rhythm, his stride smaller to match her short paces. She glanced up at him, into the soft gaze, and forced a smile. 'You're right, Billy. They don't need me mollycoddling them all their lives, do they? And it's our chance now.' She breathed out sharply. 'And Lord knows we waited long enough for this time together. We've earned it.'

Billy grunted softly. 'We can have adventures: a new house, trips out on the bike, new roads to travel. Fun times ahead for us, my darlin'.'

'And what about Buddy? What about our lovely boy, all those miles away?'

'You have to let him lead his own life now.'

'He hasn't texted us in ages.'

'He texted last Sunday morning, a week ago,' Billy sighed. 'He said he was fine. He said he'd been talking to some fellas in Kansas City about putting a blues band together.'

'Oh yes, a week ago. He's not the best communicator, is he? It seems longer than that.' Dawnie glanced up into the air. A seagull was flying in an arc over their heads. The wind took its wings and tossed it backwards. Billy glanced in the same direction and then reached into his inside pocket, pulling out a small digital camera.

He pointed the lens towards the sea and then swirled towards the sand dunes, focusing and waiting for the shutter to snap.

'There's some grand stuff to photograph here.' He pushed the camera back inside his jacket. 'I've heard there are honey buzzards, goshawks and red kites. I'd love to take some photos of a white-tailed eagle. There are some not far from here; I read about it in a book.'

Dawnie squeezed his hand. 'I'll never forget the picture you took at Martin Mere Wetlands, the one of the two swans and the little cygnets swimming in formation downstream. The one that won the competition.'

'That's how I got this camera, remember: it was first prize.' Billy patted his jacket, aware of the small hump in his inside pocket. 'But I'm looking forward to getting close to some new species here. I'd love to take some better pictures of kingfishers, too...'

'We should put some of your photos on the walls, Billy. It cost enough to frame them,' Dawnie mumbled. 'We can use them to cover up the horrible magnolia paint of number thirteen Maggot Street.' She sighed. 'I'll have to buy some different coloured paints and liven the place up a bit.'

Billy shrugged. 'It's just six months in Margot Street. We'll be dandy. And my photos are all packed away in crates...'

She elbowed him gently, a gesture of mischief, her former sad mood lifting. 'Well, you'd better organise a trip to the DIY shop this week, because I can't stare at those bland walls any longer. I rang the owner and he said it was all right to paint the walls as long as I pick a neutral colour. So, we need to pick up a few pots of paint.' Her eyes twinkled with mischief. 'There's one I've seen, Jewelled Sunset, bright flaming orange it is – or a bright pink, Fandango Fuchsia – and a feature wall in a deep nautical blue, just like the sea... I mean, that's almost neutral.'

Billy caught the playful sparkle in her gaze and gave a throaty laugh. 'Well, I'll be leaving the creative stuff to you, my darlin'. Just pick the pots of paint and get the brushes and we can spruce the house up any way you like. You're the boss of all that stuff.'

Dawnie took a deep breath. 'Homemaker, am I?' She thought for a moment, then stood still, her feet planted in the sand. Billy was staring at her. Dawnie folded her arms. 'Right. Let's go back to the bike now, Billy, and stop somewhere for a coffee on the way back to Maggot Street, shall we? Then maybe we can look in a few estate agents' windows. I know they'll all be closed but we can still window-shop. Let's see what's out there in our price range.'

She moved her hands to her hips. 'You're right about this being our time together, Billy. We need to get a shift on and start this house hunting. After all, we're making our final move now until they take one or other of us out in a box.' Her face was determined beneath the dark curls. 'So, we need to find the perfect home, the me-and-you-together-forever, happy-ever-after place we deserve, Billy Murphy, where you can fall asleep to the sound of the sea and wake refreshed and happy in the morning, no nightmares. What do you say to that?'

Billy smiled at her, his eyes crinkling, the pupils large with love. 'I'd say you were exactly right, darlin'.' He wrapped an arm around her shoulders as they turned back and began to stroll across the expanse of soft sand towards the car park. 'In fact, I'd say you were always right about just about everything.'

Dawnie nodded, her mouth firm and resolute. 'Okay, Billy, here we go, onwards and upwards towards our new future.' She gazed up at him and winked. 'You can buy the coffee. And I'll have a nice slice of cake with mine.'

'Cake, coffee, whatever you want.' Billy slowed down to fall in step with her stride. 'I'd give you the moon if I could, darlin'. You know that. But we'll start with some coffee and cake for the now, will we?'

5

Malcolm's hands twitched at the curtains in the lounge. Gillian was bustling behind him, adjusting the photograph on the mantelpiece; James in his uniform, his face serious. She sighed and moved across the room, laying the table. Malcolm knew it must be ten to two: they always ate at two, on the dot. On Sundays it was always roast beef or lamb, occasionally pork or chicken, potatoes, vegetables and gravy. Malcolm narrowed his eyes: he was watching two women talking to each other on the street, a tall blonde one and a shorter one with dark curls and gold-rimmed spectacles. They were both in their fifties, in jeans and matching green sweatshirts. Malcolm frowned. 'I wonder what they're doing.'

Gillian's voice chimed from behind him, accompanied by a dull clunk that told him she had polished his knife and fork and was putting it by his polished dinner plate. 'Who, dear?'

'Those two mad women from number fifteen. You know, the feminists, the ones who wear jeans all the time.'

'Audrey and Sylvia? What does it look like they are doing, dear?'

'They are knocking on his door.'

'Whose door?'

'The Hell's Angel's door, him with the big bike and the skinny women, the blonde one and the dark one, his two wives.'

Gillian sighed. 'Are you sure, Malcolm?'

'They have a cake. Audrey is holding it and they are knocking at number thirteen. I don't think he's in though. I saw them go out on the motorbike earlier today, just after lunch. He hasn't moved that Transit van, though, and I distinctly told him yesterday in the letter that he should move it at once...'

'What's it like, Malcolm?'

'The Transit van?'

'No, the cake.'

'I don't know, Gillian – it's in a cake tin. But I expect it's a fruit cake.'

'It might be an iced cake, with jam and cream. A nice Victoria sponge.'

Malcolm's voice became louder, irritated. 'For all I know, Gillian, it's one of those cakes the hippies make. You know, full of drugs, full of cannabis.'

'Can of what, Malcolm?'

'Bis.'

'Can of bis?' Gillian caught her breath. 'Oh, cannabis. They have made them a cake full of cannabis?'

'They're turning away. The feminists are going to take the cake back to their house. Oh no – look. Here they are now, on the bike.'

'The feminists?'

'No, Gillian, you're being silly. The Hell's Angel and wife number two. They've just arrived. He's stopped the bike. They are getting off it and now they are talking to Audrey and Sylvia. Now Audrey has given the dark-haired wife the cake tin and she's laughing. She's just kissed her on the cheek.'

'Who has?'

'Now that man from across the road has toddled across and

joined them and they are all laughing. You know, Vincent Stocker from number fourteen, that lad who lives with his old mother, Dilly.'

'I'm just fetching the potatoes, Malcolm. I'm just going to get them out of the oven or they'll burn. Then I'll bring the veg and the gravy. It's almost two o'clock.'

'They are all laughing, Gillian. And Vincent Stocker has given the Hell's Angel a beer bottle – it looks empty – and they are both having a rare old time talking together. The skinny woman with the dark hair has taken the bottle and now she's saying something and everyone is nodding their head and the big man looks very pleased with himself.'

'I'm just serving up the roast, dear.'

'Oh no! Oh, my goodness me... no!'

'What, Malcolm? What's happened?'

Malcolm lurched back from the curtain, alarmed, letting the fabric fall from his fingers, almost bumping into Gillian, who stood behind him clutching a brimming gravy boat as she leapt back in shock. The gravy slopped over, covering the back of her hand and she yelped in pain. Malcolm yelled louder, his face twisted in horror.

'She saw me, Gillian, the woman with the dark hair. She saw me here, watching her behind the curtains and she waved at me then the big man turned and saw me and waved and smiled. I've been spotted.'

Gillian held the gravy boat aloft and, shaking her left hand in the hope that the cool air might soothe the burn, she scuttled to the table. 'Never mind that now, Malcolm, your dinner is ready. Come and sit down.'

Malcolm tutted at his wife, as if she had irritated him somehow, and then he ambled across towards the table, his slippers making no sound on the carpet. He sat down, picked up his knife and fork and attacked the meat as if it was about to fight back, as if the roast lamb had just driven a Harley Davidson outside his house or parked a Transit van too close to his space. Gillian stared at the reddening patch on her hand, at the plates of food, the grey meat, the grey cabbage, the matching gravy and steaming potatoes, and sighed.

* * *

Dawnie turned the beer bottle upside down and shook it. Drops of water leaked onto the concrete, suggesting that Dilys had washed it out properly before sending it back for a refill. Dawnie chuckled. 'Well, I'm so glad your mother liked the home brew.'

'We both did,' Vinnie murmured. He glanced up to the bedroom above, wondering if the blonde sister was upstairs, if she was watching them.

Aude nodded towards the cake tin that Dawnie was hugging in her other hand. 'I hope you like carrot cake, Dawnie.'

'We love it,' Dawnie beamed. 'It was always my go-to cake for my great-grandchildren. They couldn't get enough of it. I'd ice it and cover it with little bits of orange jelly sweets, cut in the shape of carrots and little Caleb would—' She caught Billy's serious gaze and clamped her lips together. She beamed at the faces around her optimistically. 'Well, why don't you all come in with Billy and me now and have some cake?'

'I made it for *you*,' Sylv grinned.

Billy approached the door, holding out a key. 'Come in, will you all? You're all welcome. We'd be delighted if you'd step inside for a bite and maybe some of the home brew.' His eyes met Vinnie's hopeful expression. 'Sure, and we haven't had a housewarming party yet. The place isn't straight – we've hardly moved in – but I'd be a happy man if you'd all join us...'

He led the way inside, followed by his neighbours and then Dawnie. By the time she had reached the kitchen, Billy was already opening fresh beer bottles from beneath the sink. She placed the cake tin on the counter. 'We've got some veggies in, Billy, and some cheese. What shall we make?'

Billy beamed at her. 'I thought we'd knock up gnocchi with some vegetables and some white sauce. We have plenty of potatoes. It won't take long, and we've enough for the five of us.' He wrapped an arm around his wife. 'Dawnie and I, we love entertaining and cooking together.'

'Gnocchi sounds delicious,' Aude nodded, running a hand through her blonde hair. Vinnie was hunched over, looking awkward. 'I don't know. I left my mother by herself.'

Dawnie was chopping mushrooms. 'Shall I go over and fetch her?'

'I could go over to your house and carry her back?' Billy offered as he mashed cold potatoes in a large bowl for the gnocchi.

'She might be asleep.' Vinnie looked around him at the cardboard boxes piled high with utensils and pots. One box contained rusty tools and there were metal shapes that could be parts of a motorbike. Another box was full of clothes. Vinnie stared at a blue lace garment that he thought might be a bra. He shrugged nervously. 'What's your sister called, Dawnie?'

'Lorraine.' Dawnie thought of her sister who ran a B&B in Blackpool. Lorraine was nothing like her: younger, taller, broader, blonde. She smiled. 'Ah, she's a one, our Lorraine. She's had three husbands and she's looking out for a fourth.' She winked in his direction. 'Do you like blondes, Vinnie?'

Vinnie nodded, feeling his cheeks tingle. 'Where is she now, your sister?'

'She's in Blackpool. But no doubt she won't be able to stop

herself from visiting here, once we're settled. I'll have to introduce you.'

Vinnie coughed, his cheeks reddening, and he stared at his hands. Billy passed bottles and glasses to his three guests and began adding flour to the bowl and kneading gnocchi. Sylv took a swig of her beer.

'So, did you say you're renting here while you look for a place to buy?'

'Yes. We'd like somewhere with a nice view of the sea. I saw a lovely cottage in an estate agent's window this afternoon.' Dawnie reached for a beer. 'So sweet. Three bedrooms, a little garden with roses, even a pond for the fish.'

Billy chuckled. 'I'd never be able to stand up in the place. It has the low beams and low ceilings. It'd make me feel like a giant stuck in a kennel.'

'Billy likes big houses, farmhouses with huge rooms, space for his Harley, maybe a barn or two and room for his drum kit,' Dawnie giggled.

'Do you have a drum kit?' Vinnie's mouth gaped open.

'Oh yes, and it's all set up in the guest bedroom. Guests will have to sleep downstairs.' He chuckled. 'The third bedroom's not big enough for it and anyway I have the spare bike parts and my photographs in boxes in there.' Billy noticed Vinnie's astonished expression and a thought popped into his head. 'Do you want to see the kit?'

'Can I?' Vinnie's eyes gleamed.

Sylv leaned forward. 'Me too, please. I was in a brass band when I was a youngster and I played a snare. I've never played a full kit though.'

Dawnie began to grate some cheese. 'Go on, Billy. Take Vinnie and Sylv up and show them the kit. I'll finish the gnocchi and make the sauce.'

'And I can help, if you need a sous-chef?' Aude offered.

'It's a deal,' Dawnie smiled.

Billy wiped his hands on a tea towel, leaned over and pecked Dawnie's cheek. 'That'd be grand. Thanks, darlin'. We'll only be ten minutes.'

Dawnie winked at Aude. 'Don't make it more than twenty or it'll all be cooked, eaten and washed up.'

Billy led the way upstairs two steps at a time, Sylv bustling after him and Vinnie following, his movements hesitant. Aude picked up a knife and began chopping onions. Dawnie was dropping perfect pieces of gnocchi into a pan of bubbling water and heating oil in another, adding onions and mushrooms. Aude's voice was soft.

'You seem a very happy couple, you and Billy.'

Dawnie rolled her eyes, her face mock-romantic, and giggled. 'He's the best man there is, my Billy.'

'You have kids, don't you, and grandkids?' Aude wiped her eyes from the strength of the onion fumes. Dawnie did the same and nodded.

'Two grown kids, Lindy and Buddy. A granddaughter, Fallon, and three great-grandkids.'

'You must miss them.'

'Oh yes, I do, even though they're all a handful.' Dawnie nodded even more emphatically and waved a hand in front of her face, to dispel tears and the steam from the bubbling gnocchi water. She felt she should say something, move the conversation on, so she asked, 'Have you any kiddies, Aude?'

'No, sadly.' Aude pressed her lips together. 'It's just me and Sylv.' She rolled her eyes towards the ceiling and grimaced. 'It's very quiet up there.'

Dawnie chuckled. 'Billy will be telling them all about John Coghlan's cymbal.'

* * *

Billy was beaming at Sylv and Vinnie. 'I've had this kit for a long time. I've been building it, replacing bits, upgrading it, but this cymbal has been with me since 1977. I remember exactly when I got it. Dawnie and I wanted to treat ourselves to a night out. I'd been away for a while and we'd missed each other, and so we went to Manchester to see Status Quo in concert. I got myself invited back-stage afterwards to chat to the roadies and then I got talking to the drummer. Ah, he was a lovely fella, John Coghlan was. We talked about drums and venues and then he gave me one of his old cymbals. And this is it, still good to this day.'

'Incredible.' Sylv spoke reverently, touching the cymbal with light fingers. 'I've seen Status Quo five times. I saw them in Torquay once with Aude.'

'I've never seen them live.' Vinnie was still staring at the kit, his mouth open. 'I've always wanted to play the drums, though. Billy, I was thinking, could I just sit on the seat and hold the sticks up, like a real drummer?'

Billy handed him a pair of wooden drumsticks. 'Be my guest, Vinnie. Here you are.'

Vinnie eased himself around to the back of the kit, moving the round seat gently and sitting down with care. He bounced up and down on the seat a few times, making himself comfortable, and a grin spread across his flushed cheeks. 'This is good.' He held the sticks in the air and felt his confidence swell like a gust of wind. 'How do I look?'

'Like Keith Moon,' Sylv suggested.

'Or John Bonham.' Billy thought of his favourite drummer.

'I'd love to be a drummer,' Vinnie breathed. 'Do you know who my favourite is?'

'Ginger Baker?' Sylv was confident.

'No, I know, the Animal one from *The Muppets*?' Billy gave a cheeky wink.

Vinnie waved the sticks in the air and shook his head, the curls of the fringe above his eyes shifting from side to side. 'I like Ringo Starr.'

Billy patted his shoulder. 'Why don't you just give the cymbal a quick bash, Vinnie? It's a nice feeling, playing drums. It always helps me, when I'm a bit wound up, just to play a few licks.'

Vinnie thought about it. He imagined himself playing in a room, bright lights blazing overhead, girls in short skirts screaming adoringly below the stage. One of them was blonde, and looked exactly like Dawnie's sister. He brought both hands down with a crash. His foot found a pedal and he stomped hard as he thrashed at the cymbals with both sticks. Billy clapped and cheered, and Vinnie launched into a drum solo with all his energy.

* * *

Dawnie heard the insistent rapping of the front door knocker over the cacophony of the percussion upstairs. Sylv lifted her voice above the noise. 'Oh no – I can guess who that will be.'

'I'll get it. Can you keep an eye on the cooking? Dinner's almost ready,' Dawnie yelled. She wiped her hands on a tea towel and rushed towards the front door, screeching as she passed the stairs, 'Billy! Billy, can you tone it down a bit up there? I can hardly hear someone knocking at the door.'

The drumming stopped. Dawnie tugged open the front door to meet the gaze of a gaunt man in his seventies, his hair grey-brown and thinning on top. She looked him up and down. He wore a baggy cardigan, grey shirt and trousers, and tartan slippers on his feet. His arms were folded. When she met his eyes, he was grinning his teeth. He spat his words through them. 'What in hell's name do you think you are doing, woman?'

Dawnie frowned. She knew it had to be her neighbour from number eleven by his angry expression, and she truly sympathised with him, as the noise level upstairs had been clearly unacceptable, even to her. But she wasn't about to be addressed as 'woman' by anyone, and certainly not by someone she'd never met before who was leaning into her hallway with a seething face, so she fluffed her dark curls and said, 'What am I doing? I'm making gnocchi. Everyone's welcome here. Do you want to come in and join us for dinner?'

'No, I most definitely do not.' He folded his arms even more emphatically. 'It's Sunday afternoon, for goodness' sake.'

Dawnie offered him a perplexed expression. 'You must be our neighbour from number eleven. I'm Dawnie Smith. Can I offer you a brew? A pint of beer? Do you want to meet Billy, my husband, and say hello? He's just upstairs, practising his paradiddles...'

Malcolm actually stamped his foot. 'I don't want anything. Just stop that bloody noise, will you, or I'll be forced to call the police.'

Dawnie reached out and put a hand on Malcolm's arm. He winced, as if thinking she was about to give him a Chinese burn. She smiled sweetly into his face.

'Oh, the noise. You should have said. It was probably just Billy letting off steam on the drums.' She met Malcolm's eyes and beamed at him. 'The doctor has told him to bash the kit hard every once in a while, so that he'll de-stress. It keeps his aggression levels down.' She patted Malcolm's hand encouragingly. 'It stops him hurting anyone. That's why we moved house. He's like a caged lion when he's stressed. You should have seen what he did to our last neighbour...'

Malcolm's eyebrows shot up, and his frown deepened. Dawnie pushed the door closed so that only her face was peeking out. 'But

I'll ask him to stop playing now. Don't worry. He's probably calmed down. I don't think he'll murder anyone tonight. And oh, by the way, it was so nice to meet you.' She shut the door with a click.

As she turned round, Aude was behind her in the hall, a hand clamped across her mouth to stop the giggles. On the stairway, three figures loomed in shadow, listening: Billy, Sylv and Vinnie had heard every word. Billy rushed down and swept his wife off her feet, his eyes crinkling with amusement.

'Darlin', you are a wicked, wicked woman, so you are. No wonder I married you all those years ago.' He chuckled. 'But will we go and eat now? I'm starving, and after Vinnie's drum solo I have a real thirst on me.'

Dawnie squeezed his thick sausage fingers in her hand. 'It's all ready now, Billy. Yes, let's all go and sit down at the table.' She sighed and murmured to herself. 'I can't help thinking, though: I think we might have upset our next-door neighbour, just a teeny bit.'

6

'We had a lovely dinner last night, Mam, and home-made beer with it. And everybody helped with the food. Billy's a great cook, and Dawnie is too.'

'Nobody invited me round to eat at number thirteen.' Dilly folded her arms. 'I was here by myself until eight o'clock, Vinnie, freezing cold in my cardie, with a sandwich, watching Bruce Willis on television. Why ever didn't you come and get me?'

'I thought you'd be tired, Mam. I thought you'd want to rest. I mean...' Vinnie offered his most apologetic expression. 'I was playing the drum kit in the spare room. You'd have found it too noisy.'

'Not at all. I like a bit of proper drumming. Besides, I'm glad you're making friends. I mean, since you and that Sally split up, you've hardly made any new friends at all. You've been living here with me for how long? Nearly seven years now, Vinnie, so it's about time you started to gad about a bit.' Dilly pressed her lips together. 'I wouldn't have minded trying the gnocchi, though, or having a bit more of the home brew. It was tasty.' She poked her son with a long skinny finger. 'And I wouldn't have minded seeing Dawnie give a piece of her mind to Moaning Malcolm from number eleven. Both him and his wife, Mrs Frosty-knickers, they had it coming. The way they used to moan to everybody in the street about poor Jason and Darren and Jamie, those nice lads who lived there before. They made their lives a misery. No wonder they left and moved to Exeter. I wouldn't want to live in Exeter, mind. There's no sea to see.'

Vinnie folded his arms. He didn't like his mother mentioning Sally. It hurt him too much to think about it again. They'd lived together in a flat in Bideford. He had tried his best to make his ex-girlfriend happy, eleven years of working overtime in the carpet shop to buy her nice things, to take her to nice places. He remembered the skiing holiday in Austria, how lovely Sally had looked in the red one-piece ski suit, her blonde hair tucked in a red woollen hat with a pom-pom on the end. But she had flirted with the ski instructor and the barman, with her pouty lips and her long eyelashes, and Vinnie had felt left out. That was how Sally had always made him feel. Then she had left him for Joe, the man who worked at the railway station clipping the tickets; he had his own bungalow with a gravel drive, and he owned an open-top car.

The others before Sally hadn't been much better. Sonia had left him for the supermarket manager. Nicola had told him he was too serious and she had laughed when he'd cried. She had said she'd fallen for his doe eyes and beautiful curls but she'd wanted a man who'd be the boss. Vinnie didn't want to be the boss. He wanted someone to love him for who he was, someone he'd love back with all his heart. But at least he wasn't being dumped and laughed at now. At least, now he was living with his mother, he was safe from any risk of heartache.

But his mind was drifting to Dawnie, how cheerful and confident she was. Her sister must be the same. Vinnie had found out the name of the blonde sister – it was Lorraine – and Dawnie had said her sister would come to visit soon. Vinnie felt his heart knock in his chest. He was fifty-two but he was still young and capable of feeling love. He had his own hair, his own teeth; he was fit and muscular and he could scrub up to look smart if he wanted to. But he craved someone to care about him just a little bit, someone to snuggle up to him, to ruffle his soft curls and kiss his cheek. He closed his eyes and imagined Lorraine nibbling his ear.

'Vinnie, you're day-dreaming again, love.' Dilly patted his arm. 'I could do with a cup of tea. And my eye is properly painful today; you wouldn't be a love and fetch my drops? Then I thought we could have a nice sandwich and watch the serial on TV this afternoon, the one about the young woman who comes to live in the sleepy village and solves all the gory murders. Or should we get out a DVD? A nice Jean-Claude van Damme? What do you say?'

Vinnie opened his eyes and stared at his mother. 'All right, Mam. I'll put the kettle on, shall I?'

She blinked at him and gave her sweetest smile. He heaved himself from the sofa with a sigh as Dilly reached for the TV remote, and he trundled sadly towards the kitchen. He loved his mother. He'd do anything for her. But the truth was that each day was the same for him: it was empty, repetitive, each moment lacked something vital to bring his life alive. He knew what his problem was: it came to him each night before he fell asleep and it whispered loudly in his ear. He was lonely, and the loneliness slithered over his life like a cold snake and stole his confidence and made him shiver inside his own skin. He longed for someone warm, someone who would make his blood sing again. Behind him the television crackled to life and Vinnie heard his mother chuckle at something on the screen. She was watching action movies again. He sighed and filled the kettle.

* * *

Dawnie rolled more paint on the lounge wall over the old magnolia wood chip and stood back, blinking at the colour. Saffron Sizzle was more orange than yellow, and it shone in the sunlight that streamed through the window. Dawnie decided the pale curtains with the thin red stripes would have to go: she was in a home-making mood, dressed in jeans and one of Billy's t-shirts, her short platinum hair tied up in a red flowery scarf. She nodded: the paint would do the trick, bring in the sunshine and banish the dullness.

She and Billy had bought the tins of paint from a local DIY shop this morning and she had started decorating straight away. She couldn't wait to finish the whole lounge. Two walls would be in the stunning saffron colour and the rest of the room would be painted in a creamy pale yellow, Daffodil Dream. Billy needed calm colours in his home to help him relax, she knew that. He was out on his bike again, although he'd promised to be back as soon as he could, once he'd found a good local bike shop. He wanted to source a horn cover for the Harley, whatever that was. Dawnie pushed the roller along the paint in the tray and sloshed more colour on the walls. The room was too quiet so she hummed a tune for a moment, and then she paused.

She wondered if Malcolm next door could hear her humming and if he'd come round to complain. She'd turn the volume up: she chuckled and began to bawl out 'Maggie May', which was the bawdiest song she could think of since it was about a Liverpool prostitute who robbed a sailor. She stopped singing at the end of the song and the room was filled with silence. There wasn't a sound from next door, not the rustle of a voice in conversation or the rattle of a radio. Dawnie didn't like silence. Suddenly, she remembered a folk song called 'The Cuckoo's Nest', which she thought was fairly bawdy as it was about a woman losing her maidenhood, so to speak, so Dawnie began to sing that at the top of her voice with the intention of emphasising the raunchiest bits. It was a pretty song, despite the somewhat chauvinistic lyrics, Dawnie thought, but she threw herself into the rendition, slathering the walls with paint and wiggling her hips as she sang.

At the end of the song, she thought about following it up with the Sex Pistols' hit about misbehaving in the rigging, but the silence had returned to the room. Dawnie felt a pang of loneliness: she was a woman with a paintbrush in her hand, in a room full of unopened boxes and an unpleasant blue faux-leather sofabed and dull red striped curtains in a small terraced house in Maggot Street that didn't feel like home. She wondered when Billy would be back. She'd enjoyed herself last night, having dinner with neighbours, chattering to new people around a table, sharing home-brewed beer. She'd taken an immediate liking to Aude and Sylv from number fifteen: they were very friendly and had a ready smile and a sense of humour. And she'd liked Vinnie: he seemed a quiet sort, a bit shy but nevertheless, sensitive and good-natured.

Dawnie stopped painting, her saffron roller aloft, as a thought occurred to her: Vinnie had asked her what her sister's name was. Dawnie frowned. She knew for certain that she hadn't mentioned Lorraine to Vinnie at all. How did he know she had a sister? She shook her head and began to paint the walls in long strokes.

The front door clicked, and Billy called cheerily from the hallway. 'I'm home, darlin'.'

'I'm in here, lover.' Dawnie raised her voice although Billy was just outside the door. 'Did you bring me anything tasty back – apart from your hunky self?'

Billy stood in the doorway, filling the space, a giant of a man in a leather jacket, his hair dishevelled from the crash helmet he had pulled off. 'I stopped off at the estate agents we looked into yesterday and got us some house details.' He offered some papers to Dawnie. 'And I found a grand bike shop and, while I was there, I met this young fella.'

A tall, slender man emerged from behind Billy. He wore a leather jacket and had thinning fair hair that curled over his ears, and he peered through steel rimmed spectacles. He was a little younger than Billy, probably in his sixties, and he smiled as he met Dawnie's eyes, holding out slim fingers. 'You must be Dawnie. I've heard all about you. I'm Lester Wainwright.'

'Pleased to meet you, Lester,' Dawnie smiled, shaking his hand and staring at the helmet under his arm. 'You've come here on your bike, then?'

Lester nodded his head towards the front door. 'I left the Harley outside, next to Billy's, although Billy's bike is in much better shape than mine.'

Billy clapped his new friend on the shoulder. 'Lester's a doctor, darlin'.'

Dawnie's eyes flitted briefly to the printed details from the estate agents. Her gaze took in a photo of a huge majestic-looking house with a wild garden. She looked back to Lester. 'Doctor, eh? That might be useful. I've a sore knee that aches something rotten in the mornings. And I swear Billy's hearing is going.'

Lester shook his head, smiling. 'Doctor of entomology, I'm afraid: PhD from Reading, many years ago. I used to write books. I'm mostly retired now, although I still do a few bits and pieces; articles, photographs.'

'I'll have to get one of your books, Lester.' Dawnie's eyes gleamed. 'I love reading about insects and worms. I particularly love spiders; my last home in Bolton was full of them.'

Billy's face shone with enthusiasm. 'Lester lives two streets away, in Mary Street. He's got a big shed out the back, full of spare parts. So, put down your brushes and get your jacket on, darlin'. We're going round there now.'

'I'd love you to meet my wife Ursula, Dawnie.' Lester clutched his helmet in an embrace. 'She doesn't get out enough. She's not keen on the bike. But I know she'd love to meet you.'

Billy pointed at Dawnie's jacket and helmet, lying on the blue sofabed. 'Come on, darlin'. We can drive round there now. It's grand to meet another fella with a love of the bike and I'm dying to see what you have in the shed, Lester.'

'I can't go yet – I'm not dressed up,' Dawnie protested. 'Look at me, Billy – jeans and a baggy t-shirt and this old headscarf.'

'You look grand, darlin'.' Billy wrapped his arms around his wife. 'Come on, grab your things and we'll get along to Mary Street now, will we?'

'It'll be lovely to meet your wife, Lester. Okay, Billy, the painting can wait. Just give me a few moments to wash the brushes, though.' Dawnie rushed into the kitchen, making a clanking noise, bustling in the sink, and then she hurried back and reached for her leather jacket, her helmet and the estate agents' details. Billy was already opening the front door.

* * *

Gillian was polishing the table, spraying from a can and then rubbing the wood with a pristine yellow duster. Malcolm moved past her, his hip edging her to one side, and took his place at the window, twitching the curtains with nimble fingers. 'They are outside our house again, Gillian, the people from number thirteen.'

Gillian sighed. 'Why don't you go out for a nice walk, Malcolm? You always feel better after a stroll. The weather's lovely.'

'And bump into *him*? Don't be silly, Gillian. I told you what his other wife said to me. He's aggressive, dangerous.'

'I was thinking about making us a nice salad for—'

'Good Lord, there are two of them now.'

'Two what? Hell's Angels?'

'Two bikes. The Hell's Angel man has a friend, and he has a bike. They've parked them both right up next to the Honda Jazz.'

'I expect they'll move them soon, dear.'

'There's a whole pack of Hell's Angels living next door now. Whatever will we have next? An orgy?'

Gillian sighed and sprayed more furniture polish on the table. The heavy scent caught in her throat and she coughed.

'Oh look, a woman's come outside.'

'His wife, probably?'

'No, this is a different woman. Come and look, Gillian, before she puts the helmet on. This one's got short white hair,' Malcolm gulped, indignation constricting his throat. 'He's got three wives in there. Three!'

Gillian shook her head and sidled up to the window. Malcolm's face had reddened, broken veins purpling in his cheeks. He took a breath and puffed out air.

'I'll write it all down. I'll put the date in the log and record that there are two Hell's Angels next door, two bikes and the bigamist man has three wives.' He turned to Gillian, his face an expression of horror. 'Not two now, but three wives!'

Gillian returned to the table and lifted the duster. 'All three wives look exactly the same – they just have different hairstyles. It's the same woman, Malcolm.'

Malcolm wasn't listening; he pressed his nose to the window as Billy started up his engine. He watched Lester climb astride his Harley and Dawnie, in her helmet, clamber on the back of Billy's bike. As they all chugged away slowly, Malcolm narrowed his eyes.

'He thinks he can do what he likes, the Hell's Angel next door. He thinks he's a big man and he can just carry on as he pleases, ignoring rules of common decency. Well, he can just think again. I'll teach him how we behave in Margot Street, Gillian. I'll teach him a lesson.'

7

As soon as Dawnie entered the house, an end terrace with a garage attached and a garden to the rear, she could smell the warm scent of baking. Lester led her and Billy into the kitchen and called out to his wife to come and meet his new friends. A woman with honey-coloured hair that came to her shoulders, and pretty dimples in her cheeks, rushed over with open arms. She smelled of sweet honeysuckle.

'So pleased to meet you. I'm Ursula.'

Dawnie hugged her. 'Pleased to meet you too, Ursula. I'm Dawnie Smith. I can hear an accent. Is it German?'

'I am from Würzburg, in Bavaria, although I've been living over here for five years. Come into the conservatory, Dawnie. I will make us some tea. I have made cake already.'

Billy and Lester shuffled past the women, each with the same sheepish expression on his face. Billy patted Dawnie's shoulder, and Lester muttered, 'Will you both be all right if Billy and I spend some time in the shed?'

Ursula nodded, her voice soft in reply. 'It will give us time to get to know each other. Off you go, Lester, and take your new friend with you. Dawnie and I are going to eat cake and drink tea together.'

Lester and Billy slunk away towards the garden. Ursula picked up a tray with a tea pot and cups and led the way to the conservatory, which overlooked a neat patio and a flower bed. Through the sparkling glass, Dawnie could see Billy and Lester outside, fumbling at the locked door of a large wooden building, their heads close together. Ursula smiled. 'I don't think we'll see those boys for at least an hour. Can I offer you something to eat?'

Dawnie sat in a wicker chair and accepted a cup of tea and a generous portion of cake, filled with cream and chocolate. Dawnie licked her lips.

'*Kirschtorte.*' Ursula cut a liberal slice for herself. 'I hope you like cherries.'

Dawnie shovelled a dainty forkful into her mouth, looking around at the neat conservatory with cream blinds, wicker chairs with soft cushions and a small table on which Ursula had placed the tray. Next to it was a book entitled *Brilliant Bugs*. It had a chocolate brown cover featuring a glossy photograph of a huge beetle with long creepy legs and beady eyes. The author's name was Dr Lester Wainwright. Dawnie glanced at Ursula; in her floral blouse and dark trousers, she sat stiffly in her seat and smiled a little awkwardly at Dawnie.

'Great cake.' Dawnie thought she would put her hostess at ease. 'Did you make it? I bet you have plenty of time to cook, what with Lester studying insects and being out on his Harley all the time.'

Ursula's face was troubled as she nodded slowly. 'He is always busy, writing, taking photographs or fixing up his bike. I like to keep myself occupied.'

Dawnie studied the other woman. Her skin was smooth apart from laughter lines around her eyes. She could be in her late fifties or early sixties. It would be polite to ask her to talk about herself.

Dawnie raised inquisitive eyebrows. 'Do you work in Barnstaple, Ursula?'

Ursula chuckled. 'No, I don't work now, not since I came to England. In Germany I was a receptionist in a hotel. That is where I met Lester.'

Dawnie slurped her tea and nodded encouragingly. 'How did you meet him?'

Ursula's eyes shone with a soft light. 'Seven years ago, I was a divorcee and I met Lester. He had a broken relationship, a wife who had taken him for granted and then taken everything he owned. He needed a fresh start. Every year, the local Bavarian club would invite over their English riders, both clubs were affiliated together, and they all stayed in the hotel where I worked. Lester was part of the group. We met that year and struck up a sort of friendship.' Ursula patted her warming cheeks with soft fingers. 'The truth was I was very taken with him. He was such a gentleman and I thought he was so intelligent and well-spoken. Then, the next year, he came back and we met again. I suppose you would say we dated. We emailed each other, telephoned for a year and then, five years ago, he asked me to marry him and I said yes and came over to England to live here.' She beamed. 'And we bought this house and settled down. Lester has tried to retire but he's still very busy. And that is our story and we are very happy.'

Dawnie clapped her hands. 'That's lovely. Do you have any children, you know, from your first marriage?'

'One son, Meinke. He is still in Würzburg with his wife Frida and their daughter Liesel, my granddaughter.'

'You must miss them all.' Dawnie had finished her tea. The plate with the crumbs of cake lay on her lap.

Ursula nodded. 'Oh, yes.'

'I miss living with my daughter too, and granddaughter and great-grandchildren.' Dawnie met Ursula's eyes. 'My son Buddy is in the USA. I'm not sure what he's up to. I think he's playing in a band.' She sighed. 'Kids are a worry, aren't they, even when they are grown up.'

Ursula let out a long breath. 'And the men, too. Lester is out riding his Harley Davidson in the wind and the rain and when he is late to come home, I think of terrible things that might have happened to him and I worry so much. I don't drive myself. I don't like it, all the busy cars roaring past. It is as much as I can do to take the bus into town. So of course, when Lester is on his motorcycle, I worry.'

'I know what you mean about worry. Billy can be a real problem around the house, especially when he hasn't slept properly and he's all wound up like a caged animal. But I'm used to his ways now. He's done his own thing for most of our married life and he'll never change.' She lifted another forkful of cake, her head filled with images of the past. The room had become quiet, the women sitting still, immersed in their private thoughts. Dawnie took a breath and gave a determined smile. 'This is a beautiful house you have, Ursula. '

'It is very comfortable. Lester and I have made many improvements. We added on this conservatory two years ago. It is my favourite room to sit in the afternoon with tea.' She giggled softly. 'I am becoming very English.'

Dawnie's eyes lit up. 'Talking of houses, I don't suppose you could help me to choose somewhere to view...' She reached over to her jacket and pulled out the estate agents' leaflets, folded in her inside pocket. 'Billy brought these back today. We're looking for a house so that we can settle down somewhere close to the sea, for Billy. We want to buy a house that will be perfect for the pair of us, and soon.'

Ursula took the papers, reached for a pair of half-moon glasses and put them on, gazing with interest at the details. Her face brightened. Dawnie leaned forward, balancing the remains of the cake on her knee. 'What do you think?'

'This one is nice – and Chulmleigh's so beautiful,' Ursula sighed. 'A lovely detached cottage, all original beams from the 1700s. But it is modernised inside, the kitchen is small but pretty. Or this one, in Saunton, with the large windows – this is very grand. It is called Chestnut House: it says in the print that it is only five minutes' drive from the sea. I love the views around Saunton. And it is such an imposing building. Would five bedrooms be too many for you, I wonder, Dawnie?'

'Not for Billy,' Dawnie cackled. 'He'd use three of them as man-caves: he'd put his bike parts in one bedroom, his drum kit in another and he'd set up the third as a workshop.'

Ursula's laughter tinkled. 'Oh, these men.' She covered her mouth with dimpled hands but tears shone in her eyes. 'They will be the ruin of us. But we love them so much.'

'You're right, Ursula. But this house move is really important for us both now,' Dawnie grinned. 'I think the world of Billy but it's been tough going for us both for most of our married life, so I won't settle for second best now. I want the perfect place. We deserve it. Billy deserves it after all he's had to put up with…'

'Is it me you're talking about?' Billy grunted good-humouredly from the doorway, making Dawnie jump and her cheeks flush. 'I can feel my ears burning up.'

Lester was leaning over his shoulder, grinning. 'Billy and I have had a great time talking about bikes in the shed, *Liebling*.' He walked over and kissed the top of Ursula's honey-coloured hair. 'We might be able to help each other out with a few odd jobs and we can share spare parts too.'

Ursula stood up. 'I will get you both a cup of tea and some cake. More tea for you, Dawnie?'

'Oh yes, please. Sit down next to me, Billy. Ursula has found us a house I want to go and view. We'll ring them up and book an appointment. It's called Chestnut House; it has five bedrooms, a huge garage and it's only a few minutes from the sea. What do you think?'

'Five bedrooms and a garage?' Billy's eyes gleamed. 'That could be ideal. I'd have plenty of room for my bike and my drum kit. I could even buy another classic bike... or two.'

* * *

Billy slowed the Harley down outside number thirteen Margot Street, and stopped the engine. Dawnie gazed over his shoulder at the curtains in number eleven from her pillion seat. There was no sign of movement inside the house. She slid from the seat and took off her helmet. 'Billy, I've been thinking. I'm going to go and call in on our neighbours.'

'Malcolm and his wife? Shall I come along with you?'

'No.' Dawnie bundled her jacket and helmet into Billy's arms, adjusted the floral headscarf and met his eyes. 'I want to pop in and apologise to them. I was a bit over the top last night, telling him tales about you being dangerous. I want to try to build some bridges. It might be best if I just go by myself for the first visit. Both of us together might be too much for them. You never know, Billy, he might start shouting and I don't want you to have to deal with that. I'll try to make the peace.'

She kissed Billy's cheek through the raised visor of his helmet and he threw an arm around her shoulder. 'All right, darlin'. You know best. While you're gone, I can have a little look at these bits and pieces Lester gave me.' He brandished a fist full of metal he'd pulled from his pocket, washers or nuts – Dawnie wasn't sure.

She flashed her eyes at him. 'I was hoping you'd get some of the painting done: you could finish that wall in the lounge.'

He patted her shoulder. 'Leave it all with me, darlin'. I'll sort it all.'

'If I'm not back home in half an hour, send a rescue party,' Dawnie chortled. 'Malcolm might have murdered me...'

Dawnie waited for the front door to click. After Billy had gone inside, she took a deep breath, pulled her t-shirt straight, ignoring the blot of saffron paint on the hem, and adjusted her floral head-scarf, teasing strands of platinum hair over the top. Then she knocked firmly with a clenched fist at the door of number eleven and waited. She knocked again. Almost immediately, someone peered through the curtains. Through the slice of opened door, Dawnie saw a woman with neat white hair, the fringe held back with a grip, her ample figure encased in a blue flowery dress. The neighbour frowned at Dawnie. 'Yes?'

Dawnie offered her most compelling smile. 'Mrs Frost, isn't it? I'm Dawnie Smith. My husband and I live next door at number thir-teen.' She paused, hoping the woman would introduce herself properly.

'Yes?'

'I wonder if I might come in a moment.'

Gillian Frost pressed her lips together. 'Malcolm is out.'

'Please?' Dawnie raised her eyebrows encouragingly. 'I just wanted to apologise.'

Gillian's expression seemed to soften at the word apologise. She opened the door a little more. 'All right, just for a moment.'

Dawnie followed her neighbour into a tidy lounge with a cream carpet and a brown leather suite. In the corner was an oak table and the door to the small kitchen was open, revealing a white cooker and cream cabinets. The room smelled of furniture polish. Dawnie waited to be asked to sit down but Gillian Frost turned squarely to face her, as if they were about to begin a bout of armed combat. 'Well, what do you want?'

'Mrs Frost, I was hoping your husband would be in too.'

'He's gone out for his constitutional.'

Dawnie frowned, wondering why Gillian hadn't joined him on his walk. She stared into the woman's narrowing gaze and immediately knew there was no chance of a neighbourly cup of tea, let alone a biscuit. She breathed in. 'Well, as I was saying, Billy and I have rented the place next door and I wanted to make sure we didn't all get off on the wrong foot.'

Gillian folded her arms and said nothing.

'I may have been a bit rude to your husband last night. I'm afraid he caught me at a bad moment.' Dawnie almost giggled, a nervous choke in her throat. She turned it into a cough. 'The drumming outburst was a mistake. It won't happen again. And about the bike too, and the Transit van being in your way – we'll make sure it's parked closer to Sylv and Aude's Fiat so it won't inconvenience you...'

She looked hopefully at Gillian, who still said nothing, but continued her hard stare. Dawnie was reminded of being at school, years ago, scolded by a particularly heartless headmistress who was trying to shame her into obedience. Dawnie thrust out her chin. Her encounter with Gillian made her feel exactly the same, except Dawnie was seventy, not seven years old.

She tried the charismatic grin again. 'I hope that will go some way to sorting things out between us.'

Gillian nodded. 'I'll tell Malcolm about it when he gets back.'

Dawnie glanced around the room. There was a picture on the mantelpiece: a young man in uniform with a serious expression. Dawnie picked it up to examine the soldier's face.

'Put that down,' Gillian snapped.

Dawnie glanced at her, her face apologetic. 'I'm sorry. I just thought...' She placed the photograph back carefully. 'Is that your son?'

Gillian nodded. 'James.'

'Is he still in the forces?'

Gillian looked away. The silence in the room felt cold and Dawnie shivered. She thought about mentioning her own children, Lindy Lou and Buddy, but Gillian's face was set hard and her eyes glittered. Somehow it didn't feel right. Instead, Dawnie offered a broad grin. 'It's a lovely photograph.'

Gillian nodded curtly and folded her arms.

'And...' Dawnie's smile broadened; it was now so wide it made her cheeks hurt. Her mind moved quickly for something to say that would create a sense of harmony. 'We're neighbours, so I hope that means we can become good friends.'

'Friends?' Gillian's face held a doubtful expression.

Dawnie racked her brain in a desperate attempt to be sociable. 'You know, help each other out, remind each other about putting out the bins, move heavy furniture together and swap recipes and such.'

Gillian pursed her lips, making her mouth appear like a tightly stitched sock. 'Recipes?'

For a moment there was silence. Dawnie's mind raced, realising that Gillian disapproved of her suggestion, trying to find any way to endear herself to her neighbour. Then suddenly, unable to stop herself, she began to chatter about the first idea that came into her head.

'Recipes. Different dishes, exotic ones, traditional ones. I make a great hotpot. I could give you the recipe. Billy does a good Irish stew, not that we have it very often. We hardly had it at all when my children were growing up, of course, with Billy being away a lot, but we did have the hotpot, proper Lancashire hotpot all the time, three times a week, and I do a great spotted dick. I bet you'd love to try some spotted dick with jam... and custard...'

Dawnie gave up. Gillian was staring at her. She breathed out again, in defeat. 'Well, I'll be off now, shall I? It was nice talking to you...' She searched for the woman's name but it occurred to her that she didn't know it, so she settled for a formality. 'Mrs Frost.'

Gillian nodded. 'I'll show you out, Mrs Smith.'

'Ms Smith. Billy's my husband and he's a Murphy but I've always been...' Dawnie recognised the blank lack of interest on Gillian's face. She considered hugging her neighbour but decided it was probably too early in their relationship. Dawnie adjusted her headscarf, flicked her fringe and grinned.

'Well. I'll get off home now, shall I? Next door?' She gave a wild laugh and made a rush towards the exit. 'Have a good evening then and – we'll be as quiet as possible – not that we are normally quiet, mind, but we'll do our best and – and – and give my love to Malcolm.'

Dawnie heard Gillian close her front door sharply behind her. She breathed out in relief and realised she didn't have a key to number thirteen. She rapped on the front door with her fist, forgetting that it had both a bell and a knocker, and when Billy opened the door she threw her arms around him with a desperate gasp.

'Let me in quickly and get the home brew out, Billy, or the brandy. I need a stiff drink. I've just been through the silent inquisition ordeal next door and I'm definitely not going back in there again – ever.'

8

'She has a northern accent, dear. She's certainly not from these parts.'

'Outsiders? Well, of course they are.'

'Then she said she'd give me some recipes, Malcolm.'

'Whatever for?'

'Lancashire hotpot, I think, and spotted dick.'

'I mean why did she offer to give you recipes? Your cooking is quite adequate normally. And you know I don't like hotpot. The woman must be raving mad.'

'She did apologise to me, though.'

'I wish I'd been here, Gillian. I wouldn't have accepted an apology. Oh no, no apology, not without conditions attached.'

'She seemed very friendly.'

Malcolm rested his chin on his chest. 'It's not *her* I'm worried about, it's *him*. I mean, she told me about his history of aggression, and we can see he's a thug from the way he walks about with that leather jacket on.'

'Oh, and she promised he wouldn't play the drums again. And he's moved the Transit van to give you more room.'

'I noticed that. What else did she say?'

'Not a lot, dear. Oh, there was one thing. She said he's a good cook but he wasn't used to cooking very often because he'd been away a lot.'

Malcolm's jaw became slack. 'Away? As in away, inside, in prison?'

Gillian turned away and moved to the table, lifting up the can of polish and the duster. 'I don't know. I suppose so, yes.'

'For GBH, no doubt. And dealing in stolen goods. Drugs even.' He turned to his wife, his eyes glassy behind the frames. 'Gillian, we're living next door to a criminal. This is terrible. We have to warn people, make sure everyone in the street knows the dangers. It's our duty.'

* * *

It was Friday morning and a beam of sunshine soft and yellow as melting butter illuminated the freshly painted walls in the lounge. Dawnie had found a leopard print throw and some matching cushions to cover the dull blue sofabed. The room seemed warmer, more homely. Billy and Dawnie stood together, arms around each other's waists, surveying the space, now tidy, clear of all boxes and with one of Billy's framed pictures on the wall. Beneath his leather jacket, Billy wore his clean Foo Fighters t-shirt and his best jeans. Dawnie's red curls framed her face and she sported leather trousers and a sparkling gold vest. She patted the red wig, teasing a curl from her eyes. 'How do I look, Billy?'

'Ah, you're a vision,' he sighed, kissing the tip of her nose.

She waved a hand around the room. 'The walls are lovely now, and your photo is the centrepiece.'

'It's the curlew I photographed a few years back.'

'I'm glad you found the picture, Billy – it looks nice against the saffron yellow wall.'

'I think Lester would appreciate it.'

'He's an entomologist, love – they only like worms and bugs…'

'He's fascinated by all wildlife and nature. He's a good fella. We'll have to pop round there again soon or invite them round here.'

'I liked Ursula too. I think she's a bit, you know, lonely, Billy. I'll maybe drag her out with me one night. We could go dancing.'

He squeezed her arm. 'Whatever you fancy doing, darlin', is fine by me. But we have an appointment at one o'clock. Shall we get going? It's a beautiful day to be out on the bike, for sure, and we've a house to view.'

* * *

The estate agent was standing by his BMW outside Chestnut House, a majestic building with a brick frontage, as Billy and Dawnie rode up the gravel drive. He glanced up from his clipboard and back again. When Billy and Dawnie dismounted, the estate agent came over and extended his hand to Billy. 'Simon Mountjoy.'

'Billy Murphy.' Billy shook the estate agent's hand energetically. 'And this is Dawnie Smith.'

Simon Mountjoy glanced at Dawnie as she tugged off her helmet, his eyes flicking over the curly red hair and the gold vest beneath her jacket, then he turned back to Billy. 'Well, I think you're going to be impressed by Chestnut House. The Myttons have decorated it tastefully in the five years they've been here. They are looking to go back to South Africa, where they have family. Shall we go inside? Follow me, please.'

The estate agent pivoted on his heel and forged ahead towards the house, his walk brisk. Dawnie noticed that Simon Mountjoy had a very narrow bottom and slim legs as he strode along in his navy suit. His smartly cut dark hair lifted a little in the light breeze. He couldn't be more than thirty years old. He reached the oak front door and turned to Billy with a practised smile.

'This place has been on the market for just over a week but you're the third people to view. Shall we go round the side of the house and start with the boot room?'

They followed the estate agent along a little path and waited as he pushed a long key into a lock. They entered into a narrow room, where coats hung on pegs and wellingtons and shoes were inverted on racks, the soles spotless. Two huge metal bowls were empty on a plastic mat, bags of dried dog food neatly stacked to one side. Simon Mountjoy nodded towards Billy. 'The owners are out currently. Shall we go and see the kitchen? It certainly is the heart of this home.'

Dawnie followed Simon and Billy into a square room with three large windows with gingham curtains. A long quartz worktop occupied one wall, with scarlet and cream tiles. Dawnie glanced around at a Belfast sink, several pristine food-processing machines of various sizes in chrome and cherry red, a gleaming kettle and, just behind them, a spotless cream Aga cooker. In the centre of the room were a square oak table and four chairs. Dawnie glanced at Billy. 'This is lovely, isn't it?'

'Oh, it is. We could live here, darlin'.'

'Is the cooker gas or electric, Simon? Or wood or solid fuel?' she asked but the estate agent had already turned towards the door. Simon led them into a hallway with cream floor tiles and into a dining room, where there was a long formal table with a chandelier above it. The window contained two identically-framed photographs, one of a couple smiling for the camera in their wedding clothes and another of a bespectacled young man in a gown and mortar board, holding a rolled certificate tied with purple ribbon, his face beaming with pride.

They crossed another hallway into a lounge with an open fireplace, a wood burning stove and a neat stack of logs. There was a cream three-piece suite and a large rug on the oak floor. There were oak beams above their heads and on the wall a stag's head gaped, its glassy eyes focused ahead. Dawnie muttered, 'I don't like that, Billy.' He took her hand and they followed the estate agent into a vast hallway.

'Shall we look at the bedrooms, Mr Murphy?' Simon suggested, leading the way up a winding carpeted staircase, the white walls displaying wedding photographs of the couple and several more framed snaps showing their son in various poses from childhood to adolescence. At the top of the stairs, Simon indicated a large blue bathroom with a free-standing bath with gold taps and a spacious shower cubicle at the end, and the fourth bedroom, currently a spare, with white walls and a cream duvet. Simon turned to Billy. 'You aren't local?'

'Ah, we're renting locally,' Billy grinned. 'While we find the perfect place. We're cash buyers.'

'Our other home is up in Bolton,' Dawnie added chirpily. 'It's a big Victorian semi. It has four bedrooms and an attic and a cellar. Our children and granddaughter and great-grandchildren are living there.'

Simon didn't seem to hear: he gave Billy his full attention. 'I don't expect Chestnut House to be on the market for very long, Mr Murphy. As I say, there has been a lot of interest. If you look through the window in the master suite...' He moved expertly to the largest bedroom and pointed to the double-glazed frames. 'You can see the sea from here.' He held back the curtains and Billy nodded. Dawnie eased her husband to one side, peering beneath his arm.

'Oh yes, I can see: it's just a thin line at the moment. Very nice view, though.'

'I expect the tide is out, darlin'. But it's not far away: we'd be on the beach in minutes from here. And there's plenty of room for my bike and the Transit.'

Simon offered Billy his practised smile. 'The garden is three quarters of an acre. Shall we go outside, Mr Murphy?'

'That'd be deadly.' Billy beamed at his wife. 'Let's go and see the garage, shall we? And I think there are fruit trees outside, an orchard. I might even be able to make my own cider.'

Dawnie turned and followed the men who were in conversation together, one small bottom in a navy suit and one larger backside in jeans, walking down the stairs towards the front door. She felt her fingers clenching into fists.

* * *

'He didn't speak to me at all, Billy.' Dawnie clung to Billy as he manoeuvred the Harley through evening traffic, skilfully passing a black Audi that was taking up far too much of the road. 'I mean, it didn't matter what I said to him – he totally ignored me. He wouldn't even look in my direction.'

Billy shrugged huge shoulders. She heard his raised voice drift back. 'It was a nice house, though, Dawnie. I could live there. All those apple trees in the garden. And three good-sized sheds and a double garage.'

'That's not what I'm saying.' She made her hand into a fist and resisted the urge to tap him hard on the back: he was driving, and she loved him too much to hurt him, even through the thick leather of his jacket. Instead, she raised her voice against the wind. 'I mean, Simon Mountjoy was so rude. I tried to get involved with the conversation but he acted like I wasn't there and spoke directly to you, as if what I thought didn't matter.'

Billy said nothing for a while. He was looking around himself, negotiating a roundabout. Then Dawnie heard him mumble. 'He was all right, the Simon one. He was only the estate agent – you don't need to pay mind to him. The house was grand, though.'

'He put me right off the place.' Dawnie squeezed her eyes closed. 'It's happened to me before, being ignored. It's just typical. Because I'm an older woman, these men think I'm invisible or not important at all.' Her fingers caught the red threads of her wig as the hair blew into her eyes. 'Invisible, me? I mean, I may not be seventeen but I'm hardly dowdy... it's not as if I'm not noticeable, is it?' She leaned her face against the leather of his back and felt Billy chuckle. He muttered something about his beautiful wife being hard to ignore and how she was the loveliest woman on the planet.

Dawnie gritted her teeth. She loved Billy but sometimes he could be exasperating: he just didn't understand how it felt to be a woman of a certain age. She would have liked him to have stood up for her, to have said something like, 'This is my wife Dawnie, Mr Mountjoy. We're buying the house together and she's just spoken to you but you ignored her. I won't have it.'

But he hadn't noticed. And she, Dawnie, in her tight leggings and gold sparkly top and curly red wig had been sidelined, ignored and treated as some has-been woman who had nothing to offer any more, just a mere bystander to the transactions of an estate agent and the big man who held the purse strings. Dawnie blew air through her mouth, exasperated. She wouldn't be ignored. She would fight back.

'Billy. Are you listening to me? I won't put up with it.'

'Right, darlin'. Of course you won't.'

Dawnie clutched her arms tightly around his waist. He was strong and immovable, as solid as ever. But he didn't understand how she was feeling right now. Being unnoticed smarted, an open wound. She'd rushed through her life so far, an impatient adolescent and bride, a busy mother, at times a lone parent, then a doting grandmother. She'd spent all her adult life being a good wife and mother, but just as soon as she'd slowed down to take notice of what was going on around her, it became clear how others viewed her: she was merely someone's wife, someone's mother, an older woman who didn't count for anything. Dawnie suddenly felt the surge of determination that always followed injustice. Her good looks may have faded, but her appearance didn't define her: she was still the same woman, a woman of substance with a good heart, so how dare someone assume she was of no importance any more? It made her fume. There was no way she would drift into old age and become as decayed and dust-laden and worn out and rickety as the old furniture in the house they were renting. Dawnie was determined she would not be overlooked. There was still plenty of life left in her yet. An idea filled her head and she thrust out her chin.

'Billy, I've decided. I'm going to organise something nice for our neighbours, something that will bring the residents of Maggot Street together and show them how to have fun.' A wide grin spread across her face. 'Yes, I know exactly what I'll do. It's time to give all our neighbours a properly good time and get them to sit up and take notice.'

9

Dawnie had decided she would look business-like but display the carefree air of a holiday rep at the same time, so she had chosen a smart pair of jeans, a light jacket, a colourful blouse and a trilby hat over her short hair. She added bright earrings and a huge necklace of matching beads and a clipboard. She rapped at the door of number fourteen, her face already set in a smile. It was Tuesday, half past five in the afternoon: Dawnie knew Vinnie worked at the garden centre as a buying administrator, but she hoped he might be home by now. She glanced at the clipboard, at the names on her list so far. Aude and Sylv had said yes straight away: they'd jumped at the idea of a day trip to Plymouth. Of course, Lester and Ursula had been up for it; as soon as she and Billy had popped round, Ursula had agreed to go, putting the kettle on and offering delicious cake.

And, equally unsurprisingly, there had been no reply from the Frosts when she'd called round. Dawnie pressed her lips together: in almost four weeks at Margot Street, she had only spoken to Malcolm Frost once, when he knocked at the door of number thirteen to complain about the noise of the drums and the parking, and she'd only spoken to Mrs Frost once – she still didn't know her first name – to apologise. Dawnie mused: they were strange neighbours, the Frosts, not at all welcoming. She'd never met anyone like them before, not in any of the places she'd lived, and she'd had some interesting neighbours in her time.

Dawnie was thinking of Mrs Willis, a little round woman who had lived in the tiny terraced house next to her in Raikes Way when she and Billy were first married and Lindy Lou was a newly-born baby. Billy was away from home and Pat Willis kept a watchful eye on Dawnie and her little one, popping round each day to chat and to cuddle the baby. Mrs Willis, who looked ancient to Dawnie then but was probably only in her forties, worked in a biscuit factory and brought round 'freebies', as she used to call them, always mispronouncing the names of the brands and offering her a conspiratorial wink. 'Dawnie, love, I got you some coconut *mellows* and some *alibees*. No, none of them was pinched; they're all above board, love.'

Dawnie used to adore the foil-wrapped Alibi biscuits with the mint centre; the coconut mallows she'd give to Tasker, an old mutt who belonged to an equally old gentleman called Derek Cuthbertson several doors down. Tasker used to call round every house in the street once a day for scraps and, where none were given, he'd leave a smelly memento on the doorstep.

Dawnie was smiling at the recollection as the door creaked open and a small woman with a pair of heavy-framed glasses peered out. Her hair was long and pale, wound around her head and fastened with a clip. She waved a thin hand over her eyes and spoke in a soft Welsh accent.

'I'm sorry – I'm not buying anything today. I've got enough pegs to last me the rest of my days and if you're the Jehovah's Witnesses, I'm not religious.' She blinked at Dawnie. 'You don't look much like a Jehovah's Witness in that hat, mind.'

Dawnie beamed. 'I'm Dawnie Smith from across the road.'

'Oh, you're the home brew woman who's moved in with the man on the motorbike? Well, the home brewed beer is very nice, I can tell you. You're the one who told Malcolm Frost where to get off, am I right? You'd better come in. I don't like this draught around my ankles.'

Dawnie wasn't aware of a draught – it was a warm May day – but she followed the old lady into her house. It was chilly inside. The woman sat on the sofa, which was covered with a brown woollen throw with long tassels.

'I'm Dilly Stocker. I hope you don't mind if I don't offer you tea, Dawnie. Vinnie will be here any moment now; he finishes at five; he'll be on the bus, coming back from work. He'll make us a nice brew. Was it Vinnie you wanted to see?'

Dawnie brandished her clipboard. 'I'm organising a trip to Plymouth, to go dry slope skiing.'

'Well, I don't know about it all. Is there snow in Plymouth now? I can't say I'm surprised, mind. They say it's a strange place, Plymouth, always very windy and cold there.'

Dawnie smiled. 'I've got Aude and Sylv on board for a skiing trip and our friends Ursula and Lester from Mary Street. Sylv will drive her car and Lester has a four-seater, so we've space for four more people. I was going to ask Vinnie and Mr and Mrs Frost next door – they have a car.'

'Oh, they won't go, Malcolm and Mrs Frosty-Knickers. I can tell you that, Dawnie. They are very...' Dilly met Dawnie's eyes with a serious gaze. 'Very antisocial. And they aren't very neighbourly. You could ask them, mind, but they'll say no.' She patted Dawnie's hand and her gaze became more intense. 'What is it, dried sloping skiing? Do you have to be young to do it? You see, I haven't been out anywhere in a while.'

Dawnie scratched her head beneath the trilby. 'I'm sure it would be all right for you to come with us, Dilly: I mean, they do an introduction for beginners and you can have up to twelve people in a group.'

Dilly took Dawnie's fingers in hers, a claw of a hand with raised purple veins like little twigs. 'I want to go. I've never done anything like it before. Tell me what happens to you when you go. What do they do to you?'

'They have... it's like false snow, like white AstroTurf; it's all outside and we'd be in a beginners' group.' Dawnie smiled, taking in Dilly's serious face. She waved her clipboard like a real holiday rep. 'We'd all be in a group together; they show us how to walk on skis and we'd have a little slide down the teaching slope.'

'But what about me? I've never skied before. And I'm eighty-six, mind.'

Dawnie squeezed Dilly's hand. 'There's no age limit mentioned on the website. Just come anyway. You'll be fine. I've skied a couple of times, but I was no good at it. We'll stick together: we'll just laugh and have fun. If they don't let us on the slopes, maybe we can just sit down and watch the others.'

'All right. I haven't got any skis. Or one of those fancy ski suits.'

Dawnie grinned. 'They give you skis. As long as you are well-covered and warm, you don't need specialist clothes.'

'I have a tracksuit somewhere in a bottom drawer.' Dilly nodded. 'And maybe I could borrow one of your husband's crash helmets, from his motorbike?'

Dawnie sat upright. 'If you want to go, Dilly, I'll put your name down. You and Vinnie can travel in the car with Sylv and Aude. I've booked us in provisionally for this Sunday afternoon.'

The front door rattled and Vinnie burst in, his cheeks red. 'Hi Mam, I'm back. The bus was full up today so I decided to walk—' He stopped and stared at Dawnie, pushing his hands through his curls. 'Dawnie? You've had your hair cut off.'

Dawnie whipped off the trilby, pushed fingers through her hair and replaced the hat. 'I'm a woman of many styles, Vinnie.'

Vinnie continued to stare so Dilly pointed a bony finger in his direction. 'Put the kettle on, will you, Vinnie. Dawnie is organising a trip to go on the dried skiing in Plymouth and we're going with her. You're not working Sunday afternoon, are you?'

'No, it's a day off.' Vinnie's face brightened. 'I love skiing. I'm quite good at it. I remember when I went to St Johann with—' His face clouded suddenly and he put his head down, walking briskly towards the kitchen. 'I'll make us all a brew, shall I, Mam? How – how do you like your tea, Dawnie? Sugar and milk?'

'Just milk: I'm sweet enough.'

Dilly met Dawnie's eyes meaningfully. She leaned forward and lowered her voice. 'It's a shame for him, such a lovely lad, he is. My Vinnie's had his heart broken, you know. Several times. They weren't my sort of women, the ones he hooked up with, mind. They all told him he was too nice for them, then they dumped him and broke his heart. Slappers, they were, if you ask me, all of them. Put his name down for the dried skiing, will you, Dawnie? It'll be good for him to get out a bit with young people his own age.'

Dawnie shook her head, perplexed. She was surely more than fifteen years older than Vinnie and Dilly was his mother and she was quite ancient, although Dawnie had to admit she had plenty of pluck. She wondered if Dilly was referring to Aude and Sylv as the young people of Vinnie's age. She flourished her pen. 'I'll put you both down then, shall I? That's great.'

* * *

It was Saturday night and Dawnie couldn't sleep. She wasn't worried about the ski trip: it was all organised. There would be two cars for the six people and Dawnie and Billy would take the Harley.

Lester and Ursula would go together in their car – Ursula would not ride on the motorbike – and Sylv and Aude would take Vinnie and Dilly. The Frosts at number eleven hadn't answered when she'd called, and she had tried twice. The skiing trip was all booked and they'd have a great time. But she'd been awake since midnight and it was three-thirty in the morning. Dawnie couldn't sleep. She was thinking about her children.

Lindy Lou had phoned her after dinner and they'd talked for almost an hour while Billy was in the hall tinkering with the Harley. For once, Dawnie couldn't get a word in. Lindy had chatted about her job in the school serving dinners and how she'd been promoted to the role of a supervisor; about how Stewie was doing well at the factory, enthusiastically educating everyone on the shop floor about the hazards of plastic waste. Lindy had asked briefly about Dawnie and Billy and how the house hunting was going, but then she'd talked about how she and Stewie had moved into Dawnie's old bedroom, decorating the walls a bright sail-white instead of the damson paint Dawnie had enthused about three years before, and how there was so much space now some of the old furniture had been recycled. Fallon had her own room; baby Milo had moved into the freshly painted nursery and Willow and Caleb were much more settled in bunk beds.

Lindy had been bursting with anecdotes: weekend picnics, a trip out in the old Renault Espace to West Houghton, scrumptious family meals cooked from scratch. It seemed that Fallon was blossoming into a brilliant mother, independent and creative, attending local parent and baby groups, reading bedtime stories, now that... At this point, Lindy had paused and asked about her father, how Billy was enjoying the sea air.

But Dawnie had known what Lindy had been about to say. She'd held her phone in her fist, a smile on her face, her eyes glistening with tears. She'd understood the words that hadn't been uttered: now that Dawnie was not there to take over, to interfere, things were much better. Of course, Lindy hadn't been intentionally dismissive: she loved her parents and was full of gratitude that they'd left them in the house to make their own home and to find their own way. They were flourishing. Dawnie was delighted that they were doing so well, but something deep down still hurt.

After the call had finished, she had put her mobile phone away, checked that Billy was still in the hall working on his bike, and cried silent tears. She had wanted to howl aloud, to let the pain bubble and surface as a keening cry, but she wiped wet eyes on the back of her hand and felt her breath shudder. Then she had taken her phone out again and stared at Lindy's number. Moments ago, it was if they had almost been in the same room but now her daughter was so distant, Dawnie felt alone. She searched for Buddy's number and texted him without thinking.

How are you, Buddy? How is the band? I am missing you.

She hadn't pressed *send*. Billy had come back into the room, asking her if she'd help him find a tiny metal washer he'd dropped onto the hall lino. Her eyes were sharper than his. She had followed him without a word and found it straight away. Then, an hour later, she wondered if she should send the message to Buddy or if she was just behaving stupidly, a lonely mother, a clucking hen with an empty nest, who had no use any more and was in the throes of a final lonely squawk. She had held her breath and pressed *send* but of course, so far, she had received no reply.

Dawnie rolled over in the bed and clutched the pillow. She felt the weight of Billy as he turned towards her, snuffling and mumbling something in a hoarse voice. Dawnie hugged the pillow and felt tears come quickly. She snuffled, tried to swallow them. It would be so easy to give up, to break open, to cry hot tears: she missed her children and the ache sliced her open like a hot knife. But she caught her breath and swallowed hard, determined to fight, to take back control of her emotions. Billy had said it so often: the kids had their own life; they were thriving and it was an opportunity for her to lead her own life. She knew he was right, so why did she keep coming back to the lonely place, the impasse, an empty mother whose children didn't need her any more? Why couldn't she move forward? Billy had done so without a second thought.

She felt Billy roll over, almost crushing her. He murmured something else, his voice rising, a nervous edge. She put out a hand and it rested on his bare chest. The hairs were damp, matted, and as she slid her fingers to his face she felt sweat on his brow. 'Billy?' Then he was wrestling, his arms moving like pistons, confused and pushing her away.

'Billy.' Dawnie raised her voice. He was breathless, rolling from side to side, his eyes still closed, trying to tug himself from his nightmare. Dawnie straddled him and gripped his arms, feeling his sweat dampening the pink pyjama top.

'Billy, Billy, wake up. It's all right, love, I'm here. Wake up.' He embraced her, too hot, damp with fear, and she squeezed him tight. 'Billy, are you all right?'

He was panting; emerging from the shock, clasping her so hard it hurt the bones beneath her flesh. He gulped air like he was drowning. Dawnie clutched his shoulders, stroking his back like she would do to calm a child. She felt his muscles relax; his breathing was slowing down. He pushed her back so that he could stare at her and even though the room was blanketed in shadows she could see his glazed eyes. Still confused, he breathed her name twice, in an effort to calm himself.

'I had a bad dream...'

Dawnie nodded and pulled him against her, kissing his damp neck. 'I know, Billy.'

He shook his head roughly, pushing away images she couldn't see. 'It's been a while since I had one of those nightmares. I thought I was all grand now, I thought that the dreams had gone.'

'It's just a one-off. They'll go now we're here, Billy. I'm sure of it, love. We're here by the sea, we'll find our own place, breathe in the fresh breeze from the waves, stare up at the moon in the sky, and we'll sleep like babies.'

'I thought I'd got rid of all that stuff. I feel like an eejit.'

Dawnie stroked his hair, the thick mane tangled beneath her fingers. 'It'll be fine. I promise. Just me and you and no more bad memories or dreams or worries. All that's behind us now.'

Billy allowed himself to fall back on the pillow and he breathed in gratefully. 'In the dream, I was locked up behind a wall, behind bars. I couldn't breathe. There was hot sand in my mouth, choking me. I was trying to get out, scrabbling in the earth; my fingers were bleeding and suddenly I was falling through the air fast.'

Dawnie put a cool hand on his brow. 'That dream again? Don't worry, Billy. Close your eyes and try to get back to sleep. No more nightmares.' She touched his hair, leaned over and kissed his lips. 'We're fine now. No more worries. All fine. Just me and you, together, forever.'

10

When Billy and Dawnie arrived astride the Harley at the ski centre, everyone else was waiting. Dawnie slid from the saddle and pulled off her helmet to reveal a smiling face topped with a glossy black bob. Beneath the leather jacket, she had a bright pink sweatshirt with the slogan 'Old skiers don't die – they just slide downhill', and a pair of leggings in psychedelic colours. She was ready for the slopes. She thrust out her chin as she noticed Vinnie staring at her. 'This is me in sloping-off mode, Vinnie. Get used to it.'

She chuckled and gazed around at the group. Aude and Sylv were in jeans and matching black jumpers. Ursula was in a neat pair of light blue jeans and a pretty blue sweater. Lester was wearing his biker jacket, despite having brought the car. Vinnie was smartly dressed, a pale shirt, a dark jacket and brand new denims, but Dilly was the most noticeable. She was wearing a shell suit in purple that she must have owned in the 1980s, zipped to the neck. With a wide red lipstick grin, her thick-framed glasses that made her eyes gleam and a jaunty blue beret over her coiled white hair, she looked ready for action. Dawnie smiled. 'Right, shall we go in?'

Billy was still straddling the bike, his helmet on, the visor flipped up to reveal an anxious expression. He leaned over to Dawnie. 'I'm not coming with you, darlin', if that's all right with you.'

Dawnie looked perplexed for a moment and leaned closer to him. 'How do you mean? You aren't coming skiing?'

'No, I don't think I will at the minute.' He looked away for a moment, then turned to her, his eyes shining. 'I think I'll take a little ride over to Tavistock, over the moors by myself. There are blue-bells out in the woods and I have my camera in my pocket.' He gazed into Dawnie's eyes for a moment. 'I have a map with me. I might ride up as far as Princetown and Postbridge.'

Dawnie sighed, gazing into his eyes and reading his thoughts there. He needed time by himself. She patted his arm. 'All right, love. It's almost two o'clock now. Our lesson is for ninety minutes and then, I suppose, we'll all grab some refreshments.' She sighed. 'We'll see you back here in two hours, okay?'

Billy nodded and started the engine, dropping his visor over his eyes. Dawnie watched as he rode off, man and machine forming a single solid shape that diminished into the distance. She turned back to the group with a smile on her face. 'Right – anyone for skiing?'

Vinnie's face creased with anxiety. 'Where's Billy gone?'

Dawnie scratched the black bob wig with blue fingernails. 'He's off to Dartmoor. He's not one for skiing and I think he'll enjoy a ride out and a look around.'

'Oh, he will,' Lester nodded. 'There are some great butterflies to be seen: there are still a few marsh fritillary butterflies left. I should have gone with him.'

'Not today, *Liebling*.' Ursula smiled up at him and threaded a possessive arm through his. 'We will take quality time for you and me this afternoon.'

Lester's eyes gleamed and he kissed the top of his wife's blonde head. 'Whatever you say, *Schätzchen*.'

'Right, shall we go?' Dawnie felt herself slipping into the role of holiday rep again. 'We'll go inside, meet our instructor and get our skis on, shall we? Then, I don't know about the rest of you but I can't wait to get on the piste.'

Dilly caught Dawnie's eye and sniggered. 'You and me both, love. I'm always ready for a tipple. Gin and tonic's my favourite, mind, but I'm partial to your home brew. Anything, really.'

* * *

The young man who greeted them was in his twenties, his hair shiny and blond, a neat matching beard on his tanned face. He was wearing orange salopettes, a white t-shirt emblazoned with the word 'Instructor' in bold black letters, and he was tall and muscular. He shook Dawnie's hand. 'Mrs Smith?'

Dawnie clasped the outstretched hand, noticing blond hairs on the tanned skin. '*Ms* Smith, but yes, I made the booking. Are you our instructor?' She gave his orange salopettes a hasty glance and chuckled. 'I thought you were one of those prisoners in Guantanamo Bay.'

He frowned, confused by her joke and the fact that she still held his hand in hers. He smiled optimistically. 'I am your instructor for ninety minutes on the beginners' slope. My name is Günther.'

Ursula perked up at the sound of the young man's crisp accent. She beamed at him, sidling next to Dawnie.

'*Günther? Bist du Deutscher?*'

The young man took her hand, smiling. '*Nein, ich bin Österreicher.*'

Aude poked Sylv in the back and whispered, 'What are they saying?'

'Not a clue.'

Dawnie put her palm on Aude's shoulder. 'I think Ursula thought she'd found a fellow countryman but our instructor might be Austrian.'

'I've been skiing in Austria,' Vinnie confirmed. Günther looked around at his party, anxious: there were a lot of older women in the group and they were all smiling at him with a vacant expression that suggested none of them had skied before. He gave a little cough. 'We are a beginners' group. Have any of you ever been on a slope?'

Ursula called out, waving enthusiastically. 'I've been a couple of times, but that was years ago, when I was much, much younger.'

'Me too.' Lester took his wife's hand. 'But I'm sure we'll soon get the hang of it again.'

'I'm not going skiing,' Dilly chimed. 'I'm observing everyone else while I'm wearing my skis.'

'I've skied a few times,' Vinnie nodded confidently. 'I've been on blue slopes and red ones.'

'I thought all snow was white, isn't it?' Dilly's face was alarmed. 'I never heard of red snow. It must be covered in the blood of all those skiers who fell over.'

Dawnie grabbed Dilly's arm. 'Oh, don't worry – we'll just walk up the slope, put on the skis and look a million dollars.'

Günther shook his head. 'Shall we all get ourselves suited and booted? Then we'll go outside to the slopes.'

Ten minutes later, Günther and Vinnie stood at the top of the white beginners' hills in their skis, confident and ready. Aude and Sylv puffed behind them, followed by Ursula and Lester. Dawnie was helping Dilly to shuffle along. In her shell suit and blue beret, she was unimpressed.

'The sun is shining. It's not even snowing. It's warm. And this is some funny snow, Dawnie. It's not like proper snow. It's not even cold. It's like a big white welcome mat you'd have at the front door.'

'It's just like white AstroTurf,' Sylv agreed.

'We use Perma-Snow here,' Günther explained. 'It is much easier to ski on and safer if you have a tumble.' He glanced anxiously towards Dilly. 'Right. Now I will show you how to get to grips with basics. Walking first and maybe later we can try to slide down the teaching slope.'

'Can I go off by myself?' Vinnie asked.

'Maybe, once I am sure you know what you are doing, you can just ski around here a little.'

'But I need a bigger slope.'

Dilly shook her head. 'I'm not sure I won't fall flat on my face with these big things on my feet, Dawnie. Let me hold onto you, will you?'

'We'll be fine, Dilly,' Dawnie grinned. 'Let's just pose in the skis and you grab onto my arm.'

'Okay, everyone.' Günther took a deep breath, his eyes flicking towards Dilly. 'First, let's see how we do when we try to move around a little on the skis, shall we?' He rolled his eyes towards the heavens. 'This could take a little time.'

Fifty minutes later, Aude and Sylv were skiing down the beginners' slopes like experts, their cheeks pink, their faces beaming. Vinnie was doing his impression of James Bond being followed by assassins in the ski chase in *The Spy Who Loved Me*. Goggles on his face, his curls lifted on the breeze, he was at full pelt, leaning to one side then the other, a dashing expert. Ursula and Lester were skiing together. Ursula first, with panache and grace, and Lester next, his expression that of a little boy who had truanted from school and was playing in the snow, his face shining with mischief.

Günther was standing at the top of the beginners' slope, his hands on his hips, concentrating on Dilly, who was hugging Dawnie's arm, refusing to let go. 'Will you both be all right just standing here by yourselves?'

Dawnie's voice was encouraging. 'Shall we see if we can take a giant step for womankind, Dilly?'

'I can't move.' Her voice trembled a little. 'I might fall over. My hip hurts a bit and I can't see anything through my bad eye now.'

Dawnie raised her voice over the screams and yelps of excitement on the slopes around her. 'But are you enjoying yourself, Dilly?'

'Oh yes. I'm having such fun up here.' She glanced at the instructor. 'The view is magnificent. But I want to ski, just a little bit, so that I can say I've done it. It can't be so difficult down that small ramp there. I just want to go home and be able to say that I'd skied on the dried slope.'

Dawnie looked anxiously at Günther. 'What do you think? Just down that little slope? Just once?'

'I'm not so sure.' Günther chewed his lip and ran a hand through his blond mane. 'Perhaps you should sit down and have a rest for a bit instead? After all, there's another forty minutes left.'

Dilly thrust out a determined chin. 'No. I'm going to ski down this slope if it kills me.' Günther squeezed his eyes shut. That scenario had been most prominent in his thoughts since he had met Dilly.

'Can we try it?' Dawnie gave the instructor her most assertive stare. 'Can we ski a little bit, just for Dilly?'

He breathed deeply, his eyes meeting Dilly's hopeful gaze. 'Maybe you could come down with me? I could ski down really slowly, and you could put your arms around my waist?'

'Oh, that would be lovely. I'd like that.' Dilly licked her lips.

'Right.' Günther tried to make his voice authoritative, professional. 'So, let's start from here where the descent is gentle, shall we?'

Dilly stood her ground. 'I'm not doing it without Dawnie.' She pointed to the tiny woman in the black bobbed wig, the pink sweatshirt and the luminous leggings. 'I feel safer with her next to me.'

Günther scratched his beard and considered that his job might be at stake if anything happened to his protégées. He glanced at Dilly, her puppy-dog eyes soft and trusting, then at Dawnie, whose face suggested she was not one to be crossed, and he made his decision.

'Okay. What if I ski down, and you put your arms around my waist?'

Dilly nodded and threw her ski sticks away, clamping her arms around the instructor with relish.

'Then you, madam.' Günther turned to Dawnie. 'You come down behind us on your skis really slowly, so that this lady knows that you are just behind her. Can you do that?'

Dawnie nodded. Dilly glanced over her shoulder, her arms still circling the Austrian instructor's waist, and winked mischievously at Dawnie, who edged closer, ready for take-off. Then in a moment of trust and abandon, Dilly threw herself against him, hanging on with all her might.

Günther was aware of the clinging burden around his waist and he wiped his brow. He undid the straps of his salopettes and felt fresher, cooler. He smiled encouragingly over his shoulder. 'Right, ladies. Off we go. On three. One, two...'

He set off as gently as possible, feeling Dilly's grip tighten around his waist. Instinctively, he knew Dawnie was just behind them. He brought his speed down to the slowest pace possible, but he felt Dilly's legs separate outwards and she lurched forward with a bump. Her glasses were askew as her face was pressed flat against his bottom and she was hanging on desperately to his hips. The base of the beginners' slope was not far away. They were almost there. Günther urged them steadily onwards.

Dawnie could see Dilly's body was at an awkward angle, her

face glued to the instructor's orange posterior, her gloved hands gripping the salopettes in desperation, her legs on the skis spreading apart. Dawnie couldn't help it: an orange and purple skiing pantomime horse was sliding downhill in front of her eyes and she began to laugh. The chortle spluttered from her mouth so hard she pitched forward and dropped the ski poles, putting her arms out to grasp the nearest point of safety. Her hands connected with Dilly's shell suit, grabbing the material covering her legs.

Dilly screeched, stumbling against Günther, her face sliding down the instructor's backside. In desperation, her gloved hands yanked hard at the first thing they could grasp for safety: the orange salopettes. Dawnie heard the instructor yelp and suddenly all three of them had tumbled, a bundle of legs and arms at the bottom of the ski slope.

Dawnie sat up and opened her eyes, blinking in shock. The instructor had managed to remain upright, tottering, his back to them both. Dilly was on her knees, clutching at Günther's legs, the orange salopettes folded like a concertina around his ankles and she was staring up at his bottom, the flesh bare but for a lop-sided pair of red boxer shorts. Dilly gazed up at the instructor in admiration, adjusting her spectacles for a better view as she read the label on his waist band.

'Oh, Calvin Klein. Lovely.'

* * *

Ursula and Lester had gone to the counter to buy coffee and cake, although Dilly had requested a stiff gin after the shock of seeing the instructor's bottom at such close quarters. Aude, Sylv and Dawnie were sitting with her at a Formica-topped table in the café, trying to soothe her while they looked out from the viewing gallery at the beginners' slope, where Vinnie was taking a few last turns on his skis. Dawnie patted Dilly's hand. 'Are you sure you're all right?'

'Oh yes, I'm calming down a little bit now,' Dilly chuckled. 'He was a nice man, that young Mr Grunter, he was very understanding about me pulling his pants down. And it's been a long time since I had such a lovely view.' She winked. 'I think I could get used to this skiing.'

'I'd come here again, definitely,' Sylv enthused. 'It was such fun on the slopes and we really made some progress.'

'We'll make it a regular thing, shall we, Sylv? Then maybe we can go skiing abroad. I'm glad you organised it, Dawnie. It's been fantastic.' Aude reached for her hand. 'We're so glad you and Billy came to Margot Street.'

'Vinnie's had a lovely time too. It's been good for him to get out.' Dilly was watching her son skiing with flair and energy. 'Bless him. He's a good lad, my Vinnie.' She paused for a moment, thinking. 'I wish he'd find a nice girlfriend who was good enough for him. All this business he's had of "I love you Vinnie but you're too nice so you're dumped". It makes my blood boil.'

Aude sniffed. 'In my experience, that tells us more about the sort of person who is doing the dumping. What a pathetic excuse. As if an unpleasant man is a thing to prefer or to aspire to.'

'Vinnie reminds me so much of his father, my Tommy.' Dilly swallowed hard.

Dawnie glanced across towards Lester and Ursula who were buying coffee and cake, and waved briefly. She turned back to Dilly and spoke softly. 'Tell us about Tommy.'

Dilly took a long breath and waved weak fingers. 'He was an evacuee in the war, sent from Birmingham to Wales to live with his auntie. We met when we were youngsters. Then he didn't go back: he stayed in the village and we were childhood sweethearts.' She closed papery lids with a network of pale veins, and sighed, letting her eyes flicker open. 'He was handsome like Vinnie, my Tommy: dark hair and big eyes, like a doe's. And such a sweet nature, kind and thoughtful, and he always made me laugh.' A tear trickled down her cheek, a single rivulet tracking its way down the creases of her skin. 'We grew up and got married in Llansteffan. He was a plumber by trade and after a few years we came to Devon just before Vinnie was born. I was thirty-four when he arrived, mind. We'd left it late to have Vinnie and it wasn't easy, the birth, so we decided to leave it at one child.' She paused, noticing the descending tear and wiping it away with a shaky finger. 'That was a mistake. I wish I'd had more.'

Dawnie placed a hand over Dilly's. 'When did he pass, your Tommy?'

'Eight years ago. He had a stroke; just the one was enough to do it.' Dilly paused, remembering, picturing Tommy looking smart in his best suit, his eyes closed in the coffin. She took a breath. 'Then a bit later on, Vinnie broke up with his girlfriend; she got herself another man, I think, and they threw Vinnie out – Sally, she was called – I never liked her at all. She could gad about for England, that one, and she'd spend his money like it was water. Anyway, Vinnie came back home to me, and he's been with me ever since.'

Dawnie nodded. 'My son Buddy is exactly the same. Good-natured. He meets girls who take advantage. He's independent and he's got his music, though. He's strong in his own way, like Billy, and yet fragile too. But I'd like to see him with someone who appreciates him for the lovely man he is.'

Dilly's eyes drifted back to her son on the artificial slope, skiing with vigour and confidence. 'I often wonder what will happen to

Vinnie after I've gone. Who will love him as much as I do? It worries me, a lot.'

'Six coffees and some cakes.' Ursula arrived, setting the tray down on the table. 'We'll get Vinnie his drink when he's finished skiing.'

'It took my lovely wife ages to decide on what cakes to buy everyone. I told her none of them were as good as the ones she makes herself. We bought a selection.' Lester was already in his seat, sipping cappuccino and reaching for a slice of Battenberg.

Dilly hadn't moved. 'I wish he could find someone who deserves him. He's my treasure, you know, my Vinnie.' She reached out to Dawnie, her eyes huge behind the heavy-framed glasses. 'There's no love like a mother's love, Dawnie. Nothing is greater, believe you me.'

Dawnie reached for her coffee and sighed. Her mind wandered to her own son, Buddy, somewhere in the USA, playing his guitar with people she had never met. He'd replied to her text in his usual way, just an emoji, a thumbs-up sign and a smiley face. She hoped he was happy and safe, but she didn't know where he was, or the name of the town where he was staying. She thought of Lindy Lou and her boisterous family in the ramshackle house in Little Lever. They would be out somewhere now on such a bright Sunday after-noon, probably in the countryside making lots of noise, eating ice cream, yelling with laughter and having fun.

Her eyes drifted to a plain black clock on the wall, the second hand twitching. It was almost four o'clock, two hours since Billy had left on his bike to ride around the moors. She was sure he'd arrive back outside at any time now: he could be there now, astride the Harley, his helmet under his arm, by the entrance looking out for her. Dawnie closed her eyes and smiled. He could be a handful, Billy: he was obsessed with his bike, his drum kit, his hobby photographing wildlife; at times he needed quiet space and the chance to be alone with his thoughts, but he was her rock and she was his. She would never find a man she'd love and respect more than her Billy. He was a one-off, a keeper; she'd known that from the first day they'd met. And he was never late, not ever. Dawnie sipped her coffee quickly. He would be waiting outside for her, dependable as ever.

11

Billy whistled a little tune as he pushed the Harley Davidson through the doorway of number thirteen and into the bright sunlight. He propped it carefully next to the kerb and went back inside for the soapy water and sponge, the chrome polish and the chamois leather. He was standing outside with his cleaning kit when the latch to number eleven clicked and a small round woman crept out, wearing a flowery dress reminiscent of the bedroom curtains his mother had made back in County Mayo when he'd been a teenager. He could smell the waft of her lavender perfume on the breeze and it caught in his nose. He put his bowl and materials down on the step, put his hands on his hips and grinned. 'Good morning to you, neighbour.'

Gillian was heaving a full bucket in one hand, waving a scrubbing brush in the other. She stopped for a moment, taking in Billy's height, his wiry grey mane and the bulk of his forearms with the sleeves rolled up, and froze to the spot. Billy took a step forward and reached out a hand, clutching the handle of the bucket from her grasp. 'That looks heavy. I'll take it, will I, and put it down for you?'

For a moment, Gillian didn't let go, tugging the bucket towards her as if he intended to steal it. Then she let go and Billy held the handle up in his huge fist as if the bucket was empty. Gillian's eyes were glassy with fear. 'I was about to scrub the doorstep.'

Billy chuckled and placed the pail on the ground. 'And it's a fine summer's morning for a spot of cleaning. I'm sprucing up the bike. We can clean together, in tandem, and maybe have a bit of banter; it'll take away the monotony of the job.'

Gillian hadn't moved. The scrubbing brush was still clenched in her fist. She frowned. 'Banter?'

Billy gave her a charming smile. 'I don't think we've been introduced. I'm Billy Murphy.'

'Mrs Frost. Gillian Frost.'

'Well, sure and it's a pleasure to meet you, Gillian.' Billy dipped his sponge in soapy water and began to attack the mudguards. 'And it's a lovely day in June. It's my favourite month. I was born in June.'

Gillian stared at Billy, at the pail on the floor full of clean water and detergent, and back at Billy. Her mouth worked before she had any idea what she was saying. 'Yes. My birthday is in June too.'

'Really? Well, there's a turn up for the books. Mine's on the thirtieth.'

Gillian ground her teeth. 'Twenty-eighth.' She was not sure what Malcolm would say if he caught her talking to the Hell's Angel next door. He was upstairs taking an afternoon nap as he often did after lunch. He wouldn't wake until four. She felt suddenly alone.

Billy squeezed his sponge. 'We'll have to arrange a knees-up. It might be good craic to celebrate both dates together, what do you say, Gillian? A party, maybe?'

Gillian was speechless. She was watching water stream from the throttled sponge in the big man's fist. She wondered if he had done that to people, squeezed the life from them. His wife had said he had been aggressive, and Malcolm had found out that he'd been in prison so she simply said, 'Yes.' It came out as a squeak. She thought about washing the step, but that would mean turning her back on the Hell's Angel and she was unsure of what he'd be capable of, so she glued her eyes on him. He was wiping suds over the chrome of his bike, doing a thorough job, she decided.

'It's a shame you missed the skiing trip last weekend, Gillian. We had a savage time in Plymouth.'

Gillian frowned. 'Skiing?'

'Ah yes, the wife organised it. I'm sure she called on you to invite you along but you were out. They went on the dry slope skiing, even Dilly across the road. She had a lovely time; she had a turn on the skis herself. I'm sorry you missed it.'

Gillian blinked. Her mouth was numb. She didn't know what to say so she repeated her words. 'You went skiing?'

'Ah, well. I didn't go with them. It's not for me, all those crowds and noise. I was away on the bike on the moorlands, looking at bluebells and butterflies. I got some deadly photos of the flowers in the woods. The bluebells are lovely, just like a carpet all in bloom. It's grand there this time of year.'

'Bluebells?' Gillian's hand hurt from the indenting bristles of her scrubbing brush, she was squeezing it so hard. She was stunned. The big Irishman was having a conversation with her about flowers.

'It's a grand place to be living, for sure. I had a lovely tour round on the Harley by myself. I went to Postbridge. It's very calm and peaceful there; all the shade and the trees and woodlands and streams were very good for the soul, and then I came back through Princetown. Very bleak place though, Princetown – I rode past the prison. It gave me the shivers. Those places are grim, aren't they, jails?'

Gillian dropped the scrubbing brush. 'I really don't know. I have never actually been inside one myself. I – I have to go and speak to my husband. He's just inside, I mean indoors, having a snooze.'

'Well, it was nice to meet you, Gillian. I'd like to meet your ould fella sometime too – maybe we could go out on the lash together one evening.'

'Lash?'

'Ah, well. Sometimes you need to take a break from all the hard graft. I love the bike but these old classics are hard work and it can be a pain when things go wrong. Fixing them up can be murder.'

'Murder?'

'Well, it was… very pleasant to chatter to you, Gillian, but I'd better crack on.' Billy raised his hand in the air, the chamois dripping, to demonstrate how busy he was. Gillian flinched.

'Oh…' She turned quickly, stumbling into the pail of clean water, knocking it over onto the doorstep. She rushed inside, muttering something about needing to tell her husband about deadly murder. Billy frowned and then a smile broke on his face as he watched the water trickle across the concrete from the upturned bucket.

'Ah, well, that's one way to clean the step.' He chuckled to himself and picked up the chamois leather, bending over his bike. 'But I hope I haven't upset her. It was odd how she legged it, just like that. I'm not sure the poor ould dear has the full shilling.'

'Who hasn't got the full shilling, Billy Murphy? Talking to yourself again, are you?'

Billy turned round to stare at his wife, hands on hips, laughing. She was wearing cut-off denim shorts and a white t-shirt, a short pink wig and dangling earrings. A mug of tea and a large tin of biscuits had been set on the step. Billy stood up; his shirt wet, soap suds on his nose, and threw his arms wide.

'Give me a hug, wife.'

Dawnie ran into his grasp, looking up into his eyes. 'I just made us an appointment to view another house. Next Saturday at half past three. Is that all right?'

'It's dandy, darlin'. Which one are we going to look at?'

Dawnie's face shone. 'It's just yards from the sea; the house is on top of a hill and from the back garden you can look down at the waves and hear the ocean lapping against the shore. Imagine that at night, with the windows open, listening to the sound of surf rolling. We'd sleep like babies.'

Billy took in her hopeful expression. 'Is it another of your man Simon Mountjoy's houses?'

Dawnie screwed up her nose, an expression of dismissal. 'No. I'm not going to him again. This is a different agency; the woman on the phone said the owners would show us round because there was no one else available on Saturday afternoon but I told her it doesn't matter. Two sisters, apparently, who are very keen to sell. The outside looks nice in the photos. The rooms might be a bit dark but we can soon put a lick of paint on them and apparently there's a huge workshop in the garden big enough for all your stuff.'

Billy glanced at the mug and the biscuit tin, still on the doorstep. 'That's grand. Is it tea you've brought for your working man? And what can I see in the tin? Have you made a batch of cookies just for me?'

'Peanut butter cookies.' Dawnie placed the mug of steaming tea in his cupped hands and thrust the tin towards him. 'Take a couple. I'm going to give the rest to our next-door neighbours.'

Billy chuckled, helping himself to three cookies. 'Are you giving my biscuits to the mad Gillian one I managed to upset, who threw her hot water onto the front step and ran away like a scalded hen?'

Dawnie strutted towards number fifteen and knocked on the door. 'They are for Aude and Sylv. I can save a few back for the Frosts, though...'

'I wouldn't do that, not at the minute.' Billy shook his head. 'I think she said the ould fella's having a kip and when I chatted away to Gillian, she was suddenly mortified with me for some reason and scuttled off indoors. Maybe we'll call on them later and check she's all right.'

'I can always make more biscuits for them.' Dawnie knocked again and the door opened immediately to reveal Sylv, blinking behind her gold-rimmed glasses, still in pyjamas and dressing gown. Dawnie chuckled. 'It's nearly lunchtime, Sylv. Have I woken you up?'

Sylv rubbed her eyes. 'I finished work late last night. I was just having breakfast. Aude's at work now. Sorry, Dawnie: would you like to come in? I'm just having a cup of coffee. Hi, Billy.'

Dawnie followed Sylv into the hallway, shouting out to Billy with a laugh. 'Keep on cleaning, you slacker – I want the bike spotless by the time I'm back.' She listened for a moment while Billy called back a good-natured reply, then she rushed into the lounge, glancing at a huge squashy sofa covered with clothes and magazines. Dawnie's gaze took in a pretty lounge painted in cream and grey. There was a small log-effect gas fire, a television, a bird cage on a wooden sideboard and a coffee table shaped like a tree trunk. In the kitchen, there was a plate of beans on toast, half-eaten, and an almost-empty mug next to an open jar of instant coffee. A saucepan with a large wooden handle and the congealed remains of the baked beans had been left on the cooker. Dirty dishes and cups were piled in the sink. Sylv waved an arm apologetically.

'Excuse the mess. Aude and I will blitz the place when we get our days off.' She grinned. 'Then we'll be flat-out at work and wreck it all again.'

Dawnie shrugged. 'I brought you some peanut butter cookies.' She held the tin out towards Sylv. 'Do you and Aude work together?'

'Yes, when we're on the same shift. We're CNAs.' Sylv put the tin of biscuits on the kitchen counter next to Dawnie and moved to fill the kettle.

'What does that stand for?'

'Certified Nursing Assistants: we work at the local hospital. Do you take sugar in your coffee, Dawnie?'

'Just milk,' Dawnie grinned and took one of her own biscuits. 'I'm sweet enough.'

A low suggestive whistle came from the next room. Dawnie raised her eyebrows. 'What on earth was that?'

'Let's go through into the lounge.' Sylv thrust a mug of coffee towards Dawnie, reached for a peanut cookie and picked up her own mug. 'Come and meet Tequila.'

Dawnie raised her eyebrows and followed Sylv into the lounge. They sat on the squashy brown leather sofa, Sylv arranging cushions around her and putting sock-clad feet on the log-shaped coffee table. She pointed at the bird cage and her voice took on a crooning tone. 'Say hello to our neighbour Dawnie, Tequila. And be a good boy.'

The bird fluffed yellow and blue feathers and a voice rang out, not unlike Aude's. 'Give me a kiss, gorgeous.'

Dawnie approached the cage tentatively. 'Is he friendly?'

'Oh yes. He's such a good boy,' Sylv beamed. 'I could get him out if you like. He enjoys flying about a bit and exercising his wings, then he'll sit on your finger or he'll happily nest on the top of your head.'

Dawnie touched her short pink wig and imagined budgerigar excrement clogging the glossy fibres. 'Oh no, it's all right.' She turned her attention to the budgie, noticing the turquoise wings, the yellow face, the intricate zebra pattern on the back of his head and the black dots on his throat. 'Who's a pretty boy, then?'

Tequila preened for a moment, then his beady eye met Dawnie's and he retorted, 'Shut your beak. Shut your beak.'

'Charming,' Dawnie giggled and returned to the sofa. 'He's a brilliant mimic: that sounded just like you, Sylv.'

Sylv shrugged apologetically, adjusting her glasses. 'Tequila is great company for me and Aude, especially when one of us is on night shifts. But you have to be so careful what you say around him. He's really naughty with some of the things he remembers and he'll repeat them back when you least want him to.'

'Does he swear a lot?'

Sylv pressed her lips together. 'The one thing you accidentally say and immediately regret, he'll remember for ever. You know, if you say something loud, with – enthusiasm, he picks it up. I dropped nail polish on the sofa once and let out a string of swear words. That's earned itself a place in Tequila's repertoire.'

'He sounds like great fun. I can think of a few things I'd teach him to say.'

'He is completely unpredictable.' Sylv cupped her mug. 'He swears, curses; he'll chat people up and say outrageous things. Aude's sister came round for tea a few weeks ago and when she wanted more cake, Tequila asked her what her last servant died of.'

Dawnie grinned. 'Billy would love him – he'd teach him a phrase or two.'

'He begs for junk food: toast, crisps, peanuts. He'll shriek and become all attention-seeking if we have chips in the house. Of course, he never gets them.' Sylv glanced fondly at the budgie. 'But I adore him, Dawnie. He's such good company. I love having a bit of noise and fun around the house when I'm here all by myself.'

'I know; that's why I live with Billy,' Dawnie chuckled, before becoming lost in thought for a moment. 'You're right though, Sylv. I'd go crazy all by myself in a silent house. I'm used to the kids being around me and my great-grandchildren making noise and bumping about. I'm sure Tequila must be great company when Aude's away.' She pursed her lips and ran her fingers through the pink wig. 'Why do you call him Tequila?'

Sylv chuckled. 'Well he's a budgie... but he mocks people and he's a bird, so...'

'So?' Dawnie screwed up her face, thinking. 'So he's called Tequila Mockingbird?

Sylv nodded and suddenly the two women burst out laughing. Dawnie held up her coffee mug. 'It's a perfect name for him – I love it.'

A flurry of feathers and a screech came from inside the cage. 'Did anyone say Tequila? Mine's a double, darling. And make it quick.'

12

Dawnie knocked again at number fourteen. She had rapped the knocker twice, once she'd realised the bell no longer worked. It occurred to her that Dilly might be asleep, but she could be in the kitchen or out of earshot of the hard thwacking sound. Dawnie sighed. She wondered if Vinnie was at home, if Dilly had taken a tumble or couldn't get up. The old lady was in her eighties but she had been impressively plucky at the skiing. Dawnie imagined herself peering through the window and seeing the old lady slumped on the floor, then having to make a call to emergency services or bashing down the door herself, which would be difficult, and Billy was still in bed.

The door creaked ajar and Dilly blinked at her through the thick-framed glasses. 'Hello Dawnie. Red head is it today? You remind me of Lucille Ball off of *The Lucy Show*. She had the short curly red hair too. Do you remember her?'

Dawnie nodded, ruffling her copper curls, then brandished a bag. 'I brought you this. Here's your weekend's supply of home brew.'

Dilly reached out a clawed hand and took the bottles, wrapped in a carrier bag, holding it against her chest. 'Oh, look at me forgetting my manners. Come in, Dawnie. It's eleven o'clock – elevenses time. I'll get the kettle on and make us a cuppa.'

'I'd better not, Dilly. Billy and I are off to see a house later today. He's still in bed, bless him. I left him sleeping: he had a terrible night. I ought to go and wake him up.'

'Oh?' Dilly's face clouded. 'Nightmares, is it?'

'Yes, he's had them for years, on and off. I got up at eight and he was sound asleep, so I thought I'd leave him for a couple of hours.'

'I see. And can't he take some sleeping tablets?'

'He's had them.' Dawnie wrinkled her nose. 'He stopped taking them after a while.'

'Cup of cocoa then, or some sprigs of lavender under the pillow. That's what I use.'

'Thanks, Dilly. I'll try it.' Dawnie turned to go. 'Give my best to Vinnie. Billy said he'd take him out on the Harley soon if he wants to go.'

'He'd love it. He's at work right now, mind,' Dilly beamed. 'So would I. Tell your Billy I'll get on his pillion with him before too long. I'd love to go along the coast and see the sea again.'

'I'll lend you my helmet,' Dawnie chuckled as she walked away. She crossed the road back to number thirteen and noticed a familiar figure up the road waving at her. Dawnie narrowed her eyes and recognised the blonde woman in a smart cream jacket and blue denims. She called out, 'Ursula, great to see you.'

Ursula caught up with her, panting with the effort of jogging, and wrapped an arm around her friend. 'Good to see you, Dawnie. The red colour suits you.'

'Oh, I have wigs all colours of the rainbow upstairs,' Dawnie grinned, opening the front door. 'You've come to see me, I hope, and not my husband? He's still asleep.'

'Lester is in his shed, adjusting something on his bike. I thought I'd come and see you, if that's all right, Dawnie?'

'Always. Come in. I'll put the kettle on.'

Ursula watched Dawnie while she rattled around in the kitchen, making coffee and unearthing biscuits. 'You've made this place nice, haven't you? How long have you been here? A month?'

'Just over. We came on May the first. It's the sixth of June, and all I've managed to do in that time is paint the lounge and clean up the kitchen. I'd like to put up some tiles on the walls and buy some decent carpet for upstairs but we won't be here that long.' Dawnie grabbed Ursula's hand. 'We're looking at a lovely house this afternoon. It's really close to the sea. It might just be the one.' Her eyes flashed. 'This time tomorrow, who knows? We might have had an offer accepted and be on our way to buying a perfect home with a view of the ocean.'

Ursula squeezed Dawnie's hand. 'Don't move too far from me. It's nice having you here. I can just walk down from Mary Street.'

'Don't you drive, Ursula?'

Ursula shook her head.

Dawnie shrugged. 'Then Lester can bring you round on the bike.'

'I won't travel on the Harley.' Ursula sipped her coffee. 'I don't even like going in the car.'

'I'll buy somewhere on a bus route, especially for you.'

Ursula was puzzled for a moment, unsure whether Dawnie was joking, then her face brightened. 'I came round to tell you something.'

Dawnie raised her eyebrows. 'Tell away. Good news?'

'I hope so.' Ursula clutched the mug in cupped hands. 'When you and I were talking the other day, and you said how much you missed your children, I started to think about Meinke and Frida and Liesel. My granddaughter must be sixteen now; I've only seen her twice since I moved here. She was eleven when I left Würzburg.'

'She must have changed quite a lot.'

Ursula nodded. 'I feel really sad when I think about it. How we love our children and bring them up, then we spend so long apart.' Her eyes were suddenly soft with tears. 'When you think about it, Dawnie, time is the most precious thing we have. We let it run through our fingers like sand without giving it a second thought and someday soon it may all be gone...'

Dawnie pressed Ursula's hand. 'Maybe you and Lester should go to Würzburg for a visit this summer?'

'Lester did say we should take a trip back to Germany, but he'd want to go on the bike.' Ursula wiped her eyes quickly and forced a smile. 'But then I had an idea. I rang Meinke and we had a long chat. I asked him if he could get some time off work – he is an accountant – and perhaps he could come here and visit with the family.'

'That's great. What did he say?'

'He was very positive about a visit to see me. Meinke will ask his partner in the firm if he can take a week or two in July and come over here.' She pressed her hands to her face. 'I am really excited by the possibility of seeing my son again, and his family.'

Dawnie leaned forward. 'That is marvellous. It would be great to have your family over.' She took a breath. 'And that's inspired me. I'm going to text Buddy later and ask him how he's doing.' She shook her head. 'He doesn't always answer texts and it's expensive to ring the USA, but I'll definitely catch up with my boy this weekend one way or the other.' She smiled at the thought of her handsome son, tall like Billy but leaner, with his father's soft eyes and warm smile. 'And I always chatter to Lindy Lou on a Sunday, if she's not out with the family.'

'Oh, I don't know, Dawnie. These children,' Ursula breathed.

'And these men. Sometimes I think perhaps we let them define us too much. I think to myself, Ursula, you are more than a wife and a mother, you are a woman. But then the soft feelings rush back and the love brims up, and I become a carer and a cook and I forget all about myself.'

Dawnie thought about Ursula's words for a moment. She had raised two children; her last home in Little Lever had been constantly filled with the bustle of a noisy family; she'd always been busy, but she'd been fiercely independent and strong-willed. She took in Ursula's kindly smile, squeezed her hand and decided that her friend probably needed more fun in her life.

'I know what you mean.' Dawnie sat upright, her eyes bright. 'But sometimes we have to put ourselves first. I have the beginnings of a plan. Billy told me the woman next door, Gillian I think she's called, has a birthday this month. She was a bit stand-offish with me and Billy when we arrived and I think I need to do something to get to know her a bit better and bring all the neighbours together at the same time. So, I'm going to organise something.'

'A party?'

Dawnie licked her lips. 'I can do better than that. I know what we all need. A special girls' night out.'

'Who's having a girls' night out?'

Dawnie saw the shock in Ursula's eyes as she stared over her shoulder. Her face had become pale. Dawnie whirled round. 'Billy?'

Billy ran a hand over his bald head. He had shaved off all the long grey curls. 'Ah, well. I decided it was time for it all to go.'

'You look just like when we first met – the hair, I mean.' Dawnie's eyes were round with surprise: Billy's scalp was pale; his head was completely smooth.

Ursula found her voice. 'I didn't recognise you, Billy. Did you cut your hair for the summer? You will be much cooler, I am sure…'

Billy shrugged his huge shoulders. His eyes gleamed beneath

his brows. 'I don't know, I just did it. I didn't sleep well and my brain was full of dreams. Then I woke up and I needed a shower. My head felt too hot and itchy and I just glanced across at the razor and I thought it was time for a change.'

Dawnie went over to him and wrapped her arms around his waist. It wasn't the first time he'd done this, or even the second. 'You look lovely, Billy. It's taken ten years off you.'

Billy kissed the top of her red curls. 'Ah, if I get a cold head, I can always borrow one of your wigs. I think I'll look fierce in the blue one.'

'Fierce?' Ursula was alarmed.

'He means he'll look great,' Dawnie winked. 'Now I'll get you some breakfast, my fierce man, and then we'd better get off to view this fabulous house. What do you fancy? Eggs on toast?'

'That'd be grand.' Billy sat down next to Ursula. 'How's your ould fella, Ursula? Tell him I must pop in and see him in a day or two and talk about the bikes?'

'He'd like that.' Ursula sipped the last dregs of her coffee. 'In fact, you must both come round to supper soon. I make a nice *Sauerbraten*, if you like beef stew, or a *Schweinshaxn*.'

Dawnie frowned, slicing bread for the toaster. 'Is that pork?'

'Well done,' Ursula beamed. 'Pig's knuckle. Very tasty.'

'And you must come to us, Ursula. You and Lester, really soon. Billy and I love to cook.'

Billy chuckled. 'It'd be good craic, all four of us together and some home brew.'

Ursula shuffled to her feet. 'Well, I must walk back home now, Dawnie. All this talk of food has made me realise – it is almost lunchtime and I'm going to make Lester a nice *Bayerischer Wurst-salat*, sausage and salad with some bread.'

Billy leapt to his feet, rubbing the smooth scalp, still not accustomed to the feel of his head without the wiry curls. 'Let me get you a couple of pints of home brew to take with you for you both to have with your lunch.'

'Oh, can you spare some?' Ursula asked.

'Sure I can: I've got fifty bottles and three more gallon buckets brewing under the stairs at the minute.' Billy put out an arm. 'I'll walk you to the door.'

'Thank you.' Ursula turned back to Dawnie, who was cracking eggs into a sizzling frying pan. 'Thank you for the coffee, Dawnie. I hope to see you very soon, and we can talk about you coming round for supper.'

'That would be lovely, Ursula.' Dawnie raised her voice over the spitting oil. 'And thanks for popping in.'

She watched Billy grinning as he shepherded her friend out through the door; she listened to the rumble of his voice in the hallway. She took a deep breath. She remembered the last time Billy had shaved his head after a particularly bad dream in which he'd escaped from a concrete cell and had been chased through a burning desert; he was running away and was caught by the hair in barbed wire. That was five years ago, when he was in his sixties: it had been the second time the doctor put him on the sleeping tablets. His dreams had been very bad then. Dawnie hoped he was going to be all right now. This new house by the sea was going to be so important for Billy. For both of them.

* * *

Gillian was dusting the mantelpiece. She lifted the picture of James in his uniform and wiped the glass until it reflected her own sad expression. She stared at the sombre face in the photograph, the proud eyes, the immaculate uniform and she sighed. He was so young. Malcolm was in the armchair reading a newspaper. He did not look up. 'It's about time you put that photo away in a drawer somewhere.'

She ignored him, tracing a finger across the glass, around the outline of the young man, letting it rest on his face, his lips. Malcolm raised his voice. 'In the drawer, Gillian, where it belongs. Away from sight. It's all in the past now.'

Gillian turned to him sharply, her voice suddenly resentful. 'I certainly will not, Malcolm.' Silence hung in the air for a moment. It was as if the room bristled with cold. Gillian took a deep breath. 'And don't you dare ask me to do that again.' The room grew colder. 'I won't ever put him out of my sight, Malcolm. You know I won't.'

Malcolm pretended to read his paper. After a minute or two he muttered, 'All in the past.' He eased himself from his armchair and shuffled over to the window. Gillian was polishing the same spot on a brass candlestick. His fingers twitched at the curtains and he stared outside for a moment, then he gasped. 'Good Lord – it's him. He's getting the bike out with that woman. She has red hair now. He looks like a thug.'

Gillian didn't reply. Her skin was tingling with anger.

Malcolm spoke louder, hoping for a response. 'The Hell's Angel has cut all his hair off. You can tell he's a criminal, just by looking at him. He's a skinhead now.'

Gillian snorted and rubbed harder at the candlestick.

'Didn't you tell me he'd been in Dartmoor jail? In Princetown?'

Gillian waited for a moment and then muttered, her voice still bitter, 'He said he'd driven past the jail on his motorbike.'

'You told me he said the place was grim. So he knows what it's like to be in prison.'

'I can't remember what he said.' Gillian pressed her lips together and glanced at the photograph. She remembered Billy had said his birthday was in June, like her own. Like James's birthday. He would have been fifty this year; it would have been his birthday on Wednesday, the tenth. Malcolm hadn't remembered; he hadn't mentioned it.

'They are driving away, Gillian – on that bike. I don't think we want his type round here.'

Gillian sighed. 'He was perfectly all right with me.'

'Was he?' Malcolm turned, his face a mask of anger. 'You were terrified when you came in and woke me up. You said he was aggressive – he talked about murder.'

'I was thinking: I might have been wrong.' Gillian folded her arms. 'He has an accent, Malcolm. I couldn't understand him. I'm not sure of half of what he said to me.'

Malcolm breathed out, a huff of air. 'I think I need to take some firm action, Gillian. The neighbours are getting too pally with him. Didn't you say she was over at the Stockers' earlier, the wife? I think I need to do something.'

Gillian faced him, clutching the candlestick. 'Oh, for goodness' sake, Malcolm.'

Malcolm pushed his hands in his pockets determinedly. 'I'm going over there now, to talk to Dilys Stocker. She's an old lady. I should warn her. And Vincent Stocker; he shouldn't allow his mother near that man. Perhaps they are softening her up so they can rob her.'

Gillian shook her head. 'Rob her of what? The Stockers are ordinary people, like us.'

'It's no time to be weak.' Malcolm's jaw was set. 'I'm going over there now. I'm going to make sure the neighbours know exactly what sort of man he is. I'm going to tell them the truth. That Hell's Angel, he's a danger to everybody. He's a thug, a jailbird, that's what he is: he's a hardened criminal.'

13

Dilly was sitting comfortably on the sofa, her legs stretched out on a covered stool, sipping a glass of home brew and watching television when she heard someone knocking at the front door.

She called out as loudly as she could: 'Vinnie. Vinnie.'

He was upstairs, changing his clothes; he'd only arrived home a few minutes ago, but she was settled, comfortable on the sofa, unwilling to move. Besides, the writer who had turned detective was just about to solve the murder mystery. Dilly didn't particularly like the programme, but then evening television always disappointed her. She preferred the action films with a bit more sass and a bit more violence.

The knocking persisted: it was as if someone had decided that she must be a bit hard of hearing but was determined that she would respond. Dilly's hearing was excellent: better than her son's, she thought grimly as she yelled his name again. 'Vinnie, someone is hammering at the door. Come down and tell them to go away.'

He appeared at the door in a pair of knee length shorts and a white vest. 'I was just doing some weight training in my room, Mam.'

Dilly narrowed her eyes and peered at him through the good one. She could see he had been working out hard; a thin film of sweat coated his skin and his curly fringe stuck to his forehead. He was developing impressive biceps. She pointed towards the hallway. 'Vinnie, be a love and send whoever it is at the door away. I'm not expecting anyone.' She peered at him. 'Are you?'

'No.' He shrugged and trotted obediently into the hall towards the door. Dilly heard him talking to someone, a man – it wasn't Billy – the voice was decidedly strained and Billy always sounded happy. Dilly could hear Vinnie making a short retort and the man talking again, this time louder, more insistent.

Dilly turned back to the television. The novelist woman had confronted the murderer. It was the bank manager, the balding mild-mannered one no one had suspected, but now he had pulled a gun on the plucky writer, who spoke her mind bravely about how she had known he was the baddie all along and now he was gleefully bragging about all his crimes. The gun aimed at her chest didn't seem to bother her; she was assured and calm. Dilly wondered how she would behave in such a situation. Suddenly, the writer flourished her Dictaphone. She had taped the entire confession. Then the police burst in and hurled the man to the ground.

Dilly snorted. Bruce Willis wouldn't have acted that way. He'd have fired his gun and rolled on the floor through broken glass, resplendent in a white vest and gleaming with perspiration, and then he'd have spat a string of expletives at the baddie before head-butting him and wrestling him to the ground in a pool of blood. Dilly loved the richness of Bruce's vocabulary, the fighting, the way he was all muscle and brash nonchalance. There was one of his films on the men's movie channel later, one of the *Die Hard* series. She'd seen them all several times, but she wanted to see them again. She had a soft spot for Clint, especially as Dirty Harry, but Bruce was her favourite. She decided she'd curl up with a glass of

Billy's home brew later and enjoy the film, perhaps with Vinnie next to her on the sofa, if he wasn't too tired after work and weightlifting.

The credits from the murder mystery were rolling down the screen and Dilly felt the cold air blow in from the street against her ankles. The men were still gossiping in the street. Dilly raised her voice. 'Vinnie, it's draughty. Close the door and come in here, will you?'

She heard him mutter something and then the door clicked. He slunk into the room as if he had been reprimanded and plonked himself beside his mother.

'So? Who was it at the door?'

'Malcolm from across the road.'

'Oh, him.' Dilly reached for the television remote. A repeat of *The Professionals* would start soon. She remembered the cop-style series from the 1980s. She'd enjoy the action in that, although it was usually a bit too tame for her taste.

Vinnie sighed. 'Malcolm said to tell you about Billy from number thirteen. He's shaved his hair off.'

'Oh, that's a shame now.' Dilly changed channels, looking for *The Professionals*. 'I liked him with his long ponytail. Maybe he is a bit too hot, mind, now the summer's here.'

'Malcolm says he's been in jail for GBH.'

'Who has? Malcolm? He doesn't look the type.'

'No, Billy, Mam. Malcolm says both Billy and Dawnie have admitted it. He's been in prison.'

Dilly stared into the dark glass of home brew. 'He makes a good pint of stout, mind.'

Vinnie frowned. 'Malcolm says it's dangerous to associate with Billy and Dawnie and we should have nothing more to do with them. He says it's for our own good.'

'And what do you think, Vinnie?'

His brow creased, as if he might cry. 'I like them, though, both of them. And – well – I wanted to meet Dawnie's sister, the blonde one, when she comes to visit again. She seemed nice. Dawnie is so friendly and Billy's a good bloke. He promised me a ride on his Harley. No, I like them. I think Malcolm's got it wrong. What do you think, Mam?'

'I'll tell you what I think, Vinnie.' Dilly sat upright and stared at her son. 'I'll tell you straight and for nothing.' The theme tune to *The Professionals* had started to ring out, but Dilly took no notice of the television. Her eyes behind the glasses shone. 'I'm eighty-six years old. I won't have anyone telling me what to do and what to think, especially snooty Malcolm Frost and his wife. Dawnie and Billy are good neighbours, which is more than I can say for him across the road at number eleven. I like Billy. I don't care if he's been to prison for triple murder, arson, bank robbery and shooting Bambi, I couldn't care less. He's my friend, and so is Dawnie.' She swallowed more beer to lubricate her voice. 'And you'd do well not to listen to any of Malcolm Frost's rubbish, Vinnie. So, there you have it: my opinion.' She smiled brightly at her son, who was staring at her. 'Now, how about some fish and chips for tea tonight and a bit of *Die Hard with a Vengeance*?'

* * *

The bike slowed to a chug as they rode uphill, the sea a blue curve below them to their left. Dawnie realised she was hugging Billy harder than usual, her arms around his waist. He felt solid, dependable as he steered the bike round a corner and they slowed down, passing hedges and coming to a standstill at a closed wooden gate. The 'For Sale' sign told them they were at the right place: Seashell Cottage. Dawnie frowned, pulling off her helmet to reveal the red curly wig. Billy opened the gate, lifting it to prevent it dragging on the floor. The hinge was broken. He turned to take his wife's hand. 'Well, here we are.'

'It looks a bit run down.' Dawnie noticed the peeling green paint on the door, the wood bleached beneath. There was a small wooden sign, 'Seashell Cottage', hanging down at an angle: one of the nails had come loose. Grass had grown high on either side of the path. She gazed up at Billy, her brow furrowed. 'There are two sisters who live here: I just assumed they'd be tidy. They are called Miss Thick and Miss Thick. I haven't got any first names.'

Billy knocked at the door, his other hand in Dawnie's. 'They are clearly not keen gardeners. But the place can be sorted out easily enough, a lick of paint and a bit of digging.'

The door opened and two small women, both in identical shapeless cardigans, navy skirts and metal framed glasses, their hair short, faded and straight, stared out. Dawnie beamed at them. 'Miss Thick?'

'Yes,' they answered together, and didn't move.

'We've come to see the house.' Dawnie waited. 'I'm Dawnie and this is Billy.'

'So I see.' The one on the left had spoken.

'Indeed,' said the one on the right and they both turned away, walking into the shadowy hallway.

Dawnie gazed up at Billy. 'We should follow them.'

'Right, in we go, darlin'.'

Dawnie stepped into the hallway and caught her breath. High up, on a dark wooden cabinet was a round-headed owl staring at her with glassy eyes, its feathers smooth. Billy squeezed her hand. 'It's stuffed: it won't move.'

The women had disappeared behind a huge oak door to the left. Billy and Dawnie followed, stepping in to a small, dark living room. There was a chill in the air despite the sunlight outside; the room was musty. The yellow net curtains at the window hung in tatters.

Two old chairs squatted in front of an open fireplace; the hearth was blackened and covered in soot. In a glass case, a stuffed fox stared sadly at the world.

Miss Thick grunted, 'Living room.'

'Sitting room,' the other Miss Thick corrected her sister.

The first Miss Thick looked irritated. Billy surveyed the room and glanced at Dawnie. The two women had moved on into the next room. Dawnie and Billy caught up with them in the kitchen. It was square with a flagstone floor and a tiny window at the far end. There was a Formica table in the centre with two place settings, plates, knives and forks, and two glass tumblers. On the work surfaces there was a litter of potato peelings. A saucepan steamed on a well-used range, belching a starchy stench into the air. The first Miss Thick saw Dawnie staring at it.

'It's a wood-fired Rayburn.'

Her sister elbowed her sharply. 'It's an Aga.'

The first Miss Thick elbowed her back, annoyed. 'It's a Rayburn. It says so at the back.'

Her sister sulked. They led the way through a door which had been painted white, the previous bright blue colour showing beneath the flaking surface. They climbed rickety wooden stairs. Dawnie ran her fingers over the sallow wood chip on the walls. Billy patted her shoulder and gave her a meaningful look: Dawnie knew he was ready to leave. They passed a bathroom with an avocado suite and a toilet with a high cistern and dangling chain.

'Toilet,' Miss Thick explained.

'Bathroom,' her sister insisted.

They were in a small bedroom, just big enough for the double bed with a brown fabric headboard and an ancient mahogany wardrobe. Dawnie gazed at the four of them in the mirror, a tall man with a shaven head and a leather jacket, his red-haired wife clutching her helmet and two bespectacled women, like ancient schoolgirls with their arms folded.

'Bedroom one.' The first Miss Thick nodded in their direction.

'Or bedroom two. My room is bedroom one and it's next door. Follow me.' The second sister was impatient as she led the way onto a landing. A deer's head, complete with branching antlers, stared down at them, its eyes hollow and dead. The floorboards creaked beneath their feet and then they were in another equally poky room. The grey curtains were still closed. The bed was carefully made with pale sheets and blankets and a chintz counterpane. On a small sideboard stood a doll's house and a collection of china dolls in faded net and silk dresses, their eyes staring as if hypnotised. Billy leaned towards Dawnie, putting his lips against her ear. 'Do you think they've stuffed the babies as well?' Dawnie started to giggle.

Miss Thick looked at them sharply. 'My father was a taxidermist.'

Her sister shot her an impatient look. 'He stuffed things here for a living: this was his house.'

'Is he still here?' Billy asked, wondering if he was in the third bedroom, sitting up on a bed with a pipe in his hand, stuffed. Dawnie read his mind and she began to laugh, clamping a hand across her mouth to catch the sniggers.

'I suppose you'd like to see the third room?' Miss Thick asked, her brows knit crossly.

'Spare room. Father's special place.' Her sister led the way to another tiny room. There was no door, just a gaping square hole and rusty hinges. The space was cluttered with junk; boxes piled with clothes, lampshades, bric-a-brac and on the far table were an otter in a glass case, a seagull with its wings spread and its beak wide and a huge square aviary of stuffed garden birds. Dawnie grabbed Billy's hand. 'We won't go in.'

Miss Thick and her sister led the way downstairs, through the kitchen and into the dimly lit hallway. 'I suppose you'd like to see the back garden? Father's workshop is out there. It's very big. It does need a good clear-out though.'

Her sister dug her in the ribs with her elbow. 'You can take them outside. I went with the last people.'

Miss Thick was annoyed. 'I'm not going outside, Elizabeth. I have asthma.'

'I have my bunions to think of.' The sister clenched her teeth then her fists. 'I'm not going out there. I told you before, the workshop needs sorting out.'

'Then you do it,' Miss Thick lowered her voice to a hoarse whisper. 'No one will buy the house if you're so unreasonable.'

'Me? You are the one nobody likes, Margery. You're the unreasonable one.'

'Unreasonable?' Miss Thick's eyes were wild behind the metal frames. 'You are the one who still keeps dolls in your bedroom.'

'At least I have them,' the sister gasped. 'You have no one. Nobody likes you.'

'I have Father's animals. The ones in the workshop. He left them to me.'

'He did not. Tarka is mine – and Reynard. You can have the birds.'

'Don't you dare—'

'Excuse me, Miss Thick...'

The sisters turned to look at Billy at the same time, their faces equally livid. 'What?' They spoke together, an identical frown between their eyes.

Billy offered his most charming smile. 'We'll be on our way now.'

The sisters glowered, speaking directly to each other. 'Don't they want to see the back garden?'

'What about the workshop?'

'It's the best part, Father's big room, the sea view from the back gate and the path that leads down to the beach.'

'They don't want to, Margery. They've seen enough.'

'Oh, for goodness' sake, Elizabeth, don't you want to sell this house?'

'It's you who wants to sell it, Margery. I don't care at all. It was Father's house.'

'Why don't you just shut up, Elizabeth?'

'You shut up.'

'We'll be going.' Billy wrapped an arm around Dawnie, shepherding her towards the huge oak door. 'Thank you for the tour.' He gazed at them both, his eyes twinkling. 'Miss Thick... and Miss Thick... But I don't think the place is for us. Good day to you both.'

Dawnie could hear the women still screeching at each other when she and Billy reached the Harley.

'Sure, and one of them will be dead and stuffed by the morning,' Billy breathed. Dawnie collapsed into giggles and hugged him.

'I tell you what, Billy.' She smiled into his eyes. 'Let's take a ride around, look at the area a bit and then go to a pub for something to eat? After that, maybe we can take a walk together, just us and the moonlight on the beach? We don't have to rush home, do we?'

Billy lifted her up, kissing her lips. 'It sounds like we have a plan, darlin'.' He winked. 'Let's go and have some fun. But I don't think we'll be putting in an offer for Seashell Cottage.'

14

The credits scrolled down the screen to *Die Hard with a Vengeance* and Dilly stretched her legs on the footstool, rubbing the aching eye behind her glasses with the crook of her finger. Two empty beer bottles and vinegar-damp wrappings from the fish and chips were on the coffee table.

'Lovely,' Dilly purred from her armchair. 'I like a bit of Bruce Willis.'

Vinnie wriggled on the sofa and eased himself upright. 'Shall I get your eye drops, Mam? You must be ready for bed.'

'Yes, all right Vinnie.' Dilly was still thinking about the heroic John McClane and the helicopter full of baddies he'd brought down by firing his gun at the power line. That's what Bruce Willis did, and all the other movie heroes: they were brave, decisive, determined and they stood up for what was right: they inspired you to take action. Dilly rubbed her chin, thoughtfully. 'Vinnie?'

His voice came from the kitchen. 'Just getting the drops, Mam.'

'No – do me a favour. Look out of the window and see if they are still up at number eleven, will you?'

Vinnie appeared in the lounge. 'What?'

'Have a look through the window. Are the downstairs lights on at Malcolm Frost's?'

Vinnie peered through a gap in the curtains. 'Yes. The television is flickering, I think.'

'Good. Pass me my cardie. It's chilly outside, I don't wonder.'

'Outside? Where are you going, Mam?'

She was by the door, hugging her woollen cardigan around her. 'I need to make a call on Malcolm Frost.'

'What for?'

'I want to be like Bruce and say "Yippee ki-yay" to his arse.'

Vinnie frowned and followed his mother out into the street. For someone of her advanced years, she was walking quite quickly, her elbows jutting out from her body as if she was looking for a fight. Vinnie caught up with her as she rapped on the door of number eleven.

Seconds later, Gillian Frost appeared, her face alarmed, the light bright in the hallway behind her. 'Mrs Stocker? Is everything all right?'

Dilly screwed up her eyes so that her face became tough and imperious. 'Are you feeling lucky, punk?'

Gillian blinked. 'I'm sorry?'

'I want to see Malcolm. So, fetch him out, will you; go ahead and make my day.'

Gillian ducked away into the darkness and reappeared moments later with Malcolm, who folded his arms and stared into the street. 'Mrs Stocker? My wife says—'

'I need to talk to you, Malcolm Frost. I believe you've been saying things to my son about Billy Murphy?'

Malcolm adjusted his tie and drew himself up to his full height. 'I only spoke the truth, Mrs Stocker. You need to know that we're living next to a convict and it's probably best if we give him a wide berth. He's done time for GBH and it's not safe to encourage him into your home or consort—'

'Hold it right there.' Dilly waved a long finger at him as if it was the barrel of a revolver. 'I won't have you saying these things nasty about Billy, see.'

Vinnie put a hand on his mother's shoulder to calm her, his mouth open.

Malcolm noticed the waving finger and frowned. 'I'm just looking out for you, being neighbourly, Mrs Stocker. You're obviously a vulnerable target to such a devious man and—'

'And you can shut your nasty mouth.' Dilly pushed the finger towards him. 'Any more of this gossip about Billy and you'll have me to deal with, Malcolm Frost. And you know what will happen if I hear about you bad-mouthing my friend?' She waggled the finger under his nose, made a firing sound and blew down the nail. 'I'll be back.'

'I beg your pardon?'

'You'll be begging for more than a pardon when I tell my friend Billy what you've been saying. You're nothing more than a nasty piece of work. So, you can keep your gossip to yourself in future.' She turned on her heel. 'Come on, Vinnie. There's a bad smell. And anyway, it's getting cold out here.'

Vinnie followed his mother as she scuttled back to the house. His heart was swollen with pride; she was assertive and loyal. He put a protective arm around her shoulders and turned to look back. The Frosts were standing in the doorway, their faces immobile, in shock. Vinnie pointed two fingers at them, mimicking a cowboy gun, and whispered, 'Hasta la vista, baby,' before the shocked couple disappeared into number eleven and closed the door with a bang.

* * *

The moon was huge, a bronze coin reflecting shimmering light on the sea, a thin golden pathway. The waves whispered, a gentle comforting murmur as Dawnie and Billy walked along the sand in the darkness. She gazed into his face. 'I like the neighbours, Billy, all of them – Dilly and Vinnie, Aude and Sylv. And Ursula is becoming a really good friend.'

Billy made a soft sound of contentment. 'Lester's a nice guy too. I think we're going to enjoy living down here.'

'And the pub we just visited was lovely; the landlady was really sociable. We'll go there again.'

'And the fish was good. I enjoyed that, and the treacle tart and the clotted cream.'

'Billy?' Dawnie squeezed his hand. 'Do you really think we can settle here?'

He was quiet for a while. 'Are you missing the kids?'

'A bit.' She swung his hand, moving his arm back and forth. 'But you're right about letting them make their own life. I just feel the empty nest thing a little...' She sighed. 'It's Buddy, though: I've been worrying about him a lot recently. I mean, his life's all so unresolved. He's miles away, across an ocean and we can't really phone him – we have no idea how he's getting on.'

'We'll text him soon, Dawnie. Just give the young fella a bit of space.'

She exhaled. 'And then I'm worried about you, Billy.'

'Ah, you've no need.'

'But the nightmares are back, aren't they? Like they have been before – like they were when you went to see the doctor...'

'The truth is...' Billy ground his teeth together, concentrating on his thoughts. 'They don't really go away, the bad dreams – they stop for a bit, months sometimes, then they come back when I don't expect it.' He forced a chuckle. 'Ah, but don't worry about me, darlin'. I'll be just dandy. I'm just acting the maggot a bit at the moment – give me a couple of weeks and I'll be right as rain again.'

'You shaved your head, Bill...'

He shrugged. 'It'll grow back.'

'Was that because of the nightmares?'

He groaned. 'Yes – the same old stuff inside my head rattling round, the heat. I feel cooler now the hair's all off.'

Dawnie paused, turning to him and put a hand onto the smooth scalp. 'Promise me something?'

'Anything.'

'Just let it grow back a little, just so you have a little bit of curly hair.' She grinned at him, meeting the serious eyes. 'I don't want you to get a cold head.'

'Ah, all right, darlin'.' He was gazing at her. He wrapped big arms around her and she put her head against the clammy leather of his jacket and closed her eyes. The sea made a low breathing sound, like an animal snuffling in its sleep.

Dawnie hugged Billy and felt herself relax, slumping against the solid weight of his body. 'I could stay here for ever, Billy.'

They stayed in the position for a while, eyes closed, Billy resting his chin against the silk of her red curls. They were lost in their own thoughts. Finally, Dawnie wriggled and stared up at the indigo sky, the stars, the mottled moon.

Billy followed her gaze. 'It's a beautiful night.'

'I love looking up at the sky.' Dawnie hugged him closer to her. 'Sometimes it makes you feel serene, and sometimes you just feel so small and insignificant in such a big world.'

'There were times when all I wanted to do was to see the moon.' Billy's voice rumbled in his chest. 'There were times when the world was so dark, all I could see was blackness in the night, like a big blanket over my mouth, stifling me with its hot scratchy wool.' He forced a dry laugh but his eyes were sad. 'At those times I'd think about you and the kiddies and how good it would be to be with the three of you; Christmases, birthdays, holidays. All I wanted was to be home with you again.'

Dawnie nodded. Tears bloomed in her eyes and her vision blurred. 'It's always only been you for me, Billy – since the day we met in Manchester at the dance hall.'

'I'll never forget it. It was 1971 and there you were with your friends, moving around, shaking and twirling. I couldn't take my eyes off you. This beautiful dolly bird in jeans and a skimpy top, blonde hair flying round her face, dancing fit to bust.'

'Do you remember what I was dancing to?'

'It was "War" by Edwin Starr. What else would it be, eh? I thought to myself, "Go and chat her up Billy, and don't make a bags of it. She's too good looking to mess this one up." But I had to have a drink first, although I didn't want to get totally locked or you wouldn't have given me the time of day.'

'Then you came over, all shy and handsome, and asked me to dance. I was totally smitten: you were so different. All the other guys had the long locks, flowery shirts and you were tall and smart, with your cropped hair and that sexy voice.'

Billy turned to her and put his arm around her waist. 'It was Otis Redding playing: he was singing "Sitting on the Dock of the Bay". I thought I might be in with a chance of a smooch with you.'

'I could smell the whisky on you, Billy. But it was the charm that won me over. You were funny and warm and so sweet. And by the end of the evening, well – do you remember what you said to me?'

Billy grinned. 'I said, "It's Billy and Dawnie forever now." I still have the tattoo on my shoulder. I got it a month later.'

'And I have the matching one.' Dawnie chuckled. 'Then, by 1972 I was pregnant with Lindy Lou, and we got married. My mother said it would never last.'

Billy pulled her closer to him. 'Ah, and she was wrong about that, too.'

'Billy...' Dawnie turned him around and they began to walk back to the car park where the Harley was parked. 'This house by the sea that we're eventually going to find...'

'Our forever home?'

'It will make a difference to us both, won't it?'

'I promise you it will, darlin'. Me and you, coming into our own time, our own place.'

'Are you sure?'

'Sure as I am about me and you and that I'll love you till the day I die.'

Dawnie closed her eyes tightly. 'That day scares me, Billy. You know, the thought that one of us will go and one of us will be left behind.'

'Darlin', I understand that, but...' Billy's step fell in line with hers. 'One thing I learned after all those difficult years is how fear kills happiness. It takes your life away. You know, when we are scared of something, it makes everything seem worse. Finding courage isn't easy, it's not something you're born with and it's not about just being brave. For me, it's about concentrating on what we have now, me and you. What you've given me is bigger than the both of us – our love is what keeps me going.'

'I don't understand.'

'It's easy. You love me, I love you – and that love combined, it fuses; it's like alchemy, like magic, something that takes to the air and you breathe it in and it keeps you alive. Focus on that, darlin', because when you're gone and I'm gone, that magic potion which is our love will still be there, that essential bit of Dawnie and Billy joined, it'll outlast us and it's precious as gold.'

Dawnie learned against him. 'That's so beautiful, Billy.'

'So, let's concentrate on the now, will we, and find ourselves a nice house. One that's close to the sea – but doesn't contain any stuffed wildlife or warring sisters.'

'It's a deal.' Dawnie gazed up at the stars, tiny chips of diamond, and the copper circle of moon as it slid behind a straggling cloud. The sea exhaled and inhaled, soft and reassuring. She felt loved, safe, contented, and she promised herself that, whatever life would bring, she would remember this moment forever.

15

Friday the twelfth of June promised to be a hot day: the air was thick and heavy with heat and it was only half past eight in the morning. Billy was in a chirpy mood. He'd had a good night's sleep and he'd offered to nip to the corner shop in Martha Street to pick up some eggs and coffee for breakfast and some of Dawnie's favourite oat milk. Secretly, he was craving chewing gum. A smoker of rolled-up cigarettes until fifteen years ago, Billy had given up overnight but there were times like now when he had to have a stick of Juicy Fruit to chew. Dawnie had always hated him smoking but he'd always offered her the same cheeky answer. 'It comes with the territory, darlin' – gives me something to do during the long silences.' She'd always kissed his cheek – or pinched his bottom – and understood.

He was walking at a cracking pace, something he always did when he was by himself, when he heard the pounding feet of someone running behind him. He turned to see Vinnie, in shorts and vest, little ear plugs in place, listening to music. Billy waved his hand and Vinnie slowed to a trot, pulling out his ear plugs. Billy shrugged his shoulders. 'Ah, don't let me interrupt the run, Vinnie.'

'I've hardly started – where are you off to?'

'Just popping to the little convenience store in Martha Street.'

'I'll walk with you a bit. I'm not working until ten. I can start my run at the corner. I'm going towards the park.'

'Oh, talking of the park and open spaces, there's a bikers' rally on Sunday at Fuller's Field, just outside town. I wondered if you'd want to come down and look at the bikes.'

'This Sunday, the fourteenth? It's my day off.'

'My mate Lester told me about it: there will be lots of classics on display, food, cider, the usual craic.'

Vinnie's face brightened. 'I'd love to, thanks, Billy.'

'Will I call round for you about ten?'

'Great.' Vinnie looked up at the big man, at his smooth head with little bristles beginning to show through the scalp. He wondered how to phrase his next comment and decided it was best just to plunge in. 'Billy, don't take any notice of Malcolm Frost.'

Billy grinned. 'Ah, he's not such a bad ould fella.'

'I just wanted you to know… my mother and I don't care about your past, not at all.'

Billy was silent, thinking: maybe Dawnie had mentioned those years he'd been away to Dilly. He shook his head, making the memories dissipate. 'It was a long time ago, Vinnie. Ah, but I'm a different man now.' He pushed his hands into the pockets of his jeans. 'I met some great fellas in that time, though, made good friends: everything has its compensations.'

Vinnie nodded, imagining Billy in prison. He probably befriended the nice men in there. Vinnie believed that there were nice people wherever you went, the problem was simply finding them, working out who were the nice ones and who weren't. It was the same with girls: you never knew who'd love you and who'd break your heart. The thought made new words spring to his lips. 'Billy, can I ask you a question?'

'Ask away.'

Vinnie took a breath. 'Dawnie has a sister, a blonde, doesn't she?'

'Ah, she does.'

'Is she – I mean – will she come down to visit you again?'

Billy grinned. 'Lorraine's a bit of a mad one. She'll turn up, for sure. How do you know about Lorraine? Did Dawnie tell you about her?'

'I've seen her.' Vinnie felt his cheeks burning; they were standing at the corner. He tried a joke, a pun, to dissipate the embarrassment. 'I'd better jog on, Billy.' He crossed the road at a steady trot, calling over his shoulder. 'I'll see you on Sunday.'

'That you will, Vinnie,' Billy grinned, then the image of Dawnie's sister Lorraine filled his head. 'How has he seen Lorraine? In his worst dreams. Ah, but I'm not sure you want to be meeting that one, Vinnie,' he muttered to himself. 'I'm not sure any of us do...'

* * *

Aude had washed her hair and wrapped it in a towel while she was cooking. She was wearing an old dressing gown and slippers. She'd decided to make a nice curry for herself and Sylv, who'd be back from work at six; she had all day to create a wonderful thali, and making it early would give the flavours time to develop. She sauntered into the lounge to turn on the television: the constantly changing images and background rattle would be good company while she was cooking in the kitchen.

'Mine's a double and make it quick.'

Aude grinned, moved over to the bird cage and stuck her finger through the gaps in the bars to touch the budgie's feathers gently, speaking affectionately. 'Shut your beak, Tequila.'

'Shut your beak. Shut your beak.'

Aude switched on the TV, finding a news programme, listening to the newsreader talking about the crisis of funding in the NHS and she sighed. 'You're telling me about the problems in the Health Service – you haven't the first idea – you should work with me and Sylv.'

'Give me a kiss, gorgeous.'

Aude smiled in Tequila's direction. Someone was rapping on the front door. Aude turned towards the hallway. 'Be a good boy, Tequila.'

'Mine's a double. Make it quick.'

She opened the door and Malcolm Frost was staring at her, his face an expression of disgust. Aude pulled the dressing gown tightly across her body. 'Hello, Malcolm. How can I help you?'

He wore a grey cardigan and grey trousers, his arms folded across his chest. His face was serious. 'Audrey, I need to have a word with you. Is it convenient?'

Aude frowned then realised that he was implying that she'd just come out of the shower. She kept her dressing gown closed with one hand while adjusting the towel on her head with the other. 'What can I do for you?'

Malcolm leaned closer to her, his voice conspiratorial. 'It's about that man next door, the one who moved in with his bike and the wife with the wigs. He's shaved his head.'

'I know.' Aude's face was confused. 'I expect it's cooler in the summer...'

'Well, I thought you ought to know more about him, the sort of man he is: he's an ex-convict.'

'How do you know that?'

Malcolm tapped his nose. 'Something his wife said to my wife. He's done a stretch inside. GBH, I believe.'

Aude suddenly realised she was breathing faster. Anger was rising in her chest. 'He's a lovely man, Billy. We like him.'

'That's unwise, Audrey,' Malcolm tutted. 'If I were you, living next door, two women by themselves, I'd be very worried. I just thought I ought to warn you about him. It might be sensible to stay away from him. He's a criminal.'

Aude felt her face reddening. Her fists were clenched. Her mind searched for something to say and she remembered the television programme she'd just started to watch. She spat the words out without thinking. 'I'm not worried about someone who's been in prison. We all make mistakes. There are loads of problems out there to worry about rather than fuss about Billy: just look at how the Health Service is being deprived of decent funding.'

'I don't know what you mean.' Malcolm stood as tall as he could. 'Anyway, when things go wrong in Margot Street, and they most certainly will, you can't say you weren't warned. It's a disgrace.'

He turned away. His throat was suddenly dry. He'd go back to number eleven and ask Gillian to make him a cup of tea. He shook his head: Gillian had been moody and distant for a couple of days now. He couldn't imagine what had come over her. He assumed it was women's problems. His keys in the door, he thought about Aude's dismissive response and muttered, 'Feminists.'

Aude slammed the door and whirled back into the lounge, panting with rage. The news reader was still talking about the staffing crisis in hospitals. Aude let out a yell of frustration. 'He makes my blood boil, that man.' She took a deep breath. 'Malcolm Frost is just a nasty old man.'

'Nasty old man.' Tequila flapped his wings excitedly and bounced from his swing to his wheel. 'Nasty old man, nasty old man, nasty old man.'

* * *

Dawnie had boiled the kettle. The saucepan was on the little gas ring, hot water ready to boil eggs, and the bread was sliced and ready in the toaster. Billy would be home at any second. She glanced at the plastic kitchen clock that had a fork and spoon for hands: it was five past nine. She wasn't hungry, but she always enjoyed their leisurely breakfasts together. It was always a good time to sit together and chat, to talk about what to do with their day, to make plans.

To pass the time, she opened the kitchen cupboards to check what food was in stock. They needed to go shopping: there was half a bag of rice, some tins of beans, an onion with a green shoot and a few potatoes that had started to shrivel. Dawnie thought she would ask Ursula and Lester round for dinner soon. They were good company and it would give her the opportunity to cook something new. She'd seen a recipe in a magazine for pulled jackfruit tortillas. It sounded interesting and healthy, and a healthy meal meant she could make them all an indulgent pudding, something like tiramisu or pavlova. She loved cooking meringues but, gazing at the ancient gas oven that seemed capable of only one very hot temperature, she wondered if she would be able to cook anything beyond a simple casserole. She knew they had to find the house of their dreams. It was what Billy needed, without doubt.

Her mind drifted to the property details she'd been looking at online. There wasn't much out there that suited their needs at the moment. Seashell Cottage had been an amusing viewing experience, but one she wasn't keen to repeat. Billy had loved Chestnut House, but Dawnie had refused to go back and look at it again, citing Simon Mountjoy's blatant sexism and ageism as a good reason not to return. Billy had chuckled good-humouredly and didn't mention it again. Dawnie thought about what they needed in terms of an ideal home and wondered if she should make a list.

It had to be a vast house, like the one they had in Little Lever; it had to have space for Billy to move around and to have room for his hobbies, things to occupy his mind. A detached place with a garden would be preferable, if they could afford it, and they wanted to be close to the sea. Dawnie wondered if the house should be more modern; she wanted a versatile cooker, reliable heating, a luxurious bath, big double-glazed windows, but Billy was happy with a more primitive lifestyle, an open fire that needed logs to be chopped each day, a gurgling septic tank in the garden under a tin lid. Dawnie sighed. She wasn't sure they'd find somewhere they'd both be happy with, a good compromise, but they had more than four more months to search before the lease ended on number thirteen.

'Maggot Street,' she breathed. She gazed up at the kitchen ceiling. The once-white plaster was now sallow, and cracks stretched like spider webs across the length. She wondered whether to buy some colourful tiles for the walls to replace the chipped white ceramic squares above the cooker. She would ask Billy what he thought when he came back. He'd be home at any moment. Dawnie spooned ground coffee into her little coffee maker, a pink machine that would boil happily on the gas ring and fill the kitchen with a warm aroma.

Suddenly, her phone buzzed. Dawnie's brow furrowed: it was still too early in the morning for most people to send messages. She wondered if Billy had forgotten something: his keys perhaps. Then she saw the name on the screen: *rockandroll son*. His joke with her. It was Buddy – his first text to her in weeks.

She thumbed the button, her heart thumping, and read the words. Her heart was sinking already, the message was so short, but she read it eagerly and then read it again.

Hi mum im in lansing playing with a band its going well lots to tell you catch up soon bud

Dawnie felt tears fill her eyes. It wasn't much news but her boy had texted her and he was alive and well and she had been in his thoughts at least for as long as it had taken him to type the message. Dawnie read it again: the word 'lansing' puzzled her. It wasn't a verb, surely. It must be the name of a place: he said he was there. She rushed into the lounge, the idea buzzing in her head that it was a pity Buddy had never been interested in social media: if he'd been on Facebook or Instagram, she could have kept up with his movements. He was like Billy, though, not given to chatter, often wrapped in his own thoughts, but his heart was in the right place. She sat on the sofabed and lifted the laptop onto her knee.

Her fingers tapped the keyboard as she opened Google: 'Lansing, USA', and the answer filled the screen. It was in the state of Michigan. She hadn't a clue where that was: the mouse clicked on a map and Dawnie blinked at an image of the USA with a huge red dot. Lansing was on the right-hand side, the east, not far from New York. Dawnie pressed her lips together: it would be cold there in winter, she thought.

Then out of nowhere, the tears came in a big gulp, a throat full of sobs she couldn't stop. She didn't understand why she was sitting with the laptop balanced on her knees, wailing and being foolish. A feeling of hopelessness tore at her heart: her son was miles away, out of her reach, in a place that she couldn't recognise on a map, where she couldn't imagine how the buildings or the trees or the sky looked. He was miles away from her, miles from her being able to help him if he needed her, too far away for her to talk to him, to hold him in her arms.

As quickly as she had started to cry, she stopped and wiped her eyes. Buddy was a man now; he was forty-four, a musician in a band, leading his own life abroad. Unlike Vinnie across the road at number fourteen, who was living with his mother, Buddy was independent, exploring his own path. She didn't want Buddy to be like

Vinnie, she didn't want her son to be living at home. The best gift she could give to him now was to let him go. She sniffed and sat up straight, inhaled the aroma of coffee from the kitchen. She would change; she would be content with infrequent, brief, enigmatic texts: she would reply later, after she'd shown Billy Buddy's message and then she'd let her son know she was excited for him and ask how the band was going and what Lansing was like. She hoped he'd send a photo so that she could imagine him there.

The thought whispered in her ear that Lansing was ridiculously far from Barnstaple. Most people's children married and lived down the road, across town, in the next county, not in Lansing, Michigan, USA. But Dawnie was proud of her son, of both of her children. And, if she could only stop herself feeling the pangs and pains of an empty nest, she'd be proud of herself too.

The front door clicked and she looked up to see Billy in the doorway, chewing gum. He had a box of eggs and milk in one hand; in the other, he had a bunch of flowers, red and pink blooms, wrapped in cellophane. He held them out to Dawnie. 'I missed you, darlin', so I brought you these.'

Dawnie leapt up from the sofabed, the phone still clutched in her fingers, and ran over to Billy, throwing her arms around his waist. 'I missed you too, big boy. Come on, breakfast is ready and so am I. Today is a brand new day.'

16

Dawnie eased herself into the driver's seat of the Transit, a smile on her face. She felt good this morning and she thought she looked good, from the strappy sandals and bare legs to the short, glossy black hair – probably her favourite and certainly her most chic wig. She peered over huge sunglasses and called through the window. 'I'll see you in an hour, Billy.'

His voice drifted back from somewhere close to the Harley: he was polishing its chrome forks. 'Right, darlin', don't forget to pick up something nice for a picnic tomorrow.'

'For the bike show? I thought you said we could buy food there?'

'Ah, it'll be just charred burgers and buns. I thought we'd take something a bit special for lunch, all of us together. Will you pick up some quiche or a scotch egg? Maybe we could make some cheese straws?'

Dawnie leaned out of the window and raised her voice. 'You're a quiche man now, are you, Billy Murphy? Perhaps I'd better iron you a nice white shirt and dig out the dinner jacket.'

She heard him chuckle. 'Ah, you're codding me again: make sure you pick up a good bottle of something bubbly for when we get home afterwards, just me and you.'

'I'll do that, Billy.' She switched on the ignition and gazed in the driver's mirror. Billy's bike was on the pavement and the Frosts' blue car was not in its usual place. Dawnie backed the Transit steadily, deciding the Frosts must be out, which would not be unusual for a Saturday morning.

She parked easily at the supermarket, picked up a trolley and set about shopping. She had a small list from Dilly, who needed a few essentials, and Dawnie had said it would be no bother to pick up the extra groceries. She sauntered around the aisles, sunglasses perched on top of the wig, enjoying the way the short skirt allowed the air to cool the skin of her legs. In no time at all, she had piled the small trolley with goodies from the deli: cheese, bread, salad, tomatoes, yoghurts and a bottle of champagne. Billy would be pleased with her choices.

She made her way towards a till with only two people in a queue; she found herself standing behind a small round woman who was carrying a wire basket containing half a dozen items: Dawnie noticed pork chops, potatoes, milk, eggs, frozen peas, tea and bread. The woman wouldn't take long to go through the till: Dawnie smiled: she was in no hurry, just impatient to get back to Billy. The woman turned round and Dawnie beamed, patting her on the arm, her voice trilling with recognition. 'Gillian. Fancy meeting you here.'

Gillian Frost looked puzzled for a moment, her eyes cold behind her glasses, then her face relaxed. 'Oh, it's Dawn, isn't it?'

'Dawnie Smith from next door.' Dawnie rolled her eyes. 'What a way to spend a glorious Saturday morning, shopping at the super-market.' She touched the sleeve of Gillian's floral dress. 'I love this dress on you – vintage clothes are so on-trend, and the blue really suits you.'

Gillian looked away; she wasn't sure how to reply, then she muttered, 'Malcolm's outside in the car, having a snooze. He doesn't like shopping.'

Dawnie let out a gurgle. 'He's a cheeky so-and-so. He eats the food, so he should darn well help you shop for it. Mind you,' she clutched Gillian's arm. 'I'm one to talk, letting the old man off scot-free: my Billy's back home, polishing his bike for the show tomorrow. But at least he shares the cooking and the chores.' A thought occurred to her. 'Why don't you and Malcolm come with us to the bike show? It's in Fuller's Field. It'll be a lovely display and, if the weather is this good, we'll have a fabulous picnic.'

Gillian shook her head. 'Malcolm wouldn't like that, especially if it's in a field full of insects. He likes things to be clean.'

Dawnie almost said that she shouldn't care less what Malcolm liked, Gillian should come with them without him and let her hair down for once, but she said nothing. She tried a different tactic. 'I believe you have a birthday coming up this month?'

'In two weeks' time, the twenty-eighth. It's a Sunday.'

'So, how are you celebrating?'

Gillian shrugged. 'Oh, I don't normally do anything. We used to bother with those things but we don't really celebrate birthdays any more.'

'Are you crazy?' Dawnie hooted. 'You should take any chance you can. I tell you what, we should have a girls' night out, go dancing. I could invite Aude and Sylv next door, and my friend Ursula, and maybe Dilly would come – she enjoyed the skiing.'

Gillian's face was frozen with fear at the image in her mind, Dawnie dancing with abandon next to Dilly, who was doing her wild version of the same, while Gillian stood still and twitched her arms occasionally as if she was in the throes of death. The girl at the till saved her from answering as she called out a cheery hello and Gillian put her basket at the end of the conveyor belt and began to unload her shopping. Dawnie watched Gillian place each scanned item carefully in a smart white tote, her shoulders hunched. Dawnie felt sorry for her; she seemed burdened, unhappy. Then the girl at the till, a young woman in her early twenties with a high ponytail, spangled fingernails and a badge that proclaimed her name was Mia, told Gillian the total of her purchases.

Gillian rummaged in her handbag, which she'd hooked in the crook of her elbow. The tense angle of her body inside the floral dress suggested to Dawnie that something was wrong. Then Gillian uttered a groan and began to rummage with more effort. When she peered up at Mia her cheeks were red. 'I – I seem to have forgotten my purse... oh dear.'

Mia watched her tip everything from her handbag: a lipstick, a comb, a pen and a small notepad, a button, a keyring with a photograph on the end: Dawnie couldn't make out who it was, but it was only one face, a child perhaps. Gillian's expression was horrified. 'I've come without my purse – my husband is outside in the car – I could run out and ask him...'

'Oh, no, please don't worry.' Dawnie stepped forward, catching Mia's gaze. 'Just add my shopping on the end and I'll pay for the lot. This lady's my neighbour. I'll just sort it all out with my card.'

'Oh no, you can't do that, Dawn...'

Dawnie put her hand on Gillian's shoulder to reassure her and smiled at Mia. 'It's perfectly all right. Just put my shopping through as well.' She waved her credit card. 'I have my flexible friend here.'

Gillian was shaking beneath Dawn's hand. 'Are you sure, Dawn? I'll pay you back as soon as we're home...'

'It's no problem, honestly.'

Mia had already started to press some buttons on the till. A green light had come on overhead. 'Thank you,' she smiled at Dawnie. 'I'm new today. I'll just get my supervisor to help me with the till roll so that we can add your shopping to hers with one payment.'

Gillian's face was relieved. 'Thanks, Dawn: you've been very kind – I don't know what I'd have done if...'

'It's fine.' Dawnie tried her best to soothe Gillian while a busy woman in a dark blue uniform and a cap helped Mia adjust the till receipt. 'I mean, what are neighbours for?'

'Really... thank you so much, Dawn. I – I'll pay you back for the shopping as soon as you're home, I promise...'

'Oh, there's no rush...'

She watched Gillian scuttle away, hugging her handbag and her white tote and she sighed. Of course, Malcolm would probably be furious with the poor woman. Dawnie felt sorry for her. With a sigh, she began to shove her shopping in a recyclable canvas bag, starting with the bottle of champagne.

* * *

'Oh, it must have been awful for Gillian; I can imagine how embarrassed she was.' Ursula waved a cheese straw and stretched her legs out on the blanket. 'I'd have felt so humiliated.'

'She came to the door with the exact cash as soon as I arrived back.' Dawnie poured lemonade into paper cups. 'She seemed genuinely grateful.'

'Well, I'm genuinely grateful for this splendid picnic,' Lester grinned. He looked around at the stands full of gleaming machines. 'Where's Billy?'

'He's just showing Vinnie round some of the other bikes: he'll be with us in a moment.' Dawnie gazed around the field at the numerous displays, at the stalls selling paraphernalia and clothing, at the rows of tents and campervans and busy people, all engaged in the serious business of talking about motorbikes.

'There's a good turn out,' Ursula said. 'Thank you for the lift in the Transit, Dawnie.'

Dawnie scratched the curly black wig and chuckled. 'I didn't have a lift here myself. Vinnie insisted on going pillion with Billy. I half expected Dilly to be ready with a jacket and helmet but apparently she had a date with Clint Eastwood.'

Ursula helped herself to another cheese straw. 'This is a wonderful picnic, Dawnie. There won't be any left for Billy and Vinnie at this rate.'

'I tell you what, I'll go and find him...' Lester eased himself upright, dabbing his mouth with a paper napkin. 'I know where he'll be, most likely.'

'See you soon, *Liebchen*,' Ursula met his eyes and watched thoughtfully as he moved away. She sighed. 'We won't see either of them for half an hour. He'll go straight to the local stand and start talking to Edgars Berzin: he runs north Devon group.'

'I don't mind; there's plenty more food in the hampers. We haven't opened the goat's cheese and there's some French bread.' Dawnie sipped her lemonade. 'It's nice just spending time with you, Ursula.'

'It's good to have made such a friend. I have to say, things are much more fun now you're living here, Dawnie. Normally, I'd have come to this event on the bus and sat by myself while Lester chatted to the bike mob.'

'You really don't like motorbikes?'

'Oh, it's not that.' Ursula wafted the thought away with her hand. 'I'm delighted Lester loves his Harley Davidson and has such pleasure in riding it and having such nice friends. But at least in a car you are inside a metal box. On a bike you are so exposed. Then of course there are many road users who don't seem to notice motorcycles. Lester tells me such horror stories.'

'Billy's had a couple of near misses on the motorways over the years.' Dawnie passed Ursula another cheese straw. 'It's nice being out on the bike, though. I love the freedom of it. I used to have one myself at one time, a big Indian. I looked ridiculous on it: it was massive compared to me.'

'I think you're so brave, Dawnie. I couldn't ride on a motorbike. Just the noise of it starting up scares me.'

'I needed transport for work. I had loads of jobs over the years but there was a wonderful time when the kids were grown but still living at home and Billy and I were quite settled. It was the first time we had led a normal life together, about twenty years ago. He got a job in a car spares shop, selling and delivering spare parts. He was happy doing that and I had the best job ever. I rented a little place on the high street with a big window and I called it "Retro à la Mode". I sourced loads of clothes – antiques, stuff from the forties, fifties, sixties, anything I could get my hands on – and I sold it. I spent ages there, pressing things and pricing them and displaying hats and shoes and bags. I'd turn up in my wigs and crazy clothes, platform heels, mini dresses. Lindy Lou was married but she used to come in and help me, carrying baby Fallon in a carrycot, and we'd have such fun together. Even Buddy bought some things from me – I did really trendy menswear. Billy was happy at work and I was doing a great trade. Those were such good times.'

'I bet you were stunning. You still are. You look great in the wigs, Dawnie.' Ursula reached out and touched the short black hair. 'I admire how you have such style, such panache.'

'Oh, the truth is that I just don't care what people think, especially now I'm older. I love the way I can change my appearance to suit my mood.' Dawnie thought for a moment. 'It didn't start off that way, though. I bought the wigs to help my mum.'

'Oh?'

Dawnie ruffled the silky hair of her wig. 'My mum was ill; she was having chemotherapy and she lost all her hair. She was so anxious about how she looked, on top of the worries about her illness, so I took her to get a wig, and I got one for myself too. My kids were youngsters then, at school, so she and I would spend hours trying out different hairstyles and colours. After that, I kept the wigs up: it was too much fun to go back to one boring style. I love changing style and colour, just for the fun of it.'

'And your mum?'

'Oh, her hair grew back and she was fine,' Dawnie sighed. 'She died three years ago, my mum. She was ninety years old.'

Ursula picked up a wax-wrapped packet from the picnic basket. 'Is this the cheese? Do you think we could start on it now?'

Dawnie looked around her. There was no sign of the men. 'Why not? And there's some fresh French bread...'

* * *

'I'd love a bike like yours, Edgars.' Vinnie's face shone with admiration.

The tall Latvian put his hands on his hips and chuckled. 'It has taken me years to get it to this state of imperfection.'

'No, it's beautiful.' Vinnie ran his fingers over the leather seat and bent down to look at the chrome tank of Edgars' Harley. He could see his own face, distorted, the shape of a fiddle. 'I'm going to save up for a bike of my own.'

'Not cheap to run though, these things,' Edgars grinned, pushing a hand through thick blond hair. 'But I am a lucky man: my wife never complains about how much I spend.'

Lester sighed. 'My wife is so tolerant. She is wonderful. Ursula never grumbles about anything.'

'Dawnie had a bike once, a lovely Indian, and she sold it so that I could buy this Harley,' Billy chuckled. 'We are blessed with good women. Dawnie is the love of my life, my best friend.'

'Really?' Vinnie's voice was incredulous. He wondered if Lorraine was as kind and good-natured as her sister. He imagined riding Edgars' bike, Lorraine behind him, her blonde hair streaming in the wind.

Edgars folded his arms. 'It's good to meet you, Vinnie. I'll look out for a bike for you, if you want me to.'

'That would be great. I'm not sure what I could afford, though.' Vinnie stared gratefully at the tall lean man in a leather waistcoat and torn jeans. Then a square black bike caught his eye, parked just behind them. 'I like that trike over there.'

'Not a cheap one, that, and I know the owner well – she'd never sell it. I have a nose for a bargain though,' Edgars nodded, showing even teeth. 'I can contact you through Lester and I can text Billy too, now that I have his number.'

'I'm looking forward to getting involved in local events,' Billy beamed.

'We have a charity run soon. Billy, you must bring Dawnie and Lester, try to persuade Ursula to come. I'm going to bring Viktorija. She's working today. It is a shame she couldn't make it: she'd love to meet you all.'

'I was sent to bring these guys back for the picnic half an hour ago.' Lester put an arm around Billy and Vinnie ruefully. 'I'm afraid I got talking.'

'Come and have a bite with us, Edgars, will you?' Billy offered.

'I would, but I have to take care of this stand until my replacement arrives.' Edgars sighed.

Lester turned to go. 'The ladies will have eaten everything.'

Billy chuckled. 'That's my Dawnie. She has an appetite on her, for sure. I have no idea where she puts it.'

'Well, I look forward to seeing you all soon.' Edgars folded his arms as he watched the three men walk away. He glanced at his watch. It was just after two. He pulled a chamois from the back pocket of his jeans and began to wipe the headlamp of his Harley. He didn't notice the slim woman in her forties with fine dark hair in a ponytail, who walked up behind him and patted his shoulder. 'Sorry I'm late, Edgars – I was held up at the coffee stand.'

Edgars turned round, a grin on his face. 'Mei-Lien, it's good to see you. There has been a lot of interest in the stand and the club while you have been gone. Lester has brought some new people along. Your trike has been getting some attention.'

'Oh.' Mei-Lien lifted her shoulders, a pretence of nonchalance. 'That's good. Was it those men you just spoke to? Lester and his two friends? They passed me as I was walking over.'

'Nice guys,' Edgars agreed. 'Billy is keen to join us on club events and Vinnie, the younger fella, is after a bike of his own.'

'Vinnie?' Mei-Lien chewed her lip. 'Was he the one with curly hair and dark eyes?' She was thoughtful for a minute. 'I didn't think I'd seen him before...'

17

Billy had showered and changed into clean jeans and a black t-shirt with the slogan 'I've Spent A Lot Of Time Behind Bars' and a cartoon graphic of a pair of handlebars and a motorbike headlight. He had put the champagne on ice and set his ingredients out on the worktop for the curry paste. Dawnie had announced she was going to make herself beautiful and disappeared upstairs. Billy put the radio on and hummed along to AC/DC and Led Zeppelin as he chopped root ginger and coriander, then began to squeeze lime juice. The sweet aroma of spicy sauce filled his nostrils as he placed plates and glasses on the table.

He turned back to the laminate worktop that had seen better days and began to open a tin of coconut milk, bumping his hip on the table as he moved. He grinned and thought of the house they might buy, with a huge farmhouse kitchen, a spare room for his drums, outbuildings for his bike and the new ones he would collect. He wondered about buying a 1994 Triumph Speed Triple or a Bonneville Street Twin. He imagined working on new classic machines in his barn, listening to the whispering of the waves, the sun setting like melting honey on the water. This was the life he needed now: calm and methodical. He began to chop broccoli to the rocking rhythm of Thin Lizzy on Planet Rock: 'The Boys Are Back in Town'.

It was almost nine o'clock. Dawnie appeared in the doorway. She was dressed in a long halter-neck dress made of silver sparkly material. She had on the long blonde wig and her face shone from a luxurious soak in the bath. Billy turned down the heat on the cooker and came over to her, putting his arms around her. He inhaled the scent of vanilla.

'You smell gorgeous, darlin'.'

'Sugared caramel bubble bath.' She chuckled. 'The food smells better than I do, though. I'm so hungry.'

'You look good enough to eat.'

Dawnie flashed her eyes at her husband. 'That's the idea. But let's have this delicious curry first, shall we? I love it when you make Thai green, Billy.'

'The sauce is done, the rice is nearly ready to go – it's all under control.' Billy moved to where the champagne was chilling in a bucket of ice. 'Will we get totally locked on the bubbly tonight, darlin'?'

She followed him and circled her arms around his waist while he poured the fizzy drink into two glasses, leaning her head against his shoulder. 'It was a great idea of yours to have a date night in together. I enjoyed the bike event today and it was lovely to be with friends, but...'

He pressed a glass into her hand and raised his own. 'I know. Time together is precious.' He chimed his glass against hers. 'Cheers.'

'Cheers, handsome.' Dawnie took a sip of champagne and giggled. 'This is lovely. It will go down really well with the Thai green curry.'

'Now you're suckin' diesel. Sit yourself down and I'll serve up.'

Billy placed a bowl of steaming rice on the table and then ladled the food onto two plates. He sat down and they began to eat in silence. Then Dawnie met his eyes.

'This is delicious – you're a genius, Billy.'

'I was just imagining...' Billy sighed. 'You and me in the new house, doing this, sharing time together. Not in this manky kitchen but in our own home...'

'I thought you were happy enough here.'

'Oh, I am, darlin', for the now, but once we're in a place of our own...'

'It will be perfect.'

Billy scratched the bristles on his head. 'I was sad to lose my da last year, but the money from his house has come in handy. It was meant to be shared between me and you, and Patrick and Mary but...'

'Bless him – it was a shame that your brother didn't outlast your dad.' Dawnie forked up a mouthful of rice. 'I always liked Pat, and Mary. Neither of them made it past sixty-two.'

'Da lived to be ninety-six. I hope I have his genes. Poor Ma had such a hard life, and then she fell ill: he lived without her for over twenty years.' Billy closed his eyes for a moment. 'He was so lonely by himself.'

Dawnie squeezed his hand. 'You and I will be together for years yet.' She tossed the long silky strands of the wig over her shoulder. 'We'll be in our nineties, still having romantic meals together. Fill my glass up for me, would you, lover boy?'

Billy refilled her glass and they chewed thoughtfully for a while, then Dawnie pushed away her plate. 'I think we may have some ice cream in that little freezer box.'

Billy stood up and then stood still, listening. The radio station began to play 'November Rain' by Guns N' Roses. He moved towards Dawnie's chair, taking her hand and leading her towards the living room. The light had faded in the room and there was a pale orange glimmer from the street light outside. 'Dance with me, darlin'.'

His arm around her, her head against his chest, they swayed in the darkness. Dawnie could hear Billy's heart beneath the t-shirt, a steady thump. His hand moved to her hair, stroking the silk of the wig. She breathed out.

'This is lovely, Billy, just you and me...' Her mind flickered like a cine film, images of their family at the house in Little Lever, Caleb clambering on the furniture, Fallon drying her underwear on every radiator, Milo yelling at the top of his lungs for attention, Willow rushing around the house in one of Dawnie's wigs and a crash helmet, pretending to be on the Harley, and Lindy Lou drinking cheap Chardonnay on a Saturday night, sobbing into a tissue at the romance films on the television.

'Just me and you, like you said. Precious time.'

He murmured into her ear, his own soft words of love and she closed her eyes. Guns N' Roses became the Scorpions' 'Rock You Like a Hurricane' and Billy stood still, cupping Dawnie's face in his hands. 'I don't need soft music to tell you how special you are to me. You know that, don't you?'

He kissed her and she ran her fingers over his head as she always did, finding hard bone and bristle instead of the wiry curls. She kissed him harder, as if that would make everything in his life better. His mouth tasted of champagne and Thai green curry and she loved him for his passion, his vulnerability, his hugeness and because he was hers.

The doorbell rang, a familiar loud chime, and Dawnie was conscious that she was standing in a cooling room in the darkness. Her skin had become goose-pimpled in the thin dress. 'Billy. Who can that be?'

'I'll go.' His voice was a rumble. He flicked on the living room light and left Dawnie alone and blinking, rubbing the flesh of her arms to make herself feel warm. She listened as Billy's voice drifted from the doorway, amiable and soft. He reappeared with Vinnie just behind him. Billy chuckled. 'Vinnie wanted to ask me about the price of bikes.'

'It's just that I've been looking at my savings and I might be able to afford—' Vinnie stopped dead, staring at Dawnie in her sparkling dress and long blonde wig. He hadn't seen the blonde woman who had shouted at him in the street and called him handsome since the day Billy had arrived. He gasped and felt his heart start to race and all of a sudden, his mouth became dry. 'Lorraine?'

Dawnie frowned in surprise, shaking her head.

'It is Lorraine isn't it – Dawnie's sister? I saw you on the first day with Billy and—' Vinnie froze, realising his mistake. At close quarters he recognised Dawnie now, in the blonde wig. She was quick to help him out.

'It's me, Vinnie. Did you think...?' She was about to burst out laughing and stopped herself: Vinnie's expression was one of hurt, a crease in the middle of his brows that suggested he might cry. His voice was throaty with disappointment.

'Sorry, Dawnie...'

Dawnie rushed across the room, wrapping an arm round Vinnie's shoulder. 'It's all right, love: come in and have a glass of champagne with us. There's still some left, isn't there, Billy?'

'Oh no, no, no... it's fine... I don't like champagne...' Vinnie's face was red, his body stiffening as she linked her arm through his.

Dawnie took over. 'Billy, get Vinnie a glass of the home brew, will you and I'll have another glass of fizz.' She shepherded the unwilling Vinnie into the kitchen and pushed him down into a seat at the table. 'I want to hear all about this bike you're after, and so does Billy, don't you, Billy?'

Billy hadn't moved, unable to process what was happening,

why Vinnie was suddenly so awkward and his wife suddenly so effusive. He jerked into life. 'Ah, yes – I'm an eejit – drinks all round.' He bustled around the kitchen, bumping against Dawnie as he squeezed past the table, almost pushing his backside in Vinnie's face as he bent down to lift bottles of beer from a cupboard.

Dawnie reached over for Vinnie's hand. 'Did you enjoy the club meeting today, Vinnie? Did you meet any new people? How's Dilly?'

Too many questions flustered Vinnie. His cheeks were burning. 'She's watching Jean-Claude van Damme.'

Billy put a pint glass of beer into his hands. 'Get that lot down your neck, Vinnie.' He watched as Vinnie took an eager slurp. 'Right.' He poured champagne into Dawnie's glass. 'What sort of machine were you after getting for yourself?'

Vinnie swallowed beer, and then another mouthful. He was starting to recover. He fixed his eyes on Billy's t-shirt and read the slogan: 'I've Spent A Lot Of Time Behind Bars'. He rubbed his eyes and read it again. 'Nice t-shirt, Billy...'

'Oh, it's ancient: I've had this one for years.'

Vinnie coughed awkwardly. 'I wouldn't let Malcolm see you in it – you know how he can be.'

'We certainly do.' Dawnie still held Vinnie's hand in hers. It was warm. 'So, this bike you're after, Vinnie?'

'I shouldn't have come. It's late. It could have waited until tomorrow...'

'Not at all.' Billy topped up Vinnie's glass with the rest of the brown ale. 'I've always time to talk bikes. What sort of thing do you want?'

'Well, I'd have to have lessons...' Vinnie found the beer had calmed him a little. 'And obviously I'd have to buy the bike and then keep it in good condition. Mam wouldn't let me keep it in the hallway like you do, Dawnie...' He glanced at her in the blonde wig and felt the flush return to his cheeks. 'But I could put up a shed out the back, and...'

Billy nodded, full of enthusiasm. 'A Bonneville might be a good choice if you want a nice old classic. Or, if you want a good starter bike, a Kawasaki KLX250S.'

Vinnie was staring at him. 'How much would that be? I only have my savings...'

'I reckon I could get you started and kitted out for around three grand.'

Vinnie nodded slowly and took a long draught of beer. He wiped his mouth. 'You know, I had such a nice time today, Billy. I enjoyed the picnic, it was lovely, Dawnie, but also so nice meeting Lester and Edgars and...' He thought for a moment. 'It was such a good feeling being with all those people, like belonging to a group, like having a sort of family. And...' He took a breath. 'Well, I sort of need that, in my life.' He drank more beer and somehow his tongue moved by itself. 'I love my mam but, you know, it's lonely sometimes over there, just her and me. I haven't had much luck with women...' He glanced at Dawnie, at the blonde wig, and sighed. 'So, I thought, maybe if I joined a group like the local motorcycle club, at least I'd have some like-minded friends to spend time with and a bike would get me outdoors... and you two are so...' He gulped down the last of the beer. Billy was at his elbow with a second bottle, filling up his glass. 'So nice.'

Dawnie let go of his hand and watched him bring the glass to his lips. Her eyes flickered to Billy's face and back to Vinnie.

'I always think, Vinnie, if you're looking for love...'

She had his full attention. He brought the glass down to the table with a clunk. 'Yes?'

'If it's love you're after, it's always better not to look too hard. I find if you don't look for it, love will come and look for you.'

'Do you think so?' He was staring at her, his eyes round and soft.

'I do. The old saying about buses and girlfriends not arriving then all of a sudden two of them show up is very true.'

Vinnie raised his glass and drank more ale: he'd never heard that saying before, but he liked the way it promised hope.

Dawnie wasn't sure she hadn't made it up, but Vinnie was gazing at her as if her words were full of wisdom, so she carried on. 'There is a girl out there for you, one who deserves you. You're a lovely fella, Vinnie; you just need the right person.' Her thoughts moved for a moment to her boy, to Buddy in Lansing on stage, performing with his rock band.

'My son, Buddy, he's the same as you. He has met some women who weren't right for him: they didn't deserve him. Take that Mandy from Farnworth.' Dawnie caught Billy's eye and reached for her glass. 'No, she's best forgotten – the less said, the better. But Buddy's doing his own thing now, playing in a band in the USA and he'll find someone who's right for him by just being himself and concentrating on what he likes doing best.'

Billy sat down and opened another bottle of beer, pouring the last of the champagne in Dawnie's glass. 'Get yourself a bike, Vinnie. Make some friends. Enjoy yourself. The rest will follow, to be sure.'

'Billy's right. The woman of your dreams will come knocking on your door.'

Vinnie watched Billy top up his glass. He breathed deeply. 'Thanks, Dawnie, Billy. Thanks for all this: the drink, the advice, the help. I'm so glad I came round.'

'Ah, it's never a problem,' Billy grinned, raising his eyebrows in Dawnie's direction to check that she agreed with him.

'You're always welcome, Vinnie,' she crooned.

He took two gulps of beer. 'I'm feeling much better. Really, I am. You've made me feel so positive about the future.' He held up his glass. 'Cheers.'

Dawnie and Billy chorused, 'Cheers,' tinkling their glasses against Vinnie's.

Suddenly there was a loud thumping sound of someone banging hard at the front door. Vinnie's body stiffened, the glass in his hand. Billy frowned and elbowed Vinnie mischievously. 'I bet it's your ma, come to get you because you're drinking all the beer and she's not getting any. She'll eat the head off you when she comes in.'

Vinnie looked nervous. Dawnie grinned. 'Maybe it's mad Malcolm asking us to turn the conversation down.' She glanced at the clock and feigned exaggerated shock. 'It's gone ten. We must be breaking the curfew.'

'I'll go,' Billy offered and stood up, moving towards the living room and disappearing into darkness.

Dawnie caught Vinnie's eye. 'Billy will see you all right with a good motorbike; he'll make sure you're not ripped off and you get a good bargain.'

'Thanks, Dawnie. I'm really grateful for everything, and...' He gazed at her, his eyes round. 'Thanks for what you said about, you know, girls.'

The sound of a high-pitched raucous laugh interrupted his reverie. 'What the bloody hell is this, then?' He looked up to see a voluptuous woman striding into the kitchen. She was wearing a smart red suit, her mouth a line of vermillion lipstick, her honey-coloured hair swept up on her head. She rushed into the kitchen, picked up the champagne bottle, inverted it over her open mouth and then she slammed it down on the table. 'You've drunk the bleeding lot, Dawnie.'

Hands on hips, she gazed about her, at the poky kitchen, the unwashed dishes, the pots and pans and beer bottles. 'Well, this is a dive isn't it?' she announced. 'I can see nothing has changed, Dawnie Smith. And I had to park the BMW right up against some

stupid blue Honda that was occupying two spaces.' Her eyes moved
to Vinnie, his mouth wide open, his body cringing and taut with
horror. 'And who's this? Hello, handsome. Room for a small one
next to you, is there?' She moved to the table and wriggled closely
to him, picking up his beer glass and draining the contents in one
mouthful. Vinnie leaned away from her, his expression one of
horrified avoidance.

Dawnie gazed over the blonde woman's shoulder at Billy, who
was making a huge gesture of hopelessness, shrugging his square
shoulders. She turned to the woman and offered a resigned smile. 'I
wasn't expecting to see you. You should have phoned me to say you
were coming, Lorraine.'

18

'I was driving down to Cornwall and thought I'd visit you now you've moved to Devon. But then I forgot: I didn't have your address. I had to stop in a lay-by and ring Lindy.' She flourished a top-of-the-range phone in a shiny case. 'Anyway, I'm here now. I'm on my way to a three-day hotel convention in Bude, starting tomorrow. I thought I could stay here with you for the night – it's cheaper than a hotel. But I hadn't imagined you'd be living in such a hole. Oh, my goodness, just look at you!' Lorraine was staring at Billy. 'What have you done to your hair, Billy? You look like a convict. Dawnie, you need to put one of your wigs on that head.' She brayed at her own joke. Billy stood calmly, watching her.

Dawnie put a hand on her sister's arm. 'We can sort something out for you to stay here tonight. I'm sure we can make a space somewhere.'

'I wish I'd booked a hotel. I've been driving all day. I'm shattered.' Lorraine's eyes fell on Vinnie. 'Ooh, and who are you? You didn't tell me you had a lodger, Dawnie. I could always bunk up with you.' She put an arm round Vinnie's shoulders. 'Are you single? I'm a single woman – an hotelier by trade – I could do with someone to help me get the place ship-shape. I live in Blackpool. Sea Breeze, the place is called. It was left to me by my second husband, Roy – it was the only useful thing that man did. My third husband David decorated it – he was a builder – and I suppose indirectly he paid for the extension. So now I'm single again.' Her grip tightened around Vinnie's neck, her elbow almost constricting his breathing. 'My name's Lorraine. I'm Dawnie's younger and prettier – and more available – sister. Who are you?'

'Vinnie Stocker...' Vinnie coughed, wriggling from the death grip. 'I have to go. My mother will be waiting up. Jean-Claude van Damme will have finished. I have to make the cocoa.' His wide eyes met Billy's calm gaze. 'Thanks for the advice, Billy. I think I might be up for the Kawasaki. I'll see you tomorrow.'

'I'll see you out,' Billy murmured.

Vinnie gave Lorraine one final, terrified glance and scuttled towards the front door, Billy following him to wish him goodnight. Dawnie watched Vinnie go from the living room window. Lorraine stood behind her and shrieked with laughter. 'Well, some you win and some you don't. That one ran off like a scalded hen.'

'It's getting late, Lorraine. I can make you a bed up here on the sofa or in the spare room – I can move some of the things around up there, give it a quick tidy.'

Lorraine patted her honey-blonde hair, wrinkling her nose at the sight of the blue faux-leather sofabed with the leopard throw. 'I'm not sleeping on that thing, or in a spare room full of cardboard boxes. I thought you and I could share your bed.'

'That's Billy's bed.' Dawnie put her hands on her hips.

'Ah, it's all fine.' Billy was back in the room. 'I'll kip down on the sofa for one night, Dawnie. Let's not make a holy show of it, eh? I'll go up and find myself some bedding.' He turned away.

Lorraine cackled in triumph and put on a mocking Irish accent, calling out to him as he padded up the stairs. 'Ah, begorrah, bejaysus and the luck of the Irish to you, Billy Murphy – you'll have to kip on that horrible plastic sofabed all night. I can't imagine you'll sleep well but then you don't sleep at night anyway, do you?'

'Leave him alone, Lorraine.'

Lorraine waved a dismissive hand. 'I can't forgive him, Dawnie, for everything he put you through over the years, you bringing those kids up alone in all sorts of places, having to fend for yourself.'

'It's not your business to forgive or to judge,' Dawnie glared, her expression hardening. 'For better or for worse we said when we got married, and we've been through it together. Billy is my husband and you'll respect him while you're in my house.'

Lorraine's mouth was sulky. 'And what a house: it's a real dive, look at it. I thought you were going to buy something decent. But you let him drag you from pillar to post. How many dives has he brought you to, Dawnie? The place in Little Lever is the only good house you've lived in and you've handed that over to your kids.'

Billy arrived in the living room, hugging pillows and a duvet. He kissed Dawnie's cheek. 'You go upstairs now and have some sleep.'

'No, I'll stay down here with you, Billy. She can have the whole bed to herself.'

'She?' Lorraine gasped melodramatically, rolling her eyes as if she might faint from shock. 'The cat's mother, am I now?'

'You go on up, darlin'. Get some sleep and I'll kip down here. I'll sort a few things out in the kitchen, wash the pots and then I'll get some rest. Don't worry – I've been used to a hard bed in the past.' Billy walked into the kitchen. There was the sound of a tap running and the clatter of pans.

Lorraine pouted her red lips and called after him. 'But I need you to bring in my case from the BMW.'

Dawnie folded her arms. 'You go upstairs, Lorraine. I'll get your case. The bathroom is on the right. Tomorrow morning, I'll make you some breakfast and then you can get straight off to Cornwall.'

'I certainly will.' Lorraine ignored her sister's irritated tone. 'The conference in Bude begins with a networking lunch and I want to get some new ideas for the renovations I want to make on the hotel. I'm going for an upgrade.' She patted her hair. 'And while I'm there, I will see if I can't find an upgrade on the last husband I had.' She stared pointedly at her sister. 'It's a shame you don't do the same.'

* * *

The rain beat against the windows and the wind rattled the glass. Gillian brought a pot of tea to the table as Malcolm waited, knife and fork in his hand. She poured tea into two china cups. Malcolm snorted. 'It's nine-thirty. We're a little late for breakfast this morning, Gillian.'

Gillian gazed towards the window and shivered. 'I was thinking about washing the sheets and pillowcases today, but the weather has turned and it'll be too wet to put them outside.' She bustled into the kitchen and came back with small plates, a jug of milk, two spoons and a cardboard cereal box.

Malcolm sniffed. 'What's this?'

Gillian met his eyes. 'Muesli. I thought we'd try some for breakfast.'

'Muesli? I didn't ask for that.' His face became sullen. 'I usually have eggs, scrambled or poached or boiled eggs and two rounds of toast.'

Gillian spooned muesli into her dish, recalling Dawnie's words in the supermarket: 'He eats the food, so he should darn well help you shop for it.' Gillian had always wanted to try muesli and, based on Dawnie's encouragement, she'd decided that she'd buy some; since Malcolm hadn't come with her to the supermarket yesterday to help make the choice, he could eat what he was given. She poured milk over the cereal, fruit and nuts and took a mouthful. It was delicious. She wondered why she'd left it so long to try it for herself.

Malcolm made an exaggerated performance of chewing one mouthful of muesli, his cheeks moving from side to side like an irritated hamster. 'It tastes dry – like cardboard. It's stuck to my teeth.' He glared across the table. 'I don't like this cereal, Gillian.'

Her voice was light. 'I think it's really nice.'

'Well, I don't like it.' He pushed the bowl away, annoyed. 'Can't you make me an omelette?'

'I didn't buy any eggs.'

'What? You always buy eggs. I like eggs.'

'Well, I decided we needed a change this week.'

'You did what?'

Gillian smiled sweetly. 'I'll make you a slice of toast, Malcolm,' she munched on another spoonful of cereal, 'when I've finished my muesli.'

'No eggs? Then I'll go out and get some myself.' Malcolm shook his head and rushed over to the window. Grey droplets drizzled down outside. He put his face closer to the pane, his hot breath making a mist on the glass. 'The weather is awful – I'd have to drive, even to the little corner shop in Martha Street.' He rubbed a hand against the glass, his frustration making the glass squeak beneath his fingers. 'Oh, no – I don't believe it, Gillian.'

Gillian dabbed her lips with a napkin and reached for the china cup. 'What's the matter, Malcolm?'

'There's a car parked right up against my bumper: some sort of white BMW convertible thing. I'd never get out. I wonder whose car that is. Do you think the Hell's Angel has bought a car, or perhaps it's his wife's? It doesn't seem their style.'

Gillian shrugged. She was enjoying the muesli, wondering how it might taste with strawberries and yoghurt, or even bananas.

'I can't get out.' Malcolm's voice whined, higher and louder. 'The Transit is backed against the front and the BMW on the back bumper – I'm boxed in.' He turned round wildly and waited but his wife hadn't moved. She was drinking tea, too calmly. 'Gillian!'

'Malcolm?' She turned to him, a smile curving her lips.

He rushed into the hallway, finding a grey overcoat on the peg and a cloth cap. He started to pull on his coat, fumbling with the sleeves. 'I'll go next door and tell that man what I think of him once and for all. And if it's his wife, then I'll give her a piece of my mind, with her short skirts and her ridiculous hair and—'

'No, you won't.'

'I beg your pardon?' Malcolm's mouth fell open. Gillian arrived in the hall quicker than he had expected; she pulled his coat from his shoulders and hung it up again.

'I said no, Malcolm. I'll go next door myself, and I'll ask Dawn if she can move the Transit forward a bit. I'm sure she'll be most helpful. Then you can go out and buy yourself some eggs if you really want some.' She reached for her umbrella and opened the front door, watching the rain bounce against the roof of the Honda and trickle down the road. 'And in future, if you want something specific from the shopping, you can write a list.' She offered him a smile, her eyes crinkling. 'Or you might even break the habit of a lifetime and come inside the supermarket and do the shopping with me.'

She stepped out into the rain, pushing the umbrella up and over her head, closing the door behind her with a click. Malcolm's mouth was still open.

* * *

Billy was in the kitchen, washing the plates. He had made beans on toast and coffee for everyone. Lorraine, insisting she never ate breakfast, had polished off a plateful and was gazing at her reflection in the mirror above the mantelpiece in the living room, applying lipstick to her open mouth and trying to talk at the same time.

'The thing is, Dawnie, I'm a businesswoman. I have to look the part. This suit, for example.' She indicated the cream fitted jacket and pencil skirt. 'It was over a grand. And these shoes.' She lifted her foot to show off a cream stiletto. 'They cost me six hundred pounds, well, not me exactly...' She waved a hand at Dawnie, her own short platinum hair unbrushed, sitting on the sofabed in a shiny pink dressing gown, hugging one of the pillows Billy had slept on. 'You should take better care of yourself, Dawnie. I mean, motorbikes at your age? And those awful leathers... they don't do you any favours.'

Dawnie pressed her nose against the pillow. It smelled warm, of Billy, and she knew instinctively he had not slept well. Neither had she: Lorraine had taken most of the space in the bed and most of the duvet and had snored non-stop. 'It's time you left for Bude, Lorraine.'

'I know. This weather, though: it's no better than Blackpool.' She glanced in the direction of the kitchen and rolled her eyes. Billy had put the radio on and was listening to Planet Rock. 'You get a better type of man in Blackpool, though.'

'No one is better than my Billy. Come on, Lorraine, it's time you were on your way.'

'Charming – my own sister can't wait to push me out into the rain. Do I look all right? Is the lipstick the right colour? I mean, I want to be dressed to impress when I meet a gentleman...'

There was a crisp knock on the front door. Dawnie pulled her dressing gown tightly across her body, adjusted the thin belt and raised her voice. 'I'll go, Billy.'

She opened the door to see Gillian peering at her over rain-spattered glasses. Raindrops drummed on the roof of her umbrella. Dawnie smiled. 'Hello, come in.'

'I won't,' Gillian shivered. 'I'm all wet. I'd hate to bring in a puddle.'

'Oh, you wouldn't. Our house isn't anything special.'

Dawnie heard Lorraine's voice shrilling from the living room. 'You can say that again.'

Dawnie sighed. 'How can I help, Gillian?'

'Oh, well, it's just...' Gillian's face was apologetic. 'Malcolm can't get the Honda Jazz out. It's boxed in. I don't know who owns the white BMW but I wondered if you'd be kind enough to move the Transit forward a little bit, Dawn. Then he could get out.'

'Oh, no problem.' Dawnie glanced down at her dressing gown. 'I'll just get my coat.'

Then Lorraine bustled into the hallway with her case, tugging it across the threadbare carpet. She made an air-kissing sound near Dawnie's ear. 'Must go. Can't stay. People to see, money to make, men to impress.'

She shoved past Gillian, pushing up an umbrella, turning to make a disapproving face at the older woman as she walked away. 'I'll see you sometime, big sis. Maybe you could come up to Blackpool sometime? Girls' weekend? Text me.' The sound of her heels clacked on the pavement as she rushed towards her car.

'Whoever was that?' Gillian's eyebrows flew above her glasses.

'My sister – don't ask,' Dawnie groaned. 'But it's her car...'

Gillian turned and they watched the white BMW pass them, tyres squelching water, the horn sounding loudly.

Dawnie grinned. 'I don't see Lorraine for ages, then she shows up out of the blue, upsets everyone and vanishes into the sunset.' She rolled her eyes. 'Or into the rain in this case.'

'Thank you, Dawn.' Gillian was relieved. 'Perhaps now Malcolm will stop nagging about his car.'

'I can budge the Transit forward a bit if you need more space,' Dawnie offered.

'Oh, no: if he can't get the Honda out now, he shouldn't have passed his driving test.' Gillian turned to go, then a thought occurred to her and she put out a hand and pressed Dawnie's wrist. 'I wanted to say thank you for how you helped me out in the supermarket...'

'It was nothing,' Dawnie shrugged. 'You paid me back as soon as I got home.'

'Of course,' Gillian nodded. 'So, I've been thinking... your offer of a girls' night out for my birthday... is it still on?'

'It most certainly is.' Dawnie counted on her fingers. Today was the fourteenth; it was two weeks until Gillian's birthday. Dawnie pressed her lips together. 'Your birthday is on a Sunday – how about I organise for us to go out dancing on the Saturday evening?'

Gillian's cheeks flushed. 'I haven't been dancing in years. I'm not even sure I can.'

'Oh, you can, I promise you that. We'll have a great time.'

Gillian closed her eyes, imagining herself younger, slimmer, in the days before she had met Malcolm. Her hair had been long and dark brown; she had worn a white mini dress, dancing in the Winter Gardens with her friends Sue and Kathy to the Kinks and the Beatles and the Rolling Stones. She sighed, a long dreamy breath. 'I would like that, Dawn. Yes, I think I would like that very much indeed.'

19

Dawnie stared at the screen of the laptop, scratching her short platinum hair, embellished with a purple bow. Lindy Lou had emailed her some beautiful pictures of Fallon and the children taken at a recent family outing to Rivington Pike: all smiles, everyone clearly thriving. Dawnie smiled back at the last photo, kissing two fingers on her left hand lightly and placing them over each laughing mouth: Caleb, Willow, Milo, Fallon and finally Lindy Lou at the back, her arms around everyone. Stewie must have taken the snap on his phone. Dawnie sighed and clicked the mouse, bringing up the new specifications from local estate agents.

There was one house in particular that caught her attention: Sunnyhill. It was modern, with a huge window that ran the whole length of the back of the house, allowing sunlight to flood in. The kitchen and lounge were open plan; four bedrooms branched from a wide upstairs landing, used as an office with a high skylight. Everything was powered by gas. But there was only a small garage at the side, and it was located on the outskirts of town, nowhere near the sea. It wouldn't suit Billy. Dawnie pressed the mouse to look at another house.

She gazed at a rambling farmhouse built in the 1700s; it had a huge kitchen and flagstone floors. The beamed ceilings weren't too low. There was a barn outside and an old cider press. The line of the sea was visible from the upstairs windows: the beach was ten minutes' walk away. It would be perfect for Billy, with its huge open fires and a wild garden, but Dawnie thought it might be cold in the large rooms in the winter.

The third house was a lovely extended cottage with a huge wood-framed conservatory attached. The galley kitchen looked spacious enough in the photographs, and the en suite bedroom downstairs was huge, with potential to renovate the upstairs rooms to a modern specification. Outside was an industrial building, big enough for all of Billy's projects, with an upstairs section. It wasn't close to the sea but a little river ran through the front garden, which extended into woodland. Billy would find peace there. Dawnie decided they would go to see that one: it was called the Old Rectory.

Someone rang the doorbell: Dawnie knew immediately who it was, not only because of the lightness of the ring, but Ursula had texted that she'd be around before lunch with some exciting news. Dawnie rushed to the door and hugged her friend who, despite wearing a crisp white blouse and smart denims, was flushed and hot.

'Come in, Ursula. Shall I get us both a cool drink?'

'Oh, I have hurried here to tell you the news, Dawnie. Billy already knows – he and Lester are in the shed doing something mechanical to the Harley.'

Dawnie rolled her eyes. 'Billy said he was off on his bike to help Lester first thing this morning so I guessed they'd be in the shed. He'll come home covered in oil again,' she chuckled, leading the way to the kitchen. 'It's great to see you. Coffee, biscuits?'

'Both, please,' Ursula giggled. 'I feel very English, coming around in the morning for elevenses.'

'And I feel like I want to be Bavarian when I'm in your house,' Dawnie replied. 'With all those delicious home-baked goodies you bring out.'

'Well, that's exactly why I wanted to see you, Dawnie.' Ursula sat at the little table and folded her fingers together. 'Meinke rang. He and his family are coming to England. They will stay with us for a few days and then he wants to explore a bit, take the family to Cornwall, Dorset, the South.'

'Cornwall? I hope he doesn't bump into my sister,' Dawnie muttered. 'Ah, she'll have left Bude by now.' Her expression brightened. 'Well, it's lovely that your family are coming over. When do they arrive?'

'Tomorrow, Friday. That's why I'm here. I was hoping you and Billy would come round to dinner with us and meet them on Saturday evening.'

'Oh, that would be lovely!' Dawnie placed two mugs of coffee and a packet of chocolate biscuits on the table. 'Can I bring something to share?'

'I'm going to make some typical German food – I want it to be a real celebration. No, there's no need to bring anything, Dawnie. I just want us all to have a lovely evening together.' She grasped Dawnie's hand. 'The timing couldn't be better. I know in the summer Lester has lots of bike club events on the calendar. There are charity runs in July, money-raisers, and he will be busy, so it's perfect that Meinke is coming now. I'm just so sad he's not staying for longer.'

'I'm looking forward to the charity run next month.' Dawnie met Ursula's eyes. 'I wish you would come. It would be great, all of us being there. Are you sure I can't persuade you to ride pillion with Lester?'

Ursula took a deep breath. 'I'm not much of a biker's moll, am I?' she giggled. 'Dawnie, I'd be so afraid I would fall off, or I'd squeeze Lester too hard and he'd crash the bike, or I wouldn't be able to stay upright round the corners.'

'You lean into the corners, that's the point: you don't stay upright.'

'What if we hit a lorry? What if a car knocked us off?' Ursula grasped her mug with shaky hands and took a gulp of coffee. 'I just fret too much. Lester says that word to me all the time: "*Liebling*, you fret too much."'

'Maybe he could just go slowly and make you feel more secure? Or Billy and I could ride behind you?' Dawnie met Ursula's worried gaze with pleading eyes. 'I wish you'd come along.'

Ursula shook her head sadly. 'I'm sorry, Dawnie. I'm such a scaredy-cat: that's another of Lester's strange English phrases.' She forced a grin. 'He's always very nice about it. But I do feel a bit, you know, useless.'

'That's something you could never be.' Dawnie reached for a biscuit. 'In fact, I need your help right now. You see, my next-door neighbour—'

Ursula rolled her eyes. 'That man who always grumbles at you?'

'His wife, Gillian. It turns out she's really nice. Anyway, she has a birthday next weekend, she'll be seventy-five, and I think she'd really like a girls' night out dancing. I've asked Aude and Sylv at number fifteen and I know we can get Dilly to come with us. I hoped you'd help me organise it. It's just... I've no idea where to go – I don't know the area. I don't want to take her somewhere she feels out of place.' She squeezed Ursula's hand. 'Will you help? And come along, of course.'

Ursula's eyes shone. 'Oh, I'd love to. And I think I might know of somewhere we can go.' She leaned forward to whisper to Dawnie, thrilled by her idea. 'I think Lester has mentioned his friend Edgars from the bike club?'

'I've seen him. Latvian, tall and blond, probably in his forties? He seems a lovely man.'

'Well, I think he and his wife do a sort of disco business on the side as well as their normal jobs: they put on dance nights in one of the pubs in town on Saturdays. I'll ask Lester to give him a ring and see what he's doing on the twenty-seventh.'

'That's great. I'm so looking forward to your dinner party, and then next week we'll have a girls' night out,' Dawnie beamed. 'After that, on the thirtieth, it's Billy's birthday. I'm going to come up with something special for him, too.'

Ursula rubbed her hands together. 'And I'll tell Lester as well. I think it would be a good idea for the boys to organise something for him too.'

'A night out with the lads?' Dawnie was thoughtful. 'Do you know, that might be just what that fella of mine needs.'

* * *

'I'm not sure about this dress, Billy – not sure at all. I hate to come up with the cliché, but I haven't a thing to wear.'

Dawnie gave a despairing glance towards the bed. Three dresses, a long skirt, two pairs of trousers, a blouse and a jacket were strewn on top of the duvet. Dawnie hurled the long sparkly dress on top of the pile. 'I have no idea what will look right tonight.'

Billy pushed his hands into his jeans pocket and sighed. He gazed at his little wife in her silky dressing gown, still damp from the shower, and muttered. 'Go as you are, darlin'. You look lovely to me.'

'That doesn't help, Billy.' Dawnie clamped her lips together. 'I want to look *right*. Ursula has told her family I'm her new best friend. I don't want to let her down.'

'Ah, but it's not a fashion parade you're going to.' Billy shook his head and Dawnie threw him an irritated look.

He didn't understand it: his wife looked lovely and when he told her so, she seemed cross. He tried again. 'What about the blue wig? You haven't worn that one for a while. I like that one on you. It looks…' He chose his words carefully. 'Zany.'

'Zany?' Dawnie was horrified. 'I don't want to look like a freak show. I don't want to be ridiculous.' She picked up the blouse and jacket. 'But I don't want to be formal and uncomfortable all night.' She lifted the long skirt and held the black lacy satin against her. 'Too smart?'

Billy shrugged and glanced at himself in the mirror. In jeans and t-shirt, his scalp dark with the thick bristles, he hadn't considered what to wear at all: he'd just reached for something from the clean pile of clothing in his drawer. He scratched his head. He loved Dawnie: he wanted to cheer her up. He tried again. 'I like you in the headscarf, with a pair of jeans and that yellow top with the lacy bits on it. Will you wear that one?' She narrowed her eyes so he tried again. 'Or the shiny flowery top might go with the long daisy earrings?'

Dawnie sighed and rubbed her hands against her eyes. 'We have to be there in half an hour and I'm nowhere near ready. Did you get the wine?'

'Red and white.' Billy nodded. 'Pinot Noir, a nice Chardonnay, and I got some truffles as well, the chocolate ginger ones, like you said. Do you know, darlin', the young one who works in the corner shop, the little one with the nose rings, has a nice way with her. She reminds me of Fallon, the way she looked when we left…' He stopped. Judging from Dawnie's expression, he'd said the wrong thing, although he'd no idea what he'd said to upset her. He went over to her and put his arms around her, pulling her against his chest.

'I know you're a little bit worried about making a good impression at Lester and Ursula's, darlin'. That's because you are caring and sweet and that's why I love you.' He kissed her nose. 'But you'd never make a holy show of yourself, wherever you went. You're lovely: the loveliest person I know.'

She leaned against him and took a deep breath. 'Thanks Billy. You're sweet.' She stood back and tensed her body, making her hands into fists with determination. 'Right. The sparkly top and jeans, natural hair and headscarf it is.' She beamed at Billy to show she had made a decision and that she was grateful for his support. She had been a little harsh on him although, in truth, she'd decided that whatever she wore, it wouldn't help: she was feeling anxious about meeting Ursula's family.

'I'll be ready in less than five minutes, watch me.' She strode over to the wardrobe where her clothes bulged through the open door, a peacock's array of colour, and pulled out a black sequined vest. 'This will do fine.' She was about to discard the dressing gown when she stopped still. 'Oh, no. Billy. I just thought…'

He rubbed a hand over the bristles on his head. 'What is it, darlin'?'

'We're eating German food… we should have bought Riesling.'

20

'Let me introduce everybody. This is Frida and Liesel and this is my son, Meinke.' Ursula's cheeks were pink and her eyes shone with love. 'This is our good friend Dawnie and our good friend Billy.'

Meinke put out a hand, shook Billy's firmly and held Dawnie's fingers for a moment, smiling warmly. He was a slim man in his forties with Ursula's blonde hair, bright blue eyes and a little blond beard. He looked relaxed in an open-necked shirt and jeans. His wife, Frida, was smaller, darker, with a shy smile and neat clothes. She extended a hand to Dawnie.

'I am so pleased to meet you, Dawnie.'

Dawnie smiled. 'Your English is good.'

Liesel folded her arms. Her long hair was tied back in a pony-tail, and her eyes were dark beneath a thick fringe. She was wearing a pale t-shirt and faded jeans and her expression was one of disinterest. Dawnie decided she must be about fourteen. She stared at the wine Billy had just set down on the coffee table.

'*Warum haben sie französischen Wein mitgebracht?*'

Lester shuffled his feet awkwardly, anxious at Liesel's sullen dismissal of French wine, then he smiled brightly at Billy. 'The wine you brought is just the ticket. Thanks, Billy.'

Ursula led the way into the dining room. 'I have some bottles of *Spätburgunder* and some *Grauburgunder* too, so we'll have a nice range of red and white wine for everyone to enjoy.'

'Liesel, you may only have a little wine anyway,' Meinke spoke softly. 'One very small glass with your meal. For me, I like to try the different wines from France.'

They sat around the table and Lester poured wine into glasses. Ursula brought a huge casserole dish from the kitchen and set it down with a flourish. 'I made my own recipe of *Sauerbraten*. I hope you will like it.'

Billy sat up eagerly. 'Oh, that's the one with the cabbage. I've tried it before; it's very good.'

Ursula brought in more dishes, steaming vegetables, some sort of savoury pancakes, dark bread on a cutting board with butter, and she set them down. Dawnie was aware that Liesel was sulking and offered a warm smile in her direction, but the teenager looked away. Ursula ladled helpings of casserole onto plates. Dawnie grinned at Meinke. 'Are you having a nice time here in England?'

'Oh, yes. And the weather is lovely too. I have been to Barnstaple several times before to visit my mother and Lester, and it is a beautiful place.'

Frida patted her husband's arm. 'Meinke works too hard. It is good for him to take a holiday and have some of his *Mutti*'s home cooking.'

Ursula's voice was thick with pride. 'Meinke works in an accountancy firm; Frida also.'

'But I work only part-time now,' Frida added.

'Delicious *Sauerbraten*.' Meinke had already started to eat. He lifted his fork in apology. 'Sorry, *Mutti*, I just had to try a mouthful. It has been a long time...'

Ursula sat down. 'Frida is a good cook too: she makes lovely food. Lester and I have eaten it at your house.'

'Oh yes, I love to cook, Meinke does too.' Frida picked up her fork. 'But nothing is like mother's food for Meinke.' She smiled good-naturedly.

'And do you speak English, Liesel?' Dawnie asked sweetly. The teenager turned away, pretending not to understand.

'She does speak English, quite well. I've heard her.' Lester's voice was deliberately cheery.

'She is a little shy, I think,' Meinke said between mouthfuls. Liesel poked at her food with the fork and wrinkled her nose.

Billy was enjoying his dinner. He grinned at Liesel. 'And are you interested in the motorbikes? Will you get the chance to have a ride on Lester's Harley while you're here?'

Liesel shrugged and played with her food. '*Ich verstehe nicht was der Mann sagt.*'

Billy grinned sheepishly. 'Ah, no worries, it'll be the deadly accent she doesn't get.'

Dawnie was effusive. 'The food is lovely, Ursula. So rich and delicious. I've never had anything quite like this at home, although I do make hotpot and Billy makes an incredible Irish stew with stout.'

Ursula preened with happiness. 'Thank you, Dawnie. It is so good to have my family and my friends all together around the table. Lester, *Liebling*, please can you pour more wine?'

The adults' conversation bubbled around the table; at times people spoke over each other, stopping to chuckle good-naturedly and insist the other person went first. Lester was telling Meinke and Frida about the local motorcycle club and the charity event that would follow soon, and how he wished he could take Ursula on the pillion. Ursula patted his cheek and chatted fondly to her daughter-in-law about the best local shops. 'You should talk to Dawnie about where to buy clothes. She used to run her own antique clothes shop once.'

'Really?' Frida leaned forwards. 'Was that in Barnstaple?'

'Oh no, in Bolton. I used to source retro clothes, all sorts of fashions from the 1920s to the 1980s and sell them. I really loved doing that.' Dawnie pushed away her empty plate. 'It meant I could wear the most outrageous clothes and no one would ever comment. It sort of made me a local personality, especially with some of the youngsters.'

Liesel muttered below her breath. '*Alte Kleider für eine alte Frau.*'

Frida's face was horrified at her daughter's dismissive comment. She replied in German between clenched teeth and her eyes met Meinke's, who frowned at his daughter. Ursula leapt up awkwardly. 'I have made a *Käsekuchen* for dessert. Who would like some?'

'Cheesecake.' Lester licked his lips, his face eager. 'Me, of course.'

Dawnie glanced at Billy, who met her eyes. Without speaking, they both knew that Liesel had been rude to Dawnie: she had mocked her; she had said that old clothes were for an old woman. Billy's expression was one of confusion – he did not want to upset his friends but he felt protective towards his wife. Dawnie winked, a conspiratorial message that she was fine and Billy was to say nothing.

Ursula bustled back to the table carrying a huge cheesecake decorated with fruit, which she began to carve into slices. She placed one in front of Liesel who shook her head and looked away.

'*Nein danke, Oma.*'

Ursula's face creased with disappointment. 'Don't you want some cheesecake, Liesel? It's full of fresh fruit. I made it specially.'

Liesel wrinkled her nose and reached for the paper napkin, shredding it to pieces with nimble fingers, watching Ursula cut generous helpings for everyone else.

Dawnie took a breath and smiled at the teenager, leaning across the table and pointing to the bottle of French red wine. She spoke each word clearly for everyone to hear. '*Ich möchte bitte mehr Wein trinken.*'

Liesel dutifully reached out a hand and clasped the neck of the bottle. She held it out towards Dawnie and stopped suddenly, her mouth open. Dawnie noticed Meinke was smiling. Ursula gave a little chuckle.

Liesel's eyes were round. She spoke haltingly, her face reddening. 'You ask me for more wine in German? You speak German?'

Dawnie took the bottle, filling up her own glass, then topping Billy's and Ursula's. 'Yes, I do, enough to get by.'

'Then you understood…?' Liesel's fingers flew to burning cheeks. 'You understood the words I said tonight? All of them?'

Dawnie nodded and shrugged: it didn't really matter.

Meinke turned to his daughter. 'A little lesson, Liesel. You should never underestimate anyone.'

Frida smiled, patting her daughter's knee. 'I think perhaps an apology, in English?'

'Sorry…' Liesel's shoulders rose uncomfortably. 'And I say sorry to my grandma too…'

'Ah, there's no need to be mortified,' Billy chuckled. 'We've all been young ones. I was a total chancer at your age, Liesel, always acting the maggot. We're all having a grand time here. There's no offence taken, is there, darlin'?'

'None at all.' Dawnie sipped wine. 'Lovely wine, great company, delicious cheesecake.' She winked at Liesel. 'I was a bit naughty not to say earlier that Billy and I can speak a bit of German.'

Liesel was still flustered. 'Have you learn to speak German at school?'

'At school? No, I left school at fifteen, just a couple of CSEs to my name. I was a naughty girl in those days.' She winked at Billy.

'No, Billy and I lived in Germany for a while.' Dawnie chewed at a morsel of cheesecake thoughtfully. 'Many years ago, we were in Baumholder. The children were just tiny. It was a lovely place, though.'

'It's on the German-French border, so we could get nice wine there.' Billy winked at Liesel. 'German and French. Both of them were very good.'

Ursula smiled, looking from face to face. 'Billy is just teasing you, Liesel.'

Lester helped himself to more cheesecake. 'Billy has told me a little about his time in Germany when we've been in the shed messing about with the bikes.'

'Ah, I had a lovely BMW with the gold tank and mud guards.' Billy scratched his bristly scalp. 'I loved that bike. I sold it when we moved away.' He was quiet for a moment, thinking. Dawnie squeezed his hand.

'Can I get anyone coffee?' Ursula asked, easing herself up from her chair. 'And I can open the box of delicious truffles you brought, Dawnie.'

'Grandma, please.' Liesel spoke in her best English. 'I will like a piece of your *Käsekuchen* now. And then, when I have finished eating it, I can make coffee for everyone.' She turned apologetic eyes on Dawnie and Billy. 'If that is nice for you.'

'That would be lovely, Liesel,' Dawnie nodded. Meinke smiled at her and Billy and mouthed, 'Thank you.'

Dawnie linked her arm through Billy's and leaned back in her seat, a contented expression on her face.

* * *

They walked home, arm in arm, the stars bright in the sky. Billy listened to Dawnie chattering, his mouth a contented smile.

'And she was really nice after that. Really talkative. And her English was great.'

'It was.'

'It just shows teenagers can be moody all over the world. It must be hard sometimes, Billy, being an only child. I mean, Liesel was on holiday with her parents, but there were no other kids about. Buddy and Lindy Lou had each other and Fallon has her brood. It's much better when you're a big family.'

'It is.' Billy was thoughtful. 'But then, you don't really see your sister that much nowadays, and Patrick's been gone for a while. So, all we have is each other now, you and me.'

Dawnie hugged his arm, bringing him closer. 'And I'm so glad we have each other, Billy.' She listened to their feet moving on the pavement. 'We've come through some difficult times. Especially you.'

He nodded. 'I don't think about it so much now. But I remember there were the times when all I wanted was a cold can of cola and a good night's sleep in my own bed.'

'We came through it though, Billy.'

'Thanks to you, darlin'.'

'And thanks to you too. But it was hard being away from you, just me and the kids all alone in the house.'

'Did you not ever think...?' Billy paused. He'd never asked her before and he wondered how to word it. 'Did you not ever think of getting yourself another fella?'

Dawnie glanced up at him. 'The truth? No, I didn't, not ever.' She met his gaze and her eyes twinkled. 'I had a few offers, mind.'

'Oh, did you now?' Billy chuckled. 'The milkman and the post-man, was it?'

'No, it was Peter Clarke.'

'Peter Clarke? The fella who owned the butcher's shop on the corner?'

'He had a soft spot for me.'

'He did not. That eejit with the big fat fingers like sausages?'

'He certainly did. He was always chatting me up in the shop. Then he came round to the house one day in a suit and tie, smelling of Brut aftershave, and he asked me if I'd like to sample his pork chops.'

Billy chuckled. 'And what did you say to him?'

'I told him the whole family had become vegetarian and I made veggie burgers for the kids after that and never went near his shop again.'

Billy wrapped an arm around her. 'You're a special one, Dawnie Smith.'

'You'll think I'm even more special. I have found another house I'd like us to look at: it has a huge conservatory and an outbuilding you'll love. It'll fit dozens of motorbikes in it. It's called the Old Rectory. I think I'll book us a viewing.'

'It sounds grand.'

'And I want to plan something special for your birthday.'

'Are you taking the ould one next door out dancing next week?'

Dawnie nodded. They turned the corner into Margot Street. 'It'll be good for Gillian to have a break from Malcolm, I think. Ursula's got a venue in mind.'

'Lester said something about us going camping for a night away, me and him and perhaps the Latvian fella, Edgars. Maybe we'd do a spot of fishing. I thought I'd ask Vinnie to come along.'

'Sounds like a plan.' Dawnie felt her phone vibrate in her pocket. 'Oh, Billy, look – we've got a message.'

Billy stood still, watching Dawnie clutch her phone. 'It's late, after midnight. Who's messaging you now at this hour?' He gazed over Dawnie's shoulder as she thumbed the text.

'It's Buddy. He's sent some photos. Billy, look.'

They gazed at a picture of a street scene. There were high buildings, neon signs, a zebra crossing and, in the background, lots of cars and a yellow taxi. Dawnie breathed out. 'Buddy says he's in New York now. He's gone there with his band. He says they are doing well, playing lots of venues, becoming quite popular and – oh, Billy...'

'What is it, darlin'?'

'Buddy says he's got himself a new girlfriend.' She clicked to the next photo: Buddy was standing proudly in his jeans and shirt, his curls emerging from a blue beanie, both arms around a tall girl probably in her thirties with long dark hair and a wide smile. 'He says she's called Luciana Lopez. Look at his face, Billy. You can see he adores her.' She met his eyes. 'That's it – he'll never come home again.'

21

Dawnie had been painting the bedroom walls in dove grey: she was so keen to make sure that the room would look perfect. She and Billy had been sleeping downstairs on the sofabed at night. Billy hadn't had much rest, sleeping fitfully, wandering into the kitchen for a glass of water, up at six o'clock making toast and tea. But by Friday, the heavy stench of paint in the bedroom had been replaced by fresh warm air from the windows, flung wide all week. On Saturday morning, she stood in the centre of the room surveying her handiwork. Wigs were displayed on stands, jewellery was laid out, feather boas and glittering dresses hung from coat hangers on the picture rails around the room. The fragrance of ylang ylang emanated from diffusers.

'When the girls come round, I need it to look like a proper boudoir. I've got Prosecco and nibbles to keep us going while we get ourselves ready. I've put up a few fairy lights and a lava lamp. Do you think a disco ball would be too much?'

'Is this the room I'm going to have to sleep in tonight, darlin'? It'll look like a dance hall. I'll expect John Travolta to come jiving in wearing the white suit.'

'I'll take it all down tomorrow morning. I just want it nice for Gillian and the girls to meet and get changed before we go out.'

Billy shrugged his shoulders, huge moving mountains. 'I'll be in the shed at Lester's, fixing up his Harley.'

'That Harley will be the smartest bike in town at this rate,' Dawnie muttered under her breath. She walked over to Billy and hugged him. 'Seriously, I'll sort this room out after tonight.'

'Malcolm can't be happy about you all going out on the town.'

'It's Gillian's birthday, Billy and she's well up for it. When I told her about the Sixties Night in the Castle, she seemed really excited.'

Billy squeezed her in his arms. 'Well, you're a super organiser, darlin'. And I know how much these things mean to you, dancing and parties and strutting your stuff and the like.'

'Thanks, Billy.'

'For me, I like it quiet now. Too much noise and stuff, it's not for me any more.'

'I know, love.'

She felt him breathe out and she gazed up at him, meeting his eyes. 'We have the viewing at two. We should get going soon. We're looking at the Old Rectory – that's still all right?'

'Yes, no problem. I didn't sleep so well last night, sorry, darlin'.' Billy nodded. 'Then I'll come home, do myself a sandwich and then make myself scarce while you ladies get yourselves all dressed up to the nines.'

'You're a star, Billy.' She hugged his waist. 'I've made you some food already. And I promise – I'll have it all back to normal tomorrow.'

* * *

They arrived at the house at a few minutes past two. Billy had driven slowly and there had been several hills to crawl up, the

Harley chugging softly. Dawnie in her leathers and curly red wig held Billy's hand and stared at the Old Rectory nestling in the centre of a large garden. 'What do you think, Billy?'

The river gurgled softly below a little bridge. They walked along the path: roses, lavender and lupins swayed softly in the pretty cottage garden. The lawns had been neatly mown and there was a vegetable garden, fruit bushes and apple trees. At the front of the house was a huge wooden conservatory and the glass sparkled in the sunlight. A woman, possibly in her thirties, walked towards them, blonde hair swept up to a coil on the top of her head. She wore a navy suit, her face illuminated by a welcoming smile, and waved a hand in their direction.

'Hello. I'm Helen Ashbury from Collinson and Ashbury. You must be Mr and Mrs Murphy?' She held out a hand. Dawnie shook it.

'Dawnie Smith. This is Billy Murphy, my husband.'

'Lovely to meet you both.' Helen's smile broadened. 'Well, shall we start? Mrs Walker will be out for a while, so there's no one about in the house. We can view the place at our leisure. Do follow me.'

The estate agent led the way around the side of the house, down a path with a lawn to one side. She met Billy's eyes. 'I normally start a tour inside the house but your wife said on the phone how important the outbuilding was to you.' She waved an arm at an enormous concrete building with its doors rolled back. 'How about this? Would you like to step inside?'

They walked into the building, which was completely empty and virtually new. Steps led to a gallery above them. Billy breathed out.

'This could be an industrial building.' He shook his head in disbelief. 'It's big enough for a rock concert. I could keep dozens of vehicles in here. It's perfect.' He smiled at Dawnie then turned to Helen. 'What is it used for at the present?'

Helen frowned. 'The owner had it built intending to start a collection of military vehicles. But plans changed and they've kept it empty.'

'It is a grand place. It has it all, electricity, running water.' Billy grinned. 'I could work on my bikes and everyone else's in here and brew myself a cup of coffee and listen to Planet Rock at the same time.'

Helen smiled beatifically. 'Shall we go inside?'

'I'd like to see the house,' Dawnie agreed, grinning. 'If we can drag Billy away.'

Helen led them to the house, waving a hand towards the thick crop of trees to one side. 'All this woodland here belongs to the house. You could use it for the log fires. And the river is so pretty: it runs all around the side and under a little bridge to the front of the house.'

'It's lovely,' Dawnie murmured.

'So, the conservatory...' Helen led them into a huge room, all beams and clear glass. 'It's five years old, made of solid oak. The owners had it built when they bought the house. They have created it to maximise the light. It's lovely all year round. As you can see, it really brings the garden inside; you have it all here, nature and countryside and complete peace.'

Dawnie stood in the large room, gazing at the light green sofa and the wooden coffee table, the music system, the television, the bookcase and she put her hand in Billy's. 'This is a lovely room. I like it, don't you, Billy?'

He nodded. 'The outbuilding was savage, though. I can't get it out of my mind. How nice would it be to have a big building like that?'

Helen gave him a delighted look. 'You're cash buyers, aren't you?'

'That I am.' Billy squeezed Dawnie's hand. 'We both are, yes.'

'Good. I know Mrs Walker is keen to move quickly. Shall we see the rest of the house?'

Helen led the way into a galley kitchen. Dawnie wrinkled her nose. 'It's all right, but it's a bit smaller than it looked in the photos, Billy.'

He sighed. 'Maybe we could extend it?' His mind was still on the outbuilding. He wondered about buying an Indian and perhaps an old Triumph Bonneville. He could collect spare parts and help others with renovating their bikes. There was room to spray tanks and Billy was contemplating the designs he might create.

'It's nice, though.' Dawnie gazed at the new kitchen cupboards, the granite worktop.

'It's all bespoke. And only a few years old,' Helen enthused.

'I wanted a bigger kitchen but I suppose I could compromise.'

'Shall we go upstairs? There are three bedrooms upstairs and one down.'

The stairs were narrow and covered in thick floral carpet. Dawnie held on to the rail, the white paint flaking beneath her fingers. 'Helen, is this the older part of the house?'

'Yes.' Helen spoke over her shoulder. 'The Walkers had planned to renovate it all. This is the original cottage, which is why it's much smaller than the conservatory.' She was thoughtful for a moment. 'But it's very cosy. We have three good-sized bedrooms up here.'

They were in a room with pink satin curtains, a brass bed with a pink and white duvet and cream paintwork. There was a picture of a sunset beach with an orange ball of sun melting into a red sky. Billy hunched his shoulders. 'Well, at least there are no stuffed animals.'

Dawnie thought back to the house they'd visited last time and the Misses Thick, and she giggled. Helen looked perplexed but she smiled and led them into another room with yellow walls, dark gold curtains and a double bed, a woman's blue dressing gown folded on top, as if recently discarded. The furniture was dark: a wooden wardrobe and bedside cabinet and a gaudy yellow lamp shade with a bulb burning yellow light beneath. There was a cream bedside lamp with a fringe sitting squat on a small cabinet, and a delicate silver necklace lay next to a box of tissues. There was a dressing table with three mirrors, allowing Dawnie to see herself in triplicate, a red-haired woman with a serious face, staring at a room she couldn't imagine herself sleeping in. Dawnie was disappointed. 'It's nice but nothing special: it's a shame. These rooms are ordinary really.'

'We could decorate them, just how you'd like them, like you've done at Margot Street.' Billy's face was hopeful. 'There's a room for the drums, the last room – it's big enough, and this could be the spare room for the kiddies when they visit?'

'The smallest room, bedroom four, is used as an office current-ly.' Helen led them to another room across the landing and stood back to let Billy and Dawnie gaze through the door. There was a desk with a computer monitor, a keyboard, and photographs. Dawnie saw a photo of a couple smiling, a man and woman in their twenties, their faces filling the frame, and another framed picture of a man in uniform, his face expressionless. The curtains were cream and half-drawn, making the room gloomy despite the overhead spotlights. Helen offered her smile. 'It's a useful room, especially as an office, but it has enough space for a single bed.'

She led them to a bathroom, in which there was a basin, a toilet, white bath, a light blue shower curtain on a rail over the bath. The medicine cabinet was open. There was a cylindrical white bottle of hair conditioner next to the taps. Billy nodded enthusiastically. 'It's a bathroom. That's all you need, really.'

Dawnie wasn't so sure. She scratched the red curls. Billy was clearly keen on this place: the outside was lovely and the outbuilding was ideal for him. The house, however, was small and cramped apart from the huge conservatory. That mightn't be enough. She inhaled deeply.

'Will we take a look at the downstairs bedroom?' Billy showed Dawnie an optimistic face. 'Maybe that'll be just the ticket for us?'

'It's a nice room.' Helen led the way and ushered them into a large square room. 'This is a good size. It has a useful en suite that needs a bit of modernisation, but it has such potential.'

At the end of the bedroom was a small open door leading to the en suite, and Dawnie glimpsed the corner of a basin and grey and white coloured tiles. The bed was made tidily, a cream duvet, black piping at the edges, and there was a modern wardrobe in light pine and a matching chest of drawers. The curtains were half-drawn. A single bulb hung down, bright below an olive green lampshade. Dawnie shivered. Her hands were cold.

She gazed around the bedroom. It was uncluttered: there was little evidence of anyone's belongings, not even a pair of shoes. The décor was plain: white walls, a pine bedside cabinet with folded blue towels and something else – bottles, medicines. There was a dark green carpet on the floor. The place was clean, exceptionally clean: Dawnie could smell something sharp, like ammonia. But there was a strange sensation of emptiness, a feeling of oppression that hung all around them. Dawnie found it hard to breathe, as if something was pressing down on her shoulders, as if she was being held still. She glanced nervously at Billy. He was staring ahead at the bed, unblinking.

'Have you seen enough?' Helen's smile had vanished. 'Would you like to see the conservatory again, or perhaps we could go into the garden and take another look at the outbuilding?'

No one spoke. On the bed was a pair of pale grey pyjamas, perfectly folded. The temperature in the room had become chilled, although the summer sun streamed through the window. Dust hung on the air, the specks hovering. Dawnie shivered. Sweat trickled down her back, an icy droplet, then another. She took a deep breath. Despite the light in the room, she was surrounded by shadows. Billy's voice seemed to come from a distance. 'Whose bedroom is this?'

Helen made her voice light. 'It was Mr Walker's room.'

They stood in silence. Dawnie turned abruptly away from the room, pausing in the doorway to catch her breath. Billy was behind her. He stood still and stared at the estate agent. 'You said that Mrs Walker was selling the house? When we arrived, you said she was out, Mrs Walker?'

'That's right, Mr Murphy.'

'So, where's Mr Walker?' Billy reached for Dawnie's hand.

'I'm afraid he passed away two weeks ago. That's why Mrs Walker is selling. It's a sad story really.'

Dawnie held her breath, then whispered, 'What happened to him?'

'He was a Marine,' Helen explained. 'Quite high ranking – a Major, I think. They bought this place for their retirement and they'd started to do it up. Then Major Walker became ill. His wife nursed him here. She said the Macmillan nurses did a wonderful job supporting him, but in the end he passed quickly and Mrs Walker wants to move away, nearer to family.' Her bright smile returned. 'That's why the house is on at such a competitive price: it's up for a quick sale and it won't be on the market long.' Her smile broadened as she turned her eyes on Billy. 'Particularly with the exceptional outbuilding, perfect for someone with a hobby.'

Dawnie was watching Billy. He hadn't moved. He was staring ahead, in the direction of the bed, his shoulders hunched, his body tense beneath the leather jacket. She noticed the droplets of sweat on his brow. She linked her arm through his.

'That's great, Helen. Thank you for showing us around.' She

turned Billy, pulling him towards the front door. 'We'll have a chat about it and let you know. We have other houses to visit.'

They were at the doorway, stepping into the garden. The sunshine hit them, a blinding brightness. Dawnie blinked and turned to Helen, extending an arm, pressing her hand. 'Thank you so much for showing us around. And do say thanks to Mrs Walker...'

She tightened her grip on Billy's arm, lugging him back towards the bike. He was still gazing ahead when they reached the Harley and Dawnie handed him his helmet. 'Come on, Billy. We should get going.'

Billy shivered inside his jacket. 'Ah, I made a holy show of myself in there. I didn't know what to say to the woman when she told me all that about Major Walker. I felt terrible: the cold icy room, and the specks of dust just twirling in the air. It got into my throat. I'm an eejit.'

'No, I felt the same.' Dawnie zipped up her jacket and pushed the helmet over her curls. 'It was really uncomfortable. The room was full of sadness. I couldn't wait to get out.'

Billy still hadn't moved. 'There was the smell of death in the place. I couldn't live there.'

'I know.' Dawnie kissed his cheek. 'It wasn't for us. There will be other places.' She sighed. 'Poor Major Walker. Poor Mrs Walker. What an unhappy house.' She patted Billy's shoulder. 'Come on, love, we should be heading off.'

Billy nodded, clambering over the Harley as Dawnie scrambled onto the pillion and rested her head against the sprawl of his back. The engine rumbled to life and the bike moved away towards the descent in the direction of Barnstaple, away from the Old Rectory. Dawnie didn't look back.

22

'Who's for Prosecco? Pretzels? Nuts? I have some cheesy biscuits – and some olives.' Dawnie, still in the shiny pink dressing gown, her platinum hair damp from the shower, plonked down a tray on the bed, amid discarded clothes and underwear and poured fizzy wine into six glasses. Gillian was gazing around the bedroom, taking in the freshly painted grey walls, the array of colourful wigs, the twinkling fairy lights and feather boas.

'Dawn, surely your husband doesn't sleep in this room? It's like a lady's boudoir. Malcolm would have a fit.'

Dawnie grinned: a boudoir was exactly the effect she'd told Billy she wanted. Ursula accepted a glass of Prosecco and giggled. 'Billy is wonderful, kind and unselfish. He would do anything for Dawnie.'

'I'll make it more of a marital bedroom tomorrow.' Dawnie handed Prosecco to Aude and Sylv. 'But for now, we're celebrating – it's Gillian's birthday.'

Sylv was already trying on an electric blue wig, preening in front of a mirror. 'Is it me, do you think, Aude?'

'You look ravishing.'

Dilly was sitting on the edge of the bed, bouncing up and down, a black feather boa around her neck. She sipped Prosecco, licked her lips, pushed pretzels into her mouth and chuckled softly. 'So, we are going to dress up in all these clothes, Dawnie, and go out dancing?'

'That's the idea, Dilly. It's Sixties Night at the Castle.'

Gillian tensed. 'You won't have anything in my size. I can go in what I'm wearing.' She glanced down sadly at the floral dress, a brown and green polyester frock that came to her knees.

'I have lots of things you can wear.' Dawnie sipped from her glass. 'What size are you? Ten, twelve, fourteen? I have all sorts of clothes: I never look at the sizes. If I see something I like in the shops, I buy it – I just put a belt round it if it's too big and squeeze into it if it's too small. If all else fails, I am good enough with a sewing machine to make it stylish and unusual.' She reached into the wardrobe, moving a few heavy hangers on the rail, and pulled out a mini dress in a pattern of four black and white squares. She held it up. 'You'd look lovely in this.'

'Oh no, Dawn, I can't wear that.'

Dilly pushed a handful of peanuts into her mouth. 'Twiggy wore something like that in the sixties. I've seen pictures of her in it. If you don't want to wear it, Gillian, I will.'

'Oh, I have something else for you, Dilly.' Dawnie held out a long-sleeved maxi dress in gold Lurex that sparkled as she lifted it. 'What about this?'

'Look at that. Gorgeous.' Dilly grabbed both dresses and linked her arm through Gillian's. 'The little bathroom is across the land-ing, isn't it, Dawnie? Come on, Gillian, we're going to try these on in private… you know, like a dressing room in Biba or Chelsea Girl.'

Gillian blinked. 'But I'm not sure…'

'Oh, I'm not embarrassed: we're all girls together.' Dilly pulled her forward with new-found strength. 'Come on, my lovely. We have a birthday party to look stunning for.'

Ursula, Aude and Sylv moved towards the wardrobe. Sylv ran her fingers through her new silky hair. 'I want something to go with the blue wig.' She gasped as Dawnie handed her a blue spotted A-line mini dress. She immediately threw off her t-shirt and pulled it on, easing it over the wig, murmuring, 'Oooh, I love this.'

Aude followed suit, tugging an orange psychedelic patterned dress over her head. 'Hand me the curly red wig: it will look so *groovy* with this.' Aude flashed a grin at Dawnie. 'If that's okay, Dawnie?'

'Of course.' Dawnie handed a dress to Ursula with a flourish. 'And this is for you.'

Ursula's eyes softened as she gazed at the sophisticated black velvet dress, matching gloves and the string of pearls. 'Oh, Dawnie – are you sure I can wear this?'

'You will look like a blonde Audrey Hepburn. And for me...' Dawnie grinned. 'I'm wearing one of my old favourites – with some kinky boots.' She held up a red and yellow dress, sleeveless and so short it could have been a t-shirt. She lifted down a red floppy hat from the top of the wardrobe. 'And I don't need a wig; I'm wearing this hat and some huge sunglasses. Tonight, I'm Jean Shrimpton, the Shrimp, the first ever supermodel.'

The bedroom door flew open and Dilly stood in the centre, sparkling in her long shiny dress. She threw her arms out wide and began singing 'Goldfinger', thrusting her hips from side to side. She stopped mid-sentence and grasped her thigh in pain. 'Oh, I'll do myself an injury. Hang on. This'll deaden the agony.' Her eyes searched for the Prosecco and she leaned over, seizing the bottle. 'Well, there's not much left, is there?' She upturned the bottle over her mouth, dripping the dregs of the foam on her chin and giggled.

Gillian hovered behind her, wearing the short black and white dress, her arms hanging awkwardly in front of her. 'I can't go out in this.'

'You look exquisite, Gillian,' Ursula crooned. 'You just need some accessories: what about some big earrings and a cute hat, a Baker Boy style like John Lennon wore in *A Hard Day's Night*?'

Dawnie passed her a jaunty black plastic cap and Gillian pulled it on over her grey hair, soft strands emerging around her ears. She examined herself in the mirror, frowning. Aude put an arm around her. 'The girl's still got style. You look really chic, Gillian.'

'Do you think so?'

'What about me? Look at me. I'm Shirley Bassey.' The women turned to see Dilly in a short black wig, the feather boa draped round her neck, her arms raised in the air, her dress shimmering. 'I think I might even pull, dressed like this. What do you think, girls?'

'Pull?' Gillian folded her arms. 'Oh, we won't have to dance with men, will we? Malcolm won't like that.'

Dawnie's face was shining. 'We'll just go out there and strut our funky stuff on the dance floor and look a million dollars.' She surveyed each of the other women in turn. 'The taxi's not due for another half an hour. That's time to accessorise and make ourselves gorgeous.' She beamed towards Dilly. 'Who's for false eyelashes?'

'Me, me.' Dilly clapped her hands. 'Tonight, I'm going to be Shirley Bassey, the girl from Tiger Bay. You never know, I might even find myself a Big Spender.'

* * *

The six women slithered from the taxi: Gillian was making a vain attempt to stop her short dress from riding up her thighs. They cackled, screeched and giggled, a bright group of peacocks looking up at soft lighting inside the Castle, a red-brick pub in the centre of town. They could hear music, an insistent beat booming from the basement. Dilly wiggled her bottom and started to sing. 'I can't get no... satisfaction.'

'Pardon?' Gillian's face was visibly pale with nerves despite the blusher and orange lipstick.

'The Rolling Stones, isn't it?' Dilly's arms were moving back and forth like pistons, the feather boa hanging down her back. 'Oh, I'm ready to hit the dance floor running.'

Inside, the basement room was alive with flashing lights, slices of colours dazzling in all directions, illuminating the room. In the far corner there was a wooden bar, three bartenders busy serving drinks. On a small stage, two dark-haired women in shiny tops, baseball caps and hot pants were playing the music and moving rhythmically. In the centre of the room, a group of two men and eight or ten women in their twenties and thirties occupied the dance floor, jigging up and down. Dawnie led the way to a small empty table and everyone sat down, watching the dancers cavorting.

Gillian froze. 'Everyone's so young.'

'Perfect.' Dawnie's smile spread across her face. 'We can teach them a thing or two about the sixties.'

'Let's dance.' Aude pulled Sylv onto the dance floor and they began to jive, holding hands and twirling together and apart in well-practised moves.

'I need a drink, Dawnie.' Dilly glanced towards the bar. 'Is that the bar over there? I can smell beer but my bad eye is all blurred.'

'Are you all right to drink?' Dawnie asked. 'Do you have any medication, Dilly?'

'Just the eye drops, really. Ah, I'll be fine with just a couple.' Dilly batted her false eyelashes and clutched Gillian's arm. 'Shall we get the first round together?'

Gillian took a breath. 'The first drinks are on me – it's my birthday.' She chewed her lip, determined. 'I haven't had a vodka and lime for years. I think I'll have one now.'

'Mine's a gin and tonic,' Dilly insisted and tugged Gillian gently towards the bar. Her voice trailed over her shoulder. 'I'll see if I can get us a few free ones – on the house, like.'

'This is just great.' Dawnie clapped her hands excitedly, the music making her bob up and down. 'We're going to have such a good time.'

'First, let me introduce you to someone you must meet.' Ursula tugged Dawnie towards the stage, clambering up steps past huge booming speakers. The two dark-haired women, probably in their late thirties or forties, greeted Ursula with a smile and a hug. Ursula turned to Dawnie and pointed to the taller of the two women.

'Dawnie, this is Viktorija Berzin. She's Edgars' wife – I think you met him at the club display.'

Dawnie took her hand. 'Only briefly, at the end of the show before we went home. He and Billy chatted for ages about bikes while Ursula and I ate the picnic. Pleased to meet you, Viktorija. It's so kind of you to do the sixties music for us.'

Viktorija smiled, her face open and friendly. 'It's no trouble. Edgars and I usually do a disco night once a week here. It's fun to do a themed one, you know, sixties or eighties or rock 'n' roll.' She swept a hand through her glossy hair. 'It's good for me to take a break and get out at the weekend. Edgars is with the boys at home. Teenagers. They are a handful at the moment. Edgars is making them do their homework and he's minding Mei's little one too. He's a star.'

Ursula tugged at Dawnie's wrist. 'And this is Mei-Lien. I don't think you've met.'

The slim girl looked up from the record deck, pushed her hair back from her face and met Dawnie's eyes. 'I think I've seen you before – weren't you at the bike display?'

'Yes,' Dawnie chuckled. 'I'm surprised you recognise me. I didn't look like this.'

Mei-Lien glanced at Dawnie's dress, the white boots, the floppy hat, and then at Ursula, refined in black velvet and pearls. 'You look fantastic, both of you.'

Dawnie raised her voice over the music. 'Gillian is at the bar.' She pointed at the small woman in the black and white mini dress and shiny black cap. 'It's her birthday tomorrow so we're celebrating.'

'We'll play her some dedications.' Viktorija put her mouth to the microphone, her Latvian accent soft through the speakers. 'And a special happy birthday to Gillian for tomorrow. Now it's the Kinks with "You Really Got Me".'

Ursula smiled. 'We'd better get back to the others. We'll catch up later to chat.'

Dawnie rushed onto the dance floor towards Dilly and Gillian, who were each carrying a tray of drinks. She took Dilly's tray from her hands before the older woman tripped over the hem of her glittering dress. They returned to the small round table and were quickly joined by Aude and Sylv.

Dilly was breathless. 'I got an assortment of drinks, all sorts. We didn't pay, mind.'

'How on earth did you manage that?' Sylv was impressed.

'I told them it was Gillian's birthday and two young men at the bar bought the round for us. Lovely young men, they were. Very nice looking. And they smelled of cologne. Musty, it was, like wood shavings.'

'I can't believe we just did that, letting those men pay,' Gillian shuddered and reached for her vodka, gulping it down. 'Malcolm would be furious.'

'Malcolm can sod off,' Aude giggled. 'Sorry, Gillian. Mmm, this drink is nice. What is it?'

'I think you've got the tequila sunrise there,' Dilly chirped. She picked up the glass and sniffed it, sipping it tentatively. 'Yes, definitely tequila.'

Dawnie turned to Ursula. 'I only met Edgars briefly at the bike club, but the charity run is soon and I'll meet him there. Billy says he's really nice. Mei-Lien said she recognised me. I don't remember her.'

'She's good friends with Viktorija. I think they work together in the fitness business. I remember Edgars saying she was a Pilates teacher.' Ursula picked up a drink and sipped it tentatively. 'What's this one?'

'Southern Comfort and lemonade, I think.' Dilly took the glass from her hands and swallowed a mouthful. 'Just checking. Yes, it's the Southern Comfort.'

Dawnie gazed towards the stage to see the two dark-haired women dancing, bumping their hips against each other. Viktorija waved at her. Then she heard Mei-Lien's voice, light on the air. 'Here's a special song for the groovy girls over there who are celebrating a birthday tonight. Come on, girls: let's get you on the floor to this one. It's "Sugar Sugar" by the Archies.'

'Right, Sylv.' Aude pulled her to her feet. 'Even I remember this and I was about three when it came out.'

'I hate this song – it's such an irritating repetitive tune,' Gillian grumbled and lifted her glass. 'But I suppose I'd better dance, it being my birthday. I'll need some help though, to get me going.' She swallowed the rest of her vodka in a single gulp. 'Come on, Dilly, let's shake a leg.'

'I'm right behind you, Gilly. I might be eighty-six but I can show these youngsters how to get my groove on.'

Dawnie was giggling. 'Gillian is a changed woman, Ursula. I think we're a good influence.'

'We'd better join them and dance, Dawnie. Come on, up we get.'

'It's a good idea to keep Dilly on the floor – and Gillian, from the look of it.' Dawnie winked. 'While they are dancing, they aren't drinking.'

Dawnie allowed Ursula to tug her to the centre of the room. The lights flashed, the music boomed and six women, five wearing thigh-length dresses and one in a long, sparkling frock and a feather boa, wobbled their bottoms and thrashed their arms, huge smiles on their faces, oblivious to the glances of admiration and disbelief elsewhere in the room. 'Sugar Sugar' became 'Mony Mony', then 'Baby Come Back' dissolved into the Beatles' 'Get Back'. The six women laughed and wriggled, twirled and whooped, grinning into each other's faces, having the time of their lives.

23

'Honky Tonk Women' merged into 'Bad Moon Rising', which became 'Doo Wah Diddy Diddy' and then 'Ob-La-Di, Ob-La-Da'. Aude and Sylv, their faces glowing beneath the wigs, were leaping around trying to outdo one another with their fancy footwork and even Ursula had discovered some unusual moves, waving her hands in the air and twirling her fingers delicately. Dilly gasped, exhausted. 'I need to sit down at once.'

'I'll come with you.' Gillian was glad of the opportunity to rest her feet.

Dawnie watched them flop down at the small round table where their empty glasses had been left and she raised her voice over the music. 'Shall I get us all another drink?'

'Let's go together,' Ursula suggested.

They walked around the edge of the dance hall, which was now full of dancers jiving, twisting, rock and rolling and shuffling their feet, and found a space at the corner of the bar where the crowd of drinkers was less dense. A young man with very short hair at the sides came over to them and Dawnie found her purse at the bottom of her white PVC handbag.

'Can I have six gin and tonics, please?'

The barman smiled at her. 'Certainly.' He reached up to the optics, turning to look over his shoulder. 'Are you the birthday bunch everyone's talking about?'

Dawnie glanced at Ursula and raised an eyebrow. 'That's right. What are they saying?'

'You've brought the place to life.' The young man winked. 'People are loving the costumes. You can all come here again.'

Dawnie thrust out her chin. 'Does that mean these drinks are on the house?'

He sighed. 'I tell you what: I'll make them doubles and only charge you for singles.' He shook his head. 'You're a game old bird, aren't you?'

Dawnie put her money on the counter and lifted the tray. They walked back to the table. 'Game old bird? That was a bit cheeky.'

'Quite rude,' Ursula nodded. 'And he thinks we're in costume. I used to wear things like this all the time years ago.'

'I still do,' Dawnie retorted, bursting into peals of laughter. By the time they sat down, Dilly and Gillian were at the table waiting for their drinks. Aude and Sylv arrived, perspiring and fanning their laughing faces with their hands.

Dilly reached for a glass. 'I'm thirsty as hell. Gin, is it?'

'Me too. My, that's refreshing.' Gillian drained the glass in several gulps.

'Take it steady, Gillian,' Aude warned. 'That's a double, isn't it?'

'It's my birthday,' Gillian insisted and giggled into her hand.

A voice came from the stage. It was Viktorija. 'Right, everyone. It's competition time now. I want you all on the dance floor.' Rhythmic bass and powerful opening chords boomed through the speakers. 'It's "Keep on Running" by the Spencer Davis Group from way back in 1966. Come on, everyone. There are prizes for the best dancers. My colleague Mei-Lien is coming on down to dance with you all and she'll judge who are the best three movers and shakers.'

Mei-Lien and Viktorija showed off a few disco moves themselves from the stage, twirling round and bumping their hips.

'You can tell they both teach Pilates,' Ursula murmured. 'They have such energy. I wish I had some of what they have.'

'Come on, Gilly.' Dilly pulled her new friend's arm. 'We've got this sewn up, me and you.'

'Sylv?' Aude was upright, heading towards the busy gathering group on the dance floor, and Sylv just behind her, already wiggling her bottom.

Ursula pouted. 'We won't be allowed to sit this one out, will we?'

'We don't want to,' Dawnie whooped. She grabbed Ursula's hand and rushed into the centre of the melee, her arms in the air.

The six women danced as if it was their last moment. Lights flashed and whirled around them and, as they leapt and yelled, they were aware of Mei-Lien dancing close to them, twirling in a frenzy and moving away again. The music pounded and the women danced on, exhausted, damp with perspiration and smiling. As the song ended, Dilly clutched her chest. 'Oh, my poor ticker.'

Aude was suddenly professional. 'Are you all right, Dilly?'

'Nothing another gin won't cure, Aude. Mind, I fancy something a bit different this time.' She gave a cunning smile. 'What about some more of that Prosecco we had at Dawnie's before we came out?'

'So, the results of our competition.' Viktorija yelled over a pumping bass line. 'In third place...'

Mei-Lien scuttled over with something that looked like a box of chocolates and handed it to a young man with sunglasses and sideburns who had been jiving energetically in the crowd all evening.

Dilly raised her voice. 'Fix! It's a fix, isn't it?'

Viktorija was waving a fist above her head, all enthusiasm. 'And a well-deserved second place...'

Mei-Lien rushed over to their table and planted a bottle of Prosecco in Gillian's hand, whispering in her ear. 'Well done. Happy birthday.'

'But the winner was unanimous, voted by the bar staff who have kindly donated the prizes this evening...'

Mei-Lien was beaming as she dashed across towards the friends, holding a bottle of champagne in the air. She wrapped an arm around Dilly. 'Congratulations. You're the winner.'

Applause echoed around the hall. Dilly stood up, bowed, and then flung the feather boa in the air, blowing kisses. For a few seconds, she was Shirley Bassey, the Queen of Tiger Bay. Then she sat down and looked at the bottle label. 'What's this muck?'

Ursula gasped. 'It's Moët et Chandon. It's not muck.'

Dilly pulled a face. 'Can I swap with you, Gillian? I like the Prosecco, and anyway it's your birthday so you should have champagne.'

Gillian handed over the bottle. Her eyes were glazed, a little worse the wear for the gin and the dancing, and her voice slurred a little. 'That's fine, Dilly, but we can drink it in the taxi home. If Malcolm wants any he can whistle.'

Dawnie sipped her gin thoughtfully. 'So, is everyone having a good time?'

'Fabulous,' Sylv enthused.

'The best,' Gillian agreed.

Dilly sat back in her seat. 'Can we do this all again, Dawnie?' She thought for a moment. 'Every week?'

Aude agreed. 'It's years since I've had such fun.'

'Me too. It's been wonderful,' Dilly agreed.

'So that's agreed; we'll come dancing again together.' Ursula put an arm around Dawnie. 'And we've you to thank for organising it.'

'And you for knowing all about the disco. Viktorija and Mei-Lien are great.'

A melancholic guitar sound, swoony and sad, filtered through the speakers. 'I know this one.' Aude scratched the red wig. 'It's Fleetwood Mac. "Albatross".'

'Smooching time,' Sylv announced. 'Come on, Aude.'

'Excuse me, ladies.' The women looked up from the table to see a man, tall and bearded, in a smart tweed jacket and jeans. His hair was white and his eyes twinkled as he smiled and leaned towards Dilly. 'I couldn't help noticing you dancing before. You were the competition winner and rightly so, may I add. May I have the pleasure?'

For a moment, Dilly was confused. 'What pleasure?'

Gillian elbowed her. 'He wants to dance with you.'

'Oh.' Dilly patted her black wig. 'Well, all right, I don't mind if I do.'

Dawnie, Ursula and Gillian watched, concealing smiles, as the man, probably well into his eighties, ushered Dilly to the centre of the dance hall and put his arms around her waist. She placed her hands on his shoulder and whispered something in his ear, and he smiled as they swayed to the music.

'Well, he's no youngster – they can hold each other up,' Gillian laughed. 'Dilly did say she was going to pull. Maybe she has.'

The final guitar strains of 'Albatross' ended and the Tremeloes' 'Silence is Golden' began to play. Dilly and her new beau danced on. By now she was leaning her head on his shoulder and his hand was on her waist, precariously close to her bottom. Ursula was chuckling. 'Look at those two. Isn't it lovely, romance?'

'They'll be snogging next,' Gillian announced too loudly, clearly a little tipsy after finishing Dilly's gin.

Dawnie leaned her cheek against her hand and sighed. She was thinking about Billy, how nice it would be if he could be there dancing with her, his thick arms holding her in a tight embrace. She sighed again.

* * *

An hour later in the taxi, Dawnie was still thinking about Billy, wondering if he was at Lester's house in the shed fixing up motorbikes or if he'd come home, rearranged the boudoir into a bedroom and was waiting for her to come back. She was sleepy. It would be so easy to fall asleep in his arms now.

'He was called Ken. Ken Bradley. That's a nice name, isn't it? I liked him. Dignified, he was.'

'And was he a nice man, Dilly?' Sylv asked.

'Oh, he was lovely. Nice manners on him.'

'Manners? Niceness?' Gillian closed her eyes. 'That doesn't last.'

'He said he used to be a fisherman, years ago,' Dilly sighed, the bottle of Prosecco clutched in her bony fingers.

'Did you get his phone number?' Aude chirped.

'No, but he asked for mine though,' Dilly frowned. 'I wouldn't give it to him, mind. I thought I'd leave it at that. A one-night stand.'

'Why ever did you do that?' Ursula was curious. 'I thought you liked him.'

'Oh, I did. I was playing hard to get.'

'But you mightn't see him again.' Ursula's eyes were wide.

'You're right,' Dilly frowned. 'That was a bit silly of me, wasn't it?'

Ursula looked thoughtful for a moment. 'I'm so glad I have someone to go home to. Lester is such a lovely man.'

Gillian opened her eyes, suddenly awake. 'I've got to go home to Malcolm.'

'You must love him, though,' Ursula murmured. 'He's your husband.'

Aude made a low noise, a snort of derision. Gillian waved a hand in her direction. 'I used to love him, once. I used to love him a lot. And he loved me, too.'

'Why the past tense?' Ursula asked.

'He wasn't always such a fuddy-duddy.' Gillian giggled at the sound of the word in her mouth. 'Before we met, I used to go out dancing a lot in my teens. I was a party animal.'

Dilly snorted. 'You haven't changed, Gilly.'

'Oh, I have.' Gillian's eyes were suddenly misty with tears. 'I used to be a singer in a band in the 1960s. Folky stuff we did, Joan Baez, Bob Dylan, the Seekers. I had a good voice too – everyone said that.'

'And Malcolm?' Ursula asked gently.

'He was the guitarist.'

'No. Really?' Sylv sat up straight, remembering the fuss Malcolm had made over Vinnie playing Billy's drums. 'What changed?'

Gillian was quiet for a moment. She swallowed hard. 'Time. Time and... and then something else changed everything between us, for ever.' She wiped her eyes hurriedly. 'I don't want to talk about it.'

Dawnie sat up, shaking herself from her sleepiness, keen to change the subject. 'We're nearly home. We'll drop you off first, shall we, Ursula?'

'Thank you,' Ursula smiled, hoping to cheer everyone up: the atmosphere had become a little melancholy inside the taxi. 'We must all meet up again soon. The men have decided to go out for Billy's birthday. They're planning an overnight camping trip next weekend.' She patted Gillian's knee. 'Vinnie is going. Why don't you persuade Malcolm to go along?'

'He can be a bit antisocial,' Gillian sighed, not noticing Sylv and

Aude's mischievous glance at each other. 'I can't see him going camping.'

'Antisocial, Malcolm?' Sylv exclaimed, winking at Aude. 'No shit, Sherlock.'

'What does that expression mean?' Gillian frowned. 'Is it modern?'

Aude grinned. 'It's a reference to Sherlock Holmes: it means it doesn't take a detective to work it out. Sylv is always saying things she shouldn't. You should hear the stuff she teaches our budgerigar to say.'

Sylv giggled into her hand and hugged Aude enthusiastically.

'Wait a minute. Did you say Vinnie's going on a camping trip?' Dilly was horrified. 'I'll be all on my own. Who's going to give me my eye drops and my cocoa?'

Sylv sniggered. 'You should have given your phone number to sexy Ken.'

'I know what we can do.' Dawnie leaned forward. 'What about a film and pizza night at Dilly's while the men are away?'

'We could have a sleepover.' Dilly clasped her hands together. 'We could watch *The Terminator*. Or Rambo. I like a bit of Rambo.'

'We could each bring food and a film and choose,' Dawnie suggested tactfully.

The taxi pulled up in Mary Street and Ursula slid out. 'Goodnight, girls. Thank you all for a lovely evening. I'll bring the costume back to yours tomorrow, Dawnie.'

'Keep it. Wear it. Get Lester to take you out tomorrow. Breakfast at Tiffany's,' Dawnie shouted into the cold air.

The taxi pulled away and the women settled back into their seats, feeling the cab sway around the corner.

'It's decided,' Gillian announced. 'We'll have a girls' film night. Malcolm's going camping with Billy. It will do him good.'

'I hope so,' Dawnie murmured.

Sylv winked. 'Billy will sort him out...'

'Here we are, Margot Street,' Aude yelled as the taxi began to slow down. 'We're home.'

'Home,' Dilly breathed, stretching out her aching legs.

'And look who's waiting for you at the door, Gillian.' Dawnie reached into her purse and handed money to the driver as the taxi door was opened from the outside. Aude and Sylv rushed past Malcolm, his arms folded and his face serious, giggling together, and then Dawnie crept out into the cold night air. 'Hi Malcolm – we've brought the birthday girl home safe and sound.'

Dilly wriggled out of the taxi, pushing her hand through the black wig, rearranging her feather boa and her dress. Aude and Sylv were unlocking the front door, whispering together. Malcolm turned to Dawnie. 'You said eleven o'clock. It's almost midnight.'

Gillian emerged from the taxi and suddenly became aware of the cool breeze. Her legs folded beneath her like a concertina. She slumped forward into Malcolm's arms, holding the bottle of champagne aloft, screeching, 'We forgot to drink this, Dilly. We could open it now – you could come in for a nightcap.'

Dawnie and Dilly watched the taxi pull away as Malcolm helped his wife to stand upright. She slithered down his arm and he hiked her back up again. 'You've been drinking, Gillian.'

She laughed, mouth open, the Baker Boy cap askew on her head, her short skirt drifting up her thighs. She remembered Sylv's words and spluttered, 'No shit, Sherlock.'

Malcolm's eyes were wide as he turned on Dawnie. 'This is your doing, I suppose?'

Gillian wriggled free of his grasp and held up the bottle. 'It's Moët et Chandon and it's my bloody birthday in ten minutes. Come on, Malcolm, let's go inside and crack this open, shall we?'

She staggered through the door into the warm glow of the hallway. Malcolm scowled at Dawnie and followed his wife into the house, closing the front door crisply.

Dilly kissed Dawnie's cheek and launched herself across the road, waving the feather boa and calling, 'Goodnight, my lovely. I'll see you on the morrow.'

Dawnie adjusted her floppy hat and reached into the white PVC handbag for her keys, a smile twitching on her lips. A warm light was glowing in the upstairs bedroom – Billy was home. She pushed the Yale key into the front door and whispered softly to herself, 'And a good time was had by all.'

24

Dawnie drifted into wakefulness, her legs intertwined with Billy's: she had slept deeply. She blinked her eyes open. The sun streamed through the window onto the floor, where clothes and wigs and scarves were strewn and heaped. Billy was watching her, his shorn head on the pillow next to her, wide awake. 'Good morning, gorgeous.'

She kissed his lips. 'Did you sleep well?'

He wrinkled his nose. 'Ah, not so bad.' Dawnie heard him chuckle, her head on his chest, enjoying the low rumbling sound of his voice. 'You were quite sober last night. Did you enjoy yourselves?'

'It was great, Billy. I had to keep an eye on Dilly – and Gillian had quite a few drinks.' She smiled up into his eyes. 'She's quite good fun when she lets herself go. I think we could win the neighbours round, with a bit of effort.'

Billy made a low sound of approval. 'Right, well, I'll ask Malcolm about the camping trip today, will I? You think he'll come camping with me and Lester? He might even enjoy the craic.'

'Vinnie will come and also Edgars might go. I met his wife,

Viktorija, and her friend last night. They did the disco. They were really nice.'

Billy pulled Dawnie closer. 'It's Sunday morning. Do you think we'll stay in bed or should we get up?'

Dawnie twisted round to look at the alarm clock. 'It's gone nine. What do you want for breakfast, Billy? I'll make you whatever you want, and then I'll sort this room out and get it back to normal. It's a mess.'

'Ah, no worries.' Billy kissed her nose. 'I tell you what, darlin'. I know a little place near the coast that does a cooked breakfast. Lester says it's very good and open on a Sunday. We'll have a drive there, will we, and I'll treat you to a fry-up. Then we can come back and tidy up together.'

Dawnie stretched out luxuriously. 'It's no wonder I love you so much, Billy Murphy.' She pinched his cheek and stared into his serious eyes. 'The great thing about every day now is we can take our time. I'm assuming breakfast in the café will be on for another hour or so? There's no need to rush.'

* * *

Aude was rushing around in the lounge, looking for her shoes. The aroma of well-toasted bread hung heavily on the air. 'Ah, here they are, under the sofa.' She raised her voice. 'Is the coffee ready, Sylv? We might not have time.'

'It'll be fine: we have five minutes. That's enough time for toast and peanut butter.'

'Marmite, please,' Aude yelled back.

'Yuk!' Sylv replied, the response she always made when Marmite was mentioned.

'It stinks in here,' Aude shrieked and moved to the curtains, heaving them wide and flinging a window open. 'That's better. Fresh air.'

'Shut your beak,' Tequila screeched, fluttering inside the cage.

Sylv scuttled in from the kitchen and handed Aude a steaming mug and a piece of toast, which she handed over, using her thumb and forefinger, extending her arm full length, as if the bread was infected.

'Mmm, Marmite,' Aude cooed.

Sylv pulled a face of someone eating sour lemons and dashed back into the kitchen for a final gulp of coffee and a slice of toast with crunchy peanut butter. Aude munched, calling out with her mouth full. 'I've left my phone upstairs.'

'You'd better hurry up, Aude – we have to be out any moment now. We're due to start at ten-thirty.'

'Sometimes I'm just too tired for these bloody Sunday shifts,' Aude grumbled, as she charged into the hall.

'Only after a heavy Saturday night.' Sylv shouted back. She could hear the sound of feet thumping upstairs and into the bedroom as she emerged into the lounge.

'Give us a kiss. Give us a kiss,' Tequila chirped. Sylv approached the cage and Tequila stuck his beak through the gap in the bars and made a lunge for the toast.

Sylv poked a finger into the cage and brushed the soft feathers. 'Tequila,' she cooed. 'Who's Mummy's boy?'

'Make mine a double,' Tequila chortled and began to whistle.

Sylv filled her mouth with the piece of toast, the burned edge sticking out like a rough tongue, and muttered, 'I didn't clean your cage, Tequila.' She glanced at the time. 'Oh, go on, just a quick tidy round. I'll sort you out properly tonight.'

'Did anyone say Tequila?' The budgie fluttered on his perch as Sylv opened the wire door to the cage. 'Give us a kiss.'

Tequila hopped on Sylv's finger as she pursed her lips towards his beak. His wings quivered and he was on Sylv's head.

'Come on, Tequila, don't play silly buggers.'

'Silly buggers,' the budgie retorted and flew towards the curtains which flapped softly in the breeze, landing on the window ledge. 'Silly buggers, silly buggers.'

Sylv noticed too late. 'Oh, no.'

Tequila squawked, 'Shut your beak.' In a flurry of feathers, he rose into the air and out through the open window, vanishing towards the sky.

'Tequila!' Sylv yelled.

Aude appeared in the doorway, clutching her phone. 'What happened?'

'Did you open the window?'

'Yes.' Aude's glance flew to the empty cage, the wire door. 'Did you let Tequila out?'

'Yes.' Sylv's face was panic stricken, her eyes huge behind the gold-rimmed glasses.

Both women rushed out of the front door and into the road. Billy was astride his Harley in full leathers. Dawnie, in the red curly wig, was pulling on her helmet. She grinned. 'No hangovers today, I hope?'

'Tequila!' Sylv panted, her face desperate.

'It's a bit early, isn't it?' Dawnie was about to laugh and then suddenly her face was serious. Both women were near to tears. 'Tequila? What's happened to him?'

'He's gone,' Aude moaned.

'Did you see him? He flew through the open window.'

Dawnie shook her head. 'Sorry, Sylv.'

Billy frowned. 'Maybe he'll be back in a minute? If he can fly out, then he can fly back in again.'

'We've lost him – it's my fault. I opened the cage,' Sylv wailed.

'I left the window open.' Aude wrapped an arm round Sylv, her face reddening. 'What are we going to do?'

'We're late for work already,' Sylv groaned. 'We've got to go.'

Dawnie looked at Billy. 'We aren't in a rush to go anywhere. You get to work. We'll have a little look round for him.'

Billy slid his leg over the bike, standing tall, and pulled off his helmet. 'Ah, we'll search for the little fella. Go on, you two get off to work and don't worry. He'll turn up when he's hungry.'

Billy, Dawnie, Aude and Sylv stared up into the sky. It was cloudless, an expanse of deep blue, but there wasn't a budgie in sight. Then a crow flew overhead, its wings wide and it cawed, a deep, throaty haunting cry. Dawnie shivered.

* * *

Gillian huddled in the armchair, watching television. On the screen, a man was sieving flour into a bowl, explaining how to make the perfect Yorkshire puddings. Gillian snorted. 'I use plain flour. I don't know what it is with these modern chefs, having to mix things up all the time and experiment.'

Malcolm hovered behind her. 'Isn't it time you started on the Sunday roast, Gillian? You always begin cooking around eleven. It's almost half past.'

Gillian didn't turn around. Her back was straight as she glued her eyes on the TV chef. 'I'm not doing dinner today.'

'What do you mean you're not doing dinner today? It's Sunday. We always have Sunday dinner on a Sunday.'

'Today's my birthday,' she snapped. 'I'm not cooking.'

'You're not...?' Malcolm's hands lifted and fell of their own accord. He couldn't understand it. Routine was important, something Gillian never questioned. 'Did you want me to take you out for lunch? Is that what this is about?'

Gillian's gaze stayed firmly on the chef, who was beating eggs furiously. Her fists were clenched. 'No.'

'Is this about your birthday? Did you want a present or something? I mean, cards are just silly but I can go out and get—'

'No.' The chef was pouring batter into a tin, hot fat spattering.

'Do you have a hangover, Gillian? Is that it?'

'No, Malcolm, that is not *it*.' She turned round and shot him an irritated look then pointedly moved her eyes back to the television. The screen showed the Yorkshire puddings rising in the oven, fast-tracked to puffiness. Gillian snorted again.

Malcolm breathed out deliberately. He was mystified. He'd never really understood women's ways but Gillian had always been reliable, regular, easy-going. He made one last attempt to restore normality. 'Did you want me to make the Sunday dinner today?'

'I'm really not bothered if you stuff an entire roast dinner into your ears, Malcolm.' Gillian's teeth clicked together. 'Make yourself a sandwich, go out, stay in, put your head under a bus. I don't really care.'

He stood, winded by her words, his mind a blank. He had never heard Gillian talk this way. He wondered if it was the influence of that woman who wore the wigs next door, or the wild night out Gillian had enjoyed with her and the old Welsh lady and the feminists in number fifteen. He was about to ask her what was behind her bad-tempered mood, but he thought the better of it. An emotion lurking in the shadows of his mind, instinct or plain fear, warned him that an aggressive approach was unwise and he recalled a ballad, a slow romantic song Gillian had once sung many years ago as he played folk guitar, called 'Love Me Tender'. The memory made something ache in his heart, recalling a time long ago when he was a different man and Gillian a very different woman, one who was confident and happy, who greeted him with humour, warmth, love. He swallowed a lump in his throat.

'Can I get you something? A cup of tea?' He was desperate and when his voice came out, it was strangled with anxiety. 'A sherry, perhaps?'

Gillian sighed deeply, from the root of her being. The chef's Yorkshire puddings were crispy on the outside and golden brown. 'I don't want anything. Do what you like, Malcolm. Go away.'

He had one last attempt remaining. He drew himself to his full height. 'Gillian, is this about... about James?'

Gillian did not move. The back of her head remained where it was. She was staring at the television. There was no sound other than the TV chef, a jovial Yorkshireman, declaring the success of his puddings as he covered them with rich gravy. Then Gillian stood up and turned around slowly. Her eyes, when they met Malcolm's, were shards of glass.

'Don't you ever speak to me about James in this house. Not now. Not ever. You never have a word to say about him usually. You don't mention his birthday, you don't look at his photograph, you don't visit his grave. No, Malcolm, you leave it to me to do all that and you do nothing, because you simply don't think about him now.'

'But, Gillian, you know that I—'

'I don't care. I really don't care any more.' She sat back in the chair, gazing at the television, watching the chef carve roast beef. Malcolm knew that she was crying by the ache in her voice. 'Just go away, Malcolm. Go away.'

Malcolm stood still, not knowing what to do, then he found himself walking into the hall and up the stairs. He shuffled his feet, sadly. He stood in the bedroom, gently hitting his forehead with his fist: he had no idea what to say, what to do. He thought Gillian knew why he didn't mention James's name. It had happened a long time ago. But it still hurt too much to speak about it. He'd hidden it so deeply that he couldn't let it surface, not even to comfort her, and he knew that her heart had hardened towards him because grief for her son had set it like cement.

It was cold in the bedroom. Malcolm's skin prickled. He plodded over to the window, which had been left open to air the room, and he closed it tightly. Outside, the sky was a beautiful blue, the colour of the sea. He should have arranged to do something special, to take Gillian out on her birthday. Sadness and regret filled his chest and made his lungs and heart ache. He lay down on the bed, rubbed cold hands across his face and closed his eyes. It was too early for his afternoon nap, but his eyelids pulsed with the tension behind them and he needed to rest. He breathed out, each breath constricted by loneliness and sadness. He wondered if he should have been manlier; he should have insisted, poured Gillian a sherry, pressed it into her hand and kissed her head.

'Mine's a double and make it snappy.'

Malcolm opened his eyes wide. Fleetingly he wondered if Gillian had come upstairs, if she had changed her mind about the drink, but the voice in the room was too hoarse, not her usual compliant tone. He sat upright, his spine tense.

'Who's that? Who is it?'

'Shut your beak.'

Malcolm's heart thudded. He thought of the cricket bat he kept under the bed and reached for it slowly. Clearly there was an intruder in the house: he wondered if it was children, youths. He leaned to one side and felt for the round wooden handle. 'Come out, whoever you are.'

'Silly buggers, silly buggers.'

Malcolm frowned as something flew over his head in a flurry of wings. He ducked instinctively and raised the bat. A bird, with blue feathers and a white face, stared down at him from the top of the wardrobe. Malcolm put down the bat and caught his breath. 'It's a budgerigar...' he whispered.

Tequila preened, fluffing his feathers with his pointed beak and then flew down with a flourish, landing on the sparse hair of Malcolm's head. He screeched with delight and yelled as loudly as he could in Aude's voice, 'Nasty old man. Nasty old man. Malcolm Frost is a nasty old man.'

25

Billy strapped his camping equipment and his bag to the rack on the back of the Harley. He looked up into the sky; it was a clear day in early July, the sun was already warm on his face. Dawnie was beside him, squeezing his arm.

'You'll have a lovely time, Billy.'

He raised huge shoulders, his face a little sad. 'I'm not sure it's such a great idea, darlin'. Sure, I'll enjoy it when I get there. Lester's good company and it'll be grand. But I had my birthday last Tuesday.' He kissed her nose. 'The t-shirt and CDs you gave me were deadly and we had a lovely meal. It's the weekend now – I could be spending it with you, not sleeping outdoors with a load of fellas who are ossified on manky lager and whisky and going out to the jacks at midnight in the hedgerows.'

Dawnie reached inside his jacket, patting the old t-shirt with the image of the front of a motorbike and the slogan 'I've Spent A Lot Of Time Behind Bars'. 'You should have worn one of the new ones I gave you, Billy, not this old thing.'

'Ah, well. I just picked it up this morning. It felt, you know, old and comfortable and I'm used to it, a bit like a second skin.' Billy sighed. 'I can't get any enthusiasm for going fishing...'

'It'll be fun. A bit of bonding, outdoor cooking, baked beans bubbling over the camping stove.'

'It'd be more fun if it was just me and you,' Billy chuckled. 'Imagine us, wide awake in a little tent under the stars, planning good times to come. Now that would be grand.'

'Then we'll do that, Billy, before the summer's over. Treat this as a practice run.' She looked around her. 'Where's Vinnie?'

'He'll be here at any minute. He's mad for it, the young fella, riding pillion and sleeping under the stars.' Billy sighed. 'It's no great treat for me now.'

'And Malcolm, the local budgie-rescuing hero. He's following on in his car?'

'Ah, yes, I think so.' He smiled. 'Aude and Sylv were glad to have their bird back.'

Dawnie giggled. 'I think Malcolm was pleased to see the back of Tequila. Apparently, the budgie was flying round the bedroom swearing at him and calling him all sorts. He caught it in the end by trapping it in Gillian's nightie.'

'Tequila's glad to be back home then.' Billy glanced across the road. 'Ah, here's Vinnie.'

Vinnie was clad in denim, an unworn jacket and pristine pair of Levi's, carrying a huge bag in each hand. Dawnie shrieked across at him. 'Have you got enough luggage there? You're only going away for one night, Vinnie. It's not a fortnight in Majorca.'

A wide grin filled Vinnie's face. 'I've brought some food. Mam made us an apple pie and I've got sausages for the barbecue and extra blankets in case it's cold.'

'We'll have a grand session,' Billy chortled, winking at Dawnie. 'And I think the women will be all right too. Pizza and a good film round Dilly's, is it?'

Dawnie made a soft sound. 'I can see things turning nasty. Dilly wants to watch Bruce Willis, Ursula's bringing *Jean de Florette*, Gillian is keen on watching an entire box set by Alfred Hitchcock and I've got *This is Spinal Tap*. It's just as well Aude and Sylv are working late because according to Sylv they'd want *Mad Max* and *Thelma and Louise*, so we'd be at Dilly's eating pizza and watching all the movies until the next morning.'

Billy had attached Vinnie's luggage to the Harley. 'Well, we'll be on our way, darlin'. I'll see you around teatime tomorrow.'

Dawnie kissed his lips briefly, watched Vinnie clamber awkwardly onto the pillion seat and pull on Billy's spare helmet. The bike rumbled to life and Billy and Vinnie moved away. Dawnie waved until they turned the corner.

She was about to go into the house when Malcolm appeared, carrying a rucksack, a fishing rod and a bag that clanked with every movement, which Dawnie supposed was cooking implements. Malcolm's gaze shifted from her eyes to his car.

'Have they gone, Dawn?'

'They just left a few minutes ago.'

'I have the location set on my GPS. I said I'd follow them.' He looked miserable. 'I can't say I'm looking forward to this.'

'You'll have a great time.' Dawnie offered him an encouraging smile. 'The weather's perfect.'

She watched him bundle his luggage clumsily into the back of the Honda and start the engine. Gillian appeared at her elbow and waved a hand languidly as Malcolm pulled away.

She sighed. 'To be honest, it will be nice to have a day away from him.'

'Absence makes the heart grow fonder, Gillian?'

Gillian wrinkled her nose. 'Absence from Malcolm is probably better for my heart all around.'

Dawnie met her neighbour's eyes. 'Well I hope the men will do a bit of bonding.' She grinned mischievously. 'We women are all organised for tonight. I've got a pizza in the freezer and a bottle of Prosecco chilling.'

'I've got some nice Rioja.' Gillian's eyes twinkled. 'And *Vertigo* and *Rear Window*. I just adore Jimmy Stewart, don't you?' She put an arm on Dawnie's. 'Oh, I'm so looking forward to a night in with the girls.'

* * *

It was past six o'clock. Billy had been gazing at the same spot in the river for a long time. He hadn't caught any fish and he didn't particularly want to. It was a calm place, gurgling water surrounded by too-long grass and clusters of fragrant bittersweet. He closed his eyes for a moment, feeling the warmth of the evening sun pressing his lids. Vinnie was on his left, chattering about the carp he'd caught and thrown back and how he'd bought a brand new tent from the garden centre with a huge discount for employees.

To the left of Vinnie was Malcolm, frowning at the water and waiting for fish to appear. Billy wondered morosely if even the fish were avoiding Malcolm: he had done nothing but grumble since he'd arrived. He'd expected proper conveniences: toilets, electricity, camping equipment for hire, and Lester had grinned and said how nice it was to be close to nature and offered Malcolm the spare sleeping bag in his spacious tent as he hadn't brought either.

Lester was currently out of sight, taking photographs of insects and small aquatic creatures. He had already lit the barbecue and a thin curl of smoke filtered from where they had left the tents, filling Billy's nostrils. He wasn't hungry yet. Vinnie was talking about Dawnie, how nice she was, and how lucky Billy was to have such a loyal and supportive wife. Billy nodded and listened to Vinnie gabbling about his ideal woman.

'She'd have to be nice, Billy. I mean, I wouldn't care if she was pretty or not although pretty would be an advantage, because I'd have to look at her. And I wouldn't expect her to be domestic. I can do cooking and cleaning and anyway, I'm not that type that likes women to do everything in the home. She'd have to be my equal, you know, intellectually. Not super bright but good at conversation: she'd have to have a brain. I wouldn't mind what job she had as long as she didn't live too far away and I could see her regularly. I don't want a long-distance relationship. I like women with blonde hair. Or dark hair. Any hair really. Personality is what it's all about, isn't it? The important thing would be that she was nice. And that she liked me.'

Billy heard Malcolm mumble something about Vinnie setting his sights far too low. He should aim for a woman who would complement him; someone who'd have good housekeeping skills and be able to manage money well. A spendthrift would be no good: Malcolm warned him against these modern types who spent money like water on fripperies like mobile phones and false eyebrows. Vinnie's face reddened as he remembered Sally and her predecessors. Billy sighed and opened his eyes.

'I think you have it exactly right, Vinnie. A nice woman is the best thing you can have in life and if she likes you back, you're home and dry.'

Billy heard Malcolm making tutting noises and Vinnie changed the subject, telling Billy he was determined to buy himself a motor-bike before the end of the summer and he'd seen a nice Kawasaki online but it was too far away, in Cumbria.

Edgars was sitting under a tree several metres away where the river narrowed and a willow dipped its leaves into the water, his eyes closed, meditating. Billy decided that he liked Edgars: he was a nice fella, but full of surprises. He spoke four languages. He had his own barber's business in town, and when he wasn't working he enjoyed doing yoga and knitting all sorts of things. He had made jumpers, hats, gloves, several scarves and a balaclava for wearing on the bike. He was a strict father, insisting that his fourteen-year-old twin sons worked hard at school but although Linards was a model student, Rasmus had developed a rebellious streak and was causing the family some trouble. Edgars had laughed when he had spoken about his family; he had already decided that Linards would be a dentist and Rasmus would join his father in the barbering business where he'd be able to keep an eye on him. In his opinion, meditation and calming the mind would solve all the problems in the world, including difficult teenagers' behaviour, although Edgars admitted he would have to soothe Viktorija when he returned, as coping with the boys overnight by herself might be challenging.

Billy lifted his fishing rod and laid it down in the grass. He mumbled some excuse about seeing how the barbecue was going and ambled back to the place where they had put up the tents. The others had brought modern equipment, huge spacious tents and warm sleeping bags. Billy had his one-man tent in camouflage green, his simple rolled up sleeping bag and a blanket. He would be happier with the basics: luxuries weren't for him. When he reached their cluster of tents, Billy saw Lester piling food onto a grill over the camp fire. He grinned at Billy.

'I have put extra veggie burgers on for Edgars and I've got some beans in a pan. What do you want, Billy?'

Billy shrugged good-naturedly. 'I've caught no fish to put on. I'll be happy with anything: veggie burgers, whatever we've got on the barbie.'

'I've made a salad and Ursula has sent a cake and lots of bread rolls.' Lester waved a spatula. 'I'll put some sausages on for Vinnie. I think Malcolm has brought himself a piece of steak to cook. He told me he likes it medium rare.'

'I'll open up a few beers in a minute, will I?' Billy offered. 'It's getting a bit chilly so I reckon we'll need to crank up the fire and eat soon.'

'Good idea,' Lester agreed. 'We could all do with some conviviality around a nice log blaze.'

Billy gazed across at the river. The last of the sunlight shimmered skeins of gold on the water. A family of ducks glided along in formation, their wings oily blue, leaving long wriggling trails behind them. Billy reached into his one-man tent for his haversack, tugged out his camera and sighed. 'I'll just take a few photos, Lester, then I'll come and lend a hand with the cooking.'

* * *

Dilly was pouring Prosecco into long-stemmed glasses as Dawnie, her blonde wig twisted in a single plait down her back, sliced pizza into four generous portions. Ursula had made a fresh green salad and a large tiramisu; Gillian had brought various bags of popcorn; Dilly had supplied crisps and tortillas. Ursula placed everything carefully on the little coffee table between the sofa and Dilly's armchair. Gillian hovered behind Ursula, clutching the Alfred Hitchcock box set under her arm, repeatedly asking Ursula if there was anything she could do to help. Dilly screwed her eyes up as small as possible, sneaking a glance at Gillian's film choice, and muttered 'I've got *Armageddon*, *Hostage* and *Death Wish*, all ready to go. Which Bruce Willis one shall we do first, girls?'

Gillian hesitated. 'What about Cary Grant in *North by North West*? Or a nice Jimmy Stewart film?'

Ursula looked concerned. '*Jean de Florette* is such a moving story, beautifully filmed. I like Gérard Depardieu; at least, I liked him when he was younger...'

'You can't beat a bit of Bruce in his white vest, swearing and shooting all the baddies. Oh, I do love a bit of action.' Dilly had already started on the Prosecco. Ursula passed a glass of fizz to Gillian and they squashed up together on the sofa with Dawnie. Dilly stretched out her legs and sank back into the armchair, her lips clamped around the glass.

'Let's have some pizza,' Dawnie soothed. 'Shall we eat now?'

'Lovely,' Dilly purred, bringing the glass to her lips again. 'Right. Let's get started.' She pressed the remote expertly and the television screen burst into life, the opening sequence from *Pulp Fiction* blaring loudly.

'I haven't seen this one, mind.' Dilly leaned forward and adjusted her glasses to see the screen. 'It's got Bruce in it, though and that nice Samuel Jackson, and the young man who dances in *Saturday Night Fever*. It should be good.'

'I like *Saturday Night Fever*,' Ursula cooed. 'It was lovely. I like sensitive romance films.'

'I hope there's some dancing in it then,' Gillian said, helping herself to pizza and Prosecco. 'Some good dancing and some pleasant music. I can't be dealing with all that unnecessary shooting and swearing and sex and violence.'

Dawnie took a deep breath and clamped her lips together. She had seen *Pulp Fiction* three times and she knew full well what was coming from the first scene to the end. She refilled her glass and glanced at the other three women, their eyes shining, reflecting the colours on the screen. 'I wonder how the boys are doing...'

She watched their faces change as the film began. Ursula frowned, unsure. Dilly beamed with pleasure. Gillian looked horrified. It was going to be a long evening.

26

Smoke twirled from the blaze of the campfire towards the inky skies and Billy stretched his hands out to warm them. He licked his lips. 'The veggie burgers were deadly, Lester.'

'There's something about eating outdoors, a campfire, food cooked on the brazier, the good company of fellow men,' Lester mused, his eyes gleaming. Billy said nothing and reached for his beer, taking a swig.

'Will there be anything like this at the charity bike event?' Vinnie asked. 'You know, a party afterwards?'

Edgars reached for another veggie sausage, now a little charred around the edges, and took a bite. 'We're riding across the county in a procession. The money we raise is for the Air Ambulance.' He chewed for a moment. 'Then afterwards we're all back to Fuller's Field for a barbecue and Viktorija's doing a rock disco. My two boys are coming in the evening: it'll be a family event. It should be really lively.'

'It may be a good place to look for a bike for you, Vinnie.' Billy scratched his head. The stubble was thick now and there was the beginning of a curl to his hair. 'There'll be plenty of fellas there who might know where we can get you a nice one at a fair price.'

'I'd hate to miss the ride.' Vinnie's brow creased. 'Do you reckon I could get a pillion with someone? I'd love to come along and I can raise some money for the charity. The people at the garden centre would help if I asked them for a donation.'

'I guess you could ride with me,' Lester shrugged. 'Ursula won't get on the bike. She doesn't feel comfortable.'

'It's a shame,' Edgars agreed. 'There's a lot of fun to be had, out as a couple on the bike.' He gazed at Billy, who was staring up into the sky. 'Wouldn't you agree, Billy?'

Billy brought his thoughts down to earth and offered a grin. 'Ah, yes. Dawnie and I have had some grand times out on the Harley. And this is a good area for travelling around: lovely scenery, some interesting roads and the ocean.'

'I like it out here, under the stars at night.' Vinnie stared into the darkness. 'The river gurgling away, the dark skies, the campfire: it makes you feel calm.'

Malcolm coughed and the others realised they had forgotten he was there. 'You should have been in the Scouts, Vinnie.' He reached for his glass of lemonade. 'I was in the Scouts. It's a good grounding, proper discipline for boys.'

Billy shook his head. 'Ah, I never had much time for the old Baden Powell stuff. It never sat right with me.'

'Well, it wouldn't, would it?' Malcolm glanced at Billy's t-shirt, irritated by the slogan, the blatant flaunting of his time behind bars. 'It might have done you some good.'

'Given my time again...' Billy breathed deeply. 'I think I'd have liked to get into the photography more. I took some deadly snaps of the river earlier.'

'You'll have to show them to me.' Lester leaned forward. 'I took some close-up pictures. I got some great shots of a female Broad-bodied Chaser.'

Vinnie wondered if a joke might be appropriate: he knew what some of the men at the garden centre would say at this point. 'I'd like to meet her,' he grinned.

Billy clapped him on the shoulder. 'Strictly for the other drag-onflies, I reckon.'

'Given my time again...' Vinnie examined the other faces around him, hoping he was blending in. 'I'd have done more travel-ling. The garden centre is all right, but I'd like to have done some-thing a bit more adventurous. And I'd have liked to play the drums, be in a band.'

'You're still a young lad,' Lester chuckled. 'What are you? Fifty-something? Follow your ambitions: it's not too late.'

'It's never too late, whatever age you are.' Billy took a breath. 'I'm hoping this move, a house close to the sea, new friends, a different place, is a fresh start for me and Dawnie.'

'Some of us don't need a fresh start.' Malcolm pressed his lips together firmly. 'Some of us have lived our lives well, properly, according to the rules of common decency.'

'I had a new start for my family when we came to England ten years ago.' Edgars' eyes were earnest. 'And I'm grateful. My boys get a good education, Viktorija and I have our own businesses, we work hard and we want to settle here.' He sighed. 'For me now, I want to put something back. That's why I run the bike club, and I try to raise money for charity.'

Malcolm looked away and sipped lemonade. Then he murmured softly. 'I wonder how the ladies are getting on with their film night.'

Lester smiled, his head full of thoughts of Ursula. 'My wife has taken her favourite film. It's all in French but it's a lovely story.'

'My mam won't like a French film,' Vinnie observed. 'She likes action movies: murder and blood and lots of bad language.'

Malcolm lifted his eyebrows and was just about to comment that Gillian wouldn't stand for that sort of thing, she was far too decent, when Edgars' phone bleeped. All eyes were on him as he checked his message and groaned, 'Oh no.'

'What's happened?' Lester placed a hand on Edgars' shoulder.

'Linards has texted me. Viktorija has found cigarettes in Rasmus's jacket pocket when she put it in the wash. There's an argument going on at home.'

'Oh no, that's terrible.' Vinnie's face was shocked.

'It's a normal thing, trying cigarettes.' Billy rubbed his chin. 'Not a good habit for a youngster, though.'

Edgars stood up. 'I know Viktorija can handle this; that's why she hasn't called me. But if it's all the same with you, I'll pop home for an hour. It's only ten miles away. Our son will get a united front on this, both parents saying the same thing at the same time.'

'Will you be back?' Vinnie was concerned.

'Certainly.' Edgars pulled on his jacket. 'I'm not allowing Ras to dictate what happens to my time. I'll only be an hour or so.' He turned to go. 'That boy will have extra chores to do next week.'

Lester grabbed a torch. 'I'll walk with you to the bikes.'

Billy watched the two men stroll away. He stared up at the sky and exhaled slowly. Vinnie followed his gaze and gave a similar sigh, his voice low. 'I love it here.'

Billy lifted up a thumb and placed in over the moon. 'The moon's just like a thumbprint of wax.' His voice was soft. 'A pale yellow waxy thumbprint amid a scattering of stars.'

'It is.' Vinnie's mouth was open, staring up.

'I used to look up at the moon a lot when I was by myself, all those years ago...'

Malcolm was ready with the next question. 'Are you talking about the time when you were... away? Is that it?'

Billy hardly heard him. 'I used to stare at it up in the sky and think to myself, that's the same moon Dawnie is looking at right now, in the same sky with the same stars. And she was with the kids and I was miles away, sleeping on a hard bed, just a blanket to keep me warm. The cold got into my bones some nights.'

Vinnie held his breath. Malcolm had told them Billy had been in prison. Vinnie couldn't imagine how it must have been, being locked up, away from your family. He was filled with sympathy for Billy. He was such a nice man. 'It must have been hard for you, Billy.'

'Ah, it was.' Billy's voice was a whisper. 'But the hardest thing of all, some nights, you couldn't sleep for the silence. And then there would be a single noise; one soft sound would break the quiet, shatter it to pieces.'

'What was that?' Vinnie rubbed cold hands together.

'The worst sound I ever heard. The sound of a grown man crying.'

Vinnie's eyes were round. 'Why did they cry, the men? Was it the solitary confinement?'

'At night, the loneliness is like a rope around your neck. It chokes you. You feel so alone it hurts.'

Malcolm clicked his teeth together. 'It was your choice though, Billy. You made the decisions that led you to be sent to that place, didn't you?'

Billy came out of his reverie. 'Ah, I suppose I did so, Malcolm. You're right.'

'Then it's your fault, isn't it?'

Billy glanced at Malcolm. 'I guess it is, for sure.'

'Then you can't complain.' The light from the campfire glowed red in Malcolm's glasses and made his eyes shine. 'You were given three square meals a day; fed and clothed at the taxpayer's expense.'

Billy frowned. He hadn't expected the note of anger in Malcolm's voice. He spoke softly. 'I reckon you're right.' It was quiet for a moment, the air tingling with expectation of a new cutting comment from Malcolm, so he tried to lighten the mood. 'Ah, but I'm all right now. It's good craic here with you fellas. I'm dandy now, sitting around a campfire, chewing the fat, having a good time. And I've got a lovely wife at home and two great kids. I had a text this morning from my son – he's in New York with his band.' He turned to Vinnie and clapped him on the shoulder. 'Maybe I should put you in touch with him, Vinnie: you could ask if he needs a drummer?'

Malcolm had stood up. In the firelight his face was haggard. He clenched his fists and he was shaking. 'It's turned out all right for you, hasn't it?'

Billy was taken aback at the sudden change of mood, the immediate anger. 'How do you mean?'

'You. You came through it all, you paid your dues and now you have everything. You don't deserve it. You're just a parasite, living off everyone else.'

Billy frowned. 'I don't understand. I was just...'

'You're buying a new house, you have the classic motorbike, you think you're the big *I am*, and your son is alive and well and doing fine in New York and you're such a cool fella that everyone likes you, but I know exactly what you are, your type.' He spat the words out bitterly. 'You're the lowest of the low.'

Billy felt Vinnie shudder next to him. He rubbed a hand over his shorn head and reached out towards Malcolm. 'Hang on there, fella.'

Malcolm jerked away. 'Don't you dare touch me. I know exactly what you violent types are capable of.'

Billy raised both hands in the air. 'I wasn't going to—'

'I know what you were going to do. You were going to hit me.'

'Not at all.' Billy stood up, towering over Malcolm, who took an instinctive step back.

'Don't touch me.' Malcolm turned abruptly, bending down for his coat, shrugging it on, feeling in his pocket for his car keys. 'GBH, wasn't it, that's what you did time for? I'm not staying here, not with the likes of you, Murphy. I might get killed.'

Billy wasn't sure what to say: the words 'You're an eejit' burst between his lips.

Malcolm grabbed his luggage and his equipment and started off at a fast pace towards the car park. 'I'm going home,' he called over his shoulder.

'Malcolm, what's got into you?' Billy called out into the cold night air.

Malcolm's back was turned and he kept walking away, stopping only once to hike his luggage onto his shoulder. Billy thought he heard the man sob, a soft moan, and the words, 'My boy...' and then, 'All for the likes of you.' Then he was a dark shadow in the distance. Billy sighed and his eyes met Vinnie's, equally surprised. Neither of them had a clue what had just happened.

* * *

The music warbled, the credits rolled on the screen and the four women sat back in their seats.

'That wasn't bad at all,' Ursula mused. 'I like John Travolta. It was nice to see the dancing scene with him and Uma Thurman.'

'I liked the bit where they had to stab the woman in the heart to save her.' Gillian's mouth was open. 'I never knew you could do that.'

'She was snorting drugs, mind,' Dilly explained. 'They had to revive her with the adrenalin.'

'Shall I make us a coffee?' Dawnie offered.

'I'll do it.' Gillian was already on her feet and bustling in the kitchen.

Dilly folded her arms. 'Not enough Bruce Willis in that film for me really. But he makes a good boxer.' She reached out an arm. 'Is there more pizza and a bit more of the fizzy Prosecco?'

Ursula filled up Dilly's glass and handed it to her. She leaned over towards Dawnie. 'The charity bike run is next weekend, isn't it?'

'Vinnie's going,' Dilly whooped. 'He wants to get a bike for it. A Kacky Sacky.'

'Don't you mind him riding a motorbike?' Ursula was alarmed.

'Mind? Why ever would I mind?'

'Well...' Ursula chose her words carefully. 'Bikes can be a bit dangerous.'

'Not as dangerous as being Bruce Willis or that woman in *Pulp Fiction*.' Dilly swigged from the glass. 'Listen to me, Ursula. Life is too short to worry about things and then you don't get to do them because you're too scared.' For a moment her face was fierce. 'I might ask Vinnie if I can ride on the back with him when he gets his bike. I'd love it, getting outdoors, the wind in my face, riding past the coast and looking at the sea.'

'But aren't you worried...?'

'No, Ursula, I'm not.' Dilly took a handful of popcorn. 'I don't want my boy tied to my apron strings. I want him to be out there in the big world, enjoying himself, meeting people, having a life.'

Ursula's soft eyes met Dawnie's. 'Do you think I could do it – ride on the Harley, stay with Lester for the whole journey?'

Dawnie smiled slowly. 'Riding pillion on the charity run will be great fun. You'll love it. He'd love it.'

'I'd be so scared, Dawnie.'

'You might,' Dawnie agreed. 'For the first few minutes. But you'd be kitted up safely, with a helmet and boots and leathers, and Lester wouldn't be going fast. We'd be in a procession, all together.' Dawnie's eyes grew wide. 'Then you'd feel the exhilaration of it, the camaraderie, the bike beneath you, and it will feel safe and solid, and Lester will feel safe and solid in front of you. And you'll start to enjoy it.'

'Should I do it though, Dawnie? For Lester?'

'Yes. And for yourself. Ursula, it would be so good if you could.'

'Then I will.' Ursula grinned. 'I have to admit, I'm terrified – but I want to do it. You've inspired me, Dawnie.'

Dawnie shook her head. 'No, Ursula, you've just inspired me.'

'And when we've finished inspiring each other,' Dilly called. 'Can someone open another bottle? I'm thirsty. And then we can have another film. Maybe *Die Hard*?'

'Or a nice Hitchcock?' Gillian emerged from the kitchen with a tray of coffee.

'We should toss a coin,' Dilly suggested.

'Oh, I'm not gambling...' Gillian placed the tray down.

Dawnie sat up straight. 'I just heard something outside – an engine roaring.'

'What?' Ursula was alarmed.

'In the road.' Dawnie moved to the curtains, Ursula at her shoulder. She turned to call back. 'Gillian, there's a car revving up outside your house. It's Malcolm. He's getting out with all his fishing stuff, banging the doors.' Dawnie met Gillian's eyes. 'It's only half past ten and Malcolm is back home.'

Dilly reached for the Prosecco bottle, finding it empty, and picked up a bottle of Rioja instead. She muttered, 'Malcolm home, already? That doesn't bode too well, if you ask me.' She turned a serious gaze on Gillian and the light reflected in her glasses, making her eyes huge. 'Something has happened with the men on the camping trip. But the question is, why did Malcolm come back home?' She rubbed her hands together. 'Something funny has happened out there with the boys. Perhaps sparks have flown, a bit of argy-bargy even? Maybe there was violence, swearing, a bit of action. I can't wait to find out.'

Several days later, as soon as Billy had eaten breakfast and gone out to visit Lester to work in his shed, Dawnie called Ursula on her mobile. Fifteen minutes afterwards, she answered the knock at the front door to find her friend flushed and smiling. 'I came round as quickly as I could, Dawnie. What is this all about?'

Dawnie ushered Ursula inside, thrust a hot mug of coffee into her hands and they sat across the kitchen table like collaborators. 'I needed to talk to you, Ursula.'

Ursula's eyes shone. 'That's a coincidence. I wanted to talk to you.'

'You go first,' Dawnie insisted.

'I found this in the local newspaper...' Ursula reached into her pocket and pulled out a neatly snipped cutting. 'It's a photography competition.'

Dawnie took it and read the print. The paper was running a competition, asking for photos that reflected the beauty of the local area, to close in two weeks' time. She raised her eyebrows. 'Is Lester entering this?'

'That's the point.' Ursula's excitement left her breathless. 'He is too humble about his talents so...' She leaned forward and took Dawnie's hand. 'I am going to enter for him without him knowing and... I think you should do the same for Billy.'

'I don't understand.'

'We'll both send our husbands' photographs to the competition. I saw some of Lester's pictures from the camping trip. I'm going to enter them. They are wonderful. But I'm not going to tell him. I mean, we don't usually keep secrets from each other, but...' Her eyes shone with pride. 'He's so sensitive and modest; he won't put his own work forward. He'll say, "Oh no, *Liebling*, there will be lots of better snaps in the competition than my silly old things." If I enter using his name and my phone number, they will let me know the result and when he wins, I can break the news as a surprise. And of course, if he doesn't win, he won't be disappointed because he'll never know.'

'Billy's exactly the same: he'd shrug it off and say his pictures aren't good enough.' Dawnie was thoughtful. 'There was this lovely photo of the river, ducks swimming, and one of the moonlight reflected on the water that he took at the camping trip last week-end. Yes, we should enter their photos in secret. Then it will be a surprise if they win and if they aren't chosen, they'll never know so they won't feel like they've lost anything.' She grinned. 'It will keep their fragile egos safe.'

'Exactly.' Ursula's face was excited. 'I knew you'd understand. Now, what was it you wanted to tell me?'

Dawnie leaned back in her seat, cupping her mug in her hands. 'Ursula, do you know what happened at the camping trip last weekend between Malcolm and Billy?'

'I'm afraid I don't.' Ursula's brow was furrowed. 'Lester was in the car park after Edgars had just left to pop home. He said he saw

Malcolm come storming past him shouting about how Billy had tried to hit him and then he got in his car and drove off.'

Dawnie let out a deep sigh. 'I'm sure he didn't threaten Malcolm. Billy wouldn't hurt anyone. I spoke to Gillian about it on Monday. She shrugged it off as Malcolm being his usual grumpy self, but apparently he keeps a big record book full of details on Billy, stating all sorts of things he's done wrong – the drumming, the parking, with dates and times, and now he's logged in it that Billy was aggressive towards him.' She ran her fingers through the platinum pixie cut. Her eyes were sad and ringed with dark circles. 'Billy hasn't slept since he came back, not properly, and he has just made jokes about what happened with Malcolm, but I think he's quite upset.'

'Dawnie, everyone knows how kind and gentle Billy is, even Gillian. She'll be fine...'

'I know, but it's having a bad effect on Billy, and the charity bike run is the day after tomorrow. He's too tired to enjoy it. I think I need to do something drastic, to help him. Ursula...' Dawnie leaned forward, her face earnest. 'Several weeks ago, we went to see this house near the sea, Chestnut House. It was lovely. Billy was really taken with it.'

'Did you like it?'

'I did, but...' Dawnie chuckled. 'The estate agent was a bit dismissive with me and I threw a bit of a tantrum. I know Billy was keen on the house but I refused to deal with the estate agents again. I was being selfish.'

'That doesn't sound like you.' Ursula shook her head.

'The thing is, I've made an appointment to see it again today, at twelve o'clock, just me. If I still like it, I'll make an offer on it and surprise Billy when he gets home.'

'Is that a good idea?'

Dawnie laughed. 'It's a no-brainer. Billy loves the house and if we buy it, it will get him away from Moaning Malcolm. It's a beautiful house, lots of space, and he'd be thrilled if I'd put in an offer and it was accepted. I'm going to view it with the same estate agent, Simon Mountjoy. So, I wondered – will you come with me for moral support?'

'I'd love to,' Ursula grinned. 'That would be such fun. But won't he recognise you, this Mountjoy?'

'I don't think so. He barely looked at me the first time. I was wearing the red wig. And there are so many people called Smith so he won't remember me.' A mischievous smile curved Dawnie's lips. 'I have this smart Jaeger suit on a hanger upstairs. I got it years ago for my shop. And with no wig on and some heels and the pearl earrings, and you as my classy friend looking around the place with me, I'll be the sophisticated house buyer. And Simon Mountjoy will be putty in my hands...'

* * *

They parked the Transit across the road several metres away and walked up the drive, arm in arm, giggling. Simon Mountjoy was waiting outside the door by his BMW, clutching his brief case under his arm, slim in the dark suit, his hair neatly parted. He waved his clip board and looked from Ursula to Dawnie. 'Ms Smith?'

Dawnie extended a hand and inclined her head in what she considered to be a professional business-like fashion. 'Mr Mountjoy. Pleased to meet you. And this is my associate, Ms Wainwright.'

Ursula followed Dawnie's lead and shook the estate agent's hand firmly. 'Good afternoon, Mr Mountjoy.'

Simon Mountjoy surveyed the women, Ursula in smart jacket and perfect jeans, Dawnie in a green Jaeger suit and red lipstick, her hair shiny platinum, neat pearl earrings and a matching necklace. She raised her eyebrows. 'Shall we begin, Simon? Time is money, as they say.'

Ursula put a hand across her mouth to stifle a grin and Dawnie followed Simon, who led them to the front door and hesitated.

'Well, I think you're going to be impressed by Chestnut House. The Myttons have decorated it tastefully in the five years they've been here. They are looking to go back to South Africa, where they have family.'

Dawnie smiled, remembering that he had spoken the same words at her last visit. She decided she'd save him the trouble of going through his script. 'You're going to tell me it hasn't been on the market long and there's been a lot of interest.' He gaped at her, his mouth drooping. She continued. 'I've read the specifications from your agency, so now I need to see the house and decide for myself if it's suitable. Shall we carry on, please?'

They followed Simon into the house. His shoulders were hunched now, his head pulled into his body. They strolled through the boot room and into the kitchen.

Ursula turned to Dawnie. 'I like the cherry red colour of the range and the quartz work tops are lovely.'

'They are quartz, aren't they, Simon?' Dawnie asked, her voice clipped.

'Yes, I believe so...'

'You don't know?' Dawnie frowned. 'And the range – is it multi-fuel?'

'No, there is no gas here. It's electric. The heating is oil-fired.'

'I know that. I've seen the tank outside.' Dawnie met his eyes. 'It is a modern bunded tank, I take it?'

'Oh, I'm sure it must be.'

'I would like to know, Simon,' Dawnie replied, raising an eyebrow. 'Can you find out for me?'

'Of course. Er – shall we go into the lounge?'

Dawnie turned to Ursula and winked. 'So, what do you think of this kitchen? Is it suitable? I value your opinion.'

Ursula held back; she was tempted to gush, to say how much she'd love to cook in such a fabulous farmhouse environment, but she caught Dawnie's expression and said, 'I think it would probably be adequate.'

Simon led the way into the lounge, his clip board aloft. 'The wood burning stove in the fireplace is lovely. It throws out lots of heat.'

Dawnie recalled the new wood burner they had put in the old house in Little Lever last winter; she had bought a large one that would heat the huge room. She wrinkled her nose. 'How many kilowatts?'

'Pardon?'

Dawnie's smile was triumphant. 'I would need something with an output of at least nine kilowatts, Simon. What is the output of this one? It looks quite old.'

'Ah, well, you'd have to have a survey done of course...'

'You don't know how efficient the stove is?' Dawnie pursed her lips. She gazed around the room at the cream three-piece suite then her eyes alighted on the stag's head on the wall. 'I don't like that thing, Ursula. It's very archaic, the idea of decapitating an animal and displaying it as some sort of trophy.'

'I agree,' Ursula nodded.

'Ah well, you have to see beyond the décor...' Simon stammered.

'I'd have to purify the room,' Dawnie retorted, her face deliberately unhappy.

'To get rid of all the negative energy,' Ursula added.

'Would – would you like to see upstairs, Ms Smith?'

Dawnie nodded. 'Lead on, Simon.'

They followed him upstairs, his bottom small in the smart suit, and into the first bedroom. 'Here is the master bedroom with magnificent sea views.' Simon smiled proudly. 'Are you married, Ms Smith?'

'Is that relevant?' Dawnie asked. 'Do I need a partner in order to enjoy the magnificent sea views?'

'I think women can enjoy a sea view without the protective custody of a man,' Ursula observed. Dawnie bit her lip to stop herself from giggling. She desperately wanted to nudge her friend, to tell her not to overstep the mark, but Simon's cheeks were already burning.

'I'm so sorry, I didn't mean...' Simon stammered. 'I just thought that – you being an older lady?'

'What does that have to do with it?' Dawnie asked, her voice level.

Ursula was on form. 'I think he means you need a man to help you with your Zimmer frame, dear.'

Dawnie sighed. 'How is my age relevant to me buying this house, Simon? Do you think I might expire before I've signed on the dotted line?'

'No, not at all...' Simon screwed his eyes closed, horrified that he'd spoken out of turn. 'I just thought... I...'

'Don't think.' Ursula raised her voice. 'Just concentrate on giving us a professional tour of the house, please.'

'Of course. I'm so sorry. Follow me. Shall we go outside?'

Dawnie pressed her lips together. Ursula was magnificent. They followed Simon outside, where he showed them the garage and mentioned the acreage, the blooms in the garden, the fruit trees, hardly meeting Dawnie or Ursula's eyes. Then Dawnie shook his hand, thanked him for the tour and said she would get in touch. Simon hesitated. 'Ms Smith... I'm sorry if I unintentionally offended you before.'

'Please don't apologise.' Dawnie smiled benevolently. 'But I'd advise you not to speak unintentionally in future. Remember, women have bank accounts and they buy houses... by themselves even, sometimes.'

'Yes, my mistake. I don't usually... I mean, it won't happen ag—'

'Thank you, Simon. I'm pleased to hear that.' She linked her arm through Ursula's and they turned away together. She called over her shoulder. 'I'll give the house some thought and make my decision. Then I'll call you.'

They reached the bottom of the drive and Ursula whispered to Dawnie. 'Do you think we went too far?'

'I think we did. We're such bad women...' Dawnie burst into raucous laughter.

'I feel awful, Dawnie.'

'You were amazing.'

Ursula spluttered. 'I was so cross with how dismissive he was to you. I couldn't help the things I said: they just burst out of my mouth before I thought about them.'

'He might think before he behaves like that again to an older woman.' Dawnie squeezed Ursula's arm. 'Did you like it, the house?'

Ursula closed her eyes. 'It was lovely. Billy would love it too. That huge garage, big enough for his bike and Lester's and many more. It's perfect for you both.'

'It's a wonderful house, Ursula.' Dawnie stopped and suddenly started to cackle. 'It was hilarious when you said about the negative energy in the lounge and me needing a man to help me with the Zimmer frame.'

Ursula waved a hand in front of her face, embarrassed. 'I shouldn't have said that. I'm ashamed. It was so rude.'

Dawnie chuckled. 'I think it evened up the balance a bit.'

Ursula spluttered with laughter. 'It was certainly liberating.'

Dawnie hugged Ursula. 'You are just the most loyal, lovely friend.' They had reached the Transit and Dawnie opened the door. 'Jump in.'

Ursula hesitated, her face serious. 'So, are you going to buy the house, Dawnie?'

'We're going to drive to the nearest pub, just to get a feel for the neighbourhood.' Dawnie winked. 'We can talk about making an offer on Chestnut House over lunch.'

28

'There's a whole gang of Hell's Angels outside, right next to my car,' Malcolm murmured, his hand holding the net curtains in front of his face. 'There must be at least ten of them.'

Gillian stood silently behind his shoulder. 'There's Billy, Dawnie in her red wig, Vinnie, Lester. Oh look, Ursula is with them: she has a leather jacket on. And you know Edgars, and the dark-haired woman is his wife Viktorija. I met her at my birthday bash in the Castle.' She frowned at Malcolm. 'That makes seven, not ten, and they aren't Hell's Angels: they are friends and neighbours. And they are off to the charity run, which reminds me...' She stared pointedly at Malcolm. 'I have taken the fifty pounds from the pot you keep the water rates money in. We have enough left over to pay the next quarter so I was going to give fifty pounds to Lester and Billy for the Air Ambulance.' Her eyes flashed behind her glasses. 'If that is all right with you, Malcolm.' She breathed out. 'I think it's a fine cause and what they are doing is admirable.'

Malcolm grunted. 'I expect the feminists with the swearing budgerigar will be out in a minute from number fifteen. All the neighbours gossiping and chatting together on a Saturday morning, like there's nothing wrong with those people in number thirteen. Murphy is an ex-con, a criminal for goodness' sake. I don't know what has happened to this street since *he* moved in. It used to be a decent place.' He slunk away from the curtains, his hands in his pockets. He couldn't understand what had got into Gillian, why she was taking Billy's side against his. After all, he was the injured party. He moved over to a comfortable chair and picked up a copy of *The Telegraph* and sighed.

Gillian gazed through the net curtains and suddenly felt sad. Billy and Dawnie weren't much younger than she and Malcolm were. But they were happy; they hugged each other. They kissed each other's lips. They laughed and talked and had a good time together. Gillian couldn't remember the last time she and Malcolm had shown any affection to each other. They hardly communicated nowadays. She closed her eyes for a moment: of course, she knew when the affection had stopped. It had been so much better between them before James had been sent abroad, before what happened to him happened. She couldn't bear to think of the words. But she had been happier then, and Malcolm too. It was a long time ago, thirty years.

Now they simply existed, one day at a time. She glanced out of the windows. Billy was grinning, talking to Edgars, an arm around Dawnie. Lester was hugging Ursula, who was giggling and talking to Dawnie. Vinnie was hovering next to Edgars and Viktorija, a smile on his face. They were all clearly happy, off on an adventure, riding across the county having fun together and raising money for charity. They were doing interesting things, enjoying themselves: they felt the excitement of being alive.

Gillian turned away unhappily, her gaze meeting the sports section on the back page of *The Telegraph*, which Malcolm had placed in front of his face on the pretext of reading. He clearly preferred silence and a distance between them: it was easier and preferable to having a conversation or trying to be pleasant. This was her life now: loneliness, solitude. She could either suffer the cold silence or listen to the irritating grumbling Malcolm would offer by way of conversation. She existed from day to day, in the same house as a man she had once loved, whom she now had nothing in common with: a man who was her husband, whom she now didn't even like.

* * *

Ursula was giggling, holding out her hands to show how much her fingers were trembling. 'I only rode from Mary Street, two streets away, and I'm shaking. I was so nervous. Lester started the Harley up and it rumbled so loudly, and I felt my heart pounding. But I did it – I got this far without falling off.'

Dawnie applauded. 'You're on your way to being a professional pillion passenger, Ursula. It will be great. The sun is out, the weather is perfect. Lester will follow behind Billy and I'll wave to you all the time. You'll be fine now. Give me the thumbs up every so often to show me you're okay.'

Ursula sidled up towards Dawnie, putting her lips close to her friend's ear, her voice low. 'Did you enter Billy's photos in the competition?'

'I did. The one of the ducks and the one of the moonlight.'

'I entered a beautiful picture of a dragonfly.' Ursula's voice was conspiratorial. 'And what about Chestnut House? Did you put an offer in? Does Billy know we went to see it yet?'

'I did make an offer,' Dawnie chortled. 'It was wonderful. I offered thirty thousand pounds below the asking price. I said to Simon Mountjoy that I was Dawnie Smith and he was very smooth and friendly and he said he remembered me and my friend, meaning you. So, I said that it had been my second viewing and he was puzzled so I let him have it: I told him that Billy and I had viewed it a while ago and you should have heard him coughing and spluttering down the phone and pretending that he'd recognised me when of course he hadn't. I felt awful afterwards but at least I made the point about being made to feel invisible before.'

'And has the offer been accepted?' Ursula's eyes were wide.

'Mr and Mrs Mytton, the owners, are thinking about it over the weekend. I so hope they say yes. I told Billy what we'd done, of course, and about the offer. I wouldn't keep it from him. He's delighted.'

Billy heard his name mentioned and turned. 'Delighted, darlin'? What about? Are you telling Ursula about Buddy's text?'

Dawnie's face lit up and she grabbed Ursula's hand. 'Oh, there's more good news. I had a text from Buddy and another one from Luciana, his new girlfriend. She calls herself Luci. She sent me a film clip she'd made of Buddy on stage with his band in New York. Billy can't stop watching it. Buddy was great.'

Billy chuckled, his face flushed with pride. 'He was savage on stage. Great guitar licks. The next Hendrix. I thought he was grand.'

'And Luci seemed really nice too,' Dawnie continued. 'So friendly. And she said she was really looking forward to meeting Billy and me. I'm hoping she'll drag him over here before too long.'

'You must miss him,' Ursula agreed, her own eyes misting at the thought of Meinke and his family who were now back in Bavaria.

Edgars looked from face to face. 'We ought to get off soon. We're setting off with the rest of the group at half ten from Fuller's Field.'

Vinnie stood awkwardly. 'I don't suppose I'll be able to come now. It doesn't matter, though. Mam will be pleased to have me at home: she will be by herself, so I don't mind but it's a shame as I swapped Saturdays at the garden centre so that I could go.'

Dawnie frowned. 'Why aren't you coming, Vinnie?'

Vinnie looked nervously at Lester and Ursula. 'I don't think

there's a space for me on a bike now. I was going to ride with...
but...'

'Oh, Vinnie, didn't I tell you? We've arranged a lift for you.'
Viktorija placed a hand over her mouth, hiding a chuckle. 'I forgot
to say. I hope it's all right.' There was the throaty sound of an engine
chugging towards them, the volume increasing. Viktorija raised her
voice. 'This is your lift now. Will you be okay on a trike?'

Vinnie frowned. Billy clapped him on the back. 'Here y'are,
Vinnie. I brought you some spare togs: Dawnie's old helmet fits you
perfectly and there's a spare leather jacket of mine. The jacket's a bit
big but you'll be grand. Pull it on. We need to be getting on our
way.'

Vinnie tugged the jacket on and zipped it up: it came to his
thighs. He pushed the helmet onto his head. It fitted snugly, flat-
tening his curls. A trike, matt black and racy with gleaming steel
wheels had pulled in and stopped next to the group, the rider
calling out in a light voice. 'Hello, everyone. Sorry I'm late. Who's
my passenger?'

Edgars chuckled. 'Vinnie, meet Mei-Lien. Mei, Vinnie's riding
with you.'

Vinnie stared at the woman. He could see that she was slim
beneath the leathers she wore. Long dark hair was visible down her
back, protruding out of the helmet. Then he noticed her eyes
behind the visor, alert and dark and beautiful. Vinnie blurted,
'Thank you for offering to give me a lift.'

'Jump on,' Mei-Lien called, and Vinnie looked at everyone else
for support. He wasn't sure he could simply clamber on the back of
the trike behind this mysterious woman.

Lester patted him on the back. 'Come on, Vinnie, we need
to go.'

He wriggled across the frame of the trike behind Mei-Lien,
awkward and uncomfortable. There wasn't much room on the

saddle and his body was squashed against hers. The other riders clambered on their bikes and engines rattled and thundered to life. Vinnie noticed Ursula hugging Lester tightly and he became immediately conscious of the heaviness of his arms, the uselessness of his hands as he held them away from his body. The riders began to pull away, one by one. Mei-Lien looked over her shoulder and shouted over the noise.

'Put your arms round my waist. I don't want you falling off.'

Vinnie complied quickly in one clumsy movement before his nerves got the better of him; before he clambered from the back of the trike and ran away like a frightened chicken back into the security of his house. He was mystified by what had happened in the last few minutes of his life. He was suddenly a pillion rider behind a beautiful enigmatic woman on a slick squat trike. He couldn't believe his luck as Mei-Lien accelerated away and he tightened his hold around her small waist, feeling her sitting strong and firm beneath his grasp.

Inadvertently, Vinnie smiled: he couldn't stop himself. This was heaven, clinging to a confident, anonymous and exciting woman on a trike. Vinnie felt like the hero in *Easy Rider*. He was thinking of the song 'Born to be Wild': it was pounding inside his head, his new theme tune. He was immediately filled with happiness akin to weightlessness, just like floating in the air, like being detached from his own body.

Vinnie didn't realise that Mei-Lien was smiling too. She had recognised him straight away. He was the handsome man she had noticed at the bike show in Fuller's Field in June. She had asked Edgars about him, casually mentioning that she didn't know him; she'd wondered if he was local, if he was single. Edgars had been evasive at the time but now Mei-Lien realised that she and Vinnie had been set up together. It had been planned, deliberate. And it felt very nice indeed.

* * *

Dilly let the curtain fall from her grasp. Vinnie was gone. She had watched him go through the good eye, as he clambered up behind someone she didn't recognise onto a huge triangular bike with three wheels and she had stared as the bike rumbled away into the distance. Of course, he would be fine. He'd have a wonderful time. She wanted him to enjoy the charity run; he had spoken about nothing else all week.

Dilly wandered into the kitchen. Her hip hurt her today; there was an ache in her legs. It was still quite early in the morning; she'd normally be deciding what to have for lunch, opening a tin of oxtail soup and pouring it in a saucepan or perhaps deciding to make a cheese and tomato sandwich. But now she'd just have a cup of tea and a biscuit and sit down for a bit in front of the television, rest her legs. Her head throbbed a little; her bad eye was sore and the good one was tired. She wondered if a nap mightn't be a bad idea. She poured hot water onto a tea bag and added milk without thinking.

It was a slow walk back to her armchair. Dilly wondered if she'd overdone it all a bit recently: dressing up, disco dancing, drinking bubbly, eating pizza. But it had been worth it, she'd enjoyed it: how she had enjoyed the contact with the other women, the laughter, the friendship.

She eased herself into her chair and brought the teacup to her lips. She sipped tentatively but the hot liquid burned her mouth and she put the cup down. Her eyes searched the television stand for a DVD. There would be something she could watch: Jean-Claude van Damme or Arnold Schwarzenegger perhaps. But she couldn't really be bothered: her heart wasn't in it.

Dilly leaned her head against the hard back of the armchair and closed her eyes. Her lids felt heavy. But at least with her eyes shut, she wasn't so aware of the emptiness of the room, of the hollow silence that surrounded her.

She thought of Tommy, her Tommy. He was always wearing the same outfit whenever she thought of him: he was always in his tweed jacket and white shirt, always smart and younger than he was at the end. She never thought about him now as the man in his seventies who shuffled about the house slowly, his bones creaking. She remembered him young, upright, smiling, the soft eyes shining; the dark curls were a full head of hair, not the thin grey strands that sat closely to his head, dry hair that he seldom brushed towards the end. She missed him so badly.

And Vinnie was out now, having fun, as he should be at his age. But Dilly had no one to talk to now. Immediately she felt sorry for herself and angry at the same time: she wanted Vinnie to get out more. She always complained that he should get a life when he watched television with her each night from the sofa, one of Billy's home brew bottles in his hand, or when he pumped weights in his bedroom upstairs, making the ceiling above creak whenever he put the dumb bells down. She told him she wanted him to enjoy himself. But she was alone and lonely now, in a house that smelled stale, of last night's steak and kidney pie, where emptiness hung on the air like the space between life and death.

Dilly sighed and forced her thoughts to happier times, to Vinnie as a serious-faced toddler; to Tommy coming home from work, and she remembered how they'd hug each other and she'd have his dinner ready. Simple memories, happy times she'd taken for granted. She recalled how she'd grumble to Tommy about the ironing: she'd hated doing his shirts and he'd offer her a placid smile and say he'd do them himself and she'd become fussy and say no, it was her job, because he'd just iron more creases in and the important thing was to iron them out, and then they'd both laugh.

That's how their life together had been, ordinary but so

precious, and now there was nothing left of it and she could never have it back. Dilly imagined Tommy's smile, the warmth of his hug, his breath against her ear, the smell of the boiled sweets, the toffee brittle he'd always loved to suck that had ruined his teeth. Tears slid from between her closed lids and dampened her cheeks, but she clung to the image of him, the smell of him through his ironed shirt, the warmth of his hand on hers. She breathed softly and he was with her in her dreams, talking in his gentle voice, his arm around her waist. As she slept, her mouth moved slowly to reply to his soft words and then her lips pursed in a smile. It was as if he was really there and she remembered him exactly as he was all those years ago.

29

It was early evening when Billy and Dawnie arrived at Fuller's Field. The sun was still warm against their faces and they were cocooned inside hot jackets and snug helmets. The chrome tanks, trim and wheels from many bikes parked in close proximity flashed, reflecting blinding sunlight. An intense aroma of savoury frying onions and sausages wafted on the air. Dawnie glanced over towards the stage. Edgars and Viktorija had arrived earlier; the barbecue was busy and the disco was in full swing, people munching hot dogs and others dancing energetically to the music of Motörhead. Viktorija was on stage, her face visible beneath huge earphones, music booming through vibrating speakers. Edgars was flanked by his two teenage boys, one blond and the other with Viktorija's dark hair and eyes, both busy serving food to queues of waiting riders. Billy pointed to the entrance to the field as Lester's Harley rumbled slowly towards them. Ursula held her arms out wide, an acknowledgement of the sense of freedom on the waves in the film *Titanic*, a wide smile on her face.

Twenty minutes later, the four friends were sitting at a small table clutching paper cups of lemonade shandy and plates of food.

Ursula was complaining that her bottom was saddle-sore, and Lester was struggling to explain how, in time, she would develop a tolerance.

'But does the skin on your bottom become harder? Or do you just become more used to the pain?' Ursula giggled at the idea.

Dawnie shrugged and sipped her shandy. 'I just don't notice it now.'

'I did try to drive steadily, *Liebling*, so that you would be comfortable,' Lester apologised. 'There were just so many potholes in the road and the bike was jolting. I wanted you to have a nice easy ride.' He beamed contentedly, soft eyes shining behind his glasses. 'You were wonderful, though. I was so proud of you, going all those miles. It was lovely, riding on the bike, knowing you were behind me, feeling your arms round my waist.'

'I loved it too,' Ursula breathed.

'I was thinking...' Lester rubbed his chin. 'How about us getting away together on the bike this summer, maybe next month? I thought maybe we could go exploring.' A new thought came to him and his smile broadened. 'We could go to Europe. We could visit Germany, too – we could go and visit your family, Meinke and Frida. Of course, we'd stay in nice hotels: I wouldn't expect you to camp after a long day in the saddle.'

'That would be exciting.' Ursula turned to Dawnie. 'You could both come along too.'

'We'd have some fun, wouldn't we, all of us together. It might be a nice thing to do once we know what's happening with the house move.' Dawnie rubbed her fingers through the red strands of her wig and turned to her husband. 'Billy?'

'Uh?' Billy was lost in thought. He was staring into the distance, his eyes glazed.

Dawnie touched his hand. 'Are you tired, love? We must have travelled for miles today, up and down so many busy roads.'

Billy shook his head. 'Sorry, darlin'. I was being an eejit. I was somewhere else. What were you saying?'

Dawnie leaned forward. 'What is it, Billy? What's on your mind?'

He paused for a moment and when his voice came, it was expressionless. 'Ah, I was just thinking about, you know, Malcolm next door, how he thought I was going to punch him. I wasn't, Dawnie, I put a hand out to calm him down and he started to make a holy show of himself, shouting and accusing me of all sorts.'

Dawnie took his hand in hers. 'I know, Billy. You wouldn't hurt him. He's being a fool. It must be hard for Gillian, living with him – he's so tense and angry.'

Billy exhaled sadly. 'I hope they accept our offer on Chestnut House. I hope Simon rings us on Monday morning and says we can buy it and move in soon. It would be grand to live in that house. And, to be honest with you, Malcolm is a bit of an odd fella; he doesn't have the full shilling. I've no idea what he'll do or say next. He has some funny ideas in his head about me.'

'You're right.' Dawnie squeezed the big hand. 'I was getting quite settled in Maggot Street but it would be lovely to move to Chestnut House and we can still visit friends; we'll only live a few miles away. And we can have them all round for a housewarming party.'

Lester beamed. 'Ursula and I can visit you on the bike.' His face was flushed with delight. 'I'm so proud of her.'

'We all are.' Dawnie gave Ursula a winning smile. 'You did so well. Now you're a fully-fledged biker.'

A slow song came on over the loudspeakers, a moaning guitar sound, and Viktorija's voice from the speakers was urging couples to dance. The sky was streaked with darkening blue blurring into a melting ice-lolly of glowing sunset. Ursula grabbed Lester's hand. 'Oh, I love this one. "Parisian Walkways". Come and dance with me, *Liebling*.'

Lester made a comic face towards Billy and Dawnie, showing delight at his beloved wife's spontaneity mixed with an unwillingness to smooch to Gary Moore's sentimental guitar sound. Ursula tugged him away.

Dawnie leaned her head on Billy's shoulder. 'Have you had a good day?'

'It's been grand.' He took a deep breath. 'But to be honest with you, I'm a bit bushed.'

'Do you want to go home?'

Billy nodded. 'Ah, I think so. Let's just go back, the two of us, maybe have a drink, snuggle on the sofabed. It would be nice there, just you and me.'

'We can ring Lindy Lou and tell her about Buddy's text. Maybe she's already seen his girlfriend's film of him playing in New York.'

'I could watch it again, my boy playing rock and roll,' Billy agreed. 'Then maybe the two of us could just get an early night, have some quiet time for us both.'

'Do we need to say goodnight to the others first, Billy?'

'Let's get off home, will we?' Billy took her hand. 'I'll text Lester later, tell him I was a bit tired. He'll understand.'

They stood up, walking towards the bikes. Dawnie gazed up at Billy. 'Has anyone seen young Vinnie since we passed him and Mei-Lien on the motorway? That was over an hour ago.'

'Ah, he'll be dandy. Mei-Lien is a good driver: it's a nice little trike she has there.'

'Did you see them together, though?' Dawnie raised her eyebrows.

Billy frowned. 'Yes. She gave him a lift—'

'Oh, Billy.' Dawnie gave him a look of mock-exasperation. 'His arms were round her waist like he'd never let go and she was leaning into the embrace. Then, last time we saw them, he was resting his face against her back, a smile as big as his head.'

'He was sheltering from the wind, maybe, darlin'?'

Dawnie chuckled. 'That wasn't sheltering, Billy.' She winked and tugged his arm towards the bike. 'That was love.'

* * *

Vinnie had never felt so normal. It was as if everything he had done since this morning had slotted into an easy rhythm that felt completely natural and that would become the way of life henceforth. Talking to Mei-Lien, watching her easy laugh, sharing thoughts and feelings and history, sharing a meal in the Chinese restaurant she'd suddenly suggested they visit: it had all been second nature. He hadn't had time to worry about whether he looked all right, whether he was saying the right things, whether she liked him enough or whether she approved of his opinions or whether he was making her happy. They just fitted together, exactly like the hands they now clasped, his left holding her right as they stood in the hallway of number fourteen Margot Street. Their eyes met and they both grinned like mischievous children, trying to keep their voices low.

'Will your mum still be up, Vinnie?'

'I doubt it. It's past ten now. I think all the lights are off in the lounge except for the little lamp she leaves on in case burglars want to come in.'

Mei-Lien laughed softly at his joke so as not to wake anyone. Vinnie pushed the lounge door open. The room was crowded with shadows except for the yellow glow of a ceramic table lamp in the window. He flicked on a light and the room was illuminated, tidy, the surface of the coffee table clean and polished. There was no evidence of Dilly's late-night cocoa.

Mei-Lien took a seat on the sofa as Vinnie rushed to the kitchen to make the coffee he'd promised, the reason she'd come back to his home. As he fussed to find the most attractive mug and to measure coffee and boil a kettle, he knew that they would talk and drink and laugh quietly together and then he would kiss her properly for the first time. He was sure of it, as he was sure that she liked him just as much as he was falling for her.

They were sitting on the sofa, their elbows touching, and he watched Mei-Lien as her lips found the mug, as her mouth moved to drink coffee. He observed the way her long hair fell over her cheek, accentuating the curve of her cheekbone, and he wanted to touch her face with his fingertips.

Instead he said, 'Is the coffee all right?'

'Perfect.' Mei-Lien smiled at him. 'I'm glad you invited me back, Vinnie. This is a lovely house. It's so much tidier than my little two-bedroom flat in town.'

He spoke without thinking. 'Tidiness is overrated.'

'That's true.' She met his eyes. 'But when you have a twelve-year-old who leaves her dirty football shirts and smelly socks everywhere and is constantly demanding food and clean clothes and help with homework, it is sometimes a bit difficult to keep a tidy home.'

'You have a child?' Vinnie's eyes were wide. For some reason he'd assumed Mei-Lien was like him, single, footloose, fancy-free. He wondered if she had a husband as well.

Mei-Lien understood his thoughts and placed a hand over his. 'Grace is my daughter. Her father left us ten years ago. We never see him now.' Her gaze flickered to meet his and he stared into the soft beautiful eyes. Her voice was steady. 'I'm lucky the Pilates classes I teach with Viktorija fit around Grace's school schedule. Viktorija is so supportive. We work together as a business and hold classes in the sports centre, in village halls, prisons, all sorts of places. We're called Body Core. The disco work helps, when I can fit it around Grace. My mother is brilliant too. She's with Grace at the moment, at my place.' She shrugged. 'I promised I'd be home by eleven.' She gave a little giggle. 'Do I sound like a schoolgirl? I'm forty-six.'

Vinnie wrapped an arm around her shoulders. 'It sounds like you're doing a great job as a mum.' He spoke his thoughts out loud. 'With such a busy life, I don't expect you have much time for dating.'

'I haven't dated for years.' Mei-Lien tucked a strand of hair behind her ear and Vinnie thought his heart would melt. She looked away, at the furniture in the room, at the glowing light by the window. 'Grace is playing football tomorrow – she has a Sunday fixture in Okehampton. It's an away match, she's going in the team minibus.' She turned to stare at Vinnie. 'So, I'll be free until four.'

'Can I see you tomorrow?'

'I was hoping you'd ask.' She put her mug down. 'You could come round to my flat for lunch. I could pick you up here on the trike tomorrow morning.'

He leaned forward and his lips brushed hers tentatively. Vinnie felt the hairs on the back of his neck prickle. He kissed her, a proper kiss, his mouth on hers, and when he pulled away they were both smiling. 'I'd love that, Mei-Lien. That's a date.'

'I'll pick you up at ten then, shall I?' Mei-Lien's voice was thick with emotion. 'Maybe I can meet your mum, too.'

'You'll like her. She's not as bad as you might think when you first meet her, although she can be a bit of a handful and she loves to watch violent films.'

'There's nothing wrong with a bit of Bruce Willis.' A sharp Welsh voice came from behind them and Vinnie turned to see his mother adjusting her spectacles in the doorway, wearing a thin nightgown, her pale hair wrapped around her head.

Vinnie gasped. 'Mam.'

'Who have we here then?' Dilly approached the sofa, screwing up her eyes to see properly. 'Have you brought a girl home, Vinnie Stocker? Late night orgy, is it you're having?'

Vinnie grinned. He wondered why he wasn't cringing, embarrassed, but he simply felt happy and proud. 'Mam, this is Mei-Lien, my friend...' He was instantly amazed at how easily the words fell from his lips. 'Mei, meet my mum, Dilly Stocker.'

Mei-Lien stood up and turned, holding out her hand. 'Pleased to meet you, Mrs Stocker.'

'So, it's a girlfriend now, is it?' Dilly moved a step forward, frowning. 'Oh – I know who you are: we've already met.'

'Pardon?' Mei-Lien sounded anxious and Vinnie was immediately standing by her side.

'Mam?'

Dilly started to cackle. 'You won't remember me. Last time we met, I was dressed as Shirley Bassey. But I know who you are. You're the DJ from the Sixties Night at the Castle. You gave me first prize, a bottle of champagne. You're all right, mind.'

Mei-Lien's face relaxed and her eyes sparkled with recognition. 'Of course. I remember now. You were with the birthday group of... of ladies.'

'Vinnie.' Dilly shot him a fierce look. 'Why on earth are you drinking coffee?'

He shook his head. 'Mei-Lien and I were just...'

'Coffee, in my house?' She folded her arms. 'No. Go and get a nice bottle of Billy's home brew from the kitchen or some fizzy wine and let's have a proper drink. I might have some brandy in the cupboard, too.'

'Mei-Lien has the trike outside. She's got to drive...'

'Well, I can drink it then and she can just be polite and have a thimbleful in a glass and pretend she's going to drink it.' Dilly edged closer to the sofa. 'Go on, Vinnie – and there are some crisps in the cupboard and some rich tea biscuits and those chilli-flavoured tortilla things. Get them all out.' She stretched out a thin arm, barely covered by her filmy night gown and grasped Mei-Lien's shoulder, easing herself onto the sofa into the warm space Vinnie had just vacated. 'I want to get to know your new girlfriend better. It'll give us some time to chat while you're doing the drinks and nibbles.' She beamed at Mei-Lien. 'You have time to stay for a drink and a chat with me, don't you? I think we're going to be good friends, me and you. Why don't you just call me Dilly?'

30

The following Saturday, Dawnie was in the middle of filtering home brewed beer into clean bottles when the doorbell rang. She bustled around, turning off the little tap at the end of the tube, wiping the bottle and quickly putting on a lid, then she rushed to the door and opened it wide. Aude and Sylv were standing together, their faces grinning with expectation. Behind them, rain splashed on the grey pavement and gurgled into the gutter. Sylv beamed. 'Look at this awful weather – a typical summer's day in late July. Can we come in a minute?'

'I'm bottling beer. Of course you can come in.' She led them to the kitchen. 'I just need to fill these six bottles and cap them.'

'Shall I make us a coffee?' Aude asked.

Sylv flourished a tin. 'I've brought brownies. Can you take a break for elevenses?'

'Of course,' Dawnie replied to both women at the same time. As she bent to fill another bottle, Aude took the kettle to the tap and Sylv put the tin on the little table and leaned towards Dawnie. 'We wanted to ask you about the gossip. It's all happening around here, isn't it?'

'Gossip?' Dawnie frowned.

'Yes, lots of it.' Aude rubbed her hands together. 'Vinnie Stocker has a girlfriend.'

'We've seen him with her.' Sylv's voice was triumphant. 'She has a bike with three wheels, a very sexy black machine and there she was, in leathers, and she and Vinnie were kissing outside his house last night about half past ten. I saw them through the window.'

'And it's not the first time she's been round to his house. Or the first time they've been snogging the face off each other.'

'So, Aude and I went to see Dilly on the pretext of borrowing a DVD, and Dilly told us all about it. She said they've seen each other almost every day this week and they are all loved up. It's the real thing, apparently.'

Aude laughed. 'Then Dilly lent us *Pulp Fiction* and we watched it last night after work.' She nudged Sylv. 'Tequila's bad language has moved to a completely new level.'

'I hope he doesn't escape and fly into Malcolm's house again,' Sylv chortled wickedly. 'Because he has some very impressive vocabulary, now spoken very loudly in a perfect imitation of Samuel L. Jackson.'

'I can imagine.' Dawnie lined up the beer bottles. 'I haven't seen much of Malcolm and Gillian though. They've been very quiet.'

'I saw her down the corner shop.' Sylv accepted a mug of coffee from Aude. 'She did seem a bit down-in-the-mouth.'

'I'm not surprised, living with Malcolm.' Aude handed Dawnie a coffee. 'I heard he'd accused Billy of trying to hit him.'

'Billy wouldn't hurt anyone. With a bit of luck, we won't have to put up with Malcolm much longer.' Dawnie reached for a brownie. 'We're moving.'

'Really? When?' Aude asked, her face horrified.

'You can't move – we'll miss you.'

'It's a lovely house, about five miles away, in the middle of nowhere. We had an offer accepted on it a couple of days ago.' Dawnie bit into the brownie and chewed. 'Mmm, these are delicious. Anyway, we made an offer and the owners counter-offered and we've agreed on a sum ten grand below the asking price, so it looks like we'll be off.'

'More gossip.' Sylv rubbed her hands together. 'It won't be the same in Margot Street without you and Billy.'

Dawnie nodded. 'The first thing we'll do when we move in is have a housewarming party. You're all invited.' She waved damp fingers towards the beer. 'That's why I'm bottling the home brew today. We want to move as quickly as we can. And anyway, we're going to Ursula's and Lester's house tonight to celebrate. Billy's there already, working on Lester's bike. There's a bit of a problem: the handlebar bushes have worn out and Billy's helping him service the bike. Then they are going for a run this afternoon just to check it over and tonight we're celebrating our new house-to-be.' She leaned forward. 'Ursula and I have been a bit naughty. We entered Billy and Lester in a photography competition and didn't tell them, because they are both so modest. But their photos were incredible. One of them has to win. And the results are out at any time this weekend.'

'More and more gossip.' Aude grinned, helping herself to a second brownie. 'Things are starting to become interesting around here.'

'I know, but it's sad that you're moving away, Dawnie,' Sylv pouted and reached for the cake tin. 'You and Billy are the best neighbours we've had. Everyone will miss you.'

* * *

'I ought to pop next door and see Dawnie,' Gillian murmured as she gazed through the window. Rain was lashing against the pane.

The sky and the ground outside were a blur of battleship grey. 'I haven't seen her for ages. I miss her company.'

Malcolm grunted from his chair. It was almost lunchtime and Gillian hadn't asked him what he wanted to eat. By now, she usually had things organised. But over the last few weeks, she'd hardly spoken to him. Meals had been less regular; yesterday she'd placed a salad sandwich in front of him at half past two in the afternoon and given him a cup of milk instead of making tea. For dinner two days ago, on Thursday, she'd given him baked beans on toast. Their regular system, when meals had occurred at the same time, when Gillian had asked him for his preferences, was in the past now. It was as if she didn't care. The only thing she did regularly was to polish James's photograph on the mantelpiece. Malcolm scratched his ear and adjusted his spectacles on his nose. 'Are you all right, Gillian?'

She didn't hear him. She was gazing out of the window, her nose against the glass. She sighed and said nothing for a while, then she muttered. 'I wonder how Dilly is. I must go across and see her.'

Malcolm glanced at his watch. It was five to twelve. His stomach rumbled beneath his grey jumper. Then an idea occurred to him. He would go out in the car and buy fish and chips. That would surprise Gillian. It would be a treat. They hadn't had fish and chips in ages. There was a fish and chip shop called the Salty Plaice in town that still wrapped them in newspaper. Malcolm sighed and rubbed his eyes behind the glasses as he recalled a time long ago, before they were married, when they had shared a bag of chips. He and Gillian had been for a walk together, hand in hand, and they had sat down by the clock tower with a warm vinegar-soaked newspaper bundle on their knee, the chips burning their fingers, salt on their lips, thinking only of each other and their next kiss. He reached for his jacket, pulled it on in a swift movement and his fingers touched the car keys in his pocket. 'I'm just popping out, Gillian.'

She didn't turn to look at him or ask him where he was going. 'All right.'

'Is there anything you want from the shops?'

She shook her head.

He thought about going over to her and kissing the top of her hair, but he couldn't. His feet wouldn't move; there were unspoken words, too much space between them and it would have been easier to scale a mountain than to venture into the chasm that lay like cold hard ground between him and his wife. He coughed lightly. 'Right. I'll just get going.'

'All right.' Her voice was distant, a whisper.

Malcolm checked he had his wallet and keys as he moved towards the front door. As he opened the latch, it occurred to him that Gillian had mentioned that she and Dilly had drunk Prosecco together. Perhaps he would buy her a bottle.

* * *

'I think we're done here, Lester. It's good to go.'

'Thanks for helping me sort it out, Billy. I could hardly get the torque wrench on the drain plugs by myself. Your idea of wrapping the drain plugs in Teflon was pure genius. That should hold back the leaking. And the handlebars are perfect now.'

'I've been around Harleys for a long time, Lester. And many other engines, as a matter of fact.'

'I'm lucky to have an expert here to help me.' Lester stood up, inspecting the oil on his overalls. 'Shall we go in and get the leathers on? We can take the bikes for a spin and check everything is in good working order.'

'Good idea,' Billy said. 'I told Dawnie I'd be home this afternoon, later on. When I left her, she was bottling beer for tonight's meal.' He thought for a moment, rubbing the short wiry curls on his head. 'She's a good one, my Dawnie.'

'We're blessed with our women, Billy.' Lester patted him on the shoulder. 'As soon as we're in the kitchen, Ursula will have the kettle on to try and tempt me to stay in the warm. Then she'll offer cake or sandwiches and grumble about me taking the bike on the road in this wet weather.'

'Ah she's a good woman, Ursula.'

They traipsed into the kitchen, which was warm with the aroma of cooking. Ursula was making pastry, wearing an apron over her clothes and she smiled when she saw the men. 'Sit down at the table, Billy. I'll make you a cup of coffee. Shall I do you both a sandwich?'

Lester gave her a hug. 'We're just off for a spin on the bikes. We've given my old Harley a service. I just want to run it for a few miles, check it over.'

Ursula's face was aghast. 'In this wet weather, Lester?'

'We'll be fine, *Liebling*.'

Billy sniffed the air, his eyes closed with contentment. 'Something smells deadly, Ursula.'

Her expression changed to an immediate smile. 'I'm making lots of English things for dinner tonight. I thought we'd have Pimm's too, although it's going to be too wet to eat outside in the garden. But I've made fresh bread and pâté. I'm doing two quiches, potato salad, apple and watercress salad, pasta salad, and I'm going to make ice cream and fruit salad or a summer pudding...'

Lester wrapped his arms around her. 'You bring summer into my life every day, *Liebling*. It doesn't matter if it's raining outdoors; in here with you it's always sunny.'

Ursula's eyes shone and she hugged him back. 'You are wonderful, Lester.' She noticed Billy watching them and she giggled. 'Sorry, Billy – you must think we are two crazy people, still in love...'

'Not at all. I think you're both grand.' He beamed at them.

Lester planted a kiss on Ursula's cheek. 'We'll only be half an hour or so. A sandwich would be great when we're back, if you're not too busy.'

Billy reached for his jacket and helmet, which had been carefully placed on a kitchen chair earlier. 'Ah, not for me, Lester, Ursula. I'll head off back to Dawnie once we're done.' He caught Ursula's eye. 'I'll see you for dinner tonight, though. It's very kind of you doing all this cooking just for us.'

'I wanted to celebrate the fact that you've agreed to buy the new house Dawnie and I viewed. I can see why you're so taken with it, Billy,' Ursula smiled. 'Besides, I love the chance to cook for friends and Dawnie is in charge of the beer – she told me earlier on the phone she has several bottles.'

'It's a good job we can walk home from here, Ursula.' Billy winked at Lester.

'Once you've moved house,' Lester decided, 'you'll have to stay over in the spare room.'

'You too,' Billy agreed. 'We'll do a bedroom up in Chestnut House just for the pair of you.'

'Oh, I can't wait to see the big garage!' Lester's eyes widened behind his steel spectacles. 'You won't keep me away.'

'And the cider apples – I'll make some deadly scrumpy in the autumn,' Billy nodded.

Ursula waved her hands. 'Off you go, boys, out of my kitchen. I have plenty to do for our celebration tonight.'

Her eyes gleamed as she pressed her lips together. She wanted to tell Lester about the photography competition, how he or Billy might have something else to celebrate later in the week, how wonderful it would be if they both could win prizes. She watched them as they walked back through the kitchen door towards the shed. Through the window, she could see Lester pushing his Harley out and into the heavy drizzle, his head down. She plunged her fingers into the pastry crumb and smiled.

* * *

Dawnie surveyed the rows of gleaming brown bottles filled with best ale, capped with smart lids and labelled. She would place them under the stairs and take out several older bottles for tonight. She glanced at the wall clock. Billy wouldn't be too long; he said he'd be home by two and it was half past twelve. She had time to tidy the kitchen and sort out what she would wear this evening. The blonde wig and a long slinky dress came to mind, but if the weather persisted in raining, she'd dispense with the wig and wear jeans and a shirt.

It occurred to her that, at some point later this afternoon when the weather improved, she'd pop out to the corner shop and buy some sparkling wine, some fancy chocolates and a nice bouquet for Ursula to thank her for the hospitality and all the cooking. She smiled to herself. Life in Maggot Street wasn't so bad after all. She had made new wonderful friends; she liked all of the neighbours apart from Malcolm.

Billy had certainly been calmer this week since the offer was accepted on Chestnut House: he had slept throughout the night for the last two nights and his face was refreshed and he looked happy. His hair was growing back: he was certainly settling down.

Dawnie's face broke into a grin as she thought of her children. Since Buddy had found a new girlfriend, he was texting his parents more regularly; Luci was a good communicator too, sending photos and writing cute captions. Lindy Lou had texted Dawnie that she and Stewie had been receiving messages and pictures from them both. It felt like the family were becoming closer, somehow.

Dawnie smiled, wiping her hands on a tea towel. A ping came from her phone and her immediate thoughts were that it was a message from Billy; that he was held up at Lester's fixing his Harley, or perhaps it was Buddy or Lindy or Fallon with a new photo. She glanced at the message and her heart leapt. It was from the organiser of the photography competition. She read the words that followed eagerly. Billy's photograph of the ducks in the river had been judged to be exceptionally good and he had been awarded third place and a prize of one hundred pounds. Dawnie made little fists and jumped up and down on the spot. She couldn't wait to tell Billy. Things were really starting to look up.

31

The radio was playing 'You're My Best Friend' by Queen and Ursula was singing along as she beat the eggs and cream together in a huge bowl. She liked Queen: she loved Freddie Mercury's strong classical voice, and the romantic beauty of the ballads always made her think of Lester and she couldn't stop herself smiling.

The music ended and she frowned for a moment, trying to remember if she had enough vanilla, and she reached up to open a cupboard to look. There was a small bottle of vanilla essence on the shelf but Ursula knew the ice cream would taste even better if she used pods of real vanilla. She wiped her hands on her apron and glanced through the kitchen window. The rain was heavy and the skies were a uniform tin-grey. She would grab her coat and pop to the corner shop in Martha Street. There would definitely be vanilla pods in the store and then the ice cream would be perfect.

Ursula struggled into her navy anorak and found her purse and her phone. She checked the phone briefly to see if there was any news from the photography competition but all she found was a message about life insurance for people over fifty. She buttoned up her coat, pulled the hood over her hair and stepped outside. The rain was bouncing hard against the pavements as she lowered her head against the slanting drizzle and walked towards the end of the street with a spring in her step.

* * *

Billy manoeuvred his Harley around the mini-roundabout and into the right lane to make a turn into a side road. A glance in his mirror showed him that Lester was following just behind him. He peered to the left and noticed two cars parked by the side of the road, very close together. There had obviously been an accident: both cars were bumper to bumper. The first car was a black Range Rover; the second was a blue Honda Jazz. Two people were standing in the heavy rain facing each other, clearly arguing. Billy waved his arm to indicate to Lester that they were going to turn round and go back. Billy recognised the driver of the Honda: he was standing in a thin raincoat, his head down, looking miserable. Billy weaved through the traffic back to where the accident had been, Lester behind him, and they pulled up by the side of the road. A woman, probably in her sixties, wearing a heavy wax coat, her dark hair short under a wide-brimmed hat, was shouting at Malcolm.

'I don't know what you thought you were playing at. You hit me from behind. It's clearly your fault and there's no point you trying to deny it. You shouldn't be allowed to drive. You are clearly too old and just look at those thick spectacles. You're just a doddery old man who can't see properly.'

Malcolm shrugged, glancing into his car through the open window. The chips he'd bought for lunch, wrapped in newspaper, would be cold now. The bottle of Prosecco had fallen into the foot well. Rain water dripped down his face and he wiped his cheek with the back of his hand. Billy walked up to the two drivers quickly, his face concerned, his eyes searching for possible physical injuries. 'Are you both all right?'

'Oh, I'm fine, but it's no thanks to this buffoon,' the woman retorted, her face blotched and angry. She turned on Malcolm. 'My Range Rover is almost brand new. You stupid man. You were far too close to me and when I braked you just careered into me...'

'I'm sorry,' Malcolm stammered, looking around, bewildered.

'And so you should be. I've no idea why people your age are allowed to drive. You're a complete liability.'

Billy turned to the woman and offered her a polite smile. 'I wonder if I can help. I'm a...' He chose his words carefully. 'I'm a mechanic. Is your Range Rover all right?'

'That's not the point.' The woman's face was horrified. 'This fool just bashed straight into the back of me when I braked.'

Malcolm opened his mouth but no sound came out. Billy inspected the Range Rover. The tow bar jutted out at the back, shiny and undamaged. 'The car looks fine. You've a big tow bar there. There's no harm done to the vehicle.'

Lester was next to him, holding a hand out to the woman, shaking her fingers politely. 'Hello, I'm Lester Wainwright. It looks like just a minor bump and no one's come to any harm. I'm glad you're not injured. Your car isn't marked, thankfully. Which is more than I can say for the Honda...' He glanced at the bent bumper, the smashed headlights.

The woman pointed at Malcolm. 'It's no thanks to him.'

'You've a good strong car here.' Billy's eyes met the woman's cold blue stare. 'The roads are pretty bad because of the rain but your car's fine. Why don't you get into the car and get yourself off home into the warm and dry and we'll stay here and help this fella out?'

Lester sniffed the air: a faintly familiar sweet scent came from the woman, possibly sherry or port. He met her eyes. 'It might be better than involving the police. There will be breathalysers and the first thing they'll ask is why you braked hard in these conditions and then you have the gentleman's insurance claim to consider, and the percentage of culpability of both parties will be brought into question. It could drag on and on, in my experience.'

'It wasn't my fault,' the woman snapped. Then, nodding curtly in Billy's direction, she shrugged her shoulders. 'Since you're a mechanic and he's apologised, and my car isn't damaged, I'll give him the benefit of the doubt.' She threw Malcolm a filthy glance before turning on her heel and leaping into the Range Rover, slamming the door sharply. She drove away, leaving an arc of rainwater spraying from her wheels.

Billy put his hand on Malcolm's shoulder. 'It's not so bad. It can be fixed up. Are you okay?'

Malcolm was miserable. 'She just stopped suddenly and I couldn't stop behind her – the car just kept going.'

Billy shrugged. 'She wasn't a very pleasant woman, Malcolm, but there's no real harm done. Don't fret: we can sort it.'

Lester was waving his phone. 'Edgars has a friend who has a truck. I'll ring him and he'll tow you to a garage.'

'Tow the Jazz back home to Margot Street,' Billy muttered. 'I can fix this once we get a new bumper and a headlight. It'll be a lot cheaper than a garage.'

Malcolm stared at him. 'Can you do it?'

'Just order the parts and it'll be fine.'

'Order the parts?'

Lester put a hand on Malcolm's arm. The poor man's coat was damp, his glasses were wet and he was clearly confused and shaken. 'Leave that with me.' He smiled at Billy. 'I'll wait here in the Jazz with the bikes and let you know when Edgars arrives with his friend and the truck.'

Billy nodded, immediately understanding Lester's intention. 'Malcolm, there's a pub across the road. Let's get you in there, will we, and I'll buy you a tot of something for the shock and we can dry you out a little?'

'But I...' Malcolm stared ahead, confused.

Lester sidled into Malcolm's car, sitting in the driving seat, and reached for the cold chips. Billy wrapped an arm round Malcolm and led him across the road.

Ten minutes later, Malcolm was sitting in front of a log fire, clutching a glass of brandy, steam rising from his damp trousers. Billy held a glass of orange juice in his fist. 'How are you feeling?' he asked kindly. 'Ah, but don't be worrying about your car: it's not completely banjaxed.'

'Can you fix it?' Malcolm sipped his brandy, his face a mask of cold and shock.

'These modern cars aren't so bad... it's only a headlight and a bumper. The Range Rover tow bar just caught the front of your car.'

Malcolm stared at him. 'Are you really a mechanic? You told that woman you were.'

'Only a little fib,' Billy chuckled. 'I was an engineer in the army years ago.'

Malcolm was staring at him through steam-covered glasses. 'You were in the army?'

'Ah, I was, man and boy. When I met Dawnie we were just kids and I'd been joined up almost a year. She stuck with me through it all. We travelled all over the place, sometimes all of us as a family, sometimes just me.'

'The army?'

Billy nodded. 'I've been through a lot of service. It hasn't always been easy.' Billy sipped orange juice. 'The camaraderie was good, though. I met some grand men and made lots of friends but it was hard being away from Dawnie and the kiddies. And some places were not the best places to be for a soldier, if you know what I mean.'

'Where did you serve?'

'Ireland, the Pacific, the Middle East. I was stationed in Germany for a bit with the family. I liked it there. The Gulf was the worst for me.'

Malcolm's hand trembled around the glass. 'You were in the Gulf?'

Billy nodded slowly. 'I was. It was tough on Dawnie, me being away. The kids were almost grown up – you know, that time when teenagers want to do their own thing. Dawnie was running our home single-handed and of course she was worried about me, things being how they were.'

'Was it hard in the Gulf?'

Billy's eyes became glassy. 'Hard wasn't the half of it.' He thought for a while. 'While I was out there, I was somebody else, someone who wasn't anything like the real me. It was as if I was two characters split down the middle. They called me Murph out there – all the lads did. That was who I was then: I was just Murph, a soldier. When I got home to Dawnie and she put her arms around me and called me Billy, I wasn't sure who she was talking to. I hadn't heard my Christian name spoken for such a long time, let alone felt another human being touch me. My body was brittle, like a stick, ready to snap.'

He swigged his orange juice. 'The thirst is what I remember the most. My throat was always parched, so dry like it was stuffed with sand. I used to think all the time about a cold fizzy drink; coke, lemonade, with ice – you know the really hard ice that cracks when you crunch it. I'd stand there in the heat – it was so hot out there I thought my eyes were melting. Half the time I could hardly see because the light was so bright, and I'd just be thinking of a cold can of coke, straight from the fridge, the little droplets damp on the side of the tin.'

Malcolm was staring at him. 'You survived it, though.'

'Ah, I did, which is more than I can say for my mate Robbo. A sniper took the side of his skull clean off. I was standing right next to him. It could have been me. Inches more to one side, to the left and it would have been me, not him. I saw it all, in slow-motion as if the world had stopped turning. That was when the bad dreams started.'

'You had bad dreams?'

'It was his scream when he went down. A high-pitched scream, more like an animal's than a man's. At night times I'd deliberately keep my eyes open and stare into the darkness so that I didn't fall asleep. And I'd hear one of the fellas crying, calling out for his wife or his mother, and I'd realise that the guy couldn't sleep either. Our heads were so full of the heat and the blinding brightness and the waiting. It was like death was around every corner, in every long shadow.' He wiped a hand over his face and looked at the perspiration on his palm. 'That was in the past, going back years now, but it's still there sometimes, especially at night.'

Malcolm rested his hand on Billy's. 'My son was in the Gulf.'

Billy blinked. 'Your son?'

'James. He died out there, thirty years ago. An explosion.' Malcolm drained his brandy. 'There was nothing left of him. He was twenty years old.'

Billy's eyes rested on Malcolm, taking in the shaking of his fingers gripping the empty glass, the waxy pallor of his skin, the way his coat hung from his thin frame. He sighed. 'Ah, Malcolm, losing a child is about as bad as it gets.'

Malcolm put his glass on the table and his gaze held Billy's. His jaw trembled as he extended his hand. 'I misjudged you, Billy.'

Billy took the cold hand in his and squeezed it gently. 'You must be hungry. It's past lunchtime and your Gillian will be worried where you are.'

Malcolm shook his head sadly. 'I doubt it.'

'Let's get you back home, shall we, Malcolm?'

Billy shepherded him towards the door of the pub and outside. The rain had stopped. Across the road, Lester and Edgars, alongside a tall thin man with a bushy beard and a tattoo on his cheekbone, had secured Malcolm's car to the back of a tow vehicle. Lester saw them and waved an arm. Billy ushered Malcolm across the road to where the bearded man was grinning, holding his hand out to the other men, addressing Billy as 'brother'. Edgars clapped the man on the back. 'This is Snake. He will take you and the car home, Malcolm.' He chuckled, 'I promised Snake I'd give him a free shave at the barbers for his trouble.'

Malcolm turned to Billy. 'Thank you.' He stared at Lester, Edgars and Snake in turn. 'Thank you all.' He rummaged in his pocket. 'Let me pay you.'

Snake laughed and waved a hand. 'Not at all. Brothers help each other.'

'Then I'll give something to your charity...' Malcolm protested, turning his attention to Billy.

In the road, cars were slowing down. An ambulance rushed past, its blue lights flashing. Billy patted Malcolm on the back. 'Climb up with Snake in the truck and I'll follow on the Harley. It's time we got you safely home.'

Lester nodded. 'Ursula will be wondering where I am. I'll get back home, Malcolm, and then I'll order the parts for your car. And I'll see you and Dawnie later on for dinner, Billy.'

'I'm looking forward to it. The weather seems to be improving.' Billy nodded and looked up towards the sky. A rainbow had formed, curving behind the houses. The sun gleamed on the rooftops, reflecting the darkness of the rain and making the tiles shine.

* * *

Ursula came out of the corner shop. The rain had just stopped. She smiled, clutching her purchases: she had bought vanilla pods and some chocolate truffles that Dawnie would like. She had picked up some extra cream for the puddings, some expensive coffee beans and a bottle of brandy for everyone to share after the meal. It would be the best evening ever. She unzipped her coat and walked briskly to the end of the road. She was five minutes from home. Thoughts of slicing the vanilla pods open and releasing the sweet sticky stuff, adding it to the eggs and cream and making a delicious ice cream filled her head. She preferred making ice cream by hand, churning and freezing and churning again, tasting it occasionally to make sure it was thick and unctuous.

She reached the end of the road where the corner curved to the right and she was just about to cross to the other side when her phone buzzed. She pulled it out of her pocket and thumbed for the text as she stepped out. It was the photography competition. She scanned the words eagerly. Lester had been awarded first prize for his photograph...

The car came round the bend as if from nowhere. Ursula felt a hard bang from the right and she rose and fell. She hit the gravel hard, hearing glass break beneath her, breathing the strong smell of spilled brandy. She wondered where Lester was, whether he was safely at home yet. Then it was as if a light had been switched off and there was nothing.

32

August the seventh was the hottest day of the summer. By eleven o'clock the sun was high, bright light illuminating every corner of the town. But it was cool inside the church. Lester had asked everyone to wear bright clothes to the funeral: he said Ursula would prefer the splash of colour. Would have preferred, he'd corrected himself – she had been a happy person and not a fan of mourning clothes. His eyes were sad and his face was still a mask of disbelief. He had kept himself to himself since the accident, communicating only by phone. Billy and Dawnie had been around to the house a few times to ask him to come to stay with them. They had brought bowls of food; they had laid a hand on his shoulder tenderly and asked if there was anything they could do. Lester had said no, there was nothing anyone could do. She was gone now. And he had smiled and closed the door.

He was sitting in front of Billy and Dawnie in the front pew next to Meinke and his family, all heads bowed, and an older woman called Willa who was Ursula's cousin from Bavaria, a small, round-shouldered woman with pale hair under a neat hat. Dawnie stared at Lester's back. He was wearing his leather jacket and jeans, beneath which she knew he had a yellow shirt with butterflies on, one which Ursula had bought for him. She could tell by how he was sitting that his body was still rigid with shock; he would allow no one near him. He was cold and isolated in his grief.

The vicar, a small woman with dark hair and delicate hands that moved as she spoke, was talking about Ursula in a soft voice. She was saying how she had been the epitome of kindness to everyone, even people she had never met; how she had given money to charity, she had championed women's causes, that she had sponsored two girls, one in Cameroon and one in Nepal, and even though she was no longer with us, Ursula had made provision for their futures. Dawnie realised with a jolt that there was so much about Ursula she did not know, so much more goodness she had kept to herself.

She gazed around the church. Aude and Sylv were there, wearing their best bright summer dresses. Edgars and Viktorija wore white shirts and light jeans beneath their leather jackets. Vinnie was seated next to Mei-Lien, both wearing bright shirts and black jeans. Next to them was Dilly in a pink dress and the feather boa she'd borrowed from Dawnie. Dawnie noticed Dilly take out a large handkerchief, wipe her eyes and blow her nose. She had said before everyone had left that morning for the church that she'd liked Ursula, that life wasn't fair, that funerals made her feel that death was around every corner.

Dawnie peered over her shoulder. The church was full: there were so many people she had never met, all wearing the bright colours of summer. Then her eyes were drawn to a couple in the back row, sitting quietly, staring at the floor. The man wore spectacles and a grey suit, and the woman was in a white and navy dress and a matching hat. It was Malcolm and Gillian.

The vicar was mentioning Ursula's love of cooking, how she enjoyed welcoming everyone into her house. Dawnie stared at the oak coffin with the brass handles, surrounded by masses of flowers, and she recalled how she had hurried to the corner shop on Martha Street that afternoon to buy gifts to take to dinner at Lester's. She had arrived to see two police cars parked at an angle in the road, a Mini Cooper abandoned by the kerbside and a young man with fair hair, his head down, talking to a police officer.

Dawnie had rushed into the shop without a thought and bought chocolates and a huge bouquet of lilies for Ursula to thank her for the meal they would share together that evening. The young woman behind the counter, the one with the nose ring who reminded Dawnie and Billy of Fallon, had said there had been an accident twenty minutes earlier and a woman had been knocked down and taken away in an ambulance. Apparently, she had just come out of the shop and a car had hit her as she was crossing the road. The shop assistant said she knew her; she was a regular customer and a really nice lady. Dawnie had said what a shame it was, then she'd paid for her goods and left. When she arrived back home, Billy was with Snake and Malcolm, unloading the Honda. He said they'd be half an hour and Dawnie had told him she'd make them all a cup of tea and put Ursula's flowers in a little water to keep them fresh for later. She intended to tell him about the third place in the photography competition as soon as he came in.

Then Billy had walked into the kitchen ten minutes later, his face suddenly haggard, and Dawnie knew at once something was wrong. She had rushed to him, thrown her arms around his neck, immediately wondering if he'd had some news from Lindy Lou or Buddy. And he had told her then that Lester had telephoned him from the hospital. He'd been called in because his wife had been hit by a youngster in a car. She had stepped out into the road; it was nobody's fault, an unfortunate accident. Ursula had been pronounced dead on arrival.

The vicar started to mention Ursula's love for her son and his family, and her devotion to Lester. Ursula's untimely death had left them devastated: she would leave a gap in so many people's lives that could never be filled. Dawnie looked down at her clothes, the green Jaeger suit she had worn when she and Ursula had visited Chestnut House and she thought of her trivial revenge on Simon Mountjoy and the offer on the house that had been accepted. They would move soon. They had hopes, dreams, a future, and Ursula had none of these now. She thought about how little any of those things really mattered in comparison: a new house, pettily getting her own back on someone who had ignored her. She considered her children, living their own lives, Buddy with his new girlfriend in New York and Lindy Lou with her brood, and she looked up at Billy, his face placid, and wondered how she would feel if it had been him who had been killed.

Dawnie had pushed such fears from her mind so often during their lives together: Billy in the army so far away, her thoughts filled with worries that she'd receive a phone call that he had been hurt, or sudden news that they were flying his body home; she imagined herself explaining to the children that their father wouldn't be coming back to them again. It was a scenario she had revisited so often.

Dawnie had worried about the children, about their health, their safety at every stage in their development; she had wondered what it would be like to lose Lindy or Buddy, Fallon or one of the little ones. Life would never be the same. She couldn't bear to imagine how cripplingly bereft she would be, how empty. She had worried about her own health: how it would be if she died, if Billy was left widowed and alone like Lester. Of course, he would cope; he was a practical man, but inside he would be broken. Dawnie felt Billy's hand cover her own and she began to weep silent tears for Lester, for Ursula, for the many hollow fears she'd had in her lifetime and had never spoken out loud.

Lester somehow managed to find his way to the pulpit. He stood silently; the church was still, as if everyone was holding their breath. Then he began to speak about Ursula, how she had come into his life years ago when he had been in a dark place, how she had shone a light and warmed his heart. He spoke about how she radiated beauty, love, courage, and Dawnie thought of Ursula on the back of Lester's Harley, her arms spread like wings, laughing. A sob caught in her throat and Dawnie held it there as silent tears followed again. She kept her eyes focused on the coffin, thinking of Ursula's body inside there; how life was so fragile: at one point you had life and breath and you could laugh and be happy and then, all of a sudden, you didn't. Dawnie promised herself at that moment that she would make the most of her time left, of Billy's too, however long they both lived. And the children had their own lives to lead; she would let them soar, let them find their own places and live their lives to the full. She could let them go now. She could let all her past worries go. There was only now.

Lester clambered down and there was silence again. A gentle note from a guitar came through loudspeakers and then more soft chords from a chosen CD, Ursula's favourite. Freddie Mercury began to sing 'Love of my Life', his voice aching with emotion, and Dawnie swallowed, reaching into her pocket for her sunglasses to cover her swollen eyelids. Lester was standing in the pew with his back turned, directly in front of her, and she wanted to reach forward and comfort him, then she noticed Liesel, Ursula's granddaughter, wrap an arm around his back, bent and taut in the leather jacket. Sobs echoed from across the church and Dawnie, the sunglasses masking her own tears, watched as Dilly bent forward, her body twisted with sadness, and Vinnie held her in his arms. Meinke and Lester moved towards the coffin, and four men wearing black suits took their places to carry Ursula out to the waiting cars where the family and a few close friends would travel to the cemetery on the edge of town.

* * *

An hour later, the sunlight was still cruelly intense in the municipal graveyard as the procession walked towards the hole in the newly dug earth. The mourners gathered around the grave, quietly placed wreaths and flowers, and then finally the coffin was lowered in. The vicar spoke for a while but Dawnie wasn't listening. She was watching Lester, his face immobile and expressionless as if he too had stopped living. Billy pressed her arm gently and jerked his head to look over his shoulder. Dawnie followed his gaze. Outside the church behind the railings was a line of motorbikes, chrome and paintwork gleaming in the sunshine. There were men and women in leathers, standing with their heads bowed, row upon row of bikes, fifty, a hundred, standing silently in Ursula's memory. Fresh tears rolled down Dawnie's cheeks. Lester, Meinke and Ursula's cousin Willa sprinkled handfuls of soil over the coffin, making a dull dropping sound onto the oak, and then everyone stood in silence. No one had left the graveyard; it was as if everyone was lingering, holding Ursula's memory in their hearts. Lester moved over to Billy and Dawnie and held out his hands. 'Thank you for coming.'

'Lester.' Dawnie hugged him. She had no idea what to say.

'What will you do now?' Billy asked.

'I don't want a wake – I don't want everyone back at our house, with Ursula not there. I couldn't do it.'

Billy nodded. 'I understand.'

Dawnie patted his arm. 'What about you? How can we help?'

Lester took a deep breath. 'I'm going back with Meinke and Frida for a few days. I'm going to Bavaria, back to Ursula's own country, where she started out. I want to spend some time there and just... just think.' He smiled sadly. 'The money I won in the photograph competition – the one Ursula entered for me – will pay for me to stay for a while.'

'Will you let us know as soon as you're back?' Dawnie asked gently.

'Of course.' Lester ran a hand through his thin hair and forced a smile. 'She was everything to me. I don't know what I'll do.' He swallowed hard. 'I can't make any plans.'

Billy clapped him on the back. 'We're here for you, me and Dawnie.'

'I know. Thank you.'

They watched him shuffle away, slowly, awkwardly, as if his body was racked with pain. He was talking to Meinke and Frida, to the little cousin, Willa. Billy turned to Dawnie.

'Malcolm and Gillian came to the service.'

'I saw them,' Dawnie murmured. 'In the back row. It was nice of them to come. Gillian liked Ursula.'

Billy shifted his shoulders. 'He's not a bad fella, Malcolm. He gave me some money for the Air Ambulance and shook my hand. He said something about getting me all wrong – he thought I'd done time behind bars.' He chuckled softly. 'Perhaps it was the t-shirt I had on at the camping trip.'

'I don't think they're a happy couple, Gillian and Malcolm.'

'They lost their son, darlin', in the Gulf War. They've had it hard.'

Dawnie took his hand. 'I didn't know.'

'I forgot to say. Malcolm told me on the day that Ursula was... knocked over and, to be honest, it slipped from my head. I couldn't really think about anything else but Lester and Ursula.'

'I had no idea their son had died, though, Billy.'

'Isn't that the way of it?' Billy sighed. 'So much about people you just guess at and you've no idea what their lives are really like. You and me, we've been lucky, despite it all. We had some hard times but we have lovely kids and we have each other.'

'We do.' Dawnie leaned against him. 'We are blessed.'

'I fancy a drink. Shall we go home, darlin'? We can open up a bottle of brandy. I won't get locked, I promise – but I do need a drink.'

'Let's toast Ursula together, shall we?' Dawnie's eyes shone with tears behind the sunglasses. 'Just me and you and a bottle of brandy. We can say goodbye together.'

He took her hand and walked towards the gates, past the procession of motorbikes that had started their engines, a low rumbling of thunder, towards where he had parked the Harley.

33

Malcolm parked the Honda, polished to a shine with its new bumper and headlight, outside a small parade of shops. He clambered out and opened the passenger door.

Gillian frowned, surprised. 'Why have we stopped here?'

'I'm taking you to lunch.'

Gillian stepped out of the car and gazed up at the sign: 'La Bottega Dei Sapori'. Behind her glasses, her expression was astonished. 'It's an Italian restaurant.'

'I've booked us a table.'

'But I didn't think you liked Italian food, Malcolm. I thought you hated all foreign food.'

Malcolm raised one eyebrow. 'I thought today might be a good day to review all that.'

Inside, a young waiter with wavy hair and a warm smile led them to a small table with a red and white checked cloth. Malcolm smiled at him. 'May I have a sparkling water, and a glass of Chianti for my wife?'

Gillian was horrified. 'Wine, Malcolm? We've just come from

Ursula's funeral service and we're here, drinking wine and eating lunch as if nothing happened.'

'No, Gillian.' Malcolm's voice was firm. 'Ursula has gone and it's a tragedy. Her legacy is important, though; you told me what a cheerful, kind woman she was, how much she enjoyed her life, how she and her husband adored each other...'

'Yes.'

'I've been a fool.' The waiter was at his elbow with the drinks and Malcolm scanned the menu. 'I'll have the pasta carbonara please. Gillian, what would you like?'

She shook her head, immediately terrified of making a choice. 'I'll have the same as you – yes, that will be fine.'

'Two carbonaras – thank you.' Malcolm watched the waiter bustle away. He lifted his glass of water. 'To Ursula.'

Gillian raised her glass. 'To dear Ursula.'

They took a mouthful of their drinks and replaced their glasses carefully on the table at exactly the same time. Malcolm reached over and put his hand over Gillian's. 'I've been a complete fool, my dear. But things will change, I promise you.'

'Change?' Gillian pressed her lips together. 'That doesn't sound like you, Malcolm. You're a creature of habit.'

'Routine, my dear – and it's been the undoing of us. I've made so many mistakes.'

Gillian almost laughed, a high squeak of relief. 'I don't think I've heard you say anything like this before, Malcolm, ever.'

'I was wrong about Billy Murphy, and his wife Dawnie. When she said he'd been away, I simply assumed he'd been in prison. I didn't think or ask, I just assumed he was a criminal because of the size of him and, you know, the hair, the motorbike, the jacket... well, I thought he was a thug. I suppose I was a little bit afraid of him.'

'He's a nice man, Malcolm. They are both really kind people.'

'Oh, yes, I know that now.' Malcolm sat upright as the waiter put a steaming plate of pasta in front of him. 'He's more than that, Gillian: he's a war hero. I underestimated him completely. And Dawnie – she has been a rock for that family, for him too.'

Gillian sipped her wine and they ate in silence for a moment. Then she caught his eye and said, 'This is nice.'

'It is.' Malcolm nibbled a forkful of carbonara. 'We must do this more often.'

Gillian met his eyes. 'That would be something to look forward to.'

He was staring at her, his gaze gentle behind the glasses. 'You are a good woman, a strong woman, Gillian. You deserve much more...'

'What do you mean?'

'I used living with a routine to help me deal with the pain, and at the same time, routine was destroying what we had together.'

'I don't understand.'

Malcolm reached for his sparkling water. 'When we lost James, when he died, I couldn't speak about it. I couldn't speak to you or anyone for that matter. I was hurting and I didn't know what to do. I should have reached out – we could have comforted each other – but instead I let it go much deeper until it formed a hard ball of resentment.'

Gillian frowned. 'Who did you resent, Malcolm? Me? James?'

'Everyone.' He thought for a moment. 'But mostly myself. I resented myself for becoming the person I was: in a rut, angry, miserable, unhappy, judgemental. But I didn't know how to change.'

Gillian chewed thoughtfully. 'But you're trying to change now, Malcolm. I mean, we're here together now, enjoying lunch, trying to change, aren't we?'

'I have to change, for both our sakes. We missed James dreadfully and I have never grieved for him properly; I have never allowed you to grieve, to share it with me. I shut you out.'

'I suppose you did.'

Malcolm reached out across the table and grasped her hand. 'I have wasted so much time.' He caught his breath. 'I do love you, Gillian. And I will make it up to you.'

The waiter was hovering. 'Is everything all right, sir?'

Malcolm smiled and his face was relaxed and happy. Gillian thought how handsome he looked. With a jolt, she realised she hadn't thought about Malcolm in that way for years. 'The food is perfect, thank you. We'll have the dessert menu when we've finished.'

Gillian watched the waiter walk away. 'Dessert too?'

'I can do better than that, my dear.' Malcolm leaned forward and winked at his wife. 'Shall we have two puddings and two spoons? I thought a panna cotta and a tiramisu to share?'

Gillian smiled. 'I could get used to this.'

'Then I'll make sure you do.' He pushed his plate away. 'How was your meal?'

'Delightful.'

'I wonder how much better a carbonara would taste if it was actually cooked in Italy?'

Gillian wrinkled her nose. 'I don't know. I suppose it would be authentic...'

He took her hand again and brought it to his lips. 'I think it might be nice to find out.'

'Whatever do you mean?'

'I mean that when we've finished our meal and had coffee, I think we should go to the travel agents and ask them to show us what they have in terms of a holiday to Italy, shall we? We could go next week. I thought Florence might be nice in August, or Rome. What do you think?'

'Tuscany.' Gillian squeezed his hand. 'Tuscany at dusk would be so romantic. The countryside, the sea. Oh Malcolm, yes, let's find a little place in the hills in Tuscany.'

* * *

Dilly was walking slowly behind Vinnie and Mei-Lien, trying to appear cool and calm, but she felt warm and sticky in the pink summer dress and the drooping feather boa. In truth, she was looking at the graves, busy doing arithmetic. She was trying to work out how old the inhabitants had been when they died. Some tombstones had numbers engraved on them, clearly showing the dates and ages of the deceased but some did not and Dilly was trying to work out who had lived the longest and whether they were older than she was now when they died. She had seen an Alice, in her late eighties; there was a John, ninety-one; a Mary, ninety-four; and an Elizabeth 'Betty' Musgrave who had died aged ninety-eight. Enid Wagstaff had lived to be a hundred and one. There were some people who had died at a much younger age: Christopher had been forty, Michael just twenty-three, and little Emily was only one year old when she was 'taken by angels'.

Dilly called out to Vinnie, who was in front of her, his hand in Mei-Lien's. 'It's very warm now: everyone seems to be making their way home.'

'I'll take you home on the bus, Mam. Mei is off to teach a Pilates class this afternoon and Grace will be home from school later. We were going to take her to the pictures tonight.'

'Right, Vinnie.' Dilly put a hand to her head; it was sticky with perspiration. 'I wonder whether you could find one of those mini-supermarkets or a shop, get yourself a drink and bring me a cold one back. I fancy one of those nice iced teas you can get.'

'There's a little shop across the road,' Mei-Lien suggested, glancing at Vinnie. 'We'd only be ten minutes.'

'Perfect,' Dilly agreed. 'I'd like a few minutes to myself here. The flowers are beautiful on some of the graves, even the old ones. They smell lovely.'

Vinnie nodded and took Mei-Lien's hand. Dilly watched them walk off together and muttered to herself. 'Come on, Dilly, none of this morbid thinking. Vinnie will be all right with that one when I'm gone, mind.'

She took the path to the right towards a shady tree which hung low branches over a corner of the graveyard. There was a man in the distance, wearing a tweed suit. Dilly wasn't sure, but it looked like he had flowers in his hand. She paused for a moment and gazed back towards Ursula's grave. The vicar was talking to Lester. Meinke and his wife and daughter and the older lady, Willa, were in a group together, immobile, looking sad.

Everyone else had gone. She had seen Malcolm and Gillian go off in their car. Aude and Sylv had left just after the service; they had to go to work in the hospital. Dawnie and Billy had hugged her and promised to pop over later with some home brew. She would miss them when they moved into their new house although they hadn't set a date to leave yet.

Dilly couldn't help but feel a little morose. Some graves had beautiful flowers on them in little bowls; some had inexpensive cellophane-wrapped bouquets laid on top. On one grave there was a single red rose. Dilly wondered what her own grave might be like in the future, when her time came. She had heard Lester tell Billy that he had instructed the funeral director to make Ursula's grave a companion plot: he wanted his final resting place to be with his wife. Dilly wasn't sure if that was romantic, practical, because Lester was broken-hearted, or whether it was in fact all three at the same time.

Dilly thought sadly that she would not be buried with Tommy. Tommy had been cremated. That's what he'd wanted, Dilly had been sure of it: not that they'd ever spoken about death much but Dilly had supposed that, since he was very fastidious in his habits and he hated waste of any kind, since he'd disliked gardening and rummaging in the earth to the point of always hating dirt in his fingernails, he'd have chosen cremation for himself. Dilly didn't want to be cremated. She wanted a nice grave with a proper headstone so that people could visit and remember her. She would speak to Vinnie about it. She had saved up and the money was in the bank. Just in case.

Dilly reached the tree and decided to sit down in the shade. There was a wooden bench not far away. She walked the last few steps and plonked herself down gladly, shaking the feather boa from around her neck and coiling it on her knee. The sun was very hot now, and she was looking forward to the iced tea Vinnie would bring; she'd seen cans of iced tea advertised on television and right now she thought one would be perfect.

'May I sit down?' She looked up to see a tall bearded man with thick white hair. He was probably in his eighties. He was the man she thought she had seen in the distance, but his hands were empty; he wasn't carrying flowers now.

She shrugged. 'You can sit where you like. It's a free country.'

The man sat down and smiled. 'I thought it was you.'

Dilly shook a finger at him. 'If you're trying to pick me up, this is hardly the place...'

'It's Ken.' He smiled. 'Ken Bradley. I knew it was you when I saw the feather boa. Even without the wig, once I heard the accent, I knew it was you, Dilly.'

She gasped. 'Ken Bradley... you are the man I danced to "Albatross" with in the Castle. We had a lovely smooch together and you asked for my phone number...'

'I am, and you wouldn't give it to me. You were coy and elusive, a wonderful Welsh Cinderella. How nice to bump into you today.'

'I've been to a funeral.' Dilly folded her arms.

'At our age, that's an occupational hazard, I'm afraid.' Ken shrugged sadly. 'I come here all the time to put flowers on my wife's grave.'

'Oh, your wife? How old was she when she, you know, died?' Dilly peered through her glasses. 'Just interested in the statistics, mind.'

'Lilian was young,' Ken sighed. 'Fifty-four.'

'My friend who was buried today was in her early sixties. Too young as well.' Dilly glanced at Ken and sighed even louder. 'Tough sometimes, this life, isn't it?'

'It's all we've got, though,' Ken admitted. 'And I'm eighty-seven.'

'Oh, you're a bit long in the tooth then, like me?' Dilly suggested.

'But there's life in the old dog yet.' Ken raised an eyebrow. 'I'm always up for some fun. How about you?'

'What are you suggesting?' Dilly asked, whisking the feather boa around her neck. 'You'd better be careful, mind. My son will be back in a moment and he's a biker. He's gone to get me an iced tea.'

'Iced tea?' Ken chuckled. 'I was thinking more of offering you a ninety-nine.'

'I beg your pardon, Ken?' Dilly glared at him, her eyes bright behind her spectacles. 'I'm not that type of girl!'

'A ninety-nine ice cream cone with a chocolate flake in it and maybe a drive around the coast; we could stop off at the beach for a short stroll, a pot of tea, and take in some sea air.'

'Do you have a car?'

Ken grinned. 'My Mercedes SL is parked by the gate.'

Dilly raised an eyebrow. 'What colour is it?'

'White.'

'Good. Then I'll come for a drive with you.'

Ken leaned forward. 'And maybe dinner, afterwards, somewhere overlooking the ocean?'

'Maybe.' Dilly's eyebrow arched higher and she patted her hair. 'If you're lucky. Oh, look – there's my son and his girlfriend coming towards us. He can keep his iced tea, Ken, if we're off for a drive and dinner. I'm strictly a Prosecco girl.'

34

Hours later, Dawnie was lost in her thoughts as the full force of the shower splashed on her head, cascading droplets across her back and shoulders. She stood still, staring, letting the water trickle down her body. It didn't seem right. They had buried Ursula today yet, just a couple of weeks before, they had spent time together, laughing, chattering, sharing hopes and plans. Ursula had been so brave. During the charity run, she had ridden pillion on Lester's motorbike for the first time; she had conquered her fears of the road; she had smiled, her arms wide with abandon.

Then, a matter of days later, she had been knocked down by a teenager who had passed his driving test only months before. Of course it was not the young man's fault – Ursula had stepped out into the road; it was a blind bend – he had not been going quickly but the impact had been forceful. She had fallen and hit her head and now she was dead and the poor boy would have to live with the memory of killing her, of seeing her loom in front of his car too quickly for him to stop. It was all so tragic.

Again, as she had done so many times since Ursula's death, Dawnie had the urge to ring her friend, to pop round for a cup of coffee and a slice of cake, to chatter about this and that, their husbands, their children, life. It was too late for all that now. It would never happen again.

Dawnie's eyes were closed tightly against the water that sprinkled against her face and ran down her cheeks. Lester was going to stay in Germany with Meinke and Ursula's family for a few weeks. The break would be good for him; some time away from home might start the healing process. But, Dawnie wondered, how could he possibly ever heal? Ursula had been the love of his life. He would return to the house they'd shared, to a home where memories of Ursula sat on every shelf, stood in every corner. There would be photographs that told the story of her life, pictures of wonderful times together; there would be piles of clothes she'd chosen, that she'd worn next to her skin; in the kitchen, everything Ursula had ever touched would still be in its place; in their bedroom, the scent of her would still linger in the air. Dawnie wondered how Lester could ever get over the loss of his wife and how she and Billy could help. Then her thoughts moved to Billy and how she would cope if it had been him who had died. She couldn't bear the image and shook it away with the drops of water.

She turned off the shower, wrapped herself in a towel and stepped over the edge of the bath into the tiny bathroom. The thought that it would be nice to live in Chestnut House with its bigger bathroom and generous space flitted through her mind. It was quickly followed by another thought: she knew that houses and bathrooms and showers were not important at all. Life was important. Everything else was irrelevant.

Dawnie walked into the bedroom and was immediately struck by the bright sunlight that filtered through the window from outside; it was a glorious day. She suddenly wanted to cry. It was wrong that the weather was so warm and the sunshine so illuminating on the day when Ursula had been buried. It wasn't fair. Ursula would never see such a day, not now.

Dawnie struggled into a t-shirt and jeans, slipping her feet into trainers, and rubbed damp fingers through her short hair. She couldn't be bothered with choosing clothes, selecting a cheerful wig. She sighed. Billy was downstairs. She would go down, hug him, and then suggest they take the bottle of brandy down from the shelf in the kitchen, toast Ursula's memory, reminisce about the good times they all shared and get drunk. It would make her feel better. But when she arrived at the bottom of the stairs, Billy was waiting, wearing his bike gear. He held out her jacket and helmet. 'Here you are, darlin'. Put these on. We're going out.'

She stood still, staring at him. 'No, Billy. I thought we were going to stay here, have a drink, toast...' Her voice trailed off. She couldn't finish the sentence.

Billy shook his head. 'I've changed my mind. It's a sunny day. The open roads beckon. Let's take a ride, Dawnie: let's go to the coast and onto the moors, take in the colours of the grass and the flowers and the trees, feel the wind on our faces.' He helped her into her jacket, aware of how unwillingly she shrugged it on. 'We can stay here and mope, for sure, but the best way to remember Ursula is to look at the beauty of the world and remind ourselves that it's still out there for the taking.' He held out a hand. 'We can't bring her back but we can remember her today, outside in the fresh air, not cooped up in here crying into a glass of brandy.'

Billy drove the Harley through open roads, Dawnie clinging to him, her head resting against his broad back. For the first few miles, she kept her eyes closed, hearing the gentle rumble of the engine, feeling the rhythm of the vibrations. When she opened her eyes again and peered through the visor, they were in a narrow lane, driving down a hill past a white cottage before the bike swerved to the left and descended through a canopy of trees that leaned into the road and masked the sky, the branches knotted like folded fingers.

They drove through a little town until the houses became fewer; then the road fell away to the left to reveal paths carved like scars of brown earth, scrubby patches of grass and a steep drop down to the sea. The surf slapped against craggy rocks and sprayed into the air. Dawnie watched the foam spurt and fall into droplets and she thought about life, how it was in full flow for such a short time, only to become nothing. The ocean was an intense blue, the waves shimmering in blinding sunshine, and in the distance a line of indigo and then the swirl of sky. Dawnie tightened her grip around Billy's waist as he leaned to the right, guiding the bike up a winding hill, faded grass on either side bleached by the sun's heat.

Dawnie was lost in her thoughts for a while, the light from the sun closing her eyes, bathing her face with brightness through the visor, baking her body inside the leather jacket. She wondered if she might fall asleep and clung to Billy, aware of the solid steady body in front of her, a driver who was making decisions about which road to take, moving her steadily forward. The she felt the rhythm of the engine shift to a sluggish chugging gear and the bike came to a stop. Dawnie looked around her at open moorland, pale green grass and the rising dull red sweep of a hill, intersected with the deep scar of a path. Billy waited for Dawnie to climb off the Harley, then he was next to her, taking off his helmet. 'I thought we'd take a little walk, will we, where the view is good?'

They strode along the path, a grey scratch in the earth that intersected purple heather. It was just wide enough for them to walk together in step, their hands clasped. To the left, there was a checkboard of fields in greens and greys sweeping down towards the sea. A ribbon of sand skirted the deep blue ocean where the waves began. They climbed higher, where a group of ponies stood in long grass, turning their necks to stare as they passed, flicking their ears as the sun gleamed on their brown coats.

They wandered through scrubland, the heather pink, pale, the deep green of moss, until they reached the top of a hill. Billy pulled off his jacket and threw it down, the leather side flat against the ground, and sat on the edge, patting the lining material to encourage Dawnie to sit beside him. She flopped down with a sigh. From the high position, they gazed down at the ocean, the beach twisting around a green mound of a hill, behind which everything was intense blue water. In the distance, the ground levelled out and several trees had been bent over in the wind; they were leaning to the same side like a row of dancers, their branches stretched towards a dense tangle of scratchy leaves.

'This county is a beautiful place to live,' Billy muttered.

Dawnie nodded. She knew Billy had brought her here to think about Ursula but also to think about herself and Billy and their future. She stared at the sea, each sparkle on the surface of the waves unique, gone in a moment, followed by another sharp twinkle of light. 'We are so lucky to be here,' she breathed. 'It's lovely.'

He wrapped an arm around her; it was weighty and reassuring. 'There was a time, Dawnie, when I was on active service, that I thought I might never be able to come back to you. When I was away for months on end, all I could do was live from day to day in the hope that the next one would bring me closer to coming back home. I was so far away, living in a bubble – my existence was so different, I couldn't imagine a time when we'd be together again. It was as if I daren't hope for it.' He pulled her closer. 'But here we are now, me and you, in this wonderful place together. It's just grand, isn't it?'

'You're right.' Her voice was a whisper. 'We have so much to be grateful for. I hated it when you were away in the army. I threw myself into being a parent, living for the kids, into being so ridiculously happy to compensate for you not being there – I was just a court jester for Buddy and Lindy. I was so cheerful. I'd say, "Oh, don't worry, Daddy's coming home soon, I know he is: let's just have fun," and I'd be waiting for a letter or a phone call from you, having heard nothing for weeks, fearing that the worst had happened.'

'I wouldn't have known how to describe to you what my life was like then,' Billy mumbled. 'Lots of the lads who went home had lost the skill of talking to their wives. You know, they just went back and lived in silence. It was as if the war was still going on between their ears and they couldn't accept the peace of coming home to a place where things were normal. It was something you daren't wish for when you were away, normality. So, when you were back with the ones you loved, you didn't know how to settle alongside them and live an ordinary life.'

Dawnie nodded, remembering. 'I could tell. You'd be all chirpy with the kids, all jokes and fun and then, with me, I'd see the real Billy. You were tired, a bit stunned, and you'd go into a quiet place where I was shut out and I couldn't get through to you. And at night the bad dreams would come and I'd lie awake, listening to you living through it all over again.'

Billy kissed her. 'But you stuck it out with me. We came through it together.'

'Because I love you,' Dawnie said simply.

He took her face in his hands. 'I'd be nothing without you, darlin'. I wouldn't have made it through those times without you. That's the truth.'

'I just provided normality, the home, the family, the stable environment for you to come home to. But I was lonely, too. It was like we were that thing you use at school in geometry to draw circles, the two-legged compass. I was the leg that stays fixed and still, and you just revolved around me at a distance, going round and round, never getting any closer.' She forced a grin. 'But here we are now – we're fine. We made it through.'

'Ah, we did.' Billy gazed around at the sea, at the undulating fields. 'Me and you, Dawnie, forever.'

She leaned her head against him. 'It's our time now.' She chuckled softly. 'I miss the kids though.'

Billy's face was concerned. 'Can you be happy here with just me? Have we made the right decision? Or do you just feel like you have an empty nest and I'm not enough?'

'We are fine.' She gazed into his face. 'The kids are busy people now. They are happy, focused on what they're doing and they love us, even if they don't always text or phone. They will do their own thing, live their lives, but they'll always be our kids.' A smile flickered around her mouth. 'It's time you and I put down some roots here in north Devon, in that house by the sea. We've made friends and I know we'll miss Ursula more than I can say, but we'll move forward together and enjoy everything life throws at us. It's what living has led to and here we are. It's a new phase but it's a glorious one. Let's embrace it, Billy.'

'With both arms.' He hugged her tight and they tumbled back onto the grass. Billy kissed her mouth and then they both sat up straight, enjoying the scent of each other and the awkwardness of their fall.

A thought suddenly occurred to Billy and he chuckled. 'Malcolm believed I'd been in prison.' There were tears in his eyes, the corners crinkling with laughter. 'He believed I'd done time for GBH. I had to put him straight on it. He's been an eejit, darlin', but I think he's a nice sort of a fella really.'

'I knew he wasn't your biggest fan,' Dawnie shrugged, an exaggerated movement of surprise. 'But I've no idea why he thought you'd done time. It couldn't have come from anything I'd said to him or Gillian.'

Billy's face was suddenly serious. 'You know he lost a son in the Gulf War. He and Gillian – their boy was only a young fella. I'm not sure how well they coped with it. I think it made him a bit bitter towards people. I think he wanted to think the worst of people.'

'Poor Gillian. Poor Malcolm. We are so lucky to have our kids, Billy.' Dawnie met his eyes. 'We have so much to be happy about. We are blessed to be together.'

'Ah, we are that,' he agreed. He stared around him for a moment, breathing in the fresh air, then he rubbed his stomach. 'I'm feeling hungry. How about we get ourselves a bite to eat somewhere?'

'Is it that time already?' Dawnie asked. 'It can't be five o'clock yet.' She was about to check her phone but it was ringing in her pocket. She tugged it out, wondering if it was Lindy Lou or even Lester asking for help. She stared at it. 'It's Simon Mountjoy, the estate agent.'

She listened intently, her eyes serious, answering the crackling voice in the earpiece every so often. 'Okay. Yes... all right... oh, all right, yes. Thank you, Simon... right. I'll talk to Billy. I'll be in touch.'

Billy was staring at her, his eyebrows furrowed. 'What's your man Mountjoy after doing? What does he want?'

'It's Chestnut House. He says the Myttons have changed their mind. They aren't going back to South Africa at all.'

'So, what about the house?'

'They aren't selling it now.' Dawnie's mouth was open. 'The sale's fallen through.'

35

Dawnie blinked her eyes and stretched in the bed, making the muscles in her legs ache deliciously. She was awake now, but she'd slept deeply throughout the night. The space next to her in the bed was empty, the duvet thrown back, but something had been placed on the pillow. Dawnie blinked, sat up and picked up an envelope and a small furry toy. She examined it with a smile: it was a little teddy bear wearing a black biker jacket, a hat and dark glasses. She turned it over and the label was still attached. The price ticket told her that it had cost £9.99 and it had come from the corner shop in Martha Street. She opened the envelope, tugging out a card. It was a simple picture of the sun setting into the sea, colours merging, melting oranges and reds. Inside, she recognised Billy's handwriting, simply written:

Home is where you are xx

She picked up her phone from the side of the bed. It was past ten o'clock. There were two texts and a missed call. The first text was from Lindy Lou, simply saying that life was hectic at the moment and she'd ring in the evening. The second text was a photograph of Buddy on stage, sent from Luci's phone. Her son looked happy, ecstatic even; his eyes squeezed shut as he wrenched the notes from his guitar. The missed call was from Simon Mountjoy. Dawnie slid out of bed and pulled on jeans and a t-shirt. Sunlight streamed through the window, specks of dust dancing in the yellow beams. She'd make Billy some coffee, some breakfast if he hadn't had any; she'd hug him and thank him for the card. She smiled, hoping he'd picked up a bag of croissants from the corner shop.

There was no one in the kitchen; there were no dishes in the sink and the kettle was cool to Dawnie's touch. A packet of four butter croissants was unopened on the worktop. Billy hadn't eaten anything yet. Dawnie shook her head knowingly; it was Sunday morning. He would be outside polishing the Harley. She bustled about lazily, putting a pot of coffee on the stove, warming the croissants in the rusty oven, setting plates on a tray. The radio was rattling, Planet Rock playing Queen's 'Who Wants to Live Forever'. Dawnie thought of Ursula and sadness stopped her moving for a moment and held her still. She exhaled and shuffled towards the oven.

She carried the tray out into the sunlight. Billy was sitting on the kerbside, his bottom resting on his jacket, polishing the chrome forks of the Harley and chatting to Aude and Sylv. He looked over his shoulder and grinned. 'Hi, darlin'.'

'I've brought breakfast al fresco.' Dawnie glanced at her neighbours. 'Shall I just pop in and get extra cups and plates?'

Aude shook her head. 'I've just made a huge cooked breakfast and eaten it all.'

'Not all of it.' Sylv offered a mock-apologetic expression. 'I ate a whole plateful as well. Eggs, hash browns, fried potatoes, mushrooms, tomatoes.'

'I'm hungry.' Billy threw down the rag he was using to polish his bike and stared at the croissants. 'Thanks, darlin'.'

Dawnie kissed the top of his head, the short curls wiry against her skin. 'Thank you for the card and the little teddy. Very sweet.'

Billy beamed at her, picking up a croissant, his huge hand wrapped around the crispy exterior, his other hand reaching for coffee. 'Grand.'

Aude nodded her head towards number fourteen across the road, where Dilly and Vinnie lived. She was indicating the shiny black trike parked by the kerb. She rolled her eyes, her expression full of innuendo. 'So, it looks like someone might have stayed the night.'

Sylv nudged her gently. 'She's called Mei-Lien. She was at the funeral yesterday, holding Vinnie's hand. She seems very nice.'

The neighbours were quiet a moment. The funeral filled their thoughts, sad images playing over again. Then Aude said brightly. 'Tequila learned a new swear word this morning.'

'I stubbed my toe,' Sylv replied, waving her hands in explanation. 'It hurt. I didn't mean to say that word but it just came out.'

Aude shrugged. 'And now it's Tequila's favourite word.'

'Let's hope he doesn't escape again and swear at poor Malcolm,' Sylv chuckled. 'Talking of Malcolm, he and Gillian have gone out. We saw them go, Dawnie, about half an hour ago.'

'He's taking his missus out to breakfast,' Billy murmured. 'He stopped for a chat as I sat here cleaning the bike. He's making the most of the weather, he said.' He finished the croissant, wiping crumbs from his mouth. 'He was in a grand mood. He even said "Top of the mornin'" to me.' Billy chortled. 'In all my life I've never heard anyone say top of the mornin'.'

Dawnie sipped from her mug. The coffee was still piping hot. 'By the way, Billy, I missed a call from Simon Mountjoy.'

Aude's face was sympathetic. 'I'm sorry the house move has fallen through, Dawnie. Billy just said about it. You must be so disappointed...'

'But at least we'll have you as neighbours a bit longer,' Sylv added with a grin.

'Maybe.' Billy's eyes met Dawnie's. 'Your man Simon Mountjoy rang me when he couldn't raise you. He said he had another house come on the market just last night: he said it was perfect for us. Near the coast, five bedrooms, garage for eight cars.'

'Oh.' Dawnie was aware of two pairs of eyes staring at her, watching her reaction as the neighbours listened intently.

'So, when I've cleaned up the bike a bit, we'll go and have a look at it, will we?' Billy drained his coffee and reached for the soft rag, turning back to polish the chrome forks again. 'I said we'd see him at the place at one o'clock.' He leaned forward, applying extra attention to a gleaming spot on the forks. 'It's a special Sunday viewing just for us, he said. Simon must be keen for a quick sale.'

* * *

Crosswinds was a bungalow set back from the road on the outskirts of a village. Billy parked the bike at the top of the gravel drive next to Simon Mountjoy's BMW. Dawnie pulled off her helmet and put her hands on her hips. 'It's not very close to the sea, Billy.'

'Ten minutes' drive away.' Billy scratched his short curls, still warm where the helmet had been next to his scalp. 'I've ridden through this village before. They have a nice pub here, from the look of it. It does quiz nights and curry evenings, good craic. It might be grand living here; it has a good community feel to it.'

'Billy, Dawnie, good to see you.' Simon Mountjoy slipped from the driver's side of the BMW and held his hand out, grinning at Dawnie as if she was an old friend. 'Shall we go and see the house?'

Billy shook his hand. 'It was good of you to come out on a Sunday, Simon.'

'This house has only just come on the market.' Simon held out a hand to Dawnie, his cheeks pink with excitement. 'I wanted you to be the first to see it.'

They followed him down the drive and stared at a sprawling white bungalow, its double-glazed windows gleaming in the sunlight. Simon rubbed his hands together. 'Plenty of space for parking outside.' He glanced at Billy. 'But you wait until you see the garage.'

He slid the key into the lock. Dawnie and Billy followed him through a narrow hallway with plain white walls. There were rooms to the right and the left, a small bedroom, a snug with a television and a sofa. Simon turned to Dawnie. 'The owners, Mr and Mrs Tate, are out at the moment. Come through. Wait until I show you the kitchen. It has all-new custom-made units.'

They stepped into the kitchen, a large square room with white cupboards in a shaker style. It was clean, the granite worktops shining, the chrome fridge gleaming, the cooker and oven units pristine. 'All new,' Simon repeated. 'Just ready for someone to move in. What do you think?' His eyes caught Dawnie's and she smiled. He grinned back.

'Yes, it's nice, Simon. A good-sized kitchen.'

'I'll show you the garden room, shall I? You'll love it. It brings the outside inside.' Simon led them into a large timber framed room with huge windows, sliding doors on two sides, blinding sunlight bursting through bright glass panes onto a cream three-piece suite. He ushered them outside onto a stone patio, perfectly matching slabs of pink and grey, leading to a brick-built barbecue area, a hot tub, and beyond, a huge neatly manicured lawn flanked by fruit trees. Dawnie gazed at Billy. 'Living here would feel like being on holiday permanently.'

Billy had noticed a huge concrete building to the left. 'Is that the garage?'

'Yes.' Simon gave a triumphant smile. 'The summer house is at the bottom of the garden, near the Buddha water feature. We can go there in a moment. I thought you'd like to see the garage first.'

The garage doors slid up and open on the touch of an electric key, and Simon waved an arm. 'Go inside, Billy. Take a look.'

The garage was a huge space. Billy walked the length, his eyes wide. 'The owner has some classics here. A 2008 Jaguar XKR... an MGB Roadster. Ah, would you believe it? A 1993 Harley Davidson Fatboy.' He turned to Simon. 'Do these come with the house?'

Simon chuckled. 'There's nothing stopping you negotiating a private sale with the owner. He and his wife are moving a couple of hundred miles away so who knows what they'll want to leave behind?'

Billy allowed his fingers to trail along the leather seat of the motorbike, caressing the turquoise and white tank with an embossed red starburst symbol. The exhaust and the headlight gleamed as if new. He breathed out slowly. 'This is deadly, Dawnie.'

Dawnie was still thinking about the hot tub and the barbecue. She turned her attention to Simon. 'Shall we leave him here for a moment while we go and look at the summerhouse and the Buddha water feature?'

* * *

Dawnie sat in the snug of the Thresher's Arms, a four-minute walk from Crosswinds, still thinking about the house, about the serenity of the water feature's soft gurgle. The master bedroom had been lovely, painted in grey and pink with cream built-in wardrobes that would easily accommodate all of her clothes, her wigs and her accessories. The en suite was modern, finished in green and gold, with tall plants on each side of matching granite sinks and a huge shower cubicle set at the top of three stone steps. Billy came back from the bar carrying a pint of lemonade and a glass of red wine.

'It's a bit early for wine, Billy,' Dawnie exclaimed, grabbing the glass from him and taking a huge sip.

'The barman's a nice fella. He's called Charley. We had a bit of a chat.' Billy sat next to Dawnie on the plush red window seat.

The snug was quiet; most people were dining in the restaurant. Dawnie could hear the clatter of cutlery and smell the aroma of Sunday roast mingled with the bitter scent of beer hops. She looked around the room. There was a huge open fireplace, unlit at the moment, but she imagined the dry heat of crackling logs it would offer in winter. She met Billy's gaze. 'This would be a great place to come for a drink at Christmas.'

'There's a real community atmosphere in the bar.' Billy swallowed a mouthful of lemonade. 'They have music nights here too.' His eyes twinkled. 'I should have asked if anyone was needing a drummer.'

'So...' Dawnie placed her glass of wine on the table decisively. 'What did you think to the house?'

'Ah, the garage was deadly. I could imagine spending all day in there, darlin'.' He chuckled apologetically. 'While you're in the hot tub, not a stitch on. Then we could have a barbecue...'

She laughed. 'I hope the barbecue's not heating up while I'm in the hot tub in the altogether, Billy.'

'The garden room was grand, though. And the garden wouldn't need much doing to maintain it, just the lawn mowing and a bit of pruning the fruit bushes.'

Dawnie nodded. 'And the kitchen was so clean and modern.'

'And the big shower, room for us both at the same time, darlin'. And all those plants in the en suite.'

'It was exotic. And there was so much light in the house.'

Billy sighed. 'And we can afford it.'

'It would be a completely new start for us.'

They glanced at each other for a moment. Dawnie drained her wine. 'Shall we go back to Maggot Street, Billy?'

'I guess we should.' He took her hand. 'We have plenty to think about.'

* * *

The moon hung in a sky flecked with stars, behind the black outline of the chimney pot on the roof of number fourteen. Billy and Dawnie sat on the step, gazing across the road, mugs of hot tea in their hands. Billy indicated Mei-Lien's trike, parked outside Vinnie's house, with a nod of his head. 'I see he has his woman over there again.'

'It's true love,' Dawnie chuckled. 'I think they seem very suited to each other. She's really nice, Mei-Lien.'

'And he's a grand fella too. They are good together.' Billy sipped his tea and thought for a moment. 'You know, darlin', I love looking up at the night sky. It used to make me think of you when I was far away from home.'

'What did you think, Billy?'

'It was the big old moon in the sky that made me feel close to you, knowing you'd be at home gazing at it through the kitchen window and I'd be lying on my back, somewhere else in the world, staring at the same moon and we'd both be thinking about each other.'

She pushed her hand inside the curve of his huge fist, and it was suddenly warm. 'But now we're here staring up at it together.'

'That's everything I could want in the world now – you, me and the moon.'

There was a click from the front door of number eleven and Malcolm was standing in the doorway, wearing a dressing gown over pyjamas. Billy glanced up at him from the step. 'Hello. Are we keeping you up?'

Malcolm plucked at his burgundy dressing gown, his fingers brushing the soft material. 'Oh, no, Billy. I just heard you talking out here.'

'Too loud?' Dawnie brayed. 'That's typical of me. Sorry if I woke you, Malcolm.'

'Not at all. I just wanted to come out and have a word with you both.'

'Oh?' Billy's brow furrowed. 'Are you and Gillian all right?'

'I'm taking her off to Tuscany on Tuesday. We're driving to Bristol and leaving the car at the airport so I wondered if you could use the parking space while I was away?'

'Ah, that's nice of you,' Billy murmured.

'Gillian needs a break. We both do.' Malcolm's eyes shone behind his glasses. 'But I was thinking, when we're back in a couple of weeks, perhaps you'd like to come to dinner with us?'

'That would be grand,' Billy nodded enthusiastically.

'We'll bring some home brew round,' Dawnie offered.

'Definitely.' Malcolm smiled. 'I've heard all about this famous home brew. It would be good to try some. And, of course, I'll bring some Italian wine back. We might even cook a carbonara. Unless you'd like to let us have your recipe for hotpot and spotted dick.' He smiled, shuffling his feet. 'Well, I'd better turn in for the night. Gillian will be wondering where I've got to. She's upstairs...'

'Have a lovely time in Tuscany,' Dawnie called as Malcolm shut the door with a clunk. She tucked an arm through Billy's. 'Well, that's an extra parking space for the Transit and the Harley for the next fortnight.'

'Ah, he's a nice fella. And his missus is a good sort.'

'Have you finished your tea?'

'Nearly. Will we go in yet?'

Dawnie shook her head. 'It's nice out here. I could do with one of my wigs on though. My head is getting cold.'

Billy wrapped his arm around her, pulling her into the warmth of his body. 'Let's stay here on the step just a bit longer then.'

They sat in silence, heads touching, watching the moon slip behind the shreds of a cloud and glide out the other side. The sound of an engine roaring down the street pulled them from their thoughts. A white Mercedes SL slowed down outside number fourteen, stopping behind Mei-Lien's trike. A smart man with white hair and a tweed suit opened the door and ambled around to the passenger side. Dilly emerged, immediately noticing Billy and Dawnie. She waved her hand frantically. 'Yoo-hoo, Dawnie, Billy. We've just been to Bude for the day. We had a lovely dinner in a nice pub on the way back. You haven't met my Ken, have you?'

Dawnie cackled and put her lips close to Billy's ear. 'He's the Prince Charming she slow-danced with at the Castle.'

Ken waved. Dilly grabbed his arm in an excessive gesture of ownership. 'He's coming in for a night cap,' she hooted. 'I'll see you tomorrow and tell you all about it. By the way, Billy, I'm completely out of home brew.'

'I'll bring some round tomorrow, will I?' Billy called but Dilly had dragged her willing beau into the house and closed the door.

Dawnie leaned her head against his arm, feeling immediately warmer. 'So, Lindy rang earlier. She wants to come down here in December with Stewie and Fallon and the three kids, so that we all spend Christmas together.'

'And Buddy and his girlfriend are coming over too at the end of the year to join them. We'll all be together for a bit.' He kissed her head. 'We'll have to buy a bigger house, darlin'.'

'I know. We need somewhere with more space.'

He breathed out. 'Well, what's it to be with Crosswinds?'

'The bungalow with the lovely garden room and the huge garage and the hot tub and the Thresher's Arms pub just down the road?'

'Ah, that one. What do you think? Do we want to buy it?'

She met his eyes and grinned impishly. 'Nah.'

His smile broadened. 'It wasn't right, was it?'

'Too modern, Billy. Too perfect. It wasn't for us.'

'The garage was nice, but we'll find a better house with a big old barn outside.'

'And a huge farmhouse kitchen and apple trees for cider in the garden.'

'You're right, darlin'. We'll wait for the house we really want to come along, will we? Our together forever house.'

'A place which we know is right without having to ask each other.'

'Somewhere big and rambling in the middle of nowhere, close to the sea. We can fall asleep with the window open and the whisper of the waves in our ears.'

'Billy, yes – where we can walk on the beach together in the evening and look up at the moon.'

'I mean, it's not as if we need to move, not yet – we're all right here for the time being, darlin'.'

'Maggot Street? Yes, it's not so bad. It'll do for a month or two until we find the dream house.'

'It'll be grand until the right one comes along.'

'And it will come along. Where we're living now does the job well enough, Billy, just while we look for somewhere we can call our own. Some things are worth waiting for, love, no matter how long it takes.'

Dawnie wrapped both her arms around him. He was too broad for her to clasp her hands together and she smiled at his solid strength, pressing her head against his shoulder. They turned their gaze to the sky and Billy held up his thumb to cover the bronze moon. When he took his hand away, moments later, they were gazing at a pale yellow waxy thumbprint amid a scattering of stars.

ACKNOWLEDGMENTS

Thanks to my agent, Kiran Kataria, for her kindness, wisdom and integrity. Thanks to the brilliant Sarah Ritherdon and Nia Beynon for everything they do, and all the wonderful people at Boldwood who were involved with the creation of this book. It's a privilege to be part of such an inspirational team.

Thanks to the lovely people who support my writing: Erika, Rich, Stephanie, Kay, Rog, Jan, Jan M, Bill, Ken, Trish, Lexy, Helen, Frank, Shaz, Ian, Susie, Chrissie, Kathy N, Julie and Martin, Rach, Nik R, Pete O', Sarah and Jim, Sarah E, Mart, Cath, Slawka, Beau, Zach, Matt B, Casey B, Dianne, Jali, Ruchi, Ingrid, Katie H, Jonno, Edward and Robin.

Thanks to everyone in the NAC community; you are always in my thoughts, Thanks to Ivor at Deep Studios for the Tech and Bim for the photos.

Special thanks to Peter Blaker and all the wonderful Solitary Writers, to the hugely supportive community of Boldwood writers and to writer friends of the RNA.

Thanks to my awesome neighbours, Martin, Lindsay, Kitty, Ian,

Nina, James and Jackie, and to Jenny, Sophie, Claire, Paul and Gary, pillars of the local community.

Special thanks to our Tony for years of love, banter and bikes; to Kim, Ellen, Angela, Norman, Bridget and Debbie.

Love to my mum, who showed me books, and to my dad, who never read one.

Big love to four of my own: to Liam, Maddie, Cait and Big G.

To anyone who has read and enjoyed any of my books, a huge thank you. You have helped to make this journey wonderful.

MORE FROM JUDY LEIGH

We hope you enjoyed reading *Heading Over the Hill*. If you did, please leave a review.

If you'd like to gift a copy, this book is also available as an ebook, digital audio download and audiobook CD.

Sign up to Judy Leigh's mailing list for news, competitions and updates on future books:

http://bit.ly/JudyLeighNewsletter

Explore more fun, uplifting reads from Judy Leigh:

ABOUT THE AUTHOR

Judy Leigh is the USA Today bestselling author of *The Old Girls' Network* and *Five French Hens* and the doyenne of the 'it's never too late' genre of women's fiction. She has lived all over the UK from Liverpool to Cornwall, but currently resides in Somerset.

Visit Judy's website: https://judyleigh.com

Follow Judy on social media:

facebook.com/judyleighuk
twitter.com/judyleighwriter
instagram.com/judyrleigh
bookbub.com/authors/judy-leigh

ABOUT BOLDWOOD BOOKS

Boldwood Books is a fiction publishing company seeking out the best stories from around the world.

Find out more at www.boldwoodbooks.com

Sign up to the Book and Tonic newsletter for news, offers and competitions from Boldwood Books!

http://www.bit.ly/bookandtonic

We'd love to hear from you, follow us on social media:

 facebook.com/BookandTonic

 twitter.com/BoldwoodBooks

 instagram.com/BookandTonic